INTRODUC... ...AMIL... ...
THE DUKE OF M... ...NS

Born of wealth, pa... ...the
Pennistan siblings... ...e of
sweeping social ch... ...nal
adventure. Now adults in a world of heroes and
heroines, soldiers and spies, it is the young aristocrats'
duty to uphold their legacy by leading lives of
courage, conviction—and legendary loves. Introducing
Lynford, David, Jessup, and last but not least...

GABRIEL

Easygoing but fiery when provoked, Lord Gabriel
Pennistan is an astronomer by profession—and a spy
by invitation. His curiosity about worlds far and near
results in a variety of exciting adventures. But his
erotic encounter with a breathtaking mystery woman
may be the most thrilling and dangerous of all....

OLIVIA

High-spirited and bighearted, Lady Olivia Pennistan's
first love is her family and all who live and work at
Pennford Castle. Her second love is the warm and
sensual world of the kitchen—the perfect setting for
an uninhibited young woman to experiment with
appetites of all kinds, especially under the tutelage of
a handsome and experienced protector....

Traitor's Kiss

Lover's Kiss

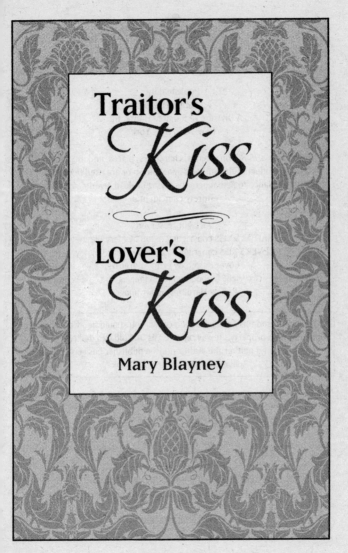

Traitor's *Kiss*

Lover's *Kiss*

Mary Blayney

BANTAM BOOKS

TRAITOR'S KISS/LOVER'S KISS
A Bantam Book / November 2008

Published by
Bantam Dell
A Division of Random House, Inc.
New York, New York

These are works of fiction. Names, characters, places, and incidents either
are the product of the author's imagination or are used fictitiously.
Any resemblance to actual persons, living or dead, events, or locales is
entirely coincidental.

Bantam Books and the rooster colophon are registered trademarks
of Random House, Inc.

ISBN 978-0-553-59212-2

Printed in the United States of America
Published simultaneously in Canada

www.bantamdell.com

OPM 10 9 8 7 6 5 4 3 2 1

Traitor's Kiss

BOOK ONE

A Private War

Le Havre, France
Winter 1813

1

CHARLOTTE! WHERE HAVE YOU BEEN? You make me cry with frustration." The vendor leaned on his cart and added a lewd gesture, leaving no doubt of his interest.

His French was of the gutter and Charlotte Parnell answered with the same accent. "Later!" she called, smiling over her shoulder and tossing her skirt so a little ankle showed. She took Georges's arm as further proof she was already occupied.

They turned down an alley and left the crowded streets behind them.

"That man is harmless, madame."

"Few men are harmless, Georges," she said, and was annoyed when a shiver came with the thought.

"The winter light is fading. Will you be warm enough with only that shawl?"

"Yes," she snapped, then closed her eyes and drew a

deep breath. "My apologies, Georges. This is a complicated venture and I am . . ." she hesitated, "uneasy. You are taking a chance and I am not sure the man is worth it."

"We are both taking a chance, madame. We do it because the money is too great a temptation to resist."

"You are so practical," she said with a little laugh. "And you are right. We will rescue a man who will be hanged as a traitor so that we have the money to save others."

"Madame," Georges began and then cleared his throat, "if he has betrayed England for France, how is it that he is in a French prison?"

"It is curious, is it not." Charlotte waved to the flower seller, who waved back. "Perhaps he has managed to offend the French as well as betray the English, or it is some political game the French are playing. In fact, Georges, I do not care as long as we are paid."

"If both sides are angry at him, the chances of his safe return are lessened. I hope that your patron agreed to pay even if this man does not survive."

"Is it murder to allow a guilty man to die in order to save ourselves?" Charlotte asked as she stopped to look at him.

"I am not sure what murder is anymore." Georges gestured to the everyday scene around them. "Despite the fact that we still eat and sleep, Napoleon has embroiled us in a fight for our lives since 1793. These last twenty years all of Europe has suffered. Even England and Russia, Austria." He ticked off the list on his fingers.

"And our small corner of the world here in Le Havre," she agreed. "We are all living in hell." Charlotte watched a man and a young woman cross the street. The girl looked back at her with curious eyes. Her companion pulled hard on her arm. "Most often a hell of our own making," she added when the girl stumbled a little as she turned away. "As for the terms of this contract, my patron and I have agreed that he will pay us a thousand pounds for the effort and double that if the man reaches England safely."

Georges nodded. They made their way past neighborhood shops competing with the vendors, who were as much entertainers as salesmen.

Charlotte paused at one shop to smile at a toddler sitting on a cushion just on the other side of the window. "It is as though we are his personal theater." Charlotte tapped her fingers on the glass.

When the tot saw her watching him, he laughed, slamming his little hand flat against the glass. Charlotte kissed her fingers, then pressed them against the pane and his hand on the other side.

The boy's mother came to him, took one look at Charlotte and Georges, scooped the child up and turned her back on them.

"Children see so much more clearly than adults," Georges said.

"And adults see exactly what I wish them to see." With a glance at her reflection she moved on. Her hair was so bright a red that anyone would know it for a wig. She loved it anyway. The color and the tousled curls always attracted attention.

As they moved out of their neighborhood, Georges dropped her arm and drifted away.

A man whistled and she did no more than wave a hand in his direction.

Charlotte did her best to move at more than a promenade and less than a hurry, not on parade to attract customers, but like a woman with a destination in mind.

At the next corner she had to wait for a cart to pass. She made a show of wrapping her shawl around her shoulders and under her arms. The trick accented the décolletage of her gown even if it did little to protect her from the cold. She would be warm enough if she kept moving.

A few steps more and a man walked up to her. This one was not as easily discouraged as the others, and with a glance, Georges was at her side once again.

She took Georges's arm, acting the lady. A curtsy gave the man an excellent view down her bodice, a reward for her dismissal.

The stranger was ready to fight for her, but Charlotte knew Georges's stare would convince him otherwise. The man settled for an insult and moved on.

"*Merci*, Georges."

"*Il n'y a pas de quoi, comme toujours*, madame."

You are welcome as always, madame. It was one of the most generous phrases anyone had ever spoken to her. The men in Le Havre had been attentive. Georges was the only one who had been kind as well as loyal. He had endured the nightmare with her, lived its consequences and never once complained.

As they rounded a corner, Georges turned from her again and went down an alley as she moved into the main thoroughfare. She attracted less attention here. Charlotte picked up her pace, entering the same alley from the other end, meeting Georges in the middle.

"This place is disgusting." The smell made her gag.

"Yes, madame," he said with pleasure, opening a barrel tucked into a doorway. The scent of lavender filled the air as he handed her a brown robe. "No one uses this alley but the night carts. You can play your role with confidence that this will be here when you return." They put the robes on over their clothes and Georges closed the lid on the lavender scent.

They left the alley together, this time attracting no attention at all. Charlotte drew a deep breath of the clean evening air, not only to clear her head, but also to prepare herself for what was to come.

GABRIEL PENNISTAN CONSIDERED himself a man of science. Not a spy. Not a murderer. Now he was all three.

Seven men executed because he had not been an effective agent. Not taken away or put on trial, but murdered in front of him. At times like this, when his memory heard the cries, smelled the horror, thought of families who were grieving, he wished he had been one of them instead of carted off as the place was set afire.

Who would think to look for him in Le Havre when he had been taken in Portugal? By his best estimate it had been eight months since the cell door slammed behind him here. Had he been forgotten or was this part of a plan?

A plan where he was left to rot with nothing to show for it but a trio of rats he had named, three failed escape attempts, an impressive beard and itchy, watering eyes, no doubt due to some damned infection.

Rational conversation brought him nothing but a spit in the face, which led to anger, which gave them an excuse to beat him. He'd learned that fast enough.

Gabe threw the rest of his cheese to the one rat brave enough to come close. The rat he had named Galileo accepted it with a bob of his head and a twitch of his whiskers, then scampered across the floor.

Relaxing against the wall, Gabriel closed his eyes and started naming each constellation and placing it in the night sky, courting the simplest of escapes. Sleep.

"Ce traitre maudit?"

He recognized the jailer's voice calling him a damned traitor followed by the sound of the key in the lock. Even as he leapt from the floor, Gabe glanced at the barred window, high above his head. His heart was pounding loud enough to be heard, the thrill of fear ratcheting up his senses. *Think, Gabriel. Use your brain, it's the best weapon you have.*

Had he fallen asleep? There was a gray light, but it was impossible to tell if it was dusk or closer to dawn. No matter the time, this was not part of the usual routine.

"Et il est anglais. Un sale cochon anglais."

No doubt he was the one the visitors wanted. He'd been told he was the only "English pig" in the place. Though probably not the only traitor.

Was this the guillotine? It was inevitable, but he would not go without a fight. He pushed the hair out of his eyes, ripped a strip from his shirt and tied it back.

He concentrated on slowing his breathing, lowered his

hands. The guillotine was inevitable, but not necessarily tonight. Could it be a government representative? Jailers looking for some amusement? The scars on his back tingled at the thought.

Or could it be freedom? He shook his head, refusing the fantasy. Without taking his eyes from the door, he reached up to the ledge and took down the sharpened spoon that was his only weapon. Tucking it in the waistband of his breeches, behind his back. He waited, half-hidden, as still as the shadows around him.

He had lived this moment in his nightmares, in his daydreams and never realized how infuriating the unknown could be. *Give me a clue of what's coming, damn it.*

The jailer had trouble with the key. That meant it was the new guard. *Turn the key to the left, then right and pull hard.*

"I thought you only came to see the condemned." The jailer coughed the deep, long rumble of consumption. "There's been no day set for this one."

Gabriel's anxiety shifted, making way for an overwhelming sense of relief. *Thank you, Maman, for insisting on a French tutor,* Gabe thought as he checked a date with Madame Guillotine off the list.

When he heard a woman's voice, low and with a cultured inflection, he wondered if he was going mad.

"Pere Milogue visits the condemned. Brother Georges and I hope to find converts."

"But an Englishman? They don't even believe in God."

He didn't know prisoners were allowed spiritual guidance. Odd.

The jailer came in followed by two others, a nun and

someone carrying a lantern. That was all he saw before the light, meager though it was, blinded him.

He squinted and relied on his other senses for information. No one spoke, the silence broken by the rats scrabbling in the corner. No one moved. What were they waiting for? Then he heard whispered words but could tell no more than the visitors did not agree with each other.

Brother Georges? Is that what the nun had said the other man's name was? Not a name he recognized.

He heard soft steps and deduced that the nun had come closer to him. Her perfume enveloped him, something blended of lavender and spice. It was a powerful distraction. Even more odd.

He clenched his fists.

His eyes had adjusted to the insult of the light and he opened them more fully. Was he overreacting? Who could be afraid of a nun and a priest?

She stood directly in front of him. Her eyes were some dark smoky color. He saw calculation rather than curiosity.

"Am I some specimen of manhood you have never seen before?"

She backed up a step. He gave her his complete attention. "Your perfume is not something I associate with religion. I can imagine a number of vignettes the three of us could act out, not one of which involves confessing my sins."

Still no reaction.

"Monsieur?" she said, whispering as if this were the exchange of a secret. "*Parlez-vous français, monsieur?*"

"*Un peu.*" He leaned closer and whispered, in French, for

her ears alone. "Yes, I speak French, but only in the bedroom."

She twirled away from him and Gabriel swore. Why was he doing his best to irritate her? Because her dark eyes were not the eyes of a woman of virtue, much less a nun.

"He says he wishes to confess." She walked to the jailer. "Please, leave us alone. We must act with speed before the devil embraces him again."

Damn. Gabe looked from the nun to the man who held the lantern, as he put his hand behind his back, reaching for his weapon. What kind of game was this?

The jailer left with a friendly nod, pulling the door closed behind him. Didn't he think it odd that a woman was in charge? Or had they bribed him for privacy?

It was more than odd. It was wrong.

"Who are you and what the hell do you want?" he asked in French and moved more deeply into the shadows. He kept his hand on his weapon.

"Brother Georges and I have come to help you." She gestured to the man, who stepped closer and raised the lantern so the light spilled into the corner where Gabriel stood. The wall at his back was his only ally.

"You sound eminently reasonable and I still do not believe you. Your eyes give you away." Gabe swore and switched to French, repeating his words and adding, "If you expect money, you've come to the wrong cell. Do you think I would look like this if I had any?"

"Il ne faut pas nous payer, monsieur." The nun answered. *They did not want to be paid?*

"Who are you?" he shouted, to the man this time, welcoming the surge of temper. Brother Georges remained silent. Was he deaf? Gabriel looked from one to the other, willing them to speak.

Gabe was about to ask a third time when the nun raised a hand to his mouth, laying her fingers against his lips. *Oh my.* The softness of her fingers, the feel of them against his lips was like a gift from an erotic gamester.

Her expression was as hard as her fingers were soft. "If you are a nun, then I am the Prince of Wales." He spoke in a whisper, ignoring the surge of lust that undermined his concentration.

"We will leave and then we will talk, monsieur."

Leave? They were going to leave? Even as he wondered if he had understood her correctly, it came to him. He had not heard the jailer turn the key when he left the cell. The door was unlocked.

He didn't need their help.

He could escape on his own.

2

BROTHER GEORGES BLOCKED his way before Gabriel had taken three steps to the door.

"Come away from there, you fool." The nun came closer to him, her dark eyes sparked with anger. "You are *not* the one in charge. I have every intention of taking you from here, but we will do it on my terms."

"I think not," Gabe said, grabbing her, pulling her in front of him. Not the wisest move, but he was the one in control now.

Her back was pressed to his chest. He felt the warmth of her, the scent of lavender and spice even through the head covering and coarse linen of her habit. He spoke as he pressed the point of his blade against the sweet-smelling flesh at her throat. "You call me a fool and I may be, but I can slash your neck before your friend here could reach me with his knife. Tell him to move from the door."

The man did move away, but toward him with his knife raised.

"No, Georges." Her voice was unruffled. "We will give him a moment to calm his foolish temper and listen."

Gabriel felt her heartbeat where he held her tight against him. She must have ice in her veins, for it was not racing nearly as fast as his.

After a long moment, Georges nodded.

The woman moved a bit, leaning into the point of the knife. Gabriel did not ease the pressure. "I will kill. Do not doubt it." Did he sound as desperate as he felt? "I trust no one, madame. Least of all two people pretending to be something they are not. I *will* escape. With you as a hostage."

"You cannot leave here without my help." She spoke softly, as though he were a wild animal. Which was not far from the truth. "At the moment you are making my work needlessly difficult. Do as I say and we will walk out of here with the guard's blessing." She moved against the knife again, and this time he eased the pressure. "You can cooperate with us *or* you can die attempting it on your own, my lord."

Gabriel froze at the use of his title. "Why do you address me so? No one here knows me as anything but 'English pig.'"

"Release me," she insisted coolly, as though she were bargaining for a new bonnet and not her life. "I will say no more until you do."

Gabriel considered. "Tell Georges to drop his knife and kick it to me." He had no idea how many more weapons the man carried, but at least Georges would have one less and he would have one more.

"*S'il vous plait*, Georges."

He nodded and tossed the knife to the floor. It landed behind Gabriel.

"*Merci*, Georges," she said.

"*Il n'y a pas de quoi toujours, ma soeur.*"

So Georges could speak. Was the man a servant or a friend? Her husband?

Gabriel released her. She stepped away, but not far. Not more than a foot.

"Before I go anywhere with you, Madame Nun," he said, making the title an insult, "tell me who you are, who sent you and what your plan is."

"I will tell you nothing but this: You will change clothes with Georges and you will trade places. First he must trim your hair and cut off some of your beard." She smiled, cynical and unfriendly. "Or everyone will think you are a prisoner trying to escape."

"He will take my place? Then he is more fool than I am." He turned to the man. "Why are you willing to do this?"

"For money."

"Of course. Why else. May you live to enjoy it." Gabriel still held his weapon at the ready as an insidious hope edged aside his doubt. "Where do we go once we are away?"

"The less you know, the better."

For whom, he thought, but did not ask again. Gabriel leaned close so he was breathing into her ear. She barely responded, but he saw her throat work as she swallowed. "I demand this. Tell me the name of the woman who thinks to save me."

When she turned to answer, her mouth was almost on his. "Not save you, my lord, only rescue you."

Her skin was lovely, her lips even lovelier. He moved a fraction closer, drawn by the scent of her, the invitation in her eyes irresistible. As she said her name, "Charlotte. Charlotte Parnell," her lips touched his. The feather touch of her mouth was like a magnet, and for a second his entire being melded with hers. She stepped back and now there was no temptation in her, only impatience.

Charlotte Parnell. Her name was not much of a concession, but this pyrrhic victory was all she would allow. He saw that by the way she turned and headed for the door.

"Decide, my lord. I will have no qualms about leaving you to the guillotine."

"I will go. If someone is paying you, then who am I to deny you your prize?"

"Very good, monsieur," she said, as though it had been a difficult choice.

Gabriel nodded and moved into the light so Georges could trim his hair and beard. The man worked with confidence and speed. Was he a barber when he was not playing at theatrics? And what were they to each other? he wondered again. Lovers? Gabriel shifted his gaze to Charlotte, standing to his right, holding the lantern.

No. Georges worked for her, not the other way around. They were not intimate. He was sure of it. Her eyes were fixed on his face, not on the barber's.

They stared at each other, and Gabriel hoped he was half as good as she was at hiding his thoughts. "You are either a consummate actress or a little mad."

She nodded, not unpleased with his comment, and lowered the lantern. Georges had finished with his barbering.

Georges undressed and Gabriel followed suit. He looked from one to the other as he worked his collar buttons, half expecting an attack of some kind. Nothing happened. Georges continued undressing. Charlotte Parnell watched.

Tugging his shirt out of his breeches, Gabriel pulled it over his head and let it fall to the floor. His cravat was long gone and his jacket used now as a blanket.

With some calculation he turned from them as he began on the front closure of his breeches.

"Stop," she commanded.

He did, because it was exactly what he had hoped for.

"They did this to you? Why?"

Holding still, he felt her fingers trace the still-sore lines on his back. Her touch was comfort and pleasure, too much pleasure after months without.

He faced her, and now that he was not entrapped by her touch, tried to decide how to use this sympathy to his advantage. Honesty. It would confuse her. Besides, it came naturally. "I was fool enough to try to escape."

She shrugged as though she had already lost interest. "Your breeches."

As he pulled them off, she was the one who moved away to gather up the clothes Georges had let fall.

They made quick work of the exchange. Georges wore a regular set of men's clothes beneath his religious garb. As he put on Gabriel's shirt he stopped and inhaled. God help him, it still smelled of the sun.

He took the pantaloons the French bourgeoisie now

favored and handed Georges his breeches. He tucked his weapon into the pocket and looked around, moving his eyes only, for the knife Georges had kicked away. On the floor nearby and just out of reach.

When Gabriel sat on the floor to exchange shoes, he sat as close to the knife as he could manage, almost had it in hand when a pair of slippers came into view.

"You would not deny Georges protection, would you, my lord? You have your knife. You will leave him his."

She nudged the knife to her partner, who picked it up without a word.

"Where is your weapon, madame?"

"Where you can never reach it."

Her complete confidence was her undoing. "Do not be so sure that your mind and body are beyond compromise, madame. Arrogance is the first step to failure. I speak from experience."

She turned from him with an abrupt, graceless step, and he counted this proof that some part of her was vulnerable

He took Georges's shoes and left the man barefoot. "Georges," he whispered, "this trade of clean for filthy, shoes for bare feet is too generous. Almost as puzzling as your will-ingness to stay behind. Who is paying you to risk your life so?"

Gabe looked from one to the other. Charlotte shook her head. With some effort he did not demand an answer. But he would have an explanation later.

By the time Charlotte Parnell was satisfied that his new clothes were as they should be, with the brown robe covering all, Georges was in the spot Gabriel had made his own, on his knees, his head lowered almost to the floor, as if praying a penance.

She handed Gabriel Georges's hat and the lantern. "Carry the light low," she whispered, "as though we need it to see our way. Keep your head down," she insisted, "and say nothing."

Pushing the heavy cell door open, the two of them began to walk toward the light at the end of the stone corridor. Gabriel's escape attempts had never won him freedom beyond this length of corridor. His previous failures dogged him as he concentrated on walking in Georges's too large shoes. He knew the spot where his first attempt had ended. There was still dried blood on the stone floor. The second and third were more vague in his memory.

The light seemed a hundred miles away as they began walking toward it. As they moved closer, elation mingled with the fear that had his hands shaking.

He concentrated on the woman next to him, dispelling the possibility of failure. Her hands were tucked in her sleeves. Even her walk was decorous. Despite that, he was sure that if the guard took one good look at that face he would know she was acting.

As they were about to step into the lighted entry, he paused, then stopped completely, frozen to the spot, two or three steps from the light.

She turned to him and nodded, her expression sympathetic for the first time. "It is the next step. This is not freedom, only the path to it."

He shook his head, doing his best to dispel the sense of disaster looming. What jail had she been in that she could understand his insane wish to stay precisely where he was, to risk no more than this?

He followed her and she made escape look easy, pausing at the guard's desk, murmuring something about prayers for his health. The man responded with another gut-churning cough and a wave toward the door. Gabriel's surprise became suspicion. Had she bribed everyone? Not with prayers, he was sure of that. With money? Her body?

As they began to move away from the guard, there was a bellow from down the hall. Every swear word he ever learned tumbled through his brain, even as the jailer reached for his weapon. It was not where he first looked. By the time the jailer gave up and grabbed a club, the roar was joined by shouting.

As Gabriel was readying himself for a fight, certain they had been discovered, the jailer insisted they leave. "They will drop the gate and it will be hours before they open it again."

Charlotte hurried him from the entry, not that he needed any encouragement. They crossed the courtyard, walked under the old-fashioned portcullis, where, as predicted, two men were wrestling with the turning mechanism.

"It's rusted open," one guard announced to the other. "Call for the soldiers!"

Gabriel followed Charlotte. They made their way down the narrow street, which emptied into a wider one. As they reached it, a handful of men in uniform hurried past. Charlotte stopped to watch them. Gabriel tugged at her arm.

"No," she said, "they will wonder if we do not appear curious."

"What about Georges? Is he in danger? What will happen to him?" He did not want to be responsible for another dead man.

When she did not answer him right away, he turned from the parade of racing soldiers to see what else had caught her attention. "How interesting that you should care, my lord," she said, considering him with curiosity. "I would wonder what kind of man you are if I did not already know." She looked back to the prison. "Georges knows precisely what to expect."

There was nothing soft about her, Gabriel realized, except for her body, which he suspected she used as coldly as she used Georges. Her feather-light kiss when she spoke her name had been as calculated as the disguise. He had not known it then but would not forget again.

"Keep your head up. Look interested."

"I am," he said, wondering what it would take to ruffle her. Nothing as simple as a kiss.

He crossed himself and tried to look religious, nodding at the comments of the crowd gathering around them. Speculation on the possibility of a prison riot. The toll the prisoners would pay for attempting it. The likelihood the guillotine would be busy tomorrow.

Sweat popped out on his brow despite the coolness in the air. Each man who looked their way was a jailer about to seize him. He kept his head down and his hat pulled low, and mumbled the Latin names for the roses his mother had treasured. His family. Was he any closer to seeing them?

Eventually a few in the crowd moved toward the prison, but the rest drifted in the direction of the boulevard. Charlotte followed them.

Moments before they reached the avenue, she took the lantern from him, doused the light and stepped into an alleyway. It was dark and smelled worse than the prison. Gabriel wondered at her sanity. Unless they *were* being followed and this was a further means to escape.

No, for they stopped after only a few steps. They were in deep shadow here, but his night vision was excellent. He watched as she pulled off her head covering, as well as the apron and brown robe.

Good Lord, he thought, as he took in the change in her appearance. Her hair was not dressed in any style, but rather a mad cap of curls and tangles that made him think she was happiest in bed.

He could not see the color of her dress, but it was not what one noticed first. Her breasts drew all the attention, and he swallowed with effort as he considered the cut of her gown, so low he was sure any moment all would be revealed.

She nodded at him. He stopped staring and mimicked her actions. Taking his robe, she stuffed it and her habit into a lavender-scented barrel that was near a boarded-up doorway. She set the lantern on top of the lid and raised her hands to her hair, not smoothing it so much as pressing it to her head. Was she wearing a wig? She shook out her skirts and took his arm. They left the alleyway, moving toward the town center. This time he did not hesitate to step from the alley, even as he sifted through explanations for his pallor and weakened appearance, so much more obvious in regular clothes. He ran a hand over his very short hair and looked up, beyond the steps he was taking, to the world surrounding him.

The boulevard was filled with people, sedan chairs and carriages. *Aha,* he thought, *it is still evening and early enough that everyone in Le Havre has someplace to go.*

Charlotte Parnell and Gabriel Pennistan joined them, walking arm in arm. "So people will think we are merely whiling away the time until we can indulge in something more strenuous."

Mixing with the crowds, feeling the air against his face, Gabe finally grasped the reality of the moment. He was free. He stopped, let go of her arm and raised his hands, making fists, as if he could grab hold of freedom.

Looking heavenward, he saw a few of the brighter stars. He slowed long enough to identify the North Star, but even this wide boulevard was too narrow to show him much of the night sky. He would find an open field and spend hours watching the stars and plan a future that had nothing to do with war or treachery.

She took his arm again and he laughed. It was all he could do to still the sound that was more hysteria than amusement. Who knew that freedom came in degrees? He had no money, no resources, ill-fitting clothes and shoes, which, in fact, belonged to Georges.

He had escaped the stone walls of the French prison, but for now he had no choice. He must follow Charlotte Parnell with no notion of their destination or her plans.

"Where are we going?" Gabriel slowed their pace.

"Walk faster." She pulled at his arm.

"No. I want answers now."

"In good time."

"Now!" He pulled her to a stop. The rest of the evening's revelers moved around them, some with curious glances.

"Do not ruin this. You could as easily die in the next few minutes as in the last few." She raised her hand to his cheek. It might have looked like a seductive gesture, but it felt more like a restrained slap.

He took her hand from his cheek at the wrist, caressing the pulse point, then holding it so she could feel his strength.

"You have no choice but to come with me," she said, pulling her hand free. "I am your jailer now."

3

SHE RAISED HER OTHER HAND and ran her thumb over his lips. He missed the first of her whispered words.

". . . to my house, where we can rid you of the smell of jail, as well as the vermin who have made themselves comfortable on you."

Mention of a bath made him itch everywhere. He moved a few steps away, amazed she would walk so close to anyone as filthy as he was.

Charlotte pulled him back to her side as a man called out, "If you wish a more willing customer, I would need no convincing."

She waved at the man, who made to follow them. "Another night, monsieur. This one is shy and will take all my time." She glanced at Gabriel as if considering some hidden quality. "Though not much of my skill."

The man laughed as he saluted her and went on his way.

Gabe ignored the insult. Tried to. As they made their way through town, he concentrated on his surroundings, memorizing the route they were taking. When they had made three consecutive left turns, he suspected she was doing her best to confuse him. When he saw the same tavern sign for a second time, he was sure of it.

After more twists and turns, they came to a narrow alleyway. She seemed to have a fondness for them. At the third gate Charlotte stopped. Pushing it open, she hurried him to the back door of a house that appeared completely dark.

She let go of his arm to use her key and Gabe considered running. The rabbit warren of streets and mews might be confusing, but it would give him a dozen places to hide.

"You would be back in jail within hours," Charlotte said softly.

"Do you read minds too?" She had not even looked at him as she spoke.

"Even a child would know you have been in prison. Your face is without color, your clothes are ill-fitting and you smell of the place." She spoke as she stepped into a small room lined with hooks for coats and a single lit candle. The hooks were empty. That was odd. Did no one live here? Or were they all out? He followed her into the kitchen without invitation and felt infinitely safer with a room in front of him and the door at his back.

"If it is so obvious that I am a villain, why did no one stop us on our way here?"

"Because they were all looking at me."

"That is definitely so." He laughed at the simple truth.

Leaning against the door, he folded his arms and took a good look her. The dress, trimmed with black lace, revealed more than it covered. "Your expression draws as much attention as your dress. You flirt with every man that passes and then give a charming show of regret, holding on to me as though I am a prize you are afraid you will lose. It is very effective, Madame Parnell."

"You saw all that?"

"I have studied the sciences for years." Her surprise was gratifying. "I have learned to observe the smallest detail." He scanned the kitchen as he went on speaking. A brace of candles cast as much shadow as light. There was no one else in the room, the only sign of life a striped cat that raised its head when they came in.

He drew in a breath, disappointed that there was not more of the scent of a home. No bread baking, the musk from people crowded together, no smell of ale from half-drunk tankards. With a twinge of annoyance he realized that if Charlotte Parnell was his jailer, then this was no more than another prison.

"You know, madame, there are several other explanations for my appearance," he said, doing his best not to sound annoyed. "I have been sick. My house burned down. My child died."

"Yes," she said dismissively, "and we may use all of those before we are done."

There was a bath before the fireplace and cans of water being kept warm on the hearth.

"Who arranged this? Is this house yours?"

Her "Yes" was terse, as though she was annoyed by his curiosity.

"Where are your servants?" Gabriel asked, his own irritation matching hers, exceeding it. "Are we alone?"

"The fewer who know of your presence, the safer it is."

"Safer for them? Or for me?"

She gave him a look implying he was not as smart as the cat that had moved near the door leading into the front of the house.

"Ah," he said. Her expression was the smallest of insults but the last straw. "Safer for them *and* for me," he said, stepping toward her, "but not for you."

He grabbed her around the waist. She was fine-boned despite her height. He could almost circle her waist with his hands. "I see a number of items I can use as a weapon. But why do I need one when I am bigger," he shook her a little, "and stronger than you are?"

Gabriel pulled her to him. He did his best to ignore the way she pressed her body to him, the way her scent awakened his lust. Letting go of her waist, he moved his hands up her arms, stopping below her jaw, caressing her, not with affection. The bones of her neck were fragile compared to the power in his hands.

Months of anger, at himself, at the French, raged through him. He pressed his thumbs into the base of her throat. "I could strangle you or snap your neck and be free once and for all."

The pulse in her neck beat steadily, her eyes were empty. *How odd.* His burst of fury faded as he studied her expression, trying to see something, *anything* of emotion. Did she not believe him capable of murder? He pressed his thumbs deeper into her throat, more as an experiment than as a threat. She must feel it, but she stood still, as if she were waiting for him to decide the color of her eyes rather than how to use his hands to kill her.

"This only works if the victim is intimidated." He was so taken aback he spoke aloud and in English. "You do not care." He eased his grip and then moved his hands to her shoulders. "I understand how you feel. One can only hide from despair for so long. There are times when death would be easier than going on."

If he had not been watching her so intently, he would have missed the flash of panic in her eyes. She twisted away from him, moved around the table, closer to the fireplace.

"Is it so painful to be honest?" he asked, following her.

"Honest?" She faced him, venom filling her words. "You want me to be honest?"

He stopped moving toward her. She had spoken in English. To make that mistake she must be very upset.

"You, who are both a traitor and a spy, want honesty?" She shook her head, speaking the last word as if it were as rare as magic. "You murdering bastard. Here is honesty. You deserve the beating that marked your back. You deserve the guillotine more than most who are sent there."

The anger ebbed, replaced by a scorn just as poisonous. "Someone is paying me well to save your life, and I need the money. There is more than one way for a woman to sell herself, my lord." The last two words were as steeped with hate as any expletive she could have used.

"Your honesty is brutal, but I find that it brings me no closer to trusting you. Tell me why you—"

"Take your clothes off," she said, interrupting him as she began to unlace her dress, still speaking in English.

With her hands stretched behind her back, her breasts were displayed even more prominently.

"I said, take off your clothes."

Her anger was gone, or at least banked, as quickly as it had appeared.

"I want some answers," Gabriel said, keeping his eyes on her as he came down the other side of the table. "Do you expect me to follow your orders with blind faith? Why do you risk your life for someone you would as soon see dead?"

"My husband died and left me with nothing. I am doing what I do best, to support myself."

That could explain quite a bit. They faced each other in front of the fire as he tried to measure the truth of her words. She did not look away as she spoke. When her dress fell to the floor, she scooped it up and tossed it on a nearby chair.

"You will do as I say, Lord Gabriel, because otherwise you will die."

No, he would not. He could make it on his own. He had a chance. A slim one. If he could find out who was paying her, then he could decide whether to follow her or not.

He took off his shirt. As absurd as it sounded, bathing was the next step to freedom.

Her corset was front-fastening and she dispensed with it as he tossed his shirt onto the chair with her dress. She raised the skirt of her chemise and stripped off her garters and stockings. Her ankles and feet were delicate. They would feel the cold of the stone floor.

Her fine lawn chemise left little to the imagination. He could see her figure and could make out the dark circle of her nipples, the shadow of hair at the V of her legs. Why exactly was *she* undressing?

He bided his time. This was not about sex any more than her costume was. His mind understood it, his body did not. As she began to fill the bath, he counted it wiser to look away from the display. As it was, undoing the buttons on his pantaloons was a struggle.

Stripped down to his small clothes, he reached for one of the buckets, following her example, filling the tub. He had lost weight. Prison food would only prolong life, not fuel strength. But he could still lift the cans, and the walk through town had not exhausted him. Fear had given him the energy. Even now it kept him alert.

"Enough," she said. "Save some water for rinsing and shaving. Climb in." She stood with her hands on her hips, watching him as he pulled off his drawers and tossed them into the fire.

He stepped into the bath and stilled. The water was too hot, or was it the feel of it that made him gasp? He stood still a moment before settling slowly with a long moan of pleasure he was sure she had heard before. This felt as good as sex. Almost. "You may kill me before dawn, Charlotte Parnell, but still I thank you. I have never, until this moment, so appreciated the bliss, the pure sensual bliss, of a bath full of hot water." He put his head back, resting it along the hard-edged rim, and closed his eyes, relaxing, for the first time since the knock on his cell door.

She tossed the soap into the water. The splash of it hitting the surface made him straighten.

"There is no time for leisure if you wish to be bound for England tonight. Wash your hair first, so I can pick the nits while you wash the rest of your body."

"I suppose that is why Georges cut my hair so short." He raised a fierce lather and then used the soap on his head, washing so vigorously he felt the beginnings of a headache. "Shaving my head would have called too much attention to my appearance."

She did not answer, but moved behind him, positioning one of the larger empty buckets at the edge of the bath. She pulled his head back, none too gently. The slosh of cool water she used to rinse his hair drew a gasp. "You are cruel, Charlotte."

Then the real torture began. She ran her fingers through his hair, stroking his scalp. Her gestures were purely practical, at least he thought they were, but the way her strong fingers moved along his head felt like a caress and he wished she would rub his shoulders, his back, all of his body.

He took a cloth from the stack at hand and spread it from one side of the bath to the other. It would help keep the water warm. If he did not find something else to think about, she would know the real reason for the cloth.

Despite the intimacy of her task, he did not trust her. He would have sex with her in an instant, but he would do it with his eyes wide open and her hands tied to the bedpost. The image did nothing to calm his arousal. *Talk, find some an-*

swers, he commanded himself. "You say I am bound for England tonight?"

No answer. He tried again.

"And you said 'someone is paying me well' to do this." He emphasized the two pieces of information he did have. She continued her work in silence.

"From what I can deduce, your patron is English. Not my father. He always insisted that we fully experience the consequences of our actions. Most likely it's my brother, Lynford. He's the oldest and heir to the title, definitely 'someone,' as you named him, and wealthy enough to pay well. He would."

She said nothing.

"I would be a fool to follow you without some details."

Silence.

He pressed on. He might not be winning the answers he wanted, but it was calming his more lascivious thoughts. "I cannot credit someone from the British government would pay well or send a woman to do this job." He waited only a beat and then answered for her, covering his aggravation with as practical a voice as he could manage. "Of course, everyone knows the government would sacrifice anything or anyone with victory so close. Before they were willing because they were so desperate. Any excuse will do to justify their actions."

He could feel the breath of a laugh on his neck. He did his best to ignore the effect it produced. At least she was paying attention.

"It could have been my brother Jess. Gamblers have an amazing range of acquaintances. He's not at all like Lynford, who never puts a step wrong."

Charlotte rubbed something in his hair and began to comb it. She was almost finished and had not said one word. He gripped the side of the bath. "Surely not my sister, Olivia? I cannot credit she would have any idea how to hire someone to effect an escape." .

"I'm finished with your hair."

Gabriel turned to face her. "Damn it, woman." He took both her hands and held them tight. "Give me something. Anything. At least tell me that my family knows I am alive."

4

CHARLOTTE SAT BACK on her heels, pulling her hands from his. He had done that all evening—react physically to his emotions, like the way he spread his arms and laughed at his first look at the sky.

His temper was just as close to the surface. She dried her fingers on her shift to keep from raising a hand to her throat and the bruise she knew would be there tomorrow.

It was not what she expected from someone who read books all day. Not this man of mercurial moods. It was hardly what one expected in a man of science.

She had thought to find a stoop-shouldered, squinty-eyed man, older than his years. Lord Gabriel Pennistan might show signs of long imprisonment, but no one would call him old or stoop-shouldered. His cheeks were as gaunt as his body, but it accentuated the fullness of his mouth. Tall and blond, he looked fit despite his months in prison.

And he had provoked her so that she had lost her temper. Charlotte tried to recall the last man who had done that. None came to mind since her husband had died. And her anger had never won anything from him but derision. She had learned and wrapped scorn around herself like a suit of armor.

Gabriel Pennistan was waiting, staring at her as if he could hear the words she was thinking.

"Why does it matter who is paying me?" she asked.

"I need some reason to believe in you," he answered. "You have my life in your hands. It may be worthless to you, but I want to clear my family name. To find some way to do right by the men who died in front of me."

"How noble, my lord." She made herself frame the words as an insult. His blue eyes darkened with anger.

She looked away. If she did not tell him, would he do something foolish? She gave in. "Viscount Sidmouth told your family that you might be alive. It was the Duke of Meryon who hired me."

"My father? I find that hard to believe."

"No. Your brother is the duke now."

Water sloshed over the rim and onto the stone floor as he straightened. "My father is dead?"

Charlotte shook her head, both yes and no. "I can only assume so."

He drew a deep, hard breath. "My father is dead," he said again. There was a long silence. "It's hard to imagine the world without him. I wonder when. How?" He gave his attention to washing and was silent awhile. "He was not a kind man. Nor approving. But he was a presence. The French government certainly hated him."

He spoke the last more to himself than to her.

"Like father like son. The new duke is forbidding and intimidating."

He eased his head back on the rim again. His eyes were closed, but there was too much tension in his body for him to be resting.

"I must wash your back and then you have to shave. But first, allow me to treat your eye inflammation. Hold still."

He followed her instruction and felt her fingers smooth something around the edge of both eyes. The relief was instantaneous.

"Oh," he breathed, "thank you, again, dear jailer. I thought the itching would have me gouging my eyes out. What is it?"

"Some magic concoction a friend supplies me with."

"The man of science is appalled by that description, but the sufferer salutes you." He sat still for a moment, holding his breath and then releasing it in a long sigh.

There it was again, a very physical response to the simplest pleasure. It went hand in hand with the intensity. With all his sensibilities so close to the surface, it was no wonder trouble found him. Who had ever thought he would make a credible spy?

Gabriel opened his eyes and stared up at her. "If you met my family, talked to them, they must have convinced you I am neither spy nor traitor."

She ignored his entreaty, turning back to her work. Yes, the duke had said his brother was too lazy to work at being a spy. Lord Jessup had described him as a man whose head was lost in whatever field of science interested him at the moment.

Lady Olivia said he was too honest. Charlotte was sure his work in Portugal had cured him of that.

"I am *not* a traitor."

There was the passion again, urging her to believe him or else. "Tell me your version of what happened."

He did not begin right away. Was it because he resented obeying a woman's demand or because he was honest? Her husband had insisted that a true spy would have a story ready, a story as close to the truth as possible.

"I went to Portugal in 1811."

"You went to Portugal in the middle of a war? With the French in control of Spain and England losing the fight?" The scars on his back were reddened by the water. She took the soaped sponge and began to wipe away the dirt, using as gentle a touch as she could manage.

"I hoped to see a colleague, Dr. Borgos, and study the Great Comet with him. He lived near Corunna in the north of Portugal. A good distance from Spain and the threat of Napoleon's marshals. Napoleon was on his way to Russia by then."

"And still a nest of intrigue and spies."

"Not at Dr. Borgos's estate. He was a respected astronomer and old. Not a threat to anyone."

She was not so sure that age and education made one less dangerous, but she wanted to hear Gabriel's story, not start a debate with him. "You went to Portugal to study the night sky. Is there not sky enough in England?"

"A friend of mine, Rhys Braedon, had an argument with his brother and was determined to head off to Portugal. I knew Borgos and knew he would welcome us. I went to see the

Great Comet. With an expert." He said the last sentence with emphasis. "It was Borgos who drew me to Portugal, not the sky. I cannot speak for Braedon, though I expect that he just wanted to move beyond his family's influence."

She listened as she carefully cleaned around the scars. Some of them were older than others. How had they not become infected? For all his bad luck, this was one disaster he had avoided. "Why did you not invite Borgos to meet you somewhere that was not so dangerous?"

"Name a place in Europe that has not felt the scourge of Napoleon. Besides, Dr. Borgos is confined to a chair. Travel is impossible for him."

He shifted his body and went on. She ran the sponge over his shoulders and down his back, slowly, feeling each muscle. How had he managed to keep his strength when he had been confined for so long? He shuddered, and she moved the sponge back up his spine to his neck. He shivered. She felt only a little guilty at what she was doing to him. A very refined kind of torture. It virtually guaranteed he would keep talking to distract himself.

"I spent nearly a year with the doctor. Rhys married Borgos's daughter and they went back to England. She was with child and Borgos was anxious that she should be safe."

He was quiet for a moment, then shook his head. "Have you ever had one of those moments, one you can look back to, a moment when you know your life changed?"

She nodded at the rhetorical question, forcing herself to continue her washing even though she felt physically ill at the memory.

"Borgos became ill. I think he had been failing the whole

time we were with him, but his daughter's farewell was heart-breaking, quite literally. Sometimes he was aware, sometimes he was not. He had me write a letter to his daughter and to his son. But his son had died in the war. That's when I knew death was near. He finished dictating the letter and looked at me. 'Thank you, Gabriel, thank you for your care and your company. Please, my son, do not waste this life.' I thought he was gone, but he looked at me again and grabbed my hand. 'Make the world a better place.' Then he died."

He lapsed into silence, and she breathed a prayer for the doctor's soul.

"I kept the letter he wrote his son as a reminder of his words. That was totally unnecessary." He added that with a harsh laugh, as if the memory was more of a nightmare. "At first I pursued the work that had brought me to Portugal. It was when I was in Lisbon reading a paper to men too old to fight or to those who were unwilling, that I realized I needed to take action, to join the fight to make the world safe from tyrants like Napoleon. I decided to buy a commission.

"The fight for Spain was fully engaged, even though Napoleon was now fighting a war on two fronts. I went to Wellington's winter camp and asked about a commission. Wellington himself met with me and asked if I would consider doing work for him that did not require a uniform. He asked me to work as a spy, using my interest in science as a disguise."

Charlotte stopped washing him and he paused as well. "You were willing to do that, my lord? Be a spy, knowing no one would receive you if they found out? That you could be imprisoned, tortured and executed without the protection of a uniform?"

"Yes," Gabriel said without hesitation. "There are some things more important than who will invite me to their next ball." He looked at her over his shoulder as if she would challenge what he said. When she began washing his back again, he turned from her and continued.

"They insisted that my interests were a good enough excuse to give me entrée almost anyplace. I had learned Portuguese. I was welcome in society and could go to the meanest tavern or the finest balls in the name of science."

She had finished bathing him, but held on to the sponge, washing already clean spots so that he would continue. All details were valuable. Already she saw him in a different light. His willingness to be a spy was not the conventional choice for the son of a duke.

"I was to go to . . ." he paused, ". . . a city where I would frequent a list of places they had me memorize, make myself known and see what I could learn. I went to the city I will not name and did as I was instructed.

"The ruse worked for a while. It is amazing what men will say when they are in their cups or think they are speaking to someone whose only interest is science. A few times I even found information on my own. Then one night I went to the tavern that was one of my regular haunts.

"When I arrived, there was a band of ruffians holding seven men as hostages. They asked me to identify my fellow spies. I refused, denying any wrongdoing. Without giving me a second chance, they shot and slaughtered all of them. I thought my body was going to be added to the corpses. They said that I was being spared even though I had betrayed those who had died. I was wanted for further questioning."

He stopped talking, and she waited for him to gather his composure.

"They poured spirits on the dead and burned the place down. As an example to others? To cover their crime? I don't know. Maybe both. They knocked me unconscious before I could do anything to stop them. I've thought about it for months now and have no idea what I did that served those men up to death."

Charlotte sat back again, letting him relive his personal hell. If one had a conscience it was a worse punishment than years in prison. Finally he drew a deep breath and continued.

"We left on a small French cutter. When we reached France we traveled by foot. At Le Havre I was put in prison and forgotten. That's my story, a total waste of more lives than my own." He let out a breath and turned his head a little. "Tell me, Charlotte, what have you done to make the world a better place?"

"I know this much," she said, not really ignoring his question, "self-pity is a waste." She turned his head away from her, pretending that she was not finished with his neck. When the silence had dragged on, she prodded him, "Were you tortured? Is that how you came to have the scars on your back?"

"No. Those are from my three escape attempts. Ludicrous failures, every one of them." He shook his head and went on. "My original captors said I was to be taken to Paris. The Minister of Police wanted to see me."

"Fouché, the French spymaster?" She nodded. "That is impressive." That part, at least, was exactly what the government had told her.

"Perhaps. I suppose so. Fouché has been in and out of favor with Napoleon and I cannot be certain he was the Minister of Police at the time, but even when he is out of favor, there are many loyal to him, or at least willing to do his bidding."

"That has been true since before the revolution," she said. "It is amazing how he is able to sell his services no matter who is in power." She walked to the table to light the candles near the shaving mirror. "Why did Fouché wish to see you?"

"I have no idea. No, no, I have a dozen ideas. He wanted to execute me more publicly. A ducal connection would attract some attention."

She shrugged. "You have only to convince Viscount Sidmouth to be set free."

"It is the truth, damn your skeptical mind." He picked up the sponge and threw it into the fire. It sizzled and was gone quickly, rather like his temper, she thought.

"It is a near version of the story Viscount Sidmouth passed on. With a critical difference."

"What is it?"

She shook her head. "You will find out when you reach London." When he would have protested, she raised her hand. "Those are my orders."

He slid back into the water.

"I *can* tell you that about six months ago word reached the War Office that you were alive. They dismissed it as unreliable information." She was surprised when he did no more than nod. Where was his temper now? "Your brother was willing to pursue it. I was sure you were dead and that he was behaving for absurdly sentimental reasons."

"You didn't say that to his face, did you?"

"No, I did not insult him, not once. We were civil. Both of us were at our icy best."

"And everyone within ten feet covered with frost or standing close to the fire, but unwilling to leave, in case they had to save one or the other of you."

"Just so." She smiled at the lanterns. This Pennistan was the youngest son. And as different from his oldest brother as possible.

"Lynford did not know that the promise of money was the best way to secure your help?"

"I convinced him."

"I wish I could have seen it."

She heard the laughter in his voice and envied him his family and their camaraderie. His brother and sister had stood with the duke, Lord Jessup insisting any amount of money would be worth Gabriel's safe return. That kind of loyalty was as rare as honesty.

She set the candles inside the reflecting lantern as she spoke, glancing back at him. "You know, if your brother were not my sponsor, I could use this information against you. I still could insist on more money to keep silent about your misadventures as a spy."

"Lynford would find you and ruin you if you tried. Jess would snub you until no one would receive you."

"It would only matter if I moved in society, and it must be clear I do not."

"Not entirely. When I switched to English, so did you. You have been speaking perfectly cultured English for the last hour. You sound as though you often have tea with the Queen." His smile invited her to share the joke.

Damn. How could she have been so careless?

"Perhaps I am the one who will blackmail *you*." His smile turned wicked. "You are neither nun nor prostitute. But perhaps you are not completely a lady either. Based on all the data at hand, I would say you are an actress. I imagine you can play any role you wish."

Let him think he had the best of her. His arrogance suited her at the moment.

He was watching her closely through narrowed eyes, and she realized the lanterns made the room brighter and her wet shift left little to the imagination.

"I'm wrong, you know. You could not play *any* role. No one would mistake you for a boy."

She moved to the chair to gather her clothes. "You will shave while I change my shift and dress. There are clothes for you on the table. If you cooperate, you will be on your way to England before dawn."

Hearing the water slosh, she stopped gathering her clothes and looked up, disappointed he had taken the towel and wrapped it around his waist as he stood.

When he saw her looking, he stepped from the bath and dropped the towel to the floor.

She shivered, but only because the room was cold. Gathering her clothes, she went through the door, stopping to pick up the cat, moving slowly so Gabriel would not know she was even a little tempted. A fool he might be. Harmless he was not.

5

CHARLOTTE AND GABRIEL stood at the door of the tavern, waiting for a group to leave. Each one of the men eyed Charlotte and did not even notice him. She was right. With her nearby he was invisible. He relaxed a little, though Charlotte had insisted that an attitude of discomfort would suit their story perfectly. Hardly heroic, but at least he was the one with her. He would bet his left arm that she was the most desirable woman any of these men had ever seen. How would he feel if they had been to bed together? Smug, he decided.

"Do you come here often?" he asked.

She shrugged.

He'd realized that conversing in French required just enough concentration to divert his mind from his predicament. There was also the absolute pleasure in having someone to talk to.

"Are you one of the three birds that give Aux Trois Oiseaux its name?"

"When it suits me."

"It does tonight. You are as exotic as the tropical bird Dr. Borgos kept as a pet."

She did not respond to his compliment and gave her shoulder to a man who came too close.

"I thought that turquoise dress was striking, but this one is even more eye-catching." He stepped back to watch her. "It's blue, that changes to violet as you move." She even wore a shawl of the same material. "Where do you find these gowns?" he asked as he admired the woman as much as the chameleon effect of the material.

"I have the gowns made at the modiste who works for whores."

"I think not. I know any number of ladies who would envy you that gown."

"Who ever said that ladies could not be whores?" She tucked her shawl more snugly under her shoulders and arms.

How many ways could she use her clothes to tempt? He cleared his throat and tore his eyes away from what she was offering. "Were you doing some reconnoitering when we passed here twice before tonight?"

"Very good, monsieur. You *are* observant." Her sultry smile made it seem as though she was captivated by something he had said. Her expression caused the next importunate man to abandon his suit. "I was hoping I had completely confused you."

"Oh, you did confuse me. Just not completely."

She gave him a genuine smile and he counted it a victory.

The common room was nearly full. He would bet Jess that this place was a brothel as well as a tavern and a place to eat. Every harbor town had as many as the traffic could bear. Like a posting house without horses, he decided.

The poor light was further compromised by the smoke from a dozen pipes floating up to the rafters. The smell of the tobacco kept company with unwashed bodies and the sweet perfume the prostitutes favored. He looked as though he belonged, if only because his clothes were similar to what the others wore. He was too blond and too tall but hoped that once they were seated no one would notice him any more than they did now.

Charlotte stood at the entrance, patting her hair and smoothing her skirts, before she took the three steps down into the room. He followed her. The high-backed benches with tables between gave as much seclusion as a private room. A good place to do business of all kinds. Even at this hour, closer to dawn than midnight. He could imagine the business being done up the stairs.

Gabriel scanned the banquettes, but it was too dimly lit to make out anything more than the shapes. Male and female. When Georges rose from the most private of the tables, Gabriel started. "How can he be here?" he whispered, so surprised he barely remembered to speak in French.

Charlotte did not answer. Gabriel had learned enough in the past year to keep silent as well. Moving to the table as she directed, he watched from the corner of his eye as Georges left through the back door.

There were tankards on the table as well as a plate of bread and cheese, untouched.

"*Mangez!*" she commanded.

He did not need to be told twice to eat. Charlotte sipped at the beer. Took a small bite from a piece of cheese. Gabriel made steadier inroads. "Cheese and ale have been the mainstays of my life this last while, but this cheese and ale are as different from that fare as you are from the Princess of Wales."

"We are both named Charlotte," she said, as if to challenge his analogy.

"I imagine that she speaks French as well as you do."

"And the list of similarities ends there."

"If your hair was not quite so red and your dress more discreet, I imagine that the two of you could easily be found at the same entertainments."

"You persist in casting me as a lady fallen on hard times." She sat back and shook her head. "I am exactly what I appear to be."

He laughed. His life was hanging by a thread, a woman was his one hope for escape, but he could not help laughing. "I have not met a single woman, whether she be prostitute or princess, who is exactly what she appears to be." Gabriel raised his tankard, saluting her. The beer was like a golden nectar, but he took only one sip.

He banished the laughter and spoke slowly. "How did Georges find a way out? Tell me," he insisted.

She reached for her own tankard but did not raise it. Instead she ran her thumb along the side of the mug.

"Tell me the truth, Charlotte."

"It was part of the plan all along." She looked him in the eye as she spoke and he decided it was the truth, if only because it was half an answer.

Before he could press her, she asked a question of her own.

"Anyone can see that you are too thin, but how is it that you have maintained your strength? You were in that place for months." She leaned closer and whispered, "I fully expected that you would be hard-pressed to walk as far as the boulevard. Prison can be completely debilitating. And you were described to me as a man of science."

He waited for her to add more, but she did not. "You mean that you found my appearance and my interests at odds?"

"Yes," she said, an edge of irritation coloring the word.

"You're not the first woman to be intrigued."

"I do expect," she said, leaning closer, "that I am the first woman who is more interested in your learning than in your body."

"Not the first," he admitted, "but certainly the first who is even after bathing me."

"Which of the sciences have you studied?" she asked, completely ignoring his comment.

"Whatever holds my interest."

"You are, then, like a dilettante in the arts."

"Yes," he said with his mouth full, then fell silent while he finished chewing and swallowing. "I have spent the last few years on the study of astronomy. That was useless in prison."

He washed the food down with a long swallow of ale. Then he pushed the empty plate aside. "But before that I spent all my time studying anatomy and how the body works. That is how I knew that I would lose my physical abilities if I did not move. Not to mention going mad from the lack of intellectual company. At first I had some money and I bribed the guards to let me out into the courtyard. When the money was gone I made myself walk my cell from my first meal to my last. I would pull myself up on the rings in the wall, grateful that was the only use they were put to. I studied the rats to see if they emulate human behavior in any way. I may write a paper on that."

"You would write of rats? What a waste of time."

"I have heard that before too. But science embraces all manner of creation and all subjects. The rat's very existence makes it of interest."

She shook her head and said no more. Gabriel allowed the silence to lengthen, hoping she would add some details of her own life.

She remained silent. So she was not a woman who was easily manipulated. She pushed her bread and cheese toward him.

Reaching out, Gabriel pretended intimacy, taking her hand instead of the bread and cheese. "Tell me how Georges escaped."

He turned her hand and began caressing the skin between her index finger and thumb.

Charlotte pulled her hand from his, reached for the bread and tore off a piece. He could play the game too, he thought, as he watched her tear the bread into crumbs.

"You planned the riot, didn't you?" The idea struck him with such clarity that he felt an idiot for not realizing it sooner.

"Very good, monsieur."

"If you knew there was to be a riot, why not let me escape then?"

"Because there was no guarantee you would survive it." She brushed the crumbs from her fingers. "And I will be paid double if you reach England alive."

"Double what?"

"A thousand pounds."

"How odd to know what your life is worth." He sat back and tried to decide if the amount was insult or compliment. "So, I am worth two thousand pounds and Georges is expendable."

"Never."

The edge to her voice and the sharp look she gave him was as good as calling him a fool. What was Georges to her? It was obvious he was more than a servant. From his observations Gabriel would say they were not lovers. There was not enough information to conclude anything more.

"Georges knows that his life is more valuable to me than yours, monsieur. Your brother understands that as well."

Her words were enough to remind him that despite the comfort of clean clothes and food he was still not guaranteed escape. It took all his discipline not to stand up and leave the room. Take his chances. At least he knew the language, was clean and was wearing a wonderfully nondescript set of clothes.

What could she do if he left? A number of answers came to mind, all of them unpleasant enough to have him keep his seat. "How many people do you know here? Or, perhaps I should ask, how much of Le Havre is in league with you?"

"Enough."

"Odd. I would have thought the French would be more difficult to suborn. Loyalty to the Emperor and all. But then, 'enough' could be two or two hundred."

"If you had been held anyplace else, your brother would have had to pay me much more, with less certainty of success. Le Havre is a natural gathering point for all sorts of intrigue," she said, with a fondness that convinced him deception was a favorite hobby of hers.

His meal was no more than crumbs on his plate and still they sat. Not for much longer, he hoped, rubbing the back of his neck. The tension was giving him an aching head and her perfume was making him ache elsewhere. "What are we waiting for?"

"A signal."

Now he did look around the room, trying to identify the person who would carry such information.

She reached across the table and patted his knuckles. "Until then, act like a besotted lover."

He raised her hand and kissed it. "I am not the actor you are, Charlotte."

She nodded in agreement and gave her attention to the room. The other patrons.

He had spent more than eight months waiting. A few more hours should be easy. It was not. To be so close to freedom and still not able to feel it was frustrating. Couple it with the constant, nagging fear of discovery, and he was about to explode.

"Eat my cheese. I am not sure when you will eat again."

He took the rough cloth serviette and wrapped the rest of the cheese and bread. "From that one sentence I can deduce

I will leave by boat and you are not sure how long it will take to reach a naval vessel in the blockade."

She did no more than raise her eyebrows and say, "Very good," and was about to continue when the agreeableness of the common room was obliterated.

The door was slammed against the wall. A troop of soldiers crowded through the doorway. Conversation stopped. It was as though everyone in the room suddenly wished to be someplace else.

Gabriel turned to look at the troop, since that was what everyone else was doing. Charlotte swore quietly and Gabriel put his hand on his knife. Did she have a weapon?

She rose slightly from her seat. *"Et voilà. Mon cher capitaine, comment vas-tu?"*

Gabe stiffened. The room was so poorly lit they might have escaped notice. Instead the captain made his way to their table. As she talked to the captain, he saw it as a ruse. How could someone who was the center of attention be doing anything illegal? It worked for her because she was, by her own admission, willing to risk everything for the money promised.

It was all he could do not to shrink down in his seat. Slide under the table to hide. Not particularly noble, but then very little about this situation was.

"Charlotte." The leader of the squad did not seem as excited to be singled out as Gabriel thought he would be. "What are you doing here with this one? I have been waiting for you since this afternoon."

"This afternoon? No, *mon cher,* it was yesterday we were to meet." Charlotte stood up and moved so the captain could not see Gabriel without moving around her. "And here I thought you had lost interest. Have your marriage plans changed you?"

"*Non*. Never," he protested, leaning closer to her.

"So you say." She did not sound convinced. "You have been looking for me everywhere?"

"I must work sometimes, Charlotte," he said, puffing up with importance. "Some English pig escaped from the prison during a riot early tonight."

"And where is the colonel while you work so hard?"

"He is busy with the mayor this evening."

Gabe watched them, listened and pretended he was invisible.

"While a prisoner is on the loose?"

"The colonel is a law unto himself, *ma chérie*. I will tell him that you are sorry to have missed him."

Charlotte laughed, and Gabe realized that the colonel was not a friend of hers.

"You know, Raoul, I was near the prison this evening. A friend had sent for me. She asked me to spend some time with her son."

Gabe had no trouble glowering now. If she used the line about his being inexperienced, he would go from glowering to angry.

"His wife died six months ago and he has lost all interest in women."

"But with your help he has recovered completely, eh?" The captain never once looked at him. Charlotte had all his attention.

"No, I am sorry to say the evening has been a failure.

Why else would we be sitting here at this hour? I even took him to Madame Rostine's to watch the live vignettes." She shook her head. "Nothing."

Rising on tiptoe, she whispered in the captain's ear, though loud enough for Gabriel to hear. "I have listened to stories all night. And the tears . . ." She shook her head.

Gabriel could feel his color rise along with his temper. He began naming Lavoisier's thirty-three elements, clenching his teeth until his jaw ached.

The captain dismissed him with a flick of his hand. "You will be free tomorrow?"

"I am sorry, but I must go to Paris. My patron there is annoyed I have been away so long."

"Delay one more day, *chérie*." He ran his hands up her arms. "Come to me here tomorrow." The captain smiled and stepped closer to kiss Charlotte. It was a long, deep kiss. The captain stepped back and ignored the round of applause. The captain bowed to Gabriel, more insult than deference. "Will that help, monsieur? Jealousy is a powerful aphrodisiac."

6

AS CHARLOTTE SMILED and kissed the captain lightly, Gabriel kept his seat, reminding himself that this was a private drama in which he had no part. The captain's words were not a personal insult.

"Perhaps, Raoul," Charlotte said. "Perhaps I can stay a day longer." She stepped away even though he had not yet let go of her arm.

Then again, seeing another man kiss a woman who was with you would arouse something in a man if not lust.

Before the guard captain could press her further, his sergeant came up to him. "No one here knows anything."

Raoul let go of Charlotte's arm and turned away, but the new man stood off to the side and could see Gabriel more easily. He looked at him with hard eyes.

Gabe wanted to raise a hand to rub at his forehead, but taking a cue from Charlotte, he did not move to hide his face.

The soldier was about to say something when his captain told him to check the private rooms upstairs. The captain turned back to Charlotte.

Surely, Gabe thought, the man he was pretending to be would try to assert himself into this scene. Doing his best to separate his character's feeling from his own, Gabe stood up and stepped beside Charlotte. "Why are you searching here for the escaped man, Captain? This place is a good distance from the prison."

"The jailer who disappeared was last seen here. It had to be investigated."

"I suspect the truth of it is that you hoped to find Charlotte here as well." He took her arm. "But as you can see, she is already occupied."

He felt the pressure of Charlotte's other hand on his arm. It was a painful pinch. Was she angry at him or afraid of the captain?

"I am sorry to have missed you, Raoul." She raised her hand from Gabriel's arm to trace a finger down the captain's cheek. "If I can delay, I will see you tomorrow. Here, in the evening. But I think we must be going now."

"I am expecting you, madame," the captain said as he stepped aside so they could leave.

The words struck Gabe as a command. He was considering the implications of that and missed what the captain said next. A ribald burst of laughter followed them out the door.

The street was quiet, the air heavier, the sky showed no stars. Would it rain?

Charlotte did not head directly for the harbor and Gabriel reasoned she was taking a more circuitous route there. The silence was exactly what his frayed temper needed. Soon he would be away from this nightmare. That last encounter had come too close to ruining it. Fear, dislodged by temper, crawled through him again. The near-empty street, the heavy skies did nothing to allay it. He needed a distraction or he would go mad.

"How long did it take you to do it?" The soft gray light of dawn seeped into his voice.

"To do what, monsieur?" Her voice matched his.

"To perfect the ability to distract men with your body, to bend them to obedience without a word."

She was silent a moment, but the smallest bit of tension echoed down her arm and through him.

"I notice details." He laughed a little. "It is how I proved my worth to Wellington's staff."

"Yes, you use your talents and I use mine." He could feel her nod as she spoke.

"I bow to you, madame. Your talent is a formidable weapon."

"I hope so. It would not be worth the sacrifice if it was not."

Sacrifice? The word stopped him in the middle of the quiet street. He waited until she raised her eyes to his. "Who is *your* jailer, Charlotte?"

Those usually guarded eyes showed that once again he had come close to a truth.

"No one owns me."

She spoke with such challenge, such conviction that he did no more than nod.

"When I am paid, it is for my services." Lest he should

have any doubts about what services she meant, Charlotte pressed her body against his.

"I am as susceptible to distraction as any other man." This was not the time or place for revelations. But the word *sacrifice* etched itself into his memory even as he spoke.

She relaxed, at least the tension around her mouth eased. Good, he thought. Let her think she was still in control. But each time he grasped a truth about her, each time he voiced it, the power shifted. In his experiments he had learned to accept small steps to success. He could be patient when he had to be.

"You must do as I tell you," she said with irritation. "I told you not to speak unless you had to."

"No man could be silent in the face of such a challenge. I had to say something. No man, even one struck with grief, will tolerate having his shortcomings discussed openly." They had been walking slowly. Now they were standing in the street. Gabriel looked back toward the tavern. It was still in sight.

She looked up at the night sky. It was a long time before she looked at him again. "I told you to be quiet because your accent is so cultured, more suited to court than a tavern. And I did my best to make you angry because it gives you color. You are too pale, and I doubt grief for a lost wife is enough explanation except in a Minerva Press novel."

"You could not tell me this before?"

"It is better for you not to know the details. More than your life is at stake." She began to walk again.

He did not move with her, compelling her to stop too.

"Exactly what else are you risking? Who? Do you mean Georges?"

"It does not concern you."

"Everything about this concerns me, Charlotte," he said, closing the small gap between them.

"Very well." Her sigh was resignation and still she was silent a moment more. "There are other people who will be served by this effort. People still trapped here in France who will have a chance at freedom if I am successful."

"That is the vaguest of explanations possible, madame. Which is the only reason I believe it at all." He offered her his arm. When she took it he wondered if she felt the same burn of awareness.

"If we are captured and they torture you, my lord, now you will have something to tell them."

"A lovely thought, madame. Thank you," he said, using that same acerbic tone she had. They walked on in silence and slowly. "Is this tediously slow pace a torture devised to drive me insane or is there a reason for it? There is no one else on the street. Who are we performing for now?"

"There is a reason. The discomfort is an added gift."

He waited.

"I had planned for us to stay at the inn until it was time to leave. Your confrontation with Raoul now means we will walk until dawn. The fact that it is torture for you is a small punishment for interfering.

"I never took into account that a man of science would have a temper so easily roused." She spoke so softly that he was not sure he was intended to hear it.

"You consider that a grave mistake?"

She nodded without looking at him. "It is one of several mistakes I have made. It reminds me that it is dangerous to assume too much. The only interest we share is keeping you alive."

"Yes, yes, it is," Gabriel agreed, wondering if she was reminding herself or warning him. "How odd. To be bound together as intimately as lovers with nothing else in common." He laughed a little. "Is it significant that we have finally found something we agree on?"

Before she could answer him, they were startled by the swell of sound that meant the door to the tavern had opened and swung shut.

Charlotte looked back. Shook her head. Gabriel followed her gaze. Two of the squad was behind them. Hard to tell if they were following them or on some other mission.

Pushing him into a nearby doorway, she put her arms around his neck. "Kiss me."

Her lips were cool against his, as though she was only vaguely interested in the experience. Gabe more than made up for her lack of enthusiasm. Not only because his life depended on it. Her soft mouth pressed to his obliterated fear, replacing it with lust. It was as irrational as it was irresistible.

He moved her so that she was the one against the door and pressed his body to hers while his mouth demanded more. A demand that drew nothing from her. He could feel the tension in her and was almost sure it was not only because she was anxious about the footsteps coming closer.

Raising his head, he saw anger in her eyes. "Give in to it, Charlotte. I know you feel this too."

He touched her lips again, wooing her, moving his lips and tongue along her mouth as though he had only to find the right spot to unleash what she guarded so desperately.

She held still until he thought he had lost the siege and then an absolute torrent of feeling poured from her. She was fierce in her passion, holding his head with her hands, her mouth opened to him. He felt her body fit with his as she raised her leg so it wrapped around his hip. He buried his face in her neck as he tried to retain some control over his body.

Time and place faded and his world was filled with the aching pleasure of passion edged with darker feelings. He felt her need match his own and wondered what he had unleashed.

"We both know what they will be doing tonight." The soldier's words carried to where Charlotte and Gabriel were sheltered, the doorway gathering in the sound so they could hear. It brought them back from their erotic adventure in an instant.

Charlotte was actress enough to hold her pose. His face buried in her neck, Gabe drew in her scent as they listened to their audience.

"His eyes were red and his clothes ill-fitting. I was sure he was the spy."

"His wife died. He was prostrate with grief."

"Not anymore." The suspicious one relented. Gabriel could feel Charlotte relax. She raised his head with her hands and looked into his eyes. She rested her lips on the corner of his mouth. Neither one of them was thinking about sex.

"Where is the justice? He's with her and we are awake all night, in the rain, watching the harbor."

Charlotte drew away. He could see she was surprised. If they knew enough to watch the harbor, what else did they know? She let go of him, no longer paying him any attention at all.

"Charlotte is too smart to be taken in by a lying, cheating spy."

Gabriel missed the rest of their comments as the two soldiers lost interest and moved on.

"Madame Rostine would pay us well for our pose, monsieur."

"You weren't acting any more than I was. I would say that we were both . . ." he paused, . . . , and then finished, ". . . we were both distracted." He chose the word quite deliberately, making a lie of her claim that she could not be so influenced.

She made a small sound that was agreement or dismissal, but not denial.

"Charlotte, I have no doubt discovery is one of the possibilities you considered. What are we to do now?"

She cupped his cheek with her hand in that gesture that was not nearly as affectionate as it appeared to be. "We are going where they think we are going and we will do what they expect us to do."

7

EXPLAIN WHAT YOU mean by that." He reached for her hand, lowering it from his cheek in a grip that was tighter than necessary.

Charlotte could feel his anger. Was it always so close to the surface? "We are going to Madame Rostine's, where I will put you in the care of one of her girls."

"Oh no." He shook his head for emphasis. "You and I are together until we reach England. I *would* be a fool to let you out of my sight before I can kiss the dirt of home."

The rain began, little more than a light drizzle. And the dense clouds promised more. That would work in her favor. "Listen to me. The soldiers will not stay long at the docks in this rain. I must go home and try to salvage what I can of my plan. I will come for you later today."

"No." He let the single word hang between them. It was enough to make her see that he would not be persuaded. "We can stand here all night, or stay at the brothel together. Or go back to your house."

"None of my men come home with me. I always use Madame Rostine's. If I took you home, it would rouse suspicion." It was the absolute truth but not the whole of it.

"You took me there once tonight."

"It was necessary. We went in the back door and only to the kitchen. For reasons I explained at the time."

"Yes, because anyone could tell I had just come from prison." He was silent a moment. "It could be that was your first mistake, Charlotte Parnell. Leaving me at the brothel, or anywhere else, will be your second mistake, because I can, and will, find you."

He released her hand and waited with that way he had of staring at her. Could he find her house on his own? He was such a fine observer she could not discount his ability to work the puzzle successfully.

The mist turned to a steadier shower and made the decision for her. "Madame Rostine's," she said with a nod. "The rain will start in earnest any minute. Hurry or we will both be wet through."

She pulled her shawl around her head, as Gabriel began to take off his jacket. "Wear this," he said. "The weave is tight. It will keep you dry. I am used to the cold."

"Stop," she hissed. "Keep it. Madame Rostine's is only a few streets away." She tugged on his arm and pulled him along. "I am a prostitute and exist only for your comfort. What I feel or need does not matter."

"I have a vested interest in keeping you healthy, Charlotte."

He kept pace with her, both of them moving purposefully as the weight of the rain grew.

"You are playing a role tonight and your part is to see me as something to be used and forgotten." By the time they reached the front steps of Rostine's, Charlotte could feel water dripping down her back, soaking through her dress, ruining it. The wet silk trapped the cold against her skin. She had to hold her body rigid to keep from shivering.

"Not afraid to show her success, is she?" Gabriel said as they hurried up the wide rise of steps leading to the portico that framed the front door.

Yes, it was an elegant house, with columns, marble, brass and windows. It was more grand than anything else on the street. Rather like Madame Rostine herself.

Charlotte ignored the brass knocker, shaped like a naked fairy, and found the familiar spot she knew would echo best.

The door opened quickly and the porter stepped back without speaking. Charlotte hurried in out of the rain, as the downpour worsened.

The servant stepped away as Madame Rostine herself came down the stairs, dressed as though she were still welcoming business, complete to the feathers rising from an elaborate coiffeur.

"Charlotte," she said with surprise, "I had not expected to see you this evening." She gestured to the porter and he moved from the door and up the stairs. "Come into the salon and warm yourself. I will have your room ready in a moment."

Charlotte swept ahead of them and into the drawing room, well aware that Madame was doing her best to flirt with Lord Gabriel. She could only hope that he would be tempted by Madame's robust beauty. She gave them a moment and then turned as they followed her into the room. He moved from the door to the fire, glancing at her with more exasperation than interest.

"I think we will be here for most of the day and perhaps into the evening."

"You have paid for the room, Charlotte. It is yours for as long as you wish." With a nod, Madame Rostine made to leave.

"Will you have someone bring Charlotte a robe so that she can change out of her wet clothes? They are an invitation to illness."

"But of course, monsieur. I will send a maid immediately." She glanced at Charlotte and with a slight tilt of her head conveyed amusement at his solicitude.

Charlotte shrugged. "He is a physician and given to detail."

"Lucky you." With that, Madame Rostine swept out, taking her cloying scent with her, leaving her cynicism behind.

Charlotte walked quickly to the fire. Gabriel went to the table and poured two brandies. Handing her a glass, he raised his to his lips.

"Drink it slowly," she said.

"Shall I call you nurse as well as jailer?"

She watched as he took one sip and then another. He closed his eyes and breathed a long, slow "Ahhhh." He took one more taste and set the glass aside.

"I am well aware that it has been months since I have had anything but watered ale."

She had been reminding herself as much as speaking to him. This situation was ripe enough for folly without fueling it with spirits. Charlotte bent to put her glass of brandy on the table, but the fabric of her dress pulled across her back, the cold of it making her gasp. A convulsive shiver overcame her, and instead of setting the glass aside, she took the brandy like medicine in one long swallow. Oh, it felt wonderful, burning its way through her, calming the chattering of her teeth against the glass.

"Let me free myself from this," he said, as he struggled out of his coat, "and I will pour you some more."

Standing with her back to him, Charlotte held her hands out to the fire. She toed off her shoes. That was a mistake. Without shoes she felt even more vulnerable.

There was a tap at the door and Lord Gabriel answered it. Charlotte glanced over her shoulder. A woman, older and leaning heavily on a stick, handed him a robe. He thanked her with quiet gravity, closed the door, strode to the fireplace and, without asking, began to work the laces arrowing down the back of the blue dress.

Charlotte stiffened, but could not deny it was the only way. It proved to be slow work. The feel of his fingers at her neck made her shiver as much as the cold did. "Rip it off," she said. "It is ruined anyway."

He hesitated only a minute and then did as she ordered. The sound of the tearing fabric brought a memory, a child crying as she was pulled from her mother's arms, the woman's dress tearing as the child refused to let go. Charlotte blamed the brandy for the image. It was one of her dreams and, please God, nowhere near the truth of what had happened.

The dress dropped in a pool around her feet. He turned her to face him, his fingers leaving a warm imprint on her cold shoulders. It was all she could do to keep from stepping into his embrace, the warmth of him almost worth the risk. She hated being this cold.

He began to undo the front-fastening corset. Charlotte raised a hand to stop him. He pulled his fingers from under hers. "Yours are still shaking," he said, his eyes kinder than his tone. "Let me help you. Or is this another way you have of courting death?"

She returned his look while she considered a choice that should have been easy. Finally, she gave up the debate, dropped her hand and looked over his shoulder.

"I've never seen stays that lace in the front," he said as he made quick work of the closure. "From the same modiste who made your gowns?"

"Yes," Charlotte said, smiling a little, still avoiding his eye. "She is quite inventive. I expect someday every whore will own one."

He finished and the unlaced stays slipped down her arms. His chest brushed against her breasts and she pressed closer.

Lord Gabriel shook his head as he stepped back. "I know your game now, Charlotte." His smile was not lecherous, not even appreciative. "And I am immune to it."

She looked down his body to where the evidence of his arousal made a liar of him.

"I correct myself," he laughed, "my mind is immune. My body is all male. And you are not a jailer but a witch."

She wore only her chemise now. It was no more than damp in spots, but wherever it touched her the cold came back. He bent down to take the edge of it. She ended that with a firm "*Non.*" When she had his attention, she added, "I am not a child. This much I can manage."

With a nod, he went back to the table and finished refilling their glasses.

"My lord?" She timed her question so that when he turned to her she was beginning to cover herself with the robe, naked except for her stockings and the black embroidered garters that were her favorite.

He came closer, but merely handed her the refilled glass. "This is not about sex, Charlotte. This is about keeping you from an inflammation of the lungs."

"You lie." She spoke without rancor. "Between a man and woman it is always about sex."

"Is that so, Charlotte? Then your world is much too small and I feel sorry for you."

"Sorry for me? You self-righteous prig." She did not even try to control the rush of fury. "Your privilege is no more than an accident of birth. Don't you dare judge me."

He smiled and she knew the anger was a mistake.

"You misunderstand me," he said, lifting her chemise from the back of the chair, folding it carefully. "You are quite right. My birth was a lucky accident, but there are men who have made their own opportunity, many of them from humble circumstances. I am not self-righteous, only disappointed the choices women have are so limited."

Charlotte nodded, regretting the anger more than the misjudgment. She belted the robe but did not button it closed.

He pulled a chair closer to the fire and gestured for her to sit.

"Do you think you are the one in charge now?" She took a seat, cradling the brandy between her palms. "Need I remind you that you remain in mortal danger and I am still the only one who can lead you from it?"

"I have not forgotten. All the more reason for me to see that you are not taken by illness."

He knelt down beside her and took her foot in his hand.

"My stockings are already dry," she said, pulling her foot out of his hand.

"Maybe, but your feet are as icy as the Thames in January." He cradled first one foot and then the other, and began massaging warmth back into them.

It felt so good. She took more than a sip of brandy.

"The cold was the most persistent discomfort in prison," he began. "I came up with a list of ways to describe it. 'The Thames in January' was one. 'A privy in Scotland' was another." He smiled at her.

Charlotte Parnell smiled back at him. "As cold as Austria in the winter." She swallowed more brandy and rested her head on the back of the chair. "I know this has everything to do with power and nothing to do with seduction." Having said it, Charlotte let herself relax enough to lose herself in the pleasure of it.

He did not answer her. Continuing his massage, he ran his fingers down the center of her foot. She closed her eyes. He used his thumb on the pad of flesh under her toes, stroking the skin, pressing harder and harder.

He worked his hands up her leg, and she had to bite her lip to hold back a moan. When he reached the garter, he did not stop, moving an inch or two higher until she thought he must feel her heat as surely as she could feel the warmth of his fingers.

He pulled the garter down her leg quickly, bringing the stockings with it. He draped the bits of lingerie on the floor near the fire and left them to dry. He took one foot in his hand again.

She reminded herself at least three times that he was a spy and a traitor. She would spend the night with him as a means to a fortune that she and her family needed.

"Charlotte Parnell, you are no more a prostitute than I am."

She opened her eyes with a start, realizing that she was almost asleep. Had she gone mad? This man was only one step away from being the enemy.

"Think what you will, my lord," she said, pulling her foot from his hand. "I may not be a prostitute, but I am a whore."

"Whore, prostitute. Is there a difference?" He stood up, towering over her. The robe was cinched in the middle but open to her waist from both the top and the bottom.

She did not cover herself, but kept her head resting on the high back of the chair. "Prostitution is a profession." She thought a moment, giving him a chance to see what she was offering. "A whore . . . you see a whore is rather like a man of science. Something you do for enjoyment, because it fascinates you, and only occasionally for money."

Bending toward her, he began to button the robe. She pushed his hand away.

"Why do you make yourself to be of so little worth?"

His tone showed mild interest, but there was temper simmering in his eyes again. He took a step back to the table, picked up his glass of brandy and finished it quickly. Charlotte felt the power begin to shift her way.

"It is you who assign the worth," she said as she tried to

calculate how much he had drunk. "I prefer to think of myself as honest as I can be under the circumstances."

"You mean the circumstances of coming to France in all manner of disguises? Deceiving everyone but a chosen few with half-truths and outright lies. Your brand of honesty is convenient," he spoke as he refilled his glass.

"Yes, it is, my lord." The last two words were an insult.

"You remind me that I am a spy." He made a gesture as if to brush the insult away. "Tell me how we are different, for are you not a spy as well?"

"I have not been named a traitor." She stood up, pulled the robe closed and faced him. "And you have. That, Gabriel Pennistan, is the real difference between our stations in life."

Any dominance she had lost in allowing him to undress her and massage her feet, she had regained with that truth.

"Are you convinced a death sentence awaits me? If so, why should I even go back to England?"

"You have no other choice. No money, no clothes, none of the papers the French are so fond of." She could see the reality of her words strike him. "Your brother sits in the House of Lords. Perhaps his influence will save you."

There was a tap at the door as she was about to mention the possibility of prison. Instead she called out, *"Entrez."* The door opened a crack. No one came in, but a man's voice carried across to them, "Your bedchamber is ready, madame."

"Merci bien, monsieur."

The servant closed the door. Charlotte considered Lord Gabriel, looking belligerent rather than loverlike. "I remind you, my lord, whether I be prostitute or whore, for now the play continues."

8

THE ROOM WAS on the third floor, and by the time Gabriel had followed Charlotte up the stairs, fatigue pulled at him. Made him wonder if he had the strength to take off his clothes before he fell across the bed.

His muddled brain was still trying to sort out the difference between whore and prostitute. What did it matter? Even slightly drunk he understood that she was the kind of woman willing to share her body and nothing more. What made him think he wanted more than her legs wrapped around him, her body welcoming his?

The door to the room was ajar. Charlotte pushed it open farther and went in. Gabriel tripped through and grabbed the frame to steady himself, then pushed the door closed until he heard it click shut. He leaned against it, trying to take in his surroundings, lit by the fire and two candles. One thing he could see quite clearly: a bed, large enough for two. He stepped toward it. He might be drunk, but he knew what that bed meant.

She used a key to lock the door, and the sound of it grating shut sent a bolt of panic through him. Gabriel grabbed her wrist. "Do not lock the door."

"You do not want privacy?" Her surprise gave way to understanding. "I will put the key on that table so neither one of us feels trapped."

"You could take it the minute I fall asleep."

"You may put it under your pillow." She made to hand it to him, the word *fool* implicit in her tone. "The room is too small to hide it."

"The table, then," he said. "You are right, I am trusting you with my life while I sleep. Worry over the key is absurd in the face of that." He stepped away from the door, barely able to stand on his own. "Did you drug me?"

"Stop being ridiculous. You were the one who poured the brandy, and my hands were shaking too much to do anything secretly. You are exhausted. I cannot credit how you have lasted this long."

She took his still-damp coat from him and went behind a screen that must be used as a dressing area or for privacy. He undressed for the third time that day. He was out of his clothes before she could turn back the covers.

He watched her, busy at the small domestic task. "Whose bed is empty while you are with me?"

She came closer to him, her smile and half-closed eyes as seductive as her body. "My life is as I choose it. I am a widow. And committed to no one." She put her hands around his neck and stood on tiptoe, pressing herself against him. She was still wearing her robe. He could feel the warmth of her nonetheless. "Come to bed with me."

With the greatest sense of sacrifice, he took her arms from around his neck. He moved back a few steps. "Is there a need to maintain the charade, Charlotte? Unless there are peepholes in this room, I do believe we are now free to act as we wish." He looked around the room as though he could spy a tiny eyehole, pleased that he could sound so practical when his body was screaming for hers.

"There are no eyes but ours, and half a day until it is safe to leave." There was not the slightest hint of confrontation in her voice, but he could see it in her eyes. "The bed is the most comfortable place in this room. And we can make it even more comfortable together."

She'd walked around the bed as she spoke, slipping off her robe, taking a moment to drape it across a nearby chair.

Her body was beautiful, not voluptuous so much as flawlessly proportioned from neck to lovely breasts to waist to hips. Legs that were trim to the ankles. Feet he now knew quite well. Her natural hair color was a summer blond. Did she ever remove her wig?

There were a hundred kinds of fool, he realized. He was man enough to know he would be the king of fools to decline what she offered. He knew what she was about. Wouldn't that be protection enough? "So the whore offers herself to me?" he said as he climbed into the bed. The pillow was as comforting as his nurse's arms. The mattress soft, the sheets as welcoming as the first blush of sleep. He counted the bed, and sharing it with her, the ultimate of the delights he had been forced to do without.

He leaned toward her, touching no part of her but her lips. It was enough to make them both want more.

"You are so wrong," Gabriel whispered as he kissed her again and again, light kisses that were filled with frustration and temptation. "This is about sex as much as it's about power." To prove it, the next kiss was deep, and neither could deny the arousal.

"I do not care if you are prostitute or princess. Come to me as Charlotte Parnell." He spoke softly. He was so close to her that he could feel her heartbeat.

"That much I can give you." She blew out one of the candles on the table next to the bed. "Charlotte Parnell is yours."

Even as she reached for him, he knew she was too easily convinced. *Charlotte Parnell is not her true name,* he thought as her hands found his chest and his shoulders, pulling him closer. It did not matter anymore. He was beyond the word *no,* spiraling into a world of want.

He kissed her mouth, her neck and then whispered in her ear, "You must know that you will have little pleasure from this. It has been months since I have been with a woman."

"Perhaps," she said, turning her head a little toward him. She wasn't smiling, even if her eyes were warm with pleasure. "It may happen quickly, but it will be satisfying for both of us."

He leaned toward her, pressing his chest to her, trailing kisses down the other side of her neck, the smell of her pulling him deeper into her thrall. He used his tongue to tease her breasts as he slipped his hand under her neck to pull her closer, cradling her body against his, moving his other hand down her back, over the sweet roundness of her hips, moving quickly. He knew he was being selfish, but his aching fullness found her wet and willing. Charlotte welcomed him, putting her arms around his neck, urging him to move so that he was more on top than beside her.

He expected the purely physical connection he needed so desperately. None of the intimacy that would make it more than a bodily function. He was wrong. She kissed him, and though there was no sweetness in it, there was a passion that was real, begging to be shared. Her hands pulled him close and her legs wrapped him closer. The comfort of the pillow and bed paled next to the feel of her whole body blending with his. Tense with the effort to restrain himself, he felt no answering tension in her. She stretched her head back. Her eyes closed.

All shared in silence, words the only part of her that she did not give him. He wanted to give her some pleasure. To give her time to enjoy the coupling. What he wanted and what his body could give were two different things. His thoughts faded in a primal pulse of need. He buried his face in her neck as he filled her body. She pressed up against him, opening to him with a generosity that made the word *whore* a tribute.

He tried to thank her, tried to do something more than fall asleep still holding her, but this drug was too powerful to resist. He mumbled one word, "Tomorrow," and closed his eyes.

CHARLOTTE COULD TELL all she needed to know about a man the first time they had sex together. If a man was physical, sex with him was about position and endurance. If he was selfish, his satisfaction was all that mattered. If he was kind, he would pay well, no matter the circumstances. And if he was cruel, she did her best to avoid the bedroom.

Worst of all, worse than cruel, was the man who came to bed a different person than the one met in the ballroom. Whose life in society was all lies. A man like her husband, so practiced in his deceit that neither she nor her mother had seen through the façade. If innocence had been her excuse then, he had seen that she never made that mistake again.

Lord Gabriel was sound asleep, lying on his side, the warmth of his body finally easing the chill and the headache that came when she had reached the end of her resources.

One of his arms was outside the covers, stretched across her stomach. In protection, not possession. If he wanted to mark possession, his naked arm would be across her naked body. No, the covers between them made it protection. And the gesture bore out her observations earlier tonight. When he had asked for a robe and warmed her feet with his hands, or even before that when he had asked what would become of Georges.

He had not been free more than a moment or two and he had begun to reassert that essential quality that prison had done its best to destroy. He was one who cared. Who cared with temper and passion and not by halves.

That made him dangerous in more ways than one.

How could he have been a spy? Temper and passion were problem enough, but if you combined those with his kindness, he was bound to die for his cause. Or was it all pretense? Was he that good an actor?

Charlotte knew she should leave. She could go to the

house and make sure all was well there and return, all before he stirred. She inched away from his warmth, his arm still loose atop her, and pushed one foot from under the covers.

She swore very quietly and fell back into the bed, her head swimming with insurmountable fatigue. Her eyes kept closing as if they had their own idea on how to spend the day. In that moment she made her decision, leaned over and blew out the remaining candle.

If taking him to her house was her first mistake, then falling asleep beside him would be her second. If she was wrong about him, if Gabriel Pennistan was capable of such deep deceit, deeper than her husband's lies, then this gesture would mean her death. Her last waking thought was that if he was not the man she thought him to be, she would rather not wake in this world.

MOVEMENT ROUSED HER. Charlotte spread her arm out without opening her eyes. The other half of the bed was empty. Anger and panic woke her completely. How could she have fallen asleep? How could she? She jerked upright and searched the almost-dark room.

Gabriel came from behind the screen and stopped at the window. Making a small opening in the heavy drapes, he stood watching the world beyond their retreat.

She bit her lip and did her best to control her anger, while she reached for the flint to light the candle on the table near the bed. "What is there to see?" she asked. "This room is at the back of the house."

"I can see that it is twilight." He spoke without turning

around. "This place is already alive with business. Madame Rostine keeps a very clean house and she will tolerate no dallying among her servants."

"And how can you know all that?"

Now he did look at her, smiling. "I have excellent eyesight." He let go of the curtains, but then pushed them apart a little so that the last of the daylight filtered into the room. "My excellent night vision also tells me something else." He came back to the bed and slid in beside her. "You are in need of more attention. You should be in fine spirits and I do not see even the smallest smile of satisfaction."

She made to rise from the bed, but he stopped her by kissing her shoulder and then the side of her neck.

There was that damnable kindness. The feel of his lips made her want to turn to him, let him lavish his sweetness on every inch of her body, but there were a thousand reasons it was unwise.

"Another one of my observations, Charlotte, is that sex changes the way things are between a man and a woman."

Less tension and more trust. She could feel it too, in the one hand massaging her neck and in the way he spoke, as though sharing his observations was as intimate an act as the kiss.

She forced herself to stiffen in his hold, knowing that despite the intimacy, his generosity was woefully misplaced.

"Leave me alone." Summoning the contempt that had been so completely eroded, she shrugged out of his reach and spoke without looking at him. "I gave you what you wanted last night. But once is entirely enough."

He stilled, then pulled her back onto the pillow, so that

he was looking down into her face. "Are you saying that we had sex because you felt sorry for me?"

"Yes." The one word came out sounding brusque and callous. Though she was well aware of his temper, she went on. "I knew it would send you off to sleep as efficiently as a drug."

"You're lying," he said with what seemed to her like real amusement. "Charlotte, my dear, you wanted it as much as I did." The humor in his eyes faded. "I could make you want me again."

He touched her lips with his, small tempting touches. Each awakening the tiniest memory and an unmistakable invitation.

She turned her head away. "Is sex all men think about?" She hoped her breath of laughter sounded like exasperation. "If it is, then I can have Madame Rostine send someone to you. Need I remind you that your life is at stake? And I must go and see what can be done to preserve it."

"I hear *fool* even though it is unsaid. How wise of you not to actually speak it." He moved away from her and she wondered if his words, that kiss, had been nothing more than a contest of wills.

"If it is time to leave, then, madame, we will go together." He left the bed and gathered his clothes.

It would mean taking him to her house. Was there any other choice? She considered the question while she watched him.

He dressed quickly and efficiently, as though clothes meant no more to him than body covering. None of the vanity of a society dandy for Gabriel Pennistan.

The scars on his back were an insult to an otherwise

impressive body. She admired what little she could see in the half-light—the narrow waist, the well-formed legs—and imagined the grim determination it took to walk endlessly around the cell for weeks that had stretched into months. She added the word *resolute* to the mental list of attributes she could make use of. And while it might not be easy to bend him to her will, once he was convinced, he would be relentless in pursuit of the goal.

Her plans were in disarray but not compromised, thank God. The only option she could see was combining the two aspects of her mission. For it was imperative that they leave Le Havre as soon as possible. Lord Gabriel would understand that.

It would be easy to let him believe that he was the sole reason for this elaborate game. It could work. It had to work. Please God, let this not be her third mistake.

9

GABRIEL STARED OUT THE WINDOW while he waited for Charlotte to dress. How long would it be before he was comfortable with a locked door, in a dark room? Exhaustion had overridden the fear last night. Now all he wanted was to be outside, breathing the less-than-pristine air of the city. Is that what his life would be reduced to: moments of panic, the urge to escape his self-made prison? Dr. Borgos would turn in his grave at such a waste of a life.

The floor creaked as Charlotte moved from the bed to the dressing area.

Had she done it out of pity? If so, it would be the only time that ever happened. It made him feel like a pathetic excuse for a man.

Jess had taught him that he should be sure to ask the wallflowers to dance. It was, he'd said, a gentleman's responsibility to ensure the comfort of all the women in his circle.

Gabe was sure that his brother had done it just to see them smile. If he was brutally honest, Gabe had done it out of pity.

Was Charlotte truly a whore? Did bedding a man mean no more than a single turn on the dance floor had meant to him?

How dearly he hoped that his occasional dance partners had never construed his gesture as pity. No moment of pleasure was worth the embarrassment, the mortification, the anger that came with the realization.

"Are you ready, my lord?"

Gabriel turned to face the woman who had spoken to him. "Where is Charlotte Parnell?" he asked, not entirely joking. There had been no sound of the door opening, so he knew who this woman must be, even if the evidence before him argued against it.

"There could not be an uglier dress." He reached out and pinched a piece of the wool to see if it felt as uncomfortable as it looked. He stepped back. "Where is your red hair? I liked that wig, as did every other man in Le Havre." He shook his head at the overall effect. "Well, at least your bonnet is bearable. Are you a governess?"

"With you by my side, I am a dowdy wife." She did not react at all to his critique, only handed him a pair of spectacles. "Put these on."

He did as she ordered but asked, "Why is this necessary?"

"Because the act continues. Last night your supposed mother hired me. And I am expensive, my lord. If you are cured of your grief, which we implied by our night together, then we would not be walking the streets together again this evening. We would be in bed. That is supposing you could afford a second night." She stepped back and considered him as though he were a work of art. "Very good."

"Did you plan this or do you keep clothes here to cover all possibilities?"

"A little of both," she answered absently as she walked around him. "A stick would be too much. Stoop a little so people will believe we are a couple."

"They believed we were a couple before."

"Yes, but only because I painted you as a man desperately in need of my services."

"A virgin. A man made impotent by grief." He nodded. "And what am I to be now?"

"A man of science, of course."

"A man of science with a mouse of a wife."

"You learn quickly."

She went to the door, picked up the key from the table and opened it.

They made their way down the back way, using the servants' stairs. The passageway that ran the length of the basement was not well lit. Noise came from the kitchen, where everyone was busy preparing dinner.

Gabriel and Charlotte blended into the shadows. Moving down the hall at a confident pace, they left through the back door. Charlotte led him through the roughly cobbled alleyway as though she had done it a dozen times before.

When they reached the boulevard she took his arm.

Anyone who bothered to look would think that she was clinging to him.

They walked toward the moonrise in silence and he looked up to fix his direction. There was a planet shining next to the new moon, a bold pinprick of light. They were headed west, but that meant nothing in a city he did not know.

There was something about this parade that did not feel right. It was more than his own anxiety. Twenty minutes ago he could not wait to breathe the night air and now he wanted to be back in the room, the bed, among the familiar.

He marked their route and watched for landmarks even as he considered his disquiet. It was not the situation that was a threat. At least not any more than it had been from the moment he stepped out of the prison.

They made their way down the street, without the twists and turns of the night before. Charlotte was not making any effort to confuse him.

That's what it was. Her tight hold on his arm was another proof. It was as though her grip was the only thing that was keeping her from breaking into a run.

Leaning down closer to her, he whispered, "What is worrying you, madame?" He tried to sound like a solicitous husband. He slowed to look into her downcast face. "Are you afraid of who we might meet on the street or what is waiting for you at home?"

He felt her surprise. She drew a long breath and swore elegantly in French. "Gabriel Pennistan, I will be so happy to see the last of you."

He took stock of that unexpected answer and then smiled. When he did not respond, she looked up at him.

HE WAS SMILING, damn him. Smiling as though he knew what she was thinking. What arrogance. She should never have stayed with him, slept beside him like some besotted woman with her first lover.

She loosened her grip on his arm. How did he know she was anxious?

No one was paying any attention to them, except for two boys who had been following them awhile. She was sure they were thinking of picking a pocket or stealing her reticule. She held it tighter.

The boys passed by, then the younger of the two turned back toward them. Charlotte watched as Gabriel looked over the tops of his glasses, giving the boy a stare that was a threat out of all keeping with his bent shoulders and shabby clothes. The boy reconsidered and moved on with a bob of his head.

"Very well done, monsieur," Charlotte said in the meekest of voices.

"I'm not so sure. He knows I am not what I am pretending to be."

"One who plays his sort of game can recognize another. Let us hope that he thinks you are a man making love to a pathetic dab of woman in hopes of winning her fortune."

"Oh yes, a far better image than thief and spy," Gabriel said with a cynical glance. "Why can I not be a tutor who longs for a wife and children and you are my last hope?"

"Because no teacher would be able to discourage a thief with only a glare."

"From whom do you think I learned that look?" he asked, with a short laugh. "My tutor was a master at it. I had years to observe firsthand the stare that could freeze a boy in his tracks."

"Tell me about your childhood." *Talk to me; tell me anything that will stop me worrying about how Georges managed.* If he and the children were safe. What if he had not been able to claim them as the orphanage had promised? It would take weeks, if not months, to reconstruct another ruse. She should have gone home last night. She should have gone with Georges. *Please, please, God, do not let my weakness result in harm. Take me, take me, but not them.*

They walked the length of the street before he answered her. He stopped at the next corner. The roadways were crowded and they would have to wait for a space before they crossed.

"You want me to tell you stories of my childhood? Of Lynford and Jess and how we used to hide from my father?" He could hear the edge in his voice. "Why are you so interested? Is it so I do not pay attention to the route we are taking? So that I am even more completely in your hands?" He directed their steps around a puddle from last night's downpour. "I think not, madame. If you will not tell me what is worrying you, we will walk in silence."

The road was clear and they crossed it. It was he who set the pace, slow and steady. Charlotte relaxed a little and allowed the less-than-amiable quiet. It would only add to the sober image they were trying to convey.

*   *   *

GABRIEL RECOGNIZED THE ALLEYWAY that led to the back of her house. She urged him past it. They were going in the front door this time. Never mind that the hour for calling was long past. That was a nicety he was sure did not matter in this neighborhood.

Light filtered through a space in the curtains of a room on the ground floor. Who was waiting for them?

Charlotte did not use a key to enter. She knocked and waited. A man opened the door. It was Georges, dressed as a butler. Not well dressed, but with a face as impassive as the best porters in London.

Gabriel could feel relief replace Charlotte's anxiety. Georges was the reason for her unease? He lived for the day when some woman cared that much for him. Georges nodded firmly and answered her smile with one of his own. Gabriel watched the wordless communication and wondered what triumph they were sharing.

Georges stepped back so they both could enter. He showed them into the small well-lit parlor. The room was far from welcoming. The one settee was old and worn. The fire unlit. There was a table with two chairs on either side. A rug old enough to be called an antique if it had not been faded from years of sun. The light was the only warmth in the place, leading anyone passing outside to think, as he had, that the room was cozy and in use.

Charlotte walked across the room and pulled the drapes fully closed. Had the bit of light been a sign that all was safe?

It was not until Georges closed the door that Charlotte

spoke. Odd, Gabriel thought. Was there someone else in the house they needed to fool? Or someone else they needed to protect?

"Georges, would you please show our guest to the second-floor bedchamber in the front of the house?"

Her voice was neither the toneless mouse nor the flamboyant Charlotte. Even as he considered what that might mean, Georges moved to obey her. Gabriel shook his head, stepping farther into the room. He folded his arms across his chest. "May I remind you, madame, that we are together until I am in England."

"It is as I said before," the woman spoke, sounding more reasonable than Charlotte had. "The less you know, the safer we all are."

"Be that as it may," he bowed to her slightly, "I will not be led away. A struggle would gain the attention of everyone in the house. You can only accept my word that your safety will not be compromised."

She closed her eyes for a long moment and he felt not one bit of remorse for making her task more difficult.

He could see Georges moving about the room as if to light more candles. Gabriel kept turning to keep him in sight, sure that the man would be willing to knock him unconscious to accommodate his mistress's wish. In the end it was as it had been in the prison. Charlotte was between the two of them.

"Exactly what are you going to do, my lord?" Charlotte asked as she turned to face him. Her curiosity was sincere, judging by the confusion in her eyes. "Call for help? In *my* house? Leave and find your way back to Madame Rostine's or to the soldiers at the tavern?"

"I have no plan, other than to cause turmoil." He looked at Georges and then at Charlotte. "It would endanger not only me, but whoever else might be in residence."

He let them consider his ultimatum for no more than a moment. "I know you must devise a new plan, and in the worst case you would sacrifice me to save your people. I will not be separated from you."

"Oh all right," she said with a sharpness that made her sound like a wife annoyed beyond endurance.

Gabriel nodded and leaned against the wall. He had what he wanted. He knew when to be quiet.

"I am sorry, Georges," she said. It was her apology that convinced Gabriel the man was more than servant. "We do not have the time to make him do as we want. Last night was rife with complications, but it has convinced me that he has every wish to see home."

"As you wish, madame." Georges nodded and turned to Gabriel. "If we are trapped I assure you that you will be the first of us to meet your maker and our secrets will die with you."

It was far from a welcome into the inner circle. More like a giant step into a pit of snakes.

10

THANK YOU, GEORGES," Charlotte said, her face as implacable as her servant's.

Did she thank him for his promise to kill? That puts me in my place.

"You are welcome, as always, madame."

"Tell me what happened last night." Charlotte pulled off her gloves. She walked to the settee but did not sit down. She clasped her hands, giving Georges her full attention.

"When the soldiers came to the beach I knew you would not be coming." Georges turned his back on Gabriel. "I gave the signal to the decoy and then talked to the soldiers awhile, long enough for me to allay their suspicions that I was there to assist in an escape." He rubbed his hands together. "I spoke to them and convinced them that I was sleeping on the boat after an argument with my wife."

"Only a man would consider sleeping on that scow of

yours." She shook her head as though erasing an unpleasant memory. "It smells of dead fish."

"*Merci,* madame," he said, as if it was the greatest compliment. "After we shared a bottle I directed their attention to a boat making its way from the harbor. I mentioned that it was unusual for someone to leave in the middle of the night."

"Very good."

"It was a fine idea, madame, to hire the other boat as a distraction. It served a purpose, even if it was not the one we anticipated."

"And the man thinks he was aiding an elopement?"

"Yes, and if he has been questioned, then he can tell the truth and that will keep him safe from the soldiers."

She nodded.

"I left to fish at first light and made my way back early, my empty boat proving the fishing was poor. I thought it was an adequate excuse, though no one asked."

"Very good," she said again, nodding with satisfaction. "We will have to adjust our plan. He will come with us. He will take your part and play the wounded soldier," she said, nodding to Gabriel. "If anyone should ask, we will say that he has a grievous head wound, was once a fisherman and we are taking him out to sea in an effort to remind him of it. His family is depending on him."

Georges nodded. "I will see to it, madame."

"We can be convincing as friend and family, I think."

She was only revealing the meanest of details. What was left unsaid?

"You, Georges, will become his partner in the fishing

venture. That will be the only change. Can it be that simple? Do you see any flaws?"

Georges considered the question for a long moment. "It will work." He eyed Gabriel. "The children are the key to making it convincing."

Charlotte nodded.

"Children?" Gabe straightened. "What do children have to do with this?"

"As I said, we will be posing as a family down on our luck." Charlotte spoke slowly. Did she think he did not understand?

"Are you telling me," Gabriel said, not bothering to hide his shock, "that you are going to endanger children to make our vignette more convincing?"

"They will not be endangered." Charlotte shook her head as she spoke. She turned from him to pick up her gloves.

"This discussion is not over, Charlotte."

"What else is there to say?" She turned to him again, her face a mask of indifference. "If we are discovered, they will be returned to an orphanage."

"And if we do escape?"

"The children will be better off in England than in an orphanage here." She walked toward the window. She straightened the drapes. Then she moved on to the first wall sconce and blew out the candle.

"You are heartless," he said with emphasis. He looked at Georges, whose face was as unreadable as ever. "Lives cannot be played with, surely you understand that. Unless you have an orphanage in England that needs more children?"

"Now you are being ridiculous." Her voice was sharp with denial.

"I do not need to know you well to understand that you have been too long from an honest life if you think to use children to further your ends."

"I do not need you as my conscience, my lord. I do what needs to be done, for reasons you cannot even imagine." She moved to the next sconce. Her back was straight. Her shoulders were tense.

"Then tell me your reasons, Charlotte. I want to see you as something other than a cold-blooded bitch."

"That is precisely what I am, and you would do well to re-member it." She whirled to face him as she spoke.

He had never in his life used that word to describe a woman. It did not seem to faze her in the slightest.

"We will have something to eat now and I will tell you what we are going to do next." She moved toward the door. Gabriel took a step to block her exit.

"What orphanage will give you children without ques-tion?"

"We are in the midst of war and there are children who lose their parents every day. There are women who would sell their children rather than feed them. I can send Georges to hire two off the street and he will be back with them in the time it takes you to shave and change your clothes."

It disgusted him even as he admitted it was true. It would be easier than buying a horse. He shook his head. "I am not worth that kind of sacrifice."

"That may be. But what your brother is willing to pay me is worth almost anything."

"Almost? I am relieved to hear that you do have limits."

"Yes. I do." She said it quietly, almost whispering it.

As before, he saw in her eyes what her stance hid. Regret. More than regret, he saw shame.

His shock faded in the light of her honesty. "If I want to see home, I must accept your choice."

She nodded and stepped closer to the door. He stopped her with a raised hand. "I will have my say. Knowledge brings power. It also brings responsibility. Now that I know what your plan is, I tell you that I will not sacrifice children even for my freedom or for your wealth. If something goes wrong, I will put them first. Before you, Georges, myself or any man who would harm them."

Charlotte looked at Georges with a slight smile. He drew on his pipe.

"This is not a choice, Charlotte. If it is that hard to accept, then you might as well end it here before anyone is put in more danger."

"No, sir, on this we agree completely." With a look over her shoulder she included Georges in the statement. He nodded. Once.

"Then I will rely on your judgment."

"As I must rely on your cooperation."

Relying did not mean trusting, he reminded himself.

"Come," she said. "You must be hungry."

Gabriel did not need Georges at his back to encourage him to follow her. Yes, he was hungry. In fact, *hunger* was too mild a word. Last night's bread and cheese had reminded his stomach that there was food worth eating.

Some unseen hand had left soup on the hob. There was a fresh loaf of bread on the table.

"Who takes care of this house and never shows himself? Or is it the cat?"

The tom stretched its length near enough to the hearth to feel the heat. It leapt up and came to Charlotte as they sat down.

"Georges is a man of many talents."

An answer that was not an answer. Hadn't Georges been fishing all night?

They both ate. Gabriel listened while Charlotte spoke between dainty spoonfuls of the chicken stew. Georges did not sit with them. He stood near the door, smoking his pipe.

"Do you remember that Raoul made me promise to come to him?"

Gabriel nodded.

"I must go to Aux Trois Oiseaux. Alone." She set down her spoon and reached for the bread.

"I will not be separated from you."

"Nonsense. For one hour."

"Five minutes would be too long."

"Monsieur," Georges said, "you will let her go or I will knock you unconscious and tie you to the chair so she can do as she wishes. It is what I should have done earlier."

It was quite a speech for Georges. Gabriel raised his hands in mock surrender. "All right," he said, and surprised them all. "It will give me a chance to become better acquainted with you."

Even Georges smiled a little at that absurdity.

"I will change and leave now," Charlotte said as she stood and scooped up the cat at her feet. She left through the door that opened into the hallway.

Gabriel watched the door, willing her to come back. He had a thousand questions. He turned his attention to Georges. Now, there was a challenge.

Gabe sat back and laced his hands across his stomach. "I notice that she never addresses me by name when you are with us. Why?"

As expected, Georges did not answer but only shrugged his shoulders.

"Which means that you do not know either." Gabe looked down for a moment and then spoke his conclusion aloud. "She protects you."

Georges narrowed his eyes and pulled out his pipe and lit it with one quick movement. Gabe straightened in his chair, pleased to see a reaction. "She cannot collect her money or complete her work from prison."

Or if she is dead, Gabriel silently added. He looked down at his empty bowl. "But I am her work here, am I not?" Gabe asked, raising his hands as he did so. "I am the cash prize."

Georges shrugged.

Gabe was learning to read those Gallic shrugs. Not in the movement of the shoulders; he read the facial expression that went with it. Georges's shrug meant *probably.*

"It is as much about protection as it is about money, isn't it? Does she protect you and me to protect herself or out of concern for our safety? Do you think she would be willing to die for you as recompense for guilt? Or for love?" Gabriel waited, but it was clear that conversation with Georges was at an end.

As he considered love with its urge to protect and defend and guilt with its endless rhythm of pain and regret, he did one thing he had wanted to do since Charlotte left the room. He pulled her near-full bowl of stew from across the table and picked up her untouched bread.

11

Aux Trois Oiseaux was busy. Charlotte stood at the top of the three steps that led down into the tavern and surveyed the crowd, seeing no one unexpected or suspicious.

Beyond the groups talking and smoking, she saw Raoul in the back corner, playing cards with three other officers. Judging by the coins in front of him, he was winning, as usual.

Very good, she thought.

She flirted her way through the room, avoiding the two prostitutes who were working the other corners. By the time she reached Raoul's table she had no doubt that he knew she was there. His surprise at seeing her convinced everyone but her.

"Charlotte!" He moved over on the bench seat. "Sit down and bring me luck."

She gestured to the coins in front of him. "You have luck without me, *mon capitaine*." She leaned across his arm as if pretending to count the coins, letting her breasts rub against his arm. "I would prefer to help you spend some of it."

His compatriots laughed as Raoul promptly stood up. He left coins for a round of drinks while Charlotte made her usual arrangement with the owner.

The room one flight up was a far cry from Rostine's, but the best that Aux Trois Oiseaux had to offer. With his winnings Raoul could afford to have it for one hour.

Its greatest virtue was the fireplace and two chairs that made it appropriate for more than an evening tryst. The bed itself was large and inviting and, as Charlotte well knew, comfortable and free from bugs.

Raoul preceded her into the room, already unbuttoning his jacket as Charlotte closed the door. Before the latch dropped, there was a knock and she opened it again to accept a tray with a carafe of wine and two glasses.

Charlotte set the tray on the table, draped her shawl on the back of a chair and turned so Raoul could unlace her dress. She let it slide down her arms and loosened her front fastening stays.

Raoul watched her as he sat and poured wine for each of them. Leaving her stays loose, Charlotte sat in the other chair.

"Thank you for the warning last night, *mon ami*." Charlotte reached for her glass, sipped the dry red wine and wished she had eaten a little more before leaving the house.

"You are welcome, Charlotte. Though I wish you would not persist in creating more work for me. You must have known that they would have all of us out looking for the damned prisoner."

"Yes, but I hardly thought they could have enough soldiers to search and guard the harbor. More are coming from the front every day." She wondered if that meant that this war would end soon. Was it information the government could use?

He sipped his wine and did not confirm or deny what she said.

"The one you were with last night. Is he the man we are looking for?"

It was her turn to neither confirm nor deny.

"I did give some thought to arresting him and leaving you as the innocent." He stretched his legs out in front of him and crossed them at the ankles. "But then I deduced that if I played my role that convincingly and he was the one, you might not be paid."

"You have been at this too long, Raoul," Charlotte said, ignoring this second attempt to wheedle information from her. "I worry that you are beginning to believe that you *are* a French military officer."

"Says a woman who has played her part so long that she has convinced herself she is a prostitute."

"Touché."

"Not that I haven't appreciated your enthusiasm for the role. That dress is as provocative as the body it covers." He took some wine, his eyes holding hers over the rim.

She felt color in her cheeks and wondered where in the world the blush had come from. "Stop trying to distract me."

She said it with a smile, and then turned serious. "You are becoming careless and I cannot afford to lose you."

Raoul was quiet a long time. "You are right, Charlotte, it is time for me to go home." He put the wine down. "But you see, I have no home to go to. No employment. No skills for which anyone would pay an honest wage." He stared into the fire as he spoke, as if he could pretend he was alone and merely thinking out loud.

"You have no family?" She asked the question quietly, well aware that he had never spoken of his life in England. His silence was more than she expected. He had not said, "No."

"You can always come to me, Raoul."

"Thank you, Charlotte." He abandoned his consideration of the fire and gave her his complete attention, shaking his head. "We both know that would not work. We were never meant to be lovers. We are too alike on the outside and much too different at our core."

"Yes, I know, but what I meant is that you could work for me at home in Sussex. There is always so much that needs to be done. And the boys so need a tutor who is as clever as they are."

"No, I could not work for you. Teach four boys and none of them older than ten years? I think not. Besides, we may not belong together but I am not immune to your charms, *ma chérie.*"

"Thank you. I think."

He raised his glass to her in an unspoken toast, and then shifted in his seat. She could almost see him push the too personal discussion out of his mind and return to the subject at hand.

"There is a good chance that I will be sent to the front before you come back."

Charlotte put her glass down and closed her eyes.

"Oh, do not worry. I will not actually go there. It will be the ideal moment for Captain Raoul Desseau to disappear."

"Good, very good, Raoul, and a great relief."

"I wanted to tell you and to advise you to be careful. The colonel grows more and more interested in you. Why did you not just bed him and be done with it?"

"Because I am not sure I would have survived his attention. Madame Rostine warned me, but I could see it myself. He is brutal if he is not satisfied, and his kind never is."

"You will be careful, then?"

"Of course I will. Thank you for the warning, if not the good-bye. I cannot imagine Le Havre without you."

"You have a new plan for tonight?" he asked, avoiding, as usual, anything that was at all sentimental.

"There is no plan for tonight but for sleep. In the morning."

"It is not as straightforward as last night's plan, is it?"

"No. More a deep disguise that will fool anyone who is still awake enough to approach us."

"You have found more of the children, then?"

She nodded.

"And your prize is as much an actor as we are?"

She shrugged. "Desperation awakens all kinds of talents and sensibilities."

As if on cue, they heard a commotion on the stairs, someone racing up as though followed by a troop of demons, and then a pounding on the door. Without a word Charlotte stood up. The door slammed open as she stepped closer to Raoul and into his arms.

GABE RESTED HIS ARM on the kitchen table and stared into the fire, mesmerized by the glimmering of the coals as they cooled. The coals were like his fear, reduced to a manageable glow but never fully smothered. Even now in the safety of the house, he could feel fear in the pit of his stomach, and an ache at the back of his head.

There was no damn clock in the room and no way of knowing how long Charlotte had been gone. He had suggested a card game at least an hour ago, but Georges had shaken his head. He appeared as stoic as a Spartan warrior. *No need to worry about Charlotte,* his expression said. *She knows exactly what she is doing.* Gabe wondered if that included sleeping with the guard captain.

He could tell, by the sound of footsteps, that they were not alone in the house. Georges did not respond at all to the noise. Odd. Gabe turned to him even as a small snore drew his attention. Georges was asleep standing up.

"Georges," he called quietly, and the man opened his eyes instantly, his whole body jerking awake. He looked embarrassed, and Gabe laughed. "Do you see now that you can trust me? I could have bashed you over the head and escaped quite easily."

Georges nodded, a flush coloring his face.

Gabe stood up, deciding instantly to press his advantage. "The children are already here, are they not?"

Georges looked at the door to the main part of the house.

"No, they have not been to see me. I can hear them. Scampering is the only way to describe how they sound. Add to that the kind of giggling sounds a little girl would specialize in, and one other, a boy. Only two, I think. I do believe that they are chasing the cat. If you wish to check on them, then I will come with you."

Georges shook his head.

"Or promise to wait here until you return."

"No," Georges said firmly.

"Then do fall asleep again," Gabe invited in a silky voice. "I will wake you if anything should require your attention. Did you know you snore?"

Georges did not react at all to the half insult. He checked his timepiece and pulled out his pipe.

"Has Charlotte been gone too long? Should we be worried?"

"*Non*," Georges replied. "She has only been gone an hour."

"You know," Gabe continued, "if she is protecting us, then we must, in our turn, do what we can to protect her." He held out his hand. "My name is Gabriel Pennistan. I am from Derbyshire. Do you know it?"

Georges shook his head. "You nag more than a fishwife. But like all women there are rare occasions when you make sense." He stared at the floor a moment. "I am from Gradsbourg."

"Ah yes, one of those European principalities ensnared by Napoleon." Gabe took his turn ignoring an insult, delighted with the information. Something, anything was a beginning.

"He destroyed us in one battle, barely noted."

"You fought hard and lost many. I read of it. You should be proud even in defeat."

Georges did not appear to be convinced.

Gabriel banged a fist on the table. "It's the truth, not false praise."

"My brother and cousin both died," Georges said, unmoved by Gabriel's vehemence. "I was nowhere near home at the time."

"Were you already working with Charlotte?"

"Yes," he said with the kind of inflection that meant there was more to the story than that.

"How long have you known her?" Gabe asked with casual interest.

"Longer than you have."

Gabe laughed. This was like the riddles he and Olivia used to play with her governess. "Longer than three days? Odd. I would have said more like three years."

"Longer. She was a lovely young lady when I met her." Georges's face gave the words a wistful edge.

"She isn't lovely anymore."

Georges narrowed his eyes.

Perhaps it was best not to play riddles with his jailer. "She is beyond lovely. Amazing, generous, resourceful." *Suspicious, secretive, hard.* He kept those harsher aspects to himself.

Georges nodded.

"Does she think she can save the world?"

"Yes, monsieur, she does." Georges smiled, actually smiled; then drew on his pipe. "I have convinced her to settle for this small corner of it."

"What is here that is so important to her?"

"She wishes only to make the world a better place, monsieur."

"Did Charlotte tell you of Dr. Borgos?" Gabe asked, angry at the way Georges was using the doctor's words to make her actions seem valorous.

"No. Doctor who?"

"You look confused," and since it was the first time Georges had asked him a question, Gabe actually believed he was telling the truth. "Dr. Borgos was a friend of mine who believed firmly in the need to make the world a better place."

"Then he and Madame would have much in common." Georges nodded and continued, "She has sacrificed a great deal to—"

Georges stopped speaking and Gabriel swore aloud as someone pushed through the outer door after the briefest of knocks. A man stumbled into the entryway, panting, coughing so deeply that Gabe feared for his heart.

Gabe stood up, the banked coal of his fear whipped into flame by a single knock on the door. He put his hand on his weapon and would have rushed forward, but Georges waved him back into a corner. Gabe felt like a coward but followed the order. He could not be easily seen there, and the fewer who saw him, the safer Charlotte would be. He leaned against the wall, not so far away that he could not help Georges if it was needed.

"It's the colonel, Georges," the man began, talking between

deep gasps for breath. "He is making the rounds of the taverns, looking for something, someone to blame for the spy's escape. Please tell me that Charlotte is here. It would be one coincidence too many after the last time."

Georges nodded as he moved to the entryway, pulling the door shut behind him. He could hear Georges talk to the messenger, something soothing and probably a lie.

When Georges came back into the room his expression was troubled.

"What happened last time?" Gabe asked even as he realized that the caller had been the new guard from his prison. The one with consumption. Another ally? Or a paid informer?

"It does not matter what happened before," Georges said. "The truth is that the colonel wants Madame in his bed and she has refused him. Quite publicly. She would be the perfect scapegoat even if she were not involved. I must go and find her."

"Will he not arrest you as well? What about the children?"

Georges swore.

"I will go," Gabe said. It was the obvious answer. "He has not seen me. I even know where Aux Trois Oiseaux is."

Georges began to argue.

"She does not have time for us to debate this. I will go. Now." He pulled on his jacket and ran a hand over his hair. "I will be the lovestruck widower from last night. Looking for her, hoping to spend yet another night with her." He grabbed his hat and held out his hand. "Give me some money. I will have to buy a drink at least or no one, much less the colonel, will believe I am innocent." Another thought struck him. "Is the guard captain going to hold her until the colonel arrives? Was this a trap?"

"The captain could be in as much danger as Charlotte if they are found together," he said, handing Gabe a few coins. "Now go and find her. Bring her back here."

When Gabriel would have gone out the back, Georges shook his head. "Use the front door. We will try for a semblance of normal." He opened the connecting door and said good-bye with the words Gabe had fully expected: "If you play me false, monsieur, I will find you and kill you as slowly and as painfully as possible."

12

GABRIEL SCANNED THE CROWD, doing his best to appear like a man with nothing on his mind but a woman.

The walk from Charlotte's house had been anything but comfortable. The cool night air had chilled the sweat that trickled down his neck. Odd that his first outing alone should make him feel more, rather than less, vulnerable. The echo of steps surrounded him, the air itself was heavy with fog, confusing the night sounds so he could not tell how near or far the others were until they were almost in front of him.

It was night and men eyed one another as they passed, each with their hand on their weapon, watching for a threatening move. He did the same, hoping they would not discover that his weapon was not much more than a bent spoon. He should have asked Georges for a pistol or a better knife.

More than once he raised his hand to rub at the back of

his neck as if that would erase the feeling that someone was keeping him in sight. He forced himself not to run, not to look back. No one stopped him or did more than exchange a curt nod.

He moved down the tavern's steps after the briefest of pauses at the top. Charlotte should have been easy to spot with her red wig and emerald green dress. He had seen her when she had come to the kitchen to have Georges do up the laces of her gown. Then she covered the ensemble with a green and gold shawl.

Neither color shouted at him in the crowded room. Most were dressed like he was, in ill-fitting, sober clothes. Some in the more shabby costumes that fishermen wore.

He spied only two women in the common room, nominally there to fetch drinks. They were far more interested in providing other services. Neither one of them was flamboyant enough to be Charlotte. Or clean enough.

As he worked his way around the room, nodding to whoever looked his way, it occurred to him that Charlotte's fresh-washed hands and face were half the reason that men found her so irresistible. Odd, he had never realized that before. Beneath the spicy fragrance that was her favorite, she was sweet, womanly, *clean*.

By the time he reached the barman he knew she was not in the room. Could she have finished her business with the captain and left? He was not with the group playing cards.

Had the colonel been there? No. He did not feel any fear or distress from the crowd. The fear was all his own.

He ordered a drink from a third woman, who appeared

from the kitchen, her tray laden. She nodded. He told her he would be near the fire, on the other side of the room.

As he found his spot by the smoky heat, the slightest pause in conversation drew his attention.

The relief he'd felt on entering was obliterated by the clutch of soldiers who stepped into the tavern. Like everyone who came in, the five men paused on the steps, thoroughly studied the room. Three of them then hurried down.

Gabe recognized the colonel easily enough. His uniform was far from fresh, but his insignia shone gold. He was fat from overindulgence, with an expression that showed he was never satisfied.

Self-preservation had Gabe tensing as the soldiers crossed the room. They pushed through the crowd, past him, to the table of officers, who had stood up as soon as they recognized the colonel. Gabe let out the breath he did not know he had been holding.

The man in charge of the squad spoke in a low voice while the colonel waited by the door with the other soldiers.

Gabriel forced himself to look away. He considered leaving through the kitchen. He would have, if the colonel did not have such an excellent vantage point.

Tension pulsed through the room. How many others were in fear for their life? Gabriel wondered.

Besides him. And Charlotte.

Even as he began to hope they would leave and he could ask for her, one of the officers crossed the room to a man who had a hat pulled low across his face.

"What are you hiding from?" the officer asked as he pulled off the man's cap. The accused would have fallen to his knees if one of the soldiers had not grabbed him by the arm. "Come with us and explain yourself." Gabriel and the rest of the assembly watched them drag the babbling man up the steps and out to the street.

He tried to convince himself that the nausea he felt was from eating too much. Not because he could easily imagine the kind of questioning that man would face. The scars on his back throbbed in sympathy.

If he had been asked to pick out the traitor in their midst, he too would have chosen the fellow with the hat. He was guilty of something. That much was obvious. It proved that there was much to be said for Charlotte's idea of hiding in plain view. Even if it did, on occasion, leave one in desperate need of a drink.

The colonel did not leave with his men. Gabe watched him scan the room one last time. "Where is Captain Desseau?" He addressed his question to the room in general.

No one answered. Gabriel turned to the fire, closed his eyes, although he was as interested in the answer as the colonel.

"You there!" The colonel came down the steps. The waitress was coming to him with his tankard, the colonel following her. *Do not hide. Stay in the open.*

The colonel and the waitress reached him at the same time.

"You, woman. Have you seen Captain Desseau tonight?"

"Yes, Colonel. He is upstairs with the redheaded whore right now."

Gabriel mentally swore in three languages and did what

Charlotte would have done. "Charlotte Parnell is upstairs with the captain? I have been looking everywhere for her."

Ignoring the colonel, he ran to the stairs. Bits of conversation reached him. One or two recognized him from last night. Another asked if he was back because she had not given him his money's worth, or because he wanted more.

He kept going, happy to have an audience.

He was furious with her. Anger exploded through him, erasing fear, worry, distress, like lava from a volcano destroying whatever lay in its path. *He had been worrying about her safety and she was in a bedroom entertaining a man?* When he heard the slower steps of the colonel following him, he tamped down his anger. He had one flight of steps to decide what to do. With an audience on his heels he would have to play this out. Breathing hard from more than his run up the stairs, he tried to think it through. The crowd had given him a script, the betrayed or enchanted lover. He could take his pick.

"The first door on the left." That helpful bit from someone longing to see a fight.

Pounding on the door, Gabriel pulled the latch up and swept into the room, trying for a melodramatic line that would sound both betrayed and enthralled.

"Charlotte," he exclaimed, his voice hoarse with what could only be stage fright compounded by fear, "you have played with my pride long enough."

"Move out of the way, you bombastic fool!" the colonel said as he helped Gabriel with a hard shove. "Desseau, what are you doing here?"

If his question had been bombastic, the colonel's was

stupid. It was obvious what the captain was doing. Or had been doing.

The captain and Charlotte stood in each other's arms—the captain's shirt unbuttoned, her dress around her waist, her front-fastening corset undone.

"I am not on duty tonight, sir. I arranged to see madame yesterday and was hoping to spend the evening with her." Desseau spoke as he did his best to right his clothes.

"Is that so?" the colonel asked, as if the guard captain might change his mind.

"Yes, sir, but if you have need of me I will come immediately."

"Give me the rest of your hour," an onlooker called out.

The colonel ignored him. "While you finish dressing I will speak with Madame Parnell." He turned to Charlotte, who had fastened her corset and pulled her dress up over her shoulders.

"Where were you last night?"

"I was here awhile and then spent the rest of the night at Madame Rostine's."

"With me," Gabriel added.

"With you?" The colonel turned to him. "Who are you?"

"His name hardly matters, Colonel. He paid me for the entire night and we were together until this morning."

The colonel seemed more annoyed than intrigued. "You were seen near the prison last night, madame."

"*Oui*, Colonel," she said. Gabe watched as she stepped away from Raoul and the colonel, coming closer to him. "I met monsieur there and we came here soon after."

Gabe judged it his moment to speak. "Your men, even

Captain Desseau, saw us here last night. They came just before it started to rain."

"This man is no more a spy than Charlotte is the wife of Napoleon." Desseau poured some wine and offered it to his colonel. "Last night, he was jealous of the few words I spoke with Madame. Only a fool would act that way around a whore."

The colonel took the wine and looked from one man to the other, finally settling on Gabriel. "You are a worthless guttersnipe. If I ran you through with my sword, no one would care."

With that, Gabriel ceased to exist for him, but the colonel stared at Charlotte with a lecherous hunger that was as close to hatred as lust. Gabriel was grateful for the crowd. They, at least, were on Charlotte's side.

As the silence drew out, one man called to her, "You are not a whore. You love every one of us, do you not, Charlotte?" Another laughed. "Be kind to the fool." To Gabriel he said, "It is your money she loves, but she is worth every sou."

The woman in question, the only woman in the room, waited with a calm disinterest that was not human. The wine-swilling tyrant had the power to decide whether she would go free, spend the night in prison, or worse. Gabe was afraid for her even if she was not. He had enough worry for the both of them, even had a little to spare for the captain, who was dressed and waiting by the door.

"Come, Desseau. Your leave is over." The colonel finished his wine in one long swallow. "Madame, we are not finished, you and I. I have a man to question and a spy network to uncover. After that I can give you my complete and undivided attention." Without a bow or any other farewell courtesy, the colonel left the room. The crowd parted and Desseau followed him without a backward glance.

Charlotte nodded to his back as graciously as the Queen at the end of an audience. Following the two officers to the door, Charlotte spoke to the crowd, which still waited there. "I am safe because you were witnesses. I thank you all for your support." She nodded to one of the men. "Jean, will you please tell the barkeep that I would like to buy everyone who supported me a drink. If only to prove that I love my fellow Frenchmen as much as I love money."

Jean nodded and hurried to the steps, the whole of the crowd following, with applause and shouts of *"Vive la France! Vive Charlotte Parnell!"*

Closing the door behind him, she fastened the latch before turning to face him. Now he saw fear in her face. "Who did they arrest?" She crossed to him and asked again. "Tell me, who did they arrest?"

"I have no idea. I know no one here." Then he realized who she was worried about. "It was not Georges."

She nodded, went to the table and drank some of her wine. "What are you doing here?" There was no concern for him, only anger.

He explained about the visitor and that both he and Georges had feared for her safety. He continued before she could laugh at him. "When I arrived and you were not downstairs I wondered if you had already been detained. Then the soldiers came in. I was bothered enough that I hoped Georges had followed me and we could devise a plan to help you. Georges, who would just as soon see me floating in a river facedown, and where were you? Up here with your lover." The anger echoed in his voice.

"Oh for God's, sake, would you stop talking lines from a poorly written play? It is only the two of us."

"Charlotte, this is no pretense," he said through gritted teeth. "I was afraid for your life."

"There was no need for that." She dismissed his concern with a curt wave of her hand. "I know exactly what I am doing."

"Pride goeth before a fall." He spoke the words slowly, doing his best to control himself. For Charlotte Parnell, control was power. He walked to the table and picked up her glass, sniffing the wine. "Do you know how close you came to arrest? If I had not been here, if Desseau had not been able to verify my story—" He stopped when he saw she looked more bored than concerned. "Is he your lover?"

"That is none of your business." She took the goblet from him. Finished the last of the wine.

"Oh, I think it is my business," he said, grabbing the glass back from her. He set it on the table.

Charlotte lifted the carafe and refreshed the glass and took a small sip as he continued speaking.

"You are being paid by my family. If you work for the Pennistans, you work for me." He took the glass from her and set it on the table. "I want to know why you were meeting with him and how it affects our escape."

"You took too big a chance coming here," she said, completely ignoring his question.

"It was a calculated risk drawn from your own example.

Hiding in plain sight. Who would expect a fugitive to be in the same room as the man searching for him, to talk to him? I am no longer a suspect. My ruse worked."

"He could have arrested you or run you through purely for sport. Did Georges tell you what a devil he is?" She clasped her hands tightly in front of her. The gesture caused her unlaced dress to slip down her arm. The lace edges of her stays rested on her nipples.

"I did not know you cared," Gabriel said, running his eyes down her body. "I noticed Desseau said little to defend you until I insisted he speak. Is he jealous? Does he see me as a competitor for your attention? It is true in more ways than one."

"In that there is no contest, my lord." The words carried as much contempt as a voice could convey. She reached up to raise the strap of fabric as she turned from him. Gabriel stopped her with a hand on her arm.

"Were you seducing him or was he seducing you?" When she would have spoken, he raised his hand and pressed his fingers against her lips for just a moment.

"Never mind. Spare me the details," he said with casual insult. "Let me imagine what you were doing, sharing a glass with an old lover. You were in his arms, but it is clear that you had not been to bed."

"You cannot begin to understand what Raoul and I share, my lord."

She reached for the wineglass again. He took it and threw it, so that it shattered against the wall. It did nothing to ease his temper. "Tell me," he demanded, ignoring her shocked gasp and the wine trailing down the wall. "Tell me why I should not be concerned that my *savior* was trysting with one of Napoleon's loyalists." Gabriel stepped closer to her. "When you are intimate with the enemy, it becomes my business."

"We are friends."

"You are friends with a man whose work it is to enforce Napoleon's laws? Or is he a spy too?" He laughed. "Not that it matters who you sleep with, unless it means you are closer to the enemy than you should be." Damnation, he was sick to death of this.

"When we are together, we are man and woman. His uniform means nothing." She pulled her dress up again, which only served to draw his attention to her dishabille.

"Now *you* are spouting lines from a third-rate play. He is a spy, isn't he?" He wanted to know every one of the secrets she guarded so zealously, tried to recall how Georges had phrased it. Georges had implied that if Charlotte were taken, Desseau would be in as much trouble as she was.

"Raoul Desseau is a friend."

"A friend," he said derisively. "Does that mean he does not have to pay you for sex?"

Her smile was a wicked little twist of the lips.

Frustration bubbled inside of him. "Having sex with your clothes on cannot be comfortable." He closed the distance between them. She backed up against one of the bedposts. "I suppose that it could add a sense of the forbidden," he continued, reaching up to play with the loose strings of her corset.

Charlotte drew a deep breath. He ran a thumb over the crest of her breasts. She shivered, but did not push him away.

"Why do you tremble? Are you pretending that my touch offends you? Or is it because you want more?"

"Let me go."

"First tell me something." Now their bodies were separated only by the clothes they wore. His fingers caressed her neck. He wanted to shake her, to make her tell him all that she knew, all that she planned. "Tell me what you and I are to each other. Not equals, by any means. I want to know what your plans are. Not be treated like a dog who must follow commands."

"The captain and I are not lovers." She tried to move away, but he stopped her with a hand on her shoulder.

"It was the fool I am playing who made that mistake. Gabriel Pennistan is not that naïve. No, you and Desseau are not lovers, any more than you and I are."

He reached into his pocket, tossing the last of his coins on the bed. "I have money now." He pulled her to him, pushing her dress, stays and shift down her shoulders so that her breasts were uncovered. He pinned her arms at her elbows. "If we are not lovers, Charlotte, take the money and give me your best imitation."

13

CHARLOTTE REMAINED COMPLETELY still for a moment. Not from indecision but from shock. How could she have so completely misjudged this man? Whether his lust was fueled by envy or fear, it was real. And not something to be toyed with. His mouth pressed against hers, not coaxing but demanding. When she would not open to him, he let go of one arm and pulled her closer. She could feel his arousal and was sure he had only one thing in mind.

As panic set in, she felt dread coursing through her. She would not be a victim again. "Let me go. Let me go." She punctuated each word with a kick, which did nothing to deter him.

"Give in to me, Charlotte," he said, raising his head, looking her in the eyes, his now darkened with lust and anger. "Give me what I am paying so much for." He pushed her back so that she was half lying on the bed. "Give in to me, or I will take what I want."

She tried to spit in his face, but it was no more than a sound.

He lay on top of her, making it hard to breathe. Or was it the terror that trapped the breath in her throat? This was not the first time she had been used to salvage a man's pride. With her husband, struggle had only made the punishment worse. She would save herself the only way she could. Charlotte turned her head and looked toward the window, imagining she was anywhere but here. It took all her might not to protest to this man whom she had—could it be?—begun to trust, but the instinctive "No, Charles" escaped her lips.

There was a moment as though they were frozen in a hideous tableau. Then he released her so quickly that she almost slid off the bed. Walking as far from her as the room would allow, Pennistan stopped at the small window that gave out onto the street. He kept his back to her. He leaned his arms against the wall and lowered his head. Their labored breathing was the only sound in the room.

Run! was the only thought Charlotte's panicked mind would allow. She pulled her chemise and stays into place and the sleeves of her dress up. *Run. Leave the tavern. Find Georges.*

Charlotte took three unsteady steps toward the chair, to gather her shawl. Pennistan must have heard her. He was across the room, pushing the door shut even as she tried to wrench it open.

"Let me out of here. Now." Her voice shook.

"Not yet," he said.

She raised her hand and slapped him as hard as she could. His head snapped sideways as the crack sounded between them. He shook his head and raised a hand to his cheek.

That was stupid, she thought, even as she was tempted to do it again. How she wished she had not stopped carrying her knife. She dropped her shawl and turned back to the table, and lifted the empty carafe. If she aimed carefully and used all her strength it would make as deadly a weapon as a knife.

He held up a hand as she turned toward him, testing the carafe, her eyes narrowed.

"You misunderstand me, Charlotte. You cannot leave like this."

"Yes, I can. It will not be the first time a whore has had enough of a client."

"That is not what I mean." He stepped away from the door, frustrated. "You cannot leave with this between us."

"There is nothing between us." She shouted the words. "How many times do I have to say that?"

He shook his head and she could see disbelief on his face. "There is the fact that I tried to force you. That I was so angry that I would have taken you against your will."

She tried to relax her hold on the carafe, to ease the cramping in her fingers, and walked toward the door, watching him the whole time.

"You can leave if you wish," he said. "You can slap me a dozen times if it will ease your upset. But I would rather you not crown me with that decanter."

She had her hand on the latch, the carafe in her other hand when he spoke again.

"I must have begun to believe my own acting. I do know that you are not the prostitute you pretend to be. It is a role you play. I know that," he insisted.

Her hand was still on the latch, but the agonized look on his face made her wait to hear what he would say next.

"Charlotte, I apologize." He bowed and waited for her to make a decision.

She wanted to run, to leave him behind. The silence lengthened and still he waited, with a patience she knew must be an effort. *The money,* she reminded herself. They needed the money and the security it brought. *Think about the future, not the past.*

Not quite trusting her voice, she drew a breath. "If you touch me again without my permission, I will hurt you badly. I promise you that."

His nod was firm, if not much more than a jerk of his head.

She set the carafe on the floor, not too far away. With fingers that were still shaking, she began to do up the laces of her stays that still hung loosely on her shoulders. It took a long few minutes to complete the simple task. Pulling the green silk up, she pressed the lace inserts into place, giving the dress the illusion of modesty.

She could no longer avoid looking at him. He had said he could read the truth in her eyes. She hoped her bland expression hid her fear, her memories.

"Shall I call a maid to lace up your dress?" he asked, his regret unmistakable.

She closed her eyes as her fear eased. "It would be unusual for me to call a maid. I have never done so before." Without looking at him, she presented her back. His footsteps were the only sound he made.

He began to fumble with the strings and she could tell

that he was upset too. A little of her apprehension escaped with her next breath.

"These tapes are not made for a man's hands."

She smiled weakly. There might be temper in him, but the gentleman had won out.

"You know, Charlotte, as I was coming up the stairs I had no other plan than to help you. Then I was going to take off on my own. I can speak the language, I have a little money. I can act. You showed me that." He kept on talking as he worked the laces. "Between the first tread and the last I realized that I know two people in this town. I suppose it is possible that I could find work. But if I stay in France until the war ends it is as good as admitting guilt. There is the chance I would be forced to enter the army of Napoleon."

She nodded. He was done with the lacing but continued talking to her back.

"I do believe that you will see me home. I hope that you know I am telling the truth."

She took several steps away and then faced him. "Yes, I believe you. Only a madman would want to stay here in France."

"I rise in your estimation," he said with a wry smile. "No longer fool or traitor. Thank you."

"That still leaves any number of other failings," she reminded him. How amazing that they could carry on a civil conversation when she, at least, was still shaking. "We should leave, my lord."

"Call me Gabriel, will you? There are no lords and ladies here." He spoke as he walked to the bed. "Or Pennistan if my given name is too intimate."

He collected the coins, threw back the covers and rumpled the sheets and pillows.

She should have thought of that. She closed her eyes and willed the anxiety away.

"Who is Charles?" he asked with casual interest.

"My husband," she said, too late realizing she should not have answered.

He stopped what he was doing with a start of surprise.

"I thought you told me you were a widow."

"I am."

"Thank you," he said.

"What are you thanking me for?"

"Telling me the truth. It was the truth, was it not?" he asked, as he turned to face her fully.

"Yes, it was, but not meant as a confidence, my lord. Rather a testament to my hatred of him. I will not let anyone even imagine him alive."

He looked down at his suit, brushed at some imaginary lint, pulled at his waistcoat. He picked up her shawl and handed it to her. "What do we do now?" he asked.

"Let me think a moment," she said and turned from him.

Gabriel considered the consequence of his horrible behavior. Charlotte Parnell would speak honestly only when she was so upset that she spoke before she thought. When she was more afraid of what would happen to her than she was of the truth. What had it taken to frighten her past bearing? The threat of rape. He could still hear the strangled gasp and a name that had brought him to his senses.

Her fear had given him the answer to one question.

Widowed from a man who had done the worst a husband, or any man, could do. He would not blame a woman for killing a husband who used sex as punishment.

He wondered if she had.

She certainly would have done whatever it took to escape from him tonight. His apology had helped and his "What do we do now?" had made it clear that he accepted her as the leader in this.

"It will be easy. Come." She gave him no more than that. Was it part of his punishment? He did not ask but followed her out of the room.

The streets were empty, the sky clear, and with it came much colder air. Charlotte pulled her shawl tightly around her shoulders as she took his arm.

He knew the only reason she could bring herself to touch him was that it would have attracted attention if she did not. They walked in silence awhile, still not comfortable with each other.

"My temper comes from my father. I did not realize that for a long time, as his is a cold and calculated rage that would strip you of all your humanity." She did not tell him to be quiet, so he kept on. "The new duke has Father's arrogance without the anger. He is cool and calculated, with all his sensibilities carefully hidden. My brother Jessup has my mother's charm and nothing from my father but perhaps his skill with cards. Olivia is so like our mother, but with a tendency to anger over the most trifling incidents. I am wondering if having a husband will change that."

He wished he had not said the word *husband*, and hurried on.

"I learned to control my temper," he continued. "Most of the time. Another gift from my tutor. I wonder if he is still alive. Thanks for a thankless task are in order."

She did not seem particularly interested in what he was saying, but he could feel her relax a little. He was learning to interpret her touch as well as read her eyes.

"When I do lose my temper, I always regret it. There was a time when my father and I did not speak for a year. I wanted to study anatomy and he refused to allow it. Called me a disgusting thrill seeker, a man who used science as an excuse for depraved behavior. I told him that I would leave forever. It was my mother who played peacemaker, as always."

Just when he thought he had nattered on quite long enough, she spoke.

"You would not defy him? Surely you have some money of your own?"

"Yes, but my mother insisted that she needed me. That she had lost one son in Mexico—he died there when his ship sank—and the other was no better than a wastrel to them."

"So you chose to study the stars?"

"In the end it was what father and I could agree on. He thought it would bore me quickly. I thought I could outlive him and return to my other interests."

"And now your father is dead."

"Yes. It seems so odd. Hard to believe. The last time I spoke to him, he seemed well enough. Gout and some pains in his back." He felt little sorrow, was embarrassed to realize that what he felt was relief. "I suppose that my life will not change much. Jessup is healthy and will someday marry an heiress who will support his gambling. Lynford is married and his wife will no doubt provide him with enough boys that in time I will be so far down the line of succession that they will all forget me." He stopped and turned to her. "That could be true already. Charlotte, do you know if the new duke has children yet?"

"Not that I know of," she said, starting them walking again. "You do not wish you were the heir?"

"Good God, no. The very thought of taking a seat in the House of Lords and listening to their endless machinations would drive me insane."

"Surely the wealth and influence is a fair trade for that."

"I hope my brother feels that way. As for me, I see now that Dr. Borgos has the truth of it. I want to do something more purposeful with my life than deal with politics. There are others better suited to that than I am. I will study science and at least *try* to find a way to make the world a better place."

She was silent a long time, but she did not laugh at him. When she did speak she changed the subject.

"You do not mention your other brother, the naval officer."

"I just did. David is the one who disappeared in the Gulf of Mexico almost ten years ago."

"No. I met him when I traveled to Derbyshire to speak with the duke."

"You must have met our bastard brother, Robert Wilton. David is dead."

"I know Wilton quite well. And Madeline, his wife."

"You are willing to swear that David is back in England?" He still would not accept it.

"The duke accepts him. The others all call him brother."

"Charlotte, I know I frightened you and threatened you

in a way that diminishes me as a gentleman..." As he spoke he took a step away from her. It made his words no less intense. "To make this up as retribution, though, is beyond cruel. David was my dearest friend, my hero. I idolized him. I raged at my father when he had him declared officially dead."

"And you were right. He is alive." She spoke in a matter-of-fact tone that moved him from incredulity to possibility.

"So you are saying that I have lost a father and gained a brother. How odd. How amazing."

"Time has not stood still while you have been away," she said. "Your family has changed. Your life in England will be different now."

"I only hope that I have a life left to live."

When they reached her house, the only light came from the candles in the salon. It was a sign of safety, he was sure. She used the key and they went in quietly. The cat came from the kitchen and followed them up the stairs. Charlotte showed him to the room at the front of the house.

She held the key in her hand for a long moment. "I must lock the door. Lock you in."

"Yes, I know." Did she realize that he only allowed it because this was the punishment he had earned for his hideous behavior?

"I will come for you when the house is awake."

He nodded, and she scooped up the cat and left quickly. Gabriel heard the key sound in the lock and still could not resist grabbing the handle and shaking it.

As he waited out the night he mulled over all he had

learned this evening. Gabe turned on his side and pulled the coverlet over his bare shoulders.

It wasn't only the locked door that kept him awake. David was alive. He tried to imagine how they had all reacted to it. Olivia would hardly remember him. Jessup would insist on collecting on the wager he had made that David would someday come home. Lynford's marriage was surely beyond the point where there would be any jealousy over this first of Rowena's beaus.

Charlotte had sworn it was the truth. Her whole life was such a tangle of lies, he wondered if she even knew what the truth was. How had she come to play such a charade? How had she even met Lynford? Charlotte Parnell was as puzzling as the appearance of a comet. He hoped she did not disappear as quickly, at least not before he had the answers he wanted.

Be honest, he berated himself. *You want more than answers.* Sex, he wanted sex. He could barely tolerate the endless temptation of her scent, her softness, the way she touched him, how she aroused him with little more than a look. He could not forget her until he made love to her again. More than once. When they were back in England, on equal footing. He would be the one seducing her.

The sounds of the house coming to life woke him from his half sleep. *The next act begins,* he thought. It felt like he was about to climb a ladder to reach a telescope, with nothing to hold on to for support. It might be worth the risk or it might be the last stupid thing he ever did.

14

CHARLOTTE SAT AT her dressing table, combing the tangles from her hair. The loose braid had unraveled during her restless night. She combed it with a familiar comforting rhythm and stared at her reflection, seeing nothing but the remnants of her dream.

Three soft taps at the door made her gasp. She dropped the brush and put her face in her hands. *Be honest with yourself at least. It is not only the dream that upsets you.*

She drew a deep breath and pushed the anxiety away, rose and unlocked the door for Georges. At least some part of her morning would be as it usually was. His "*Bonjour, madame*" was not much more than a whisper.

Turning away, she smiled. He treated her with such quiet dignity, when they both knew that acting as a lady's maid was beneath him, as well as embarrassing.

Watching him in the mirror, Charlotte saw him glance at

the bed and briefly consider the jumbled mess of sheets and covers. Without comment he came toward her, and she stood so he could lace up her dress.

"Did you have a restless night, madame?"

"You are the best of valets, Georges. So diplomatic. Always."

He glanced at her reflection and their eyes held in the mirror.

"I had the usual nightmare, that is all," she said.

"It will help you look the part."

"You mean my dark eyes and haggard face? How practical of you. You are a superior valet but would never do as a lady's maid. You are too honest by half."

He smiled, which made Charlotte smile too. She had always wondered if his rare show of emotion was part of his valet training or part of him as a person.

She sat back on the small stool in front of her mirror and considered what to do with her hair. "Do you never dream?"

"We live a nightmare, madame. Is that not enough?"

She watched him in the mirror as he worked. The silence stretched between them. His guilt upset her. Useless. Pointless. "Georges, you and I were as close to Charles as two people could be. His wife and his valet. You were not the only one taken in. I was too."

Georges shook his head, denying what he knew was the truth.

"He was the most charming man I had ever met," she continued. "He played on your loyalty and my youth." Charles's smile had seduced her from the moment they met.

Georges still did not speak, but threw the pillows on the bed as though that would adequately vent his feelings.

"You could come to England with me. You do not need to stay."

"We have had this discussion. I will come only if you allow me to help you and your mother raise the children."

"And I will say no, once again. You have done your part, and a house filled with children and not a man in sight is no place for a well-trained valet."

She turned in the chair and watched him as he walked to the bed and pulled the covers back. "You do understand, don't you, Georges? I feel obliged to care for the children."

"Yes, madame," he said wearily.

Good. At least he had given up trying to talk her out of it. Charlotte began braiding her hair again, this time in a tight pattern with a view to twisting it into an unbecoming coronet at the back of her head.

"It will end soon, Georges. Though I have no doubt that if I am sent to hell it will be this life I will live again and again. Watching for someone to betray us. Waking up with only the vaguest idea of where I am or who I am supposed to be."

Not happy with the feel of her braids, Charlotte turned to the mirror and reworked her hair. When she was finished she stood up and turned to him. "How do I look?"

"You look quite convincing, and I see you are cold."

She shivered despite her best effort not to.

"You should have let me build a fire."

"No, we agreed it would be a waste of money and fuel when I am leaving. Besides, if I am chilled, our supposed poverty will be even more convincing."

"I think the patch on the hem of your dress will do that."

He stepped back. "The coarse material is hardly worth mending. He will be better dressed."

"Which is as it should be." Taking a white cotton scarf from a basket near the table, she wrapped it around her shoulders and tucked it into the bodice of her dress.

"I brought his clothes to him this morning, madame. I do not think that he slept any more than you did."

"Hardly surprising," she said, unsure whether it was guilt or fear that had kept him awake.

"He asked if you were all right." Georges watched her reflection as she arranged the fichu, but did not look into her eyes. "Why would he ask that?"

"Because he lost his temper with me last night," she admitted. She had never lied to Georges before and was not going to start now. They knew each other better than some couples who shared the same bed. "After the colonel and Raoul left the upper room at the tavern."

Georges straightened, with menace in his eyes.

"Listen to me, please, Georges." She stood up and walked to him. "Yes, it brought back every horrible memory of Charles. It reminded me that marriage to him cost me my self-respect and my own sense of honor." She shook her head at his anger. "I am a different person now. I will never be abused that way again. I would have killed him if he had tried to take me. And I would have asked you to dispose of the body."

Georges nodded, as if her willingness to murder was as natural as her need to stroke the cat.

"But Georges," she reached out a hand and gently touched his arm, "he is as different from Charles Strauss as it is possible for a man to be. He is kind, a sensibility at odds with a temper easily roused. He apologized." She shook her head, bemused and amused now that it was over. "I hit him." She smoothed the rough fabric around her neck. "He told me to hit him again if it would make me feel better or safer. His kindness is an essential part of him, but his temper can get the better of him. Sometimes. But always he apologizes. A complicated man. I do not know how he survived prison with no more than scars on his back. Georges, it may be that he is a gentleman in the truest sense of the word." She patted his arm once more and then sat down again in front of the mirror.

"You may be right. I hardly know him," Georges said, grudgingly.

She prayed she was.

"Last night," he went on, "was the first time I have spoken with him outside of the night we went for him. In any case, kindness has been rare these last four years."

He reached into the basket, pulled out a threadbare gray shawl and handed it to her. "That white scarf makes you look more like a nun than the wife of a poor fisherman. Try this one."

Just looking at it made her shiver.

"I will have some blankets in the boat, madame."

With a resigned sigh, she pulled off the white shawl and smoothed her braids.

GABRIEL PULLED THE BANDAGE from his face and tossed it toward the children sitting across from him at the kitchen table. The older one, the boy, caught it easily and dropped it as quickly.

"I will not have my eyes covered," he snapped. "Whoever heard of a blind fisherman?"

"Your eyes are too bright," Charlotte said, reaching to collect the length of bandage. "No one would believe you are injured when they see that endless curiosity of yours."

"What? You do not think I can look a fool? You have called me that often enough." He raised his hands as if to stay an attack. "I will look down. I will stare at the ground. I will know people by their feet only. I will constantly remind myself not to look above your hemline. Surely this bloody wound you concocted on my brow is proof enough. Will it come off?"

"Yes, it is stain but it will be gone in a day."

She eyed her handiwork with a critical eye, then nodded. "All right, I will bandage only your forehead. That is as much as I am willing to compromise."

Gabriel sat down again. As she began winding the bandage around his head he wanted to ask what point there was in covering the wound she had so painstakingly drawn and stained. He watched her work in the mirror. He had to admit that the little bit of the wound that showed hinted at something far worse than she had created. Rather like a work of art, he thought.

The two children were studying them as intently as he was watching Charlotte, ignoring the last of their breakfast, the ubiquitous bread and cheese. The boy was about ten. The other child was a sweet-faced girl whose hair was a riot of unkempt curls. She was younger. Five? They were dressed in something one step up from rags. Had Georges truly found them on the street?

Neither one spoke a word. They watched him bickering with Charlotte with unconcealed anxiety.

"He always wants his own way," Charlotte said to the little girl. "Is your brother like that, *chouchou*?"

The little girl's wrinkled forehead relaxed into a grin as she nodded.

The boy's frown deepened.

"I imagine that he is almost always right, which makes it all the harder. Is that not true?"

The boy smiled this time. "*Oui*, madame. *C'est vrai.*"

"You understand that for today you must do exactly as I say. Your papa is not quite right in the head and I, your mama, am the one in charge. I know it is unusual."

"War is like that," the boy said with unexpected wisdom.

"So it is. Remember, no matter what, you are to call us Mama and Papa. Soon we will be away and safe in England."

Gabriel listened to the exchange, fascinated by any number of things. Charlotte's sweetness with the children. Her ability to act the role of mother as convincingly as she played the part of whore.

The boy's cultured French accent. This was not the language spoken in the streets. He wondered exactly where she had found these two. If they were indeed siblings. They looked enough alike to be related. More than that, they were comfortable with each other, the girl sitting very close to the boy, as if she sought comfort or protection. Or was she sitting close so she could stroke the cat, stretched across the boy's lap?

The oddest thing of all was their complete acceptance of leaving France for England. Was life here such a misery that even the unknown, the enemy, was preferable?

"Will the cat come with us?" the boy asked.

"No. He cares for the house while I am away."

The two children grinned at the idea of a cat as house-keeper, and with a neat twist of the bandage, Charlotte finished her task.

"Finish your breakfast. We leave soon for the fishing boat. And rest assured that there are cats in England."

All three of them, Gabriel included, ate one last mouthful of cheese and then stood. He drew a deep breath. *Keep the children safe. And see us all home.* He remembered the last time he had asked for help, as he begged the men holding him not to set fire to the tavern. No one had been listening that time. Or perhaps there was a grander plan than had yet been revealed. If that was so then, in the name of heaven, let this ruse be part of it.

15

CHARLOTTE NEEDED A FEW more minutes to arrange the scene to her satisfaction, finally deciding on leading while holding the girl's hand. Gabriel, as the injured papa, was to follow, allowing the boy to support him.

They made their way from the back door through the now familiar alleyway and out onto the street, just as the dead of night gave way to a deep dark gray.

Gabriel stared at the threadbare shawl that Charlotte had tied around her head and shoulders. Looking neither to the right nor left, up nor down. His occasional stumbles on the uneven cobblestones were not acting. The boy gripped his arm more tightly each time he tripped. The child was taking his role seriously.

It felt as though they walked for hours, though watching Charlotte as she walked was some distraction. In fact, it could not have taken too long, since the sky had lightened only a little as the smell of the water grew stronger, as did the sounds of waterfront life. The fishermen called to one another. He heard the creak of the boats as they were loaded with lines and nets.

As close to her as he was, Gabriel noticed the slightest of hesitations. He strained to hear what might have slowed her, but could detect nothing unusual. It took real effort not to glance up. This was surely a punishment from the devil. Inspiration sent from him to Charlotte. To have to remain so completely passive was torture. Refined and not physical, but torture nonetheless.

As they walked down the beach he saw fishing boats strung along the sand. A couple of fishermen were kneeling, watching the small family pass. They said nothing, but nodded at Charlotte. She nodded back. They stared at him with low-voiced comments among themselves. Nothing untoward from this group. What was it that had her back straighter, her body radiating a new tension?

Finally they reached Georges. Gabriel could tell by the smell of his tobacco. From what little he could see, the boat looked clean and tidy. Not at all the "scow" he had expected from Charlotte's comments.

"*Bonjour,* monsieur," she called as she walked up to Georges. "Here we are. Ready to fish all day." She sounded just the right tone of faux excitement. She and Georges shared a low-voiced conversation and then she came back to stand next to Gabriel. "The colonel is headed this way with three officers and at least a dozen soldiers."

Gabriel did not raise his head, but he raised his eyes to

stare at her. She had herself under control now, though he could tell that she was concerned.

Conscious of the children next to him, he did not ask the dozen questions spilling through his head. *Will he recognize us? Does he know Georges? What can I do if there is trouble?*

"I think," she said, "that we must board the boat slowly so that they believe we are not in a hurry." She waited. He could see the children nod their understanding. She continued. "We will help Papa on first, then I will board, you children will be last. Pierre, you sit in the back with Papa, and Claire will sit in the front with me. If the soldiers stop us I will speak to them. If they ask you a question, pretend you are afraid of them."

Pretend? He did not think any of them would have to "pretend" to be afraid.

She had no sooner finished speaking when a gunshot shattered the morning quiet. Jolted out of his role, Gabriel swore and, as another shot sounded, reached for Charlotte. He pushed her to the sand even as she pulled the screaming girl close to her. As they fell, Charlotte contrived it so that he was the one beneath them, her body sheltering the two of them. As she lay next to him he could feel her heart beating wildly. *Aha, so she did not have ice in her veins.*

"The boy?" he whispered.

"Safe with Georges." She rested her head on his back. They lay waiting. For disaster, discovery or, please heaven, deliverance.

"Listen!" a commanding voice rang out. "Every one of you. Men, women and children." It was the colonel. His voice, if not his obese body, was well suited to a battlefield. It carried to all of them along the broad strip of beach. "Not one of you is to leave until we have searched your boat."

"Did he shoot off that gun so we would listen," Gabriel whispered, "or to scare years off of our lives?"

"Shhh," Charlotte hissed. "They are spreading out in small groups, each with an officer in charge."

Gabriel's "family" resumed their tableau, though not all of them were acting. Charlotte was still giving most of her attention to the piteously weeping girl. Her brother stood as still as a statue and almost as white as marble. Georges drew on his pipe. The only sign of concern that Gabriel could see were his narrowed eyes.

Gabe let his head drop, doing his best to appear disinterested, while every part of him readied for action. The rattle of the officer's sword announced the squad's arrival.

"*Bonjour,* madame and messieurs."

He recognized that voice and with it came relief and rage. It was the damned interfering guard captain. Was this whole expedition his idea? Did the man have nothing to do but dog their every step? The effort to control his movement was so great that Gabriel started shaking.

Georges had ignored the colonel's words and the captain's presence and made to help Gabriel into the boat. Gabriel could hear low-voiced conversation between Charlotte and the captain.

It was dark enough and there was a chance that he would not be able to see clearly enough to recognize her. Them. Had Desseau seen Georges before? It seemed that Georges and Charlotte were together as often as she and the captain.

Georges had him settled in the boat, with his back to the beach. The captain came over as Charlotte made to join them.

"What kind of injury, madame?"

"Some damage to the brain. I remain hopeful that he will recover. Today will be the test, for he loved the sea and fishing."

Desseau waded into the water and came to the side of the boat. He put his arm on Gabriel's shoulder. Gabriel did not move, did not look up. He continued to stare at the coil of line until it became his whole world.

"Wait!"

The colonel's voice stilled all of them. He made his way to their gathering even as Gabriel could feel the captain tense and Charlotte swear.

"Who is this wounded man? The others say they have not seen him here before."

The guard captain began to explain, but something stopped him.

"Let the woman tell me," the colonel said.

"My husband always preferred to leave from the western shore, on the other side of the docks, but it is too far for him to walk now." Charlotte gave her explanation in a hesitant way, as though she were afraid and trying to be brave. What an actress she was. Or perhaps, in this case, no acting was required.

The colonel leaned over to raise Gabriel's face to his. Gabriel could feel sweat on his brow. It was not because the bandage fit too snugly.

"Please, Colonel." Gabriel could hear the pleading in

Charlotte's voice. "He does not like to be touched. See how he shakes."

"*Bien,*" he said, and ripped off the bandage with a wicked laugh.

Gabriel screamed like a wounded animal, bending double, covering his head with his hands, being sure to let his nasty "wound" show. After a moment, he stopped screaming, settling for a keening sound that went on and on.

"Search the boat, Colonel," Georges said, pushing Charlotte and the children out of his way. "I have known him all his life and will no doubt be with him at his death."

"Is that so," the colonel said. Gabriel could see him raise his pistol and felt the coldness of it pressed against his temple. "Shall I put him out of his misery now? Surely, madame, you would be better off as a widow."

The little girl began to scream. Her brother was finally driven to action, shouting, "No, no."

"Take care of your sister," Charlotte said to the boy. She came to the colonel. The old soldier smiled a little, still holding the gun at Gabriel's head. Gabriel did not, could not move. Images of home, his family, swirled through his head. Those memories were interrupted by Charlotte and her clean sweet smell. He drew in her scent and prayed to a God he was beginning to hope did exist.

"Please, Colonel. I beg you. The children need their father."

There was a long silence. Then the colonel put his gun away and grabbed Charlotte by the chin, ordering one of the soldiers to raise the lantern. "I know you." He looked at Desseau. "Where have I met her?"

Desseau had the look of a man caught in a trap. Or a lie. The regret was real even as he stepped away from her.

Brain damaged or not, Gabriel looked at Charlotte.

"Please, Captain. Please." She begged Desseau this time. The tears in her voice left no doubt of her fear.

"I am sorry, madame, but I must tell him." Desseau put some more distance between them.

Gabriel closed his eyes. To have come this far only to have it ruined was not possible. What kind of jokester was God to tease them this way? He would fight, fight and die, but he was not going to his death like a coward. He clenched his fists and waited.

"Colonel, she is Charlotte Parnell's sister. Her family is disgusted by Charlotte and mortified at the shame she has brought on them. Madame will not acknowledge the connection, but Charlotte herself told me."

The man is a spy, Gabriel realized. Or so besotted with Charlotte that he would risk life and honor to protect her.

The colonel looked at her with this new bit of information. "Yes, I can see the resemblance."

Charlotte turned her face from the colonel's but said nothing.

"It appears she is as virtuous as her sister is daring," the colonel added, looking over his shoulder at Desseau.

"Hardly worth your time, sir. But if you wish, I could bring her along for questioning."

"Bring Charlotte along for some questioning and I will say *merci bien,* Desseau," the colonel said, laughing, and walked on to harass someone else without another word to any of them.

Raoul Desseau scooped up the bandage and tossed it in the boat. He leaned closer and whispered, *"Bonne chance, mon ami,"* then stood. Calling to his squad, Desseau followed the colonel down the beach.

Had the man wished him luck? Gabriel tried to interpret his words as he controlled the urge to let his anxiety go in a huge breath of relief. His aborted sigh sounded like the troubled breathing of a sick man.

The boy was babbling, little Claire still sniffling as Georges helped them climb aboard. Gabriel watched them but could not rid his mind of Desseau's words.

Luck was no more than one soldier would wish another. That was what they both were: soldiers. It did not even matter what side Desseau was on. They both were soldiers for a cause that gave them purpose.

For his part, Gabriel wanted desperately to save his family name and personal honor. For that he would need all the luck he could find. With the hope of escape at hand, he felt generous enough to wish the captain the same.

He watched as Charlotte let Georges help her into the boat, where she made her way to the prow, taking the now whimpering girl, settling her on her lap, tucking a blanket around her.

Georges pushed off fully from the sand. None of them made a sound. Gabriel did not even dare breathe too deeply in case the colonel should change his mind. Would the boat sprout a leak? Or the sail rip in half? One of the children plunge overboard? This day had started out poorly. He hoped that their bad luck had run out.

Georges settled in the middle of the boat, sitting on an upturned wooden crate. He raised the sail.

Gabriel estimated the boat was about twenty-five feet. Something one man could handle alone. Yet large enough to cross the channel if necessary. Surely that was not what Charlotte planned to do.

The sail luffed as the boat tacked to catch the wind. Gabriel raised his head into it. It seemed to him it was just the sort of gesture a man on the verge of recovery might make.

The wind was at his back soon enough and the boat gained speed. With his eyes still closed, he embraced the sensations that surrounded this passage to freedom.

The noisy, fish-laden smell of the shore gave way to the salty clean tang of the sea. The water slapped the sides of the small boat with a comforting rhythm. The deck beneath his feet felt solid even as it thumped over the waves. The lines rattled against the mast as the sail pushed them farther from the shore. As they left France behind, Gabriel allowed himself to think of what it would be like to return home. Where his family was waiting. Not only his family, but the authorities as well.

Would they both be there when he arrived? Would he be held in another prison while the war department was notified of his return?

A trial was inevitable and his execution a possibility. He had a debt to pay and he would do what was needed to spare his family embarrassment. He did not allow the hope that the government would believe his story and release him.

"Is there family waiting for word of you, sir?"

Gabriel's companion had been stone silent. His question took Gabriel by surprise. "Yes. Yes, Pierre, there is."

The boy did not appear to be enjoying the trip as much as he was. His shoulders were hunched and he was a bit green. Gabriel rambled on about his brothers and sister.

He stopped short. He cursed to himself as he realized that Pierre did not have family to look forward to. "Where will you go when we land?"

"I will go where Madame Mama takes me."

The prospect of yet another orphanage did not seem to frighten him.

"My sister and I will stay together; Madame Mama has promised me that."

So the girl *was* his sister. "How is it that you speak such excellent English, Pierre?"

"I beg your pardon, sir. Madame said we were to tell you nothing other than that she will take care of us."

"Aha. I see." And damned irritating to be labeled as suspect. Charlotte would infect them all with her mistrust, he thought. He turned to look at her.

She was staring intently at the harbor. His sense of safety evaporated as thoroughly as the fog had. Were they being followed? He turned slightly, not caring that it was out of keeping with his role. Madness would claim him if he had to go another round with a Frenchman.

There was no one to see.

No boat overtaking them, only the empty water and the sun beginning to rise, coming up behind the city, casting the buildings into shadow. It was a dramatic picture in black and gray. The church spires were black arrows against the gray sky. The water was a silver blue mirror broken into pieces by the wind, reflecting no more than the colorless dawn. He would never forget the sight. It so matched the life he was leaving behind.

The sun blinking over the city's buildings changed the image in an instant. He turned back, blinded by it.

With his back to it he looked again at Charlotte.

She was watching him now, smiling. She might as well have been shouting, "We did it!" He smiled back, nodding. She shook her head in relief and disbelief, her smile growing to a grin. For the first time in the days they had known each other they were in complete agreement.

He closed his eyes and raised his face skyward again. In her smile he had caught a glimpse of the real woman. The woman who did not wear a costume or pretend a life. It stirred his curiosity. She was as confusing as the chemistry experiments that had nearly blown the roof off the dower house, and if there was one thing he liked it was puzzling things out. He would see that smile again, he decided.

16

EVEN AS CHARLOTTE watched him marvel at the sunrise, the little girl pulled at her sleeve.

"What is the man, Papa, doing?"

"Worshipping the sun, *mignonne*."

"Why?" she asked.

Her puzzlement told Charlotte this one must learn to have more fun. "He has been held prisoner by the French. This is the first sunrise he has seen in a long time. It is his way of celebrating."

The child did not ask anything else, and when Charlotte stopped watching Gabriel to look at the girl she saw the child studying the man and then the sky.

"Can you think of something you would like to celebrate, Claire?"

"*Oui*. I would dance and sing if I could have a mama, but I will be happy if I can have a kitten."

Charlotte felt the start of tears to her eyes. She knew exactly how that felt. She might be too old to admit it aloud, but she herself wanted nothing more than her own mama welcoming her home, fussing over her, tucking her into bed. A few days yet. Just a few more. With her arm around Claire, she kissed her hair. "I hope all your dreams will come true, and I can promise you a kitten."

The day dragged on, the cool damp air giving way to an unseasonable warmth that made her welcome the water and the fruit that Georges had tucked in the basket under the bench. The apples were bruised but delicious. She watched Pennistan eat his as though it were manna sent from heaven.

He saw her laughing at him and shouted above the wind and down the length of the boat, "The last time I had an apple was in Spain, at least a hundred years ago."

With a look of surprise, the boy said something to him, speaking so quietly that the words did not reach her, even with the wind to help.

"He has been in prison for one hundred years?" Claire asked.

"No, it only feels that way to him."

"What did he do that was so bad?"

Charlotte thought about her answer. What had she told Pierre? That he had lost a dangerous game, people had died because of it and he might pay with his life. It was the truth. If she had been feeling kinder toward him she would say that he had been trapped by another's deceit.

How did one explain that to a child? It was impossible when she could hardly understand it herself. "It was a terrible mistake, Claire. He was rescued and now he is going home."

"Will he live with us?"

"No, he has his own family. They are waiting for him."

"Oh," Claire said, biting her lip. "Pierre says the orphanage was like a prison." She reached out and trailed her hand in the water. Only for a second. "But I think I miss it already."

Charlotte felt those damn tears again. "New adventures can be as frightening as they are exciting. Where we are going will be far better than an orphanage."

"England." Claire nodded. "Pierre made up stories of what it will be like. No place could be that wonderful." She watched Charlotte for an answer, her eyes daring her to lie.

"Probably not," Charlotte said. "I can promise you one thing, mademoiselle. It will be better than France."

"*Bien*," Claire said, smiling a little. "I can really have a kitten?"

"But of course."

Claire grinned and settled back again. "*Merci*, Madame Mama."

"*Il n'y a pas de quoi, comme toujours, mon petite.*" *You are welcome, as always, little one.* For the first time she understood what Georges meant by that phrase. It was more than generous. It was a pledge.

"A HUNDRED YEARS, Monsieur Papa? No one could survive a hundred years in jail. You are lying."

"To me it felt like a hundred years. It was less than one."

The boy nodded, but still looked as though he was ready for a fight. He had been since the colonel had manhandled them, Gabriel suspected. "So, did Mama tell you where I am going?"

"Perhaps to prison, perhaps to the gallows, perhaps home to your family," Pierre answered promptly.

"Do you know why?" Gabriel asked despite his fear of the answer.

"People died because of you and the King must decide if you will live. I hope he has you strung up in the town square." The last sentence came out in a rush.

Aha, Gabriel thought, *there is the anger.* It seemed to surprise even Pierre, who turned red and mumbled something as he pressed a hand to his stomach.

"Do you say that because I am enjoying this trip and you are not? Or because you think being caught is a crime worthy of death?"

"I think you must have done something awful to be put into prison. Killed someone. Or betrayed your country. I think Madame was being kind when she said that the French trapped you."

No matter how free he felt in an open boat headed for home, this was the way it would be. A traitor carried the burden with him forever. "If you feel that strongly, why are you willing to talk with me?"

"If I am thinking about you, then I will not be thinking about being in this boat."

"How practical you are, Pierre."

"One must be to live, monsieur."

"Yes, one must. I suppose that is something we both have learned even if we came to it by different paths." Pierre had lost his innocence. Gabriel had lost his faith in everything but the way the stars glowed at night.

One learned so much in war that was better forgotten. Or

at least not shared with someone so young. Surely there was a less difficult subject he and Pierre could discuss. Something that would distract the boy. It was in his best interest as well as Pierre's that the child not become ill.

"Tell me," Gabriel began, "have you ever examined the stars?"

"We were in the city and rarely out-of-doors at night, monsieur."

"What a shame." What else? Something that would not remind him that Madame Mama did not want them sharing confidences. "Did they have rats in your orphanage?"

"Yes, of course. I named some of them."

"I had four that visited me regularly in prison. Only one that showed any boldness. Tell me what you observed of them at the orphanage."

They were in the midst of a very satisfactory discussion of the rats' eating habits when Georges called out.

"*Regardez,* madame." Georges raised his chin to direct her attention. He had spoken quietly, since Claire had fallen asleep.

Pierre had the makings of a man of science. How else could you explain a discussion of rats so intense that they both failed to see the ship, easily in sight? It was surely less than a mile away. The British colors flew from the stern. A punch of relief made Gabriel draw in a quick breath.

He studied the sea out to the horizon. Then he looked back toward shore. Being caught between two enemy ships was in keeping with their day's luck. Not another boat, ship or dinghy within sight. The land itself was no longer visible. The sea was the only reference point besides the sun, which was moving lower in the sky.

The British ship did not have many sails rigged. She moved slowly, as a ship on a blockade might do, even as it turned slightly, heading in their direction. Neither Georges nor Charlotte showed any concern. "Is that ship expecting us?"

"It is part of the blockade of French ports. They will stop anyone they see." Georges spoke even as he ran a small orange pennant out the halyard. The ship responded by lowering the British flag to half-staff. Then raising it again. Georges nodded and set the tiller to bring them alongside the ship.

"This is how we are to reach England." Charlotte was looking at Claire as she spoke, but the little girl was still asleep.

"I have always wanted to see a ship on the blockade," Pierre said, his enthusiasm at odds with his inclination to seasickness. "I think it must be very exciting."

"They have been patrolling the Channel for years, Pierre," Gabe said. "Since before you were born. *Boring* is probably the best word to describe it."

The boy nodded. "But there is always the chance a French ship will come along. Then it would not be boring."

They debated the subject for twenty minutes, until the two vessels were cozied together. Gabriel added "skilled seaman" to Georges's list of talents.

Once they were alongside the British ship, they stopped talking; it was a distraction the boy no longer needed. The crew was as noisy as their own small group was silent.

For his part, Gabriel was lending his whole mind and heart to the operation at hand. Moving them from the much smaller boat to the larger ship was a simple if delicate procedure. He would not cheer their escape until they were aboard.

A few minutes more and he could stop listing all the things that could still go wrong. His future was not that promising, but whatever it was would be more secure on a British naval vessel than a faux French fishing boat.

Calling actions to each other, two men from the ship lowered a rope ladder and a sling that Gabriel guessed was for those who were not up to a climb. Charlotte and the little girl were first. They did use the slinglike device. Charlotte and Georges talked with each other as he secured her and Claire in the seat, his movements sure and practical. How many times had they done this?

As the chair was raised the girl kept a stranglehold on Charlotte's neck despite the constant stream of words her "mama" was whispering into the little one's ear. She was an unconventional Madonna. As he watched, the thought flitted through his mind: Could it be, in this case at least, that Charlotte was not acting at all?

He lost the thought as Pierre startled him with a cheer when his sister was safely aboard. The boy was next. Pierre grabbed on to the rope ladder and hurried up the side as though the size of the British ship would ease his mal de mer. Gabriel followed him, without as much grace, but without embarrassing himself either. It was not until the crew began to pull the ladder up that he realized Georges was not coming with them.

He watched Georges steer the boat toward Le Havre. Not once did he look back. Why would he? The clutch of regret

Gabriel felt surprised him. There would be no good-byes between them.

He turned to ask Charlotte what Georges would do, but she was on her knees comforting Claire, who was clearly exhausted, and most likely hungry. There was no sign of Pierre. Did that mean he was busy puking over the side?

A man in an officer's uniform came up to Gabriel. "I am Mr. Burke, the first lieutenant. The captain and crew of the *Diplomat* are happy to welcome you and your family aboard, Mr. Parnell."

"Thank you, Lieutenant," Gabriel said. So they were to maintain their masquerade as a family. "I thank you and all the crew for coming to our rescue."

The lieutenant acknowledged the comment with a nod. "If the winds and tide cooperate, we should drop anchor in Portsmouth in less than a day." Someone called to him and, with a word of apology, the lieutenant left them "only for a moment."

Gabriel turned to Charlotte. "Thank you." His heart was so full of feeling that he could not think of anything more to say.

"You are welcome, Lord Gabriel. Though I am not sure that returning you home is doing you any great favor." She smiled at him with an affection that could not entirely be an act. He took her hand.

"Thank you," he said more firmly. He squeezed her hand and ran his thumb over the knuckles. He wanted to kiss her. To sweep her into his arms and let her know exactly how grateful he was. "Because of you, I will see my family. I will be allowed to plead my case. It is a greater gift than you give yourself credit for."

Was she embarrassed? She would not look at him, though she did not pull away.

The lieutenant came back to them. Gabriel tucked her hand into his arm. "As I said, we should reach Portsmouth within a day. This ship is your bit of England until then. Welcome home, sir."

BOOK TWO

A Private Peace

England
Winter to Spring 1814

17

WELCOME HOME. Gabriel accepted the words with a smile. Let them run riot through his head and heart. He blamed the water in his eyes on the wind. When his legs felt weak he did his best to rein in the maelstrom of sensibilities that ran the gamut from elation to despair. What he really wanted to do was race up to the foretop and shout his gratitude.

The lieutenant was kind enough to give him a moment to entertain his thoughts. Then he cleared his throat. "If you will collect your family, sir, I will show you to your quarters. I am sure all of you are hungry and tired."

Tired. Yes, they were, especially since that sounded like an order. Gabriel crossed the deck. He spoke to Charlotte. He discovered that Pierre was so far from unwell that he had found a bunch of boys his age and was climbing the lower rigging. Gabriel herded his group back to the lieutenant.

Amidst a flurry of introductions and an audience of curious seamen, they were shown to a cabin that must be the lieutenant's own.

"Are we displacing you, Lieutenant? My apologies," Gabriel said. In fact, it was an amazing amount of space on a ship that crammed the seamen in hammocks belowdecks. It was two rooms actually: a working space, and through a door a smaller sleeping area, with a bunk that filled most of the room.

"No, sir, this is not mine. This ship normally carries diplomats, and this cabin is designated for the head of the party. The captain thought you would be more comfortable here."

"Please thank him for us," Charlotte said, speaking to the lieutenant for the first time. "And I would also appreciate it if you would ask someone to rig a hammock in the other room."

She gave no reason for her request and the lieutenant was apparently too much of a gentleman to ask. "Of course, Mrs. Parnell" was all he said without so much as a curious look as to why a wife would not wish to sleep with her husband. The lieutenant gave all his attention to Gabriel. "We have some food on the table for you and your family, sir." Gabriel lifted the napkin covering a plate and found, of course, cheese and the Royal Navy version of bread.

"Thank you," Gabriel said with as much enthusiasm as he could muster.

"I will leave you to eat and then show you how to rig the hammocks so you can rest. The captain wants you to stay below until we are well away from these waters." With a nod, the lieutenant left the cabin.

Gabriel walked to the door.

"Are you waiting to see if he locks it?" Charlotte asked.

"Yes," he admitted. He was feeling generous at the moment. If he could make her laugh, even if it was at his expense, then he would allow it. "How long before I stop wondering who trusts me and who does not? A year? Never?"

"No one will trust you until you trust yourself," she said, walking closer.

"You mean that not all prisons have walls and locks?"

"Very good, my lord." Her face was set, her eyes unforgiving. "We know better than most that regret can hold the heart prisoner as sure as chains."

"I would not wish it on anyone."

"Oh, you are more generous than I am." Charlotte spoke with a quiet anger. "But it was an empty wish. He had no heart to be so burdened."

She turned to the children as if one had called her. It was more likely that she had regretted the words as soon as they were spoken.

"Is it odd that we have not yet met the captain?"

She was cutting the ship's biscuit into small bits and adding a little milk to it.

"I am sure the captain has more important matters to attend to."

"A mutiny to quell? A daily report to complete? They were obviously sent to collect us from Georges. We are the important matters, Charlotte."

She shrugged and shook her head, her Gallic version of "Leave me alone."

"Here, Claire," she said, "have some bread and milk and then a little bit of cheese."

"I hate bread and milk. I never want to eat it again." The tyke covered her mouth with her hands even as she spoke.

"When we reach home you may eat just the food you wish, but for now you must stay strong. Eat." Charlotte looked at Gabriel as she spoke.

"Yes, Mama," Gabriel said, hoping she was the only one who heard his sarcasm. He agreed completely with Claire. He reached for his own portion. He hoped there were no weevils, even if he did need the nourishment.

Pierre wanted only the crumbly biscuit. Gabriel took his side when Charlotte wanted the boy to eat more.

Even as they bickered over the details of their supper he marveled at how much like a family they sounded. The sulking, tired little one. The boy who wanted to play. The papa who picked his battles so carefully. The mama who was the one truly in charge.

He thought of his own mother. She'd been gone for so long he could barely recall her face. What he could remember was her infinite patience, one virtue none of them had inherited.

He saw some of that in Charlotte as she badgered the children to eat a little more. He suspected her longing to love had been buried so deep that it only showed in a loving gesture. The sweep of her hand over the child's hair. The gift of her body to a lover.

That she had the capacity to love, he had no doubt.

Would she ever speak the words *I love you*? Had his mother heard them from his father, he wondered. Not likely.

They finished the food with some effort. The children drank the milk. Charlotte and Gabriel finished the grog that had been left for them.

When Gabriel opened the door to find the lieutenant, he saw a rough-looking fellow standing to the side in the passageway. With a knuckle to his forehead the man asked permission to come in. He proceeded to clear away the plates and bowls.

Another seaman raised the table, fastening it so that it lay against the hull. The first came back. He began to hang the hammocks from bolts overhead.

Charlotte picked up Claire. She settled the child in the first hammock. Claire was asleep before she could choose between terror and curiosity. Hopefully there would be no bad dreams. Pierre was fascinated. He scrambled into his hammock with no help. Gabriel could not imagine that the swinging motion would be good for the boy's sensitive stomach. Hopefully Pierre would fall asleep as quickly as his sister had.

The first seaman moved into the small sleeping space, rigging a third hammock.

Gabriel sat in it, pulled off his jacket and pushed off his shoes. He swung his feet up and stretched out, struggling to put his jacket behind his head to use as a pillow.

He settled, watching as Charlotte pulled her dress over her head and loosed the front-lacing stays. Draping the two garments carefully at the foot of the bed, she slid between the blankets, using her chemise as a nightgown.

"I am thinking the hammock is much more comfortable than that bed," he said.

"Is that an invitation?"

"No, Charlotte," he said, more sharply than he intended. "I was asking if you would prefer to trade."

"I have had the chance to sleep in one before. I imagine that the swing of the hammock is the one sweet comfort of a sailor's life, but the bunk will suit me well enough."

"There must be comforts besides this one. The stars at night?"

"Is that enough to make up for the crowded quarters, the uncertainty of life at sea, the possibility of attack?"

"How different is that from men who live ashore? There is the same order of men aboard ship. The one with the greatest responsibility eats and sleeps better than the others. In the end, however, they all must face death with nothing but their immortal soul."

She was quiet so long, he thought she might have fallen asleep. "For some people that would be a comfort, my lord."

"Who faces death without fear?"

"Those who have sought forgiveness for their wrongs, lived a just life, always done the best they could, honored the greatest commandment." She was quiet, then added in a whisper, "Love one another."

"If any such people exist, do introduce them to me." He stifled a laugh. Her cynicism was contagious.

"There are more than you can know. If one believes your story, Gabriel Pennistan, then you are one."

He turned to see if she was joking.

She was watching him through eyes that were wet with tears. "You are one. And so am I."

"Yes, you are one, Charlotte. But the penance of this life is surely more than God would ever demand."

She turned her head away and was silent a long time. "There are times," she said, facing him again, her eyes dry, "there are times when a lie can represent a greater truth. I hope," she paused, "no, I have faith that God is not a prisoner of our beliefs or our limited imaginations."

"Not a prisoner of our beliefs," he repeated, trying to grasp her meaning. "It is as liberating a concept as I have ever heard, Charlotte Parnell." Put into words by someone most would not think to listen to.

"Liberating? Or possibly a damning one." This time she turned fully away from him. "Go to sleep, Gabriel."

"Only if you will too, Charlotte." He fell asleep before she answered him, with the thought that her command had cast a spell.

18

HE AWOKE TO dark and the sense of being bound and carried. Where was he, what was this? Fighting against the covering, he pushed up with a gasp. A hammock, he realized. He was in a hammock; the movement was the ship, taking him away from France. He was closer to home than he had been since that misguided trip with Rhys Braedon more than two years ago.

Gabriel's heartbeat steadied. His eyes adjusted quickly to the dark. Night light drifted through the overhead transom. He needed to be outside. To breathe in fresh air. He grabbed his jacket and swung himself out of the hammock, determined to sneak out without waking Charlotte. He looked to her bed to see how soundly she slept.

Her bed was empty. Her stays and dress were gone as well. Gabriel ripped the blanket from her bed, bundled it into a ball and threw it. Who was she trysting with now?

*   *   *

CHARLOTTE KNOCKED on the door of the captain's cabin and, at the "Enter," opened it and slipped in, closing the door as quietly as she could.

Robert Wilton was every inch a naval captain even if he had shed his jacket, and his weapon of choice was some sort of knife stuck in a sheath at his side.

He came to her, took her outstretched hands, kissed one and led her to the only chair. He found a seat on the cushion that ran along the base of the stern transom.

"You did it. You did it again. You are an amazing woman and I salute you."

"Thank you, Captain," she said, smiling at his enthusiasm. "And you found us with only a little delay. Equally amazing, with no road signs or mileposts to guide you."

"We both know how to do what is important to us," he said, shrugging. "You are not finished, are you? Georges stays behind yet again."

"Georges must stay behind to continue our work while I settle the children. But I am not unprotected. The two of you are cast from the same mold, and if Georges cannot be with me then I am lucky to have you."

"Is that so?" was all he said.

"Wilton, I mean that in the most chaste way possible. Why is it inevitable that all men and a good many women cannot resist the thought of the other in bed?" She settled herself more comfortably, removing the ugly head shawl and shaking her hair free. "You know it as well as I do. A smart woman makes the most of it. And a smart man takes advantage when he can."

"You have spent too much time in diplomatic circles."

"We both agree on that as well." She smoothed her skirt and told herself that his criticism of the diplomats' world was not meant as an insult. "You are an intelligent man, Wilton, only too rigid in your moral view. Even after all these years, Madeline has not helped you to see differently. How is your lady wife?"

"Very well, thank you."

She let her expression convince him that his conventional answer was inadequate. He relented with a laugh.

"She manages wonderfully without me there. I wish I were as proud of that as I should be. Whenever I come home she treats me like one of the children."

"I cannot imagine that lasts beyond your first night home." He did not answer and Charlotte realized that she probably should not have said that. "Do excuse me if that embarrasses you, Wilton. The truth is that no man or woman is too old for mothering."

"Is that so?" he said, and after a moment went on, "I have managed without one since I was ten, since my mother died. As have many of the men in the Royal Navy."

"I suppose that could be true," she said, though she thought the need for grog daily only proved she was right. "Whether they have mothers or not, the truth is that you are the luckiest man on this ship. And not only because you are the one in command. Your wife is a beautiful, capable woman who understands what you need better than you do."

"Yes, she does seem to."

She could see him smile even though he turned his attention to straightening the chart on the table between them.

"In fact, Wilton, if I could find a man who knew what I wanted before I did, as Madeline can with you, I might even be willing to marry again."

"You would?" The words seemed to be surprised out of him. He forgot the chart and gave her his full attention.

"Yes, I would," she said with a firm nod. "But you see, my dear captain, no such man exists." She laughed. "I will not marry again. It may not be easy, but the family will manage without a man to lead it. Have you word from my mother?"

"Yes, she is well, as is the household, but there is something that you should know." Wilton leaned forward, his elbows resting on his knees, his hands clasped between them. "The woman who owns the draper shop told Madeline that a gentleman came looking for Mrs. Strauss. You are not known by that name, so no one was able to work out the puzzle."

It came as a shock that her past would find her even in Sussex. But that was the truth of it. The past was never truly forgotten. "If they find out that I am Charles's widow, the worst they can do is spread vile gossip. It is not the first time someone has maligned me."

"That is in the past and you were not the one who was guilty." He took her hand, covering it with his other.

"How kind of you to say so." She squeezed his fingers, pulled her hand from his and folded both of them in her lap, trying for a composure she was far from feeling. "Yes, Charles was the reason those parents were separated from their children. Some of them forever. He was hated by more people than a debt collector. He is dead. I can swear to that. No one will find him anywhere but in that cemetery in Le Havre."

After his death she had used most of her money to go back to England and had two months of peace. Then Georges brought her the damn papers he had found. That had been four years ago.

"Let it end there."

"I wish I could, Captain, but I *am* guilty of complicity, guilty in so many other ways it hardly matters."

"So you think someone is looking for revenge?"

"I don't really know, but I have my family to consider." Her mother, the children, even the servants. She stood up. "I suppose I could leave for a while and hope whoever is looking for me will follow. I could go to Edinburgh."

"No, stay home. You have friends who will vouch for you, protect the family." Wilton assured her. He did not stand, but straightened from his relaxed position. "Sit down, my dear. Madeline and I understand the kind of family that shares no blood. We want you to stay at Taunton for as long as you want. The house is yours forever if you wish."

"Thank you, sir." No one else knew, except perhaps his wife, how truly generous this man was.

"Speaking of finding people," Wilton said, clearing his throat, "your rescue was a success on all counts, yes?"

"Yes, only it did not go as smoothly as I would have wished." She explained about the much-too-curious colonel.

"You and Georges cannot be at this much longer. You know that, don't you? Napoleon is on the road to ruin. I think he will abdicate before the end of summer. That could send the country into chaos."

"I know." She thought of Raoul Desseau and her worry for him. "Soon I will settle in Taunton. I will paint portraits, perfect the paper-cutting and silhouettes, and turn into an eccentric female. I will be content, even if the villagers never accept me."

"If you pay your bills promptly and live a quiet life, in time they will."

"My mother, perhaps, not me. I am too much a mystery." She waved away his protest. "It does not matter. I want only the quiet and my studio. I long for it the way you miss the sea when you have been too long ashore. The way Gabriel Pennistan wants nothing more than for people to believe him innocent."

"Is he innocent?" Wilton asked.

"I think he may be. He is so given to temper, and yet so intrinsically kind that it is hard to imagine him involved in such coldhearted betrayal."

"You know him that well?" He raised his eyebrows exactly like the gossiping old biddy at the drapers in Taunton.

Yes, she did, she realized. Charlotte had seen the temper, felt the kindness. It was a mistake to have spoken of it, a sure sign of her fatigue. Wilton did not need to know anything about that part of her life. "He thinks it strange the captain has not made his presence known."

"Dose him with laudanum." He drank down the last of his wine as though it would help him in the same way. "Let him sleep until we are in port."

"I trust you are joking." She pushed her wine away. "He is abed now, but his worries will compete with his exhaustion. I do not expect him to sleep well."

"Would you, if you were to meet the hangman?"

"Is that what you have heard?" She raised her hand to her throat.

"I have heard nothing since I left England," Wilton admitted. "But when I first made inquiries for the duke, Viscount Sidmouth had some particularly damning evidence. That the French Minister of Police offered Lord Gabriel Pennistan a bribe that he found irresistible." Wilton put his glass on the table with more force than necessary.

"If they had bribed him and he accepted, then why was he in prison?" Charlotte asked, hoping that the anger she was feeling did not show as clearly as Wilton's did. Had Lord Gabriel been lying when he said he did not know why he had been taken? And she had believed him so honest.

"Putting him in prison is curious, Charlotte, but both Lord Sidmouth and I agree it is a question easily answered if one has ever worked with the Minister of Police.

"No matter who is Minister, they have all learned from Fouché and release as little information as possible. I suspect that the men who were transporting him had not been told anything more than to bring him to Paris in one piece. That had one added advantage that Pennistan must have realized. If, somehow, they were stopped by the English, he would have a chance to pretend he was loyal and being held against his will. I am sure he was very comfortable until they reached Le Havre."

"Lord Gabriel admitted he was not tortured or mistreated until he tried to escape from the prison." Charlotte thought for a moment. "That should have struck me as odd. Spies are not spared as men in uniform are. They can be tortured and executed without the same considerations a soldier would have."

"Yes, and when events grew complicated his escorts put him in prison," Wilton continued. "Affairs grew even more confused and they forgot about him."

And she had called him a fool. She was the fool. "Then tell me, Wilton, if you knew he was a traitor, why did you even consider aiding his rescue? Why not let him rot in a French prison? Why did you send the duke to me?"

"I did it because I knew Meryon would pay you very well and you need the money so much more than he does."

In other words, he'd done it for her financial security and as a sort of trick *on* his family, not *for* his family.

"I knew you could manage the escape. It was a perverse stroke of luck that Lord Gabriel was imprisoned in Le Havre. No one knows it as well as you do."

"If you feel that way and want to avoid the Pennistans, then why were you willing to be here as part of this rescue?" It was too direct a question for him to give her an honest answer, and she was surprised when he did.

"I am here, madame, solely because the admiralty ordered it."

GABRIEL STARED AT THE empty bunk until he had calmed himself enough to think reasonably. She could not have gone far. Or found too much trouble. He picked up the blanket and tossed it on the bunk. He had no doubt she could take care of herself no matter the situation. Surely she would call out if she was in danger. The tangle of thoughts ran through his head as he put on his jacket, found his shoes and checked on the children. Both were sound asleep. He made his way around their hammocks to the door.

No one guarded it now. Good: no one to keep him from moving about. Bad: no one to ask about his "wife."

A ship was never quiet. At this hour most of the sounds came from creaking seams, the rigging and the wind. He found the officer on watch, avoided him. Asking about a missing passenger, especially a woman, would raise an alarm for fear she had gone overboard. The odds were good that Charlotte was exactly where she wanted to be.

He would stay near the ladder to the lower deck and wait for her. Most likely she had come above to enjoy the evening and the air.

Gabriel leaned against the mast. He turned his eyes to the night sky for the first time in two years. Cassiopeia, Ursa Major and Minor. He knew them so well that the movement of the ship was no hindrance. Nothing could obscure the Milky Way, its carpet spread out across the heavens.

The ship creaked and groaned its way west as he let the stars blur above him. Charlotte was right. How could God be limited by man's beliefs? He was greater than man, greater than this planet, greater than the cosmos spread before him.

How could God care about something as insignificant as Gabriel? And his bad choices, his time in prison, this escape were even less than he, a small part of a man, who was less than a dot in the night sky. Still, Gabriel realized, he cared, whether God did or not. He cared about life, his family, his work, his future. About the people who had touched his life: Georges, the children. And Charlotte.

He stayed as he was a few moments more. Then admitted to himself that while it might not matter at all to God or the universe, he wanted to know where she was.

Gabe circled the deck and found three seamen talking quietly and laughing.

"I beg your pardon," Gabriel started, feeling like a complete ass as he began what had to be the stupidest question a man could ask, "have you seen my wife?"

"Aye, sir, we have," one said, touching his head in what Gabe had decided was a gesture of respect. "She be with the captain."

"Has been for nearly an hour," another said.

Gabriel knew exactly what the seaman was implying and ignored it. "They are expecting me." He bit each word out, clenched his fists. He did his best to ignore their looks. He turned from them and headed for the captain's cabin.

"Three can have more fun than two, so I hear."

Gabriel froze in his steps. Then turned back to the troublemakers. Clearly ignoring the insult was not the right way to proceed. He walked to them, anger radiating in his every step. When he spoke, the effort to control his temper made his voice hard, each word slowly spoken. "Keep your filthy ideas to yourself, seaman. I have been in a French prison for nearly a year. They have shown me ways to cause pain you cannot even imagine. Do not insult my wife again."

All three seamen nodded. One with such a nervous jerk that Gabriel thought he would fall down.

"It was the grog talking, sir. He meant nothing by it."

Gabriel turned away. He hoped that one of them would test him. No one made a move. So Gabriel did his best to vent his anger with a long breath. Damn Charlotte anyway. What *was* she doing with the captain? He went on to the stateroom, where he could see candles lit. As he walked closer, he could hear voices. Then he heard a woman's laugh.

Gabriel realized that he had never heard her truly laugh before. Beneath the humor was a hint of the bedroom, intimacy and invitation. No wonder the crew was intrigued.

There was a man waiting outside this cabin. Gabriel ignored him, reaching for the door latch. The man stepped in front of him, forcing Gabe to drop his hand.

"The captain is with someone, sir."

"Yes, I know," Gabriel answered, smiling. "He is with my wife. I'm sure they are expecting me."

"No, sir, the captain said no one was to disturb them."

"You will stop me, how?" Gabriel asked. The man had no gun or sword that he could see.

"With my hands, if I must, sir."

"Oh, I wish you would try."

Before the steward could do more than raise clenched fists, the door was opened from the other side. "What goes on here?"

"This gent wants to see his wife, Captain."

Gabriel walked into the cabin without invitation. The man grabbed his arm. Then released him as quickly.

"Leave us," the captain said to the man. "Keep your mouth closed."

"Aye, sir." The crewman closed the door quietly.

Gabriel was watching Charlotte, who was less tidy than she had been before going to bed. Her hair hung down her back, now dark brown where the powder did not cover it. The simple fichu was missing from her dress. Without it, the nondescript, patched dress was not what any man on this ship would notice.

"I woke and saw you were gone. I wanted to make sure you were safe." He paused before the last word. The other words he had considered were totally inappropriate.

"You can see that I am." She smiled as if calling his bluff. "I am having a conversation with an old friend."

He turned toward the captain. Only so that she could not see how her taunting angered him. He knew her game by now and she still managed to infuriate him.

That idea was banished by shock. "Wilton! What are you doing here?" He turned to Charlotte. "Is this how the duke found you? Through our brother?"

"I am not your brother." Wilton showed that spark of temper that was the Pennistan curse.

"Oh for God's sake, yes you are."

Gabriel spoke at the same time as Charlotte. "Meryon blood runs in our veins. Both of us."

"I am the bastard and you are not. A key difference, my lord."

He used the same inflection on *my lord* that Charlotte did, the one that stripped the two words of any sense of deference.

"But here the tables are turned," Wilton said, "I am in command of this ship." Using the tip of his knife he gestured to the padded bench. "Sit down."

19

THE KNIFE MADE the captain's point with more vigor than Gabriel thought necessary. He raised his hands. "I did not come here to fight." He backed toward the other chair in the room.

"Is that so." Wilton stayed near the door, though he did tuck the knife back into its sheath. "Then why are you here?"

"Are the children all right?" Charlotte asked, standing up as she spoke.

"Yes. They are sound asleep," Gabriel answered, with a glance. Turning his back to her, he spoke to the captain: "I am here because her bed was empty. I was afraid that she might need my help."

"Your help?" Wilton gave a bark of laughter. "She is the one who rescued you."

"I am more than willing to return the favor should the

need arise." He could see Wilton bite back a smile. He chose, wisely Gabriel thought, not to say anything.

"You can see that I am perfectly safe." Charlotte gathered her shawl around her and bundled her hair into a loose knot at the nape. "I will leave you two to share brotherly affection, but I remind you, Captain, I am paid a bonus if he arrives in England alive."

Without a word to Gabriel, she swept out. He followed, then stopped, though Wilton had the door half-closed. "Our father is dead, Captain. As the new duke, my brother will surely be willing to make amends."

Wilton shook his head. "We have nothing to say to each other."

When Gabe would have said more, Wilton stepped closer. "You had best obey me, Pennistan. This is my domain. Here even your duke brother could not save you from a flogging."

Wilton closed the door. The steward hurried toward it and knocked. They were well across the deck when Gabriel heard it open. When Charlotte stopped, so did he.

"Gabriel Pennistan, you are a lying, thieving spawn of Satan," she said in a hoarse whisper. "I cannot believe that for even one minute I thought you innocent."

"Why should it matter to you that Wilton is a relation? I spoke of him before."

"Not that. W. ton tells me that Viscount Sidmouth has damning evidence of your complicity."

She was close enough to reach out and push him as she proceeded to list each one of his sins. His back was to the railing of the ship, and he grabbed both her hands as much in self-defense as in an effort to end her tirade.

"What are you talking about? What does Wilton know?"

"He has no details," she said, backing away a step or two. "Wilton says they have evidence of a bribe so tempting you could not refuse it. That the French Minister of Police, Fouché, was involved. There is talk of it being a hanging offense."

"There was no bribe." It was all he could think of to say in the face of such an outlandish suggestion.

"How convenient, my lord. Now that you are free and on your way home, you have no recollection of such an offer."

"It's absurd. You told me that Fouché is not even in Paris now."

"I also told you that even out of favor he wields more power than any man outside the army. In a matter of time, he will be back. He has more lives than a cat."

"My father agreed. He hated him, called him a liar, to his face, a man without honor and without a goal beyond his own self-interest."

"All of it true, from the stories I have heard," Charlotte said, "but a dangerous thing to say to someone so powerful."

"My father was a power himself." That prompted another thought. "If I was seen to side with the French, it would have gone a long way to discrediting the family name. I can only swear to you that I would never have done so. I am being completely honest."

"And how many do you think have said that? Honesty is not something I expect from anyone. Complete honesty is impossible."

"Your cynicism is too much a part of you. Honesty is possible. You have only to choose to believe. Tell me, are you and Wilton lovers?"

"YOU ARE INFURIATING," she said, facing him again, clenching her fists to keep from slapping him. "Words are as much a weapon to you as that absurd knife you carry."

"Not answering me is a whole different kind of honesty," he said, taking one step away from her.

"No." She managed not to shout it, but stepped even closer to him as she answered. "Wilton and I have never been lovers. He is married. I do not take lovers who are happy in their marriage."

"I believe you." He used two fingers to raise her chin. She thought she could feel his heartbeat through them.

"Now tell me that you believe what I said, Charlotte."

She shook her head.

"We have been as close to each other as two people can be. Doesn't your woman's intuition tell you something?"

She jerked back from his touch and his words.

"Or are you like me?" He reached out and ran a hand down her arm. "Every time we are this close all I can remember is how much there is left between us that is not finished."

She did not, would not, admit that was true.

"Ah, you cannot even admit it to yourself, can you? Will this help?" He took her into his arms and kissed her, softly, sweetly, but with a hunger barely held in check.

"No, my lord," she said, pushing him away. She was tired beyond bearing. "No, my lord. If you think to use sex to convince me of your innocence, you are completely mistaken."

"Charlotte," he said, sounding wounded. "I only thought to clear the air so we could talk honestly."

She laughed, and he did too.

"All right," he said between gasps of laughter, "that was a lie, I admit it."

And in that one silly moment, she believed him. Believed him innocent. Believed him.

He took her arm and they moved along the deck as though it were early evening instead of almost midnight.

"Tell me why you make all these trips to France."

She almost did. Their promenade was so natural, his question so simple.

"Is it because of the children, Charlotte? You are so solicitous of them, especially Claire. Are you her mother?"

Observant but not a genius, she thought with relief. "No, I am not their mother, and that is the truth."

"Then why?"

"Because I helped destroy their families."

"Oh, Charlotte, I do not believe a word of that."

"You are amused?" She stopped the promenade and confronted him.

"No, I would never make light of your pain, but it is so clearly impossible." He took her arm and made her walk beside him again. She had no idea who was watching, that was the only reason she allowed it.

"I am sorry I made light of your confession, Charlotte," he said again. "It is only that while you may have done some things you regret, that would disappoint me, I find the idea of murder hard to credit."

Before she could reply, they were distracted by the bell announcing the change of watch.

There was the clatter of the lines as men came down from the rigging and the thud of feet as the new crew came onto the deck. Charlotte saw a few eye them with curiosity despite the fact that Pennistan had found a spot at the stern and out of the way. All the activity gave her a blessed moment to think.

"My lord, kindness is a pathetic choice of weapons."

"Make no mistake, my dear, if I wanted a weapon, you would know," he said as he followed the progress of a man moving up the ratlines. "I will not press you anymore but will wait until you want to tell me about it. It will be a rational test of my patience."

Now she smiled. Did he turn everything into a scientific assessment? Discussing rats with Pierre. How ridiculous. And yet there was something very appealing about a man who made the best of what he was given. What if they had met in a ballroom? What if she had met him instead of meeting Charles Strauss? *Change the subject,* she commanded herself. "Did you take some time to look at the night sky this evening?"

He nodded, looking down to hide his disappointment at her change of subject.

"After all your efforts were you able to see the Great Comet with your friend Dr. Burgos?"

"Yes." He watched her for a long moment and then raised his hands in surrender. "All right, Charlotte. I promised patience. We will change the subject."

"Thank you," she replied, smiling at him, if only to see the surprise on his face again.

His surprise melted into a grin as he caught her game. He leaned to her, pressed a quick kiss on her lips and laughed as she stumbled backward. Not for all the money in the treasury would she admit that his touch had made her knees weak. He grabbed her arms and held on to her until she was steady again. Even then he did not let go right away.

"This test of who can discomfit who the most could lead somewhere interesting."

His grip was light. She had a choice.

"It would lead to an argument," she said in as dismissive a voice as she could muster, pulling out of his grasp, wondering what he was like in bed when not half drugged by spirits and exhausted. "I am not interested."

Liar. He mouthed the word, but did change the subject. "So, we are to talk about astronomy? Did you see it, Charlotte? The Great Comet?"

"Of course," she said. "That was one comet that was hard to miss. What an amazing spectacle. They do not come along very often, though. Why do you study the stars?"

"Rhys Braedon is a true lover of astronomy. Working with him made it interesting and worthwhile. Even exciting. As for me, I feel as though I own the night hours when I am alone. That anything is possible. That God created life on other planets. That their astronomers may be doing the same thing I am. Or they are centuries more advanced than we are and will be dropping from the sky to visit when we least expect it."

"Is it wise for a man of science to have such an imagination?"

"Yes, of course, where do you think great ideas come from? If Jenner had not been curious, do you think we would have a vaccination for smallpox?"

She considered the truth of that and wondered if Jenner had ever said anything as bizarre as Gabriel Pennistan had just said. She kept that to herself. "I know nothing about astronomy, not even how to tell the planets from the stars."

"It's very simple. Would you like me to show you?"

When she nodded, he stood behind her, instructing her in the way to look at the stars, to watch for the steady lights. Those were planets. From there he helped her make sense of the jumble of night lights by starting with Orion's belt and working up, and then down to the "legs." She watched the stars but was more aware of Gabriel's arm along her shoulder, his face close to hers, the way his body sheltered her.

She tried so hard to pretend indifference that her body rebelled with a violent shiver. Gabriel pulled her shawl more firmly around her.

"It is very beautiful," she said, abandoning resistance and relaxing against him. Not defeat. Surrender.

"Yes, it is," he whispered.

When she turned to him, his face was close enough to kiss, his eyes on her as though she was the beauty to which he was referring.

For a moment he was all she wanted. "Be honest, Gabriel," she whispered, "admit that this exercise in science is only an excuse to put your arms around me." She moved from his embrace, and the truth was trumped by sanity. "I think we should check on the children."

20

CLAIRE WAS SOUND ASLEEP, as was Pierre, though he was a little more restless than his sister.

Gabriel followed Charlotte into the smaller cabin. "I thought it was you who needed an excuse to be near me." He came to her, but did not take her in his arms. "Charlotte, I have put my life in your hands. You have put your life in mine. If that is not trust, then I do not know what is. If we are both looking for a reason to be together, then we need only take that trust a step further and be honest and admit what we both want."

She waited for him to be honest first.

"Did you notice, Charlotte, that your bed is big enough for two?"

She knew it was too late to argue herself out of it. She wanted him. Wanted sex with him. Only once more so that she had no time to find that his failings far outweighed his virtues.

Reaching up, she unhooked the hammock and let it trail to the floor. "Come," she said. "You see, I will admit it. You told me our first time that you would make me beg. But I will not beg. Not ever." She pressed her lips together and then smiled a little as she held out her hand. "Come to bed with me."

"You told me then that the sex we had was out of pity," he said, closing the distance between them. "Not this time."

She laughed, and was surprised to hear the genuine humor when what she was thinking was not amusing at all. "Are there any more comments we need to leave here with our clothes?"

He shrugged out of his loose-fitting jacket, letting it fall to the floor. "There will be no pity this time, Charlotte."

Closing the distance between them, she undid his shirt and helped pull it off. Then she trailed her hands down his chest. He was too thin but still felt strong. "No pity." She closed her eyes and pressed her face to his heart. "It was not entirely out of pity the first time."

He was undressed before she was, and after helping her with the laces on her dress, he stretched out on the bunk and let her entertain him with her disrobing. She had done it a hundred times at least. It was a dance she had perfected and often enjoyed. This time her clothes were an obstacle. Why stand here when she could be beside him? She wanted to hurry with the undressing, and she did.

Only to herself would she admit that she wanted Gabriel

Pennistan for the sheer pleasure of it. How long had it been since she had wanted a touch more than she wanted to see arousal as proof of her power?

With a shiver, she decided to leave her shift on and slid beside him under the blanket. He didn't complain and helped her remove the shift, pulling it over her head, remembering, bless him, not to trap her hands as he kissed her stomach, breasts, neck. When the shift was tossed aside, he captured her lips with his own. Gentle, thorough, invitation and demand, accepted and returned.

He raised his head, his bright eyes speaking passion as his lips had. She felt his heartbeat under her hands and with her lips felt it quicken. His cool supple body grew heated and tense as she pulled him close and held him. The roll of the ship, the sound of the water set the pace for them as they explored each other with a thoroughness that belied the intensity of her yearning and his need.

"I want you more than I have ever wanted any woman. I want your body, your hands, your mouth and even your mind. Your heart. Well, I know I can never have that."

How many men were honest, even in bed? In all her experience, only this one. She stopped trying to understand, to be in control, and let her mind flood with feeling. She did not so much hear his words as feel them.

"My best hope is that for a moment I will touch your heart and you will feel mine."

He matched his speech with kisses, each leaving a stream of warmth that settled in her belly and made her want more. He used his hands as he had his lips, caressing, finding new places to touch so that want was a power all its own. He cupped her with his hand and teased her with his fingers as if she were a virgin who needed to be shown each step, all the possibilities.

She moved beneath him, wanting him inside her even if it meant an end to this bit of paradise. With a laugh of purely male satisfaction he touched her, just so, and she arched against him, taking all that he could give, ready to beg. He was more generous than that, and with a kiss he plunged into her and together they left the world behind and soared through the stars.

She felt as though her heart and soul were stripped as bare as her body. He moved to lie beside her and smoothed the damp strands of hair from her face and smiled at her, then closed his eyes. "Even blind I would know you. I would recognize the feel of you, the scent of you. I could feel your heart, your pulse, and know you by any name, in any place."

He fell asleep first and she watched him until she too drifted off, comforted by the rhythm of the ship, the sounds of the night, the warmth of his body next to her.

The ship's bell woke them both though it was still night, or at least not yet dawn.

They made love again, more heated and urgent than before. The smell of land was in the air. Soon, too soon, they would be in Portsmouth.

Perhaps he slept again after; she did not. He was as honest as any man she had ever met. As true in moments of anger and passion as he was when he was considering the bits of science he had discussed with her. She made to move from the bed, before his honesty bled into her. He reached out a hand and took hers. "One more kiss." He pushed himself up

in the bunk and pulled her across him so that she was cradled in his arms.

When his lips touched hers, she realized that in a different time and place they could have meant something to each
other. She rested her head on his chest and listened to his
heart. "Gabriel, we are nothing more than two strangers
brought together by the absurdity of war."

"Hmmm" was all he said.

He had his eyes closed and she thought he might still be
half-asleep. Then he said, "We will not always be at war."

She smiled, and she felt him laugh a little. "We are changed
forever."

"For the good, if we allow it."

"Oh," she said, "you are an unbearable optimist. How
can what happened in our past make us better?"

"I don't know your past, Charlotte, but I know you now
and see the generosity and courage beneath the hardness.
Where did that come from if not your past? My father was
never the same man after my mother died, my brother much
less arrogant after he married."

"I can give you a dozen examples of the absurdity of that
but will settle for one." She moved to lie beside him, putting
as much distance between them as the small bed would
allow.

"I met Charles Strauss at the beginning of my first
London Season and married him before summer."

Gabriel reached for the blanket and drew it over them.

"He was handsome in a rugged way and one of the most
charming men I had ever met. It was all in his eyes, the way
he would lean in as you spoke, the sympathy, the amuse-

ment. He was born to be a diplomat. That is what he called himself and how society accepted him." She stopped, not at all sure how much to tell him. Suddenly not wanting to tell him anything.

"Charles Strauss?" he asked, and was quiet a minute. "I have a good memory for names and I've never heard of him."

"We did not travel in your social circles, my lord." She looked up at him and, when he only nodded, turned to stare at the ceiling again. "If we had a titled gentleman or lady at one of our soirees, it was because they considered themselves artists or egalitarians. My parents were wellborn but not wealthy, and socialized with a more artistic circle than the ton welcomed. It was the perfect place for a diplomat from a small European country to find a wife. He was from Gradsbourg. Do you know it?"

"A little."

"I learned later that the only interests Strauss represented were his own. I did not find that out until it was much too late to escape.

"My mother thought it a perfect match. He was older; to her that was a sign he would be careful with me. He planned to return to Europe; she thought that would give me a chance to bloom in a society not as constrained as England's. He was experienced; she thought that would be exciting." She stopped there. "Let me up, Gabriel. I need to dress."

He allowed her up from the bed with no hesitation, but would not be distracted from the story. "Will you tell me more?"

Once she had her shift on she felt less vulnerable. As she put her stays on over the shift, she concentrated on the ties.

It was easier if she did not look at him. "In time I understood that his diplomacy was a sham, that he made his living by helping people when they had no other recourse. Mind you, only if they had the money to pay him."

"You could not leave." It was more statement than question. "Of course you could not," he went on. "You were young, without resources, married."

She stopped dressing for a moment. "I did try to leave once. Only once." After that it was easier to hide in her art and convince herself that she was as much a victim as the ones he helped.

Before Gabriel could do more than close his eyes and shake his head, she hurried on.

"His most elaborate charade was his last. It was 1810, Napoleon was doing well and so was Charles. There were a group of English families living in Le Havre, they had been held there since the end of the Peace of Amiens."

"They had been there for seven years? Since 1803?"

"Yes. Not in prison, but not allowed to leave either. Charles was able to arrange for them to be taken to Portsmouth. It was an expensive operation. Since the revolution and Napoleon's rise to power, Le Havre had become more of a naval port and most of the ships that were not naval had to go elsewhere to unload their goods. It was a challenge finding a captain willing to take them, much less able."

She sat down beside him so that he could do up the laces of her dress. "The French authorities were bribed to ensure their cooperation, and he told me to flirt with them when money was not enough. The families paid him; some gave him all they had."

Charlotte stood and faced him. "I was the one who collected the money. I had to see and list each member of the party. Claire was not yet a year. And not at all happy at being made to stay awake so much past her usual bedtime."

She had taken the money to Charles and he had unknowingly thanked her by leaving to visit his current mistress instead of celebrating with her. "I had almost convinced myself that Strauss was doing something good. Then, the night of their departure, he sent me to distract a group of port guards. He took the families out into the harbor and aboard a ship. It was then that the captain refused to take children younger than five years old."

That made Gabriel sit up straight. "Why would he do that? I've heard that women aboard ship are considered to be bad luck, but not children."

"I am sure that if enough money was sent his way he could be convinced to reconsider, and indeed two or three of the children were allowed to go. The rest were sent ashore and the ship set sail without them. To this day I do not know if the parents accepted the decision or tried to leave. In the end, they had no choice."

She stood up and began to smooth her hair, reached for her scarf and tied it all back as neatly as she could without a comb or mirror.

"Gabriel," she said, turning to face him. "I *never* knew about the children left behind. Yes, I was a party to the effort, for a number of reasons, none of them admirable, but I did not find out about the children until later, after Strauss died."

"I believe you."

His words were calm, reassuring, as if he would never doubt her.

"Charles died a week later, killed by someone who did not care for his sort of blackmail or extortion or moneylending or peacemaking. I do not know and do not care. I think it one of my greatest weaknesses that I did not kill him myself."

She stood looking down, wondering how much honesty one man could take.

"How long ago was that?"

"A little over four years ago," she said, amazed that it had not been longer. "I felt as though I had been released from a prison. I buried him with no other mourners and went back to England."

"Did you still have family there?" he asked.

"My mother," she admitted grudgingly. "I railed and cursed her for selling me so cheaply. I went to London, swore never to use the name Strauss again, and set about making my own life there. I had some money from the sale of our things in France. I thought I would become some man's mistress if I needed to. But before the money ran out, Georges found me." She explained about the papers he had found and the list of children and what Charles had done with them. "For the last three years, Georges and I have been looking for the children, doing our best to reunite them with their parents."

"An amazing way of doing good with your life. You have found all of them?"

"Yes, and rescued all but one. The oldest boy was sold to a blacksmith," she said, remembering how the man was as cold as the metal he put in the forge. "He was to take him on as an apprentice once he was old enough. Another went to a chimney sweep. The oldest girl was sold to a bordello. I bought her back before she began to earn her keep. The rest were sent to various orphanages." Did he know that at least half of those girls would have wound up on the streets, selling themselves?

"In various guises Georges and I have 'adopted' four of them and reunited them with their families. Two did not survive long in the orphanage."

"Yes, I can imagine that. They are not the best place for the weak."

"My mother and I found ourselves with a family when we discovered that we could not locate all the parents. Claire and Pierre will join the three we already have."

Gabriel rose from the bed and began to dress.

"Nothing is more important to me than the children. I would sacrifice the money your brother has promised as well as my life and yours for them."

What could he say to that? She did not wait for an answer but reset the hammock on its hook, doing her best not to watch him as he thought about the story she had told him. It was more than she'd meant to say. But once she had started she could not stop.

She wished she could tell what he was thinking. This morning his eyes betrayed nothing. Did that mean she meant so little to him? Or was he trying to think of words worse than *whore*? Finally the wait was unbearable. "You have no questions at all?" *Stop judging me,* she wanted to shout. *I did the best I could.* When he was dressed except for his jacket, he came to stand in front of her.

"Charlotte," he said, "I do have one question."

He hesitated, and she nodded encouragement.

"Who is Georges?"

"Who is Georges? I tell you a story only a few people know and you ask me who Georges is?"

"I have waited three days to hear that story. And now that I have heard it I think what you want from me is understanding, not questions. Georges, however, is a mystery. If it is asking too much, you do not need to tell me."

"Georges was my husband's valet."

"Valet." He considered the word as though it could have more than one meaning. "Is it not odd that he would stay loyal to you after Strauss's death?"

"Yes, it is odd. But we shared a similar hell when Charles was alive. Both of us were innocent of the worst of it. He was loyal to Charles and kind to me. He is the only true friend I have in France."

"Then may I be the truest friend you have in England, Charlotte." He bowed to her.

She nodded, curtsying back. Let him believe it. They both could for a while. What would it be like to have someone to lean on and talk to, someone who did not worry the way a mother did, who understood the longing to right the wrong?

It would be wonderful, which was the very reason it could be no more than a fantasy.

21

THE PORT IS FULL UP," the lieutenant shouted over the din of the crew moving up the ropes to adjust the sails.

Gabriel nodded, amazed at the *Diplomat*'s ability to maneuver in the tight space, to find a spot—or was it assigned?—to drop anchor.

"It will be a while before we can take you ashore, sir. Captain must send word we have passengers and wait for instructions. Excuse me." The lieutenant moved off to call instructions to someone aloft.

"Do not even think about making a trip to shore on your own, Pennistan." Charlotte might give the appearance of a mouse of a woman, but her voice was that of his jailer.

The children had ended Gabriel and Charlotte's morning together: Claire insisting that she wanted to go on deck. Pierre refusing to unlatch the door "until Mama and Papa allow it." Charlotte hurried to act as mediator while Gabriel put his shoes on. By the time he joined them she was playing her role again. She had tucked away that part of herself, the essence of her, that she had given him the night before and again this morning.

He'd thought about that, trying to determine what they had had through the night that was missing now. Her jailer demand that he not consider escape brought the answer to him as clearly as the ship's bell ringing. She had trusted him. In the dark, curled together, warmed by lovemaking, she had opened her heart to him.

Now she seemed to be doing her best to recover her authority, reminding him that he was her prize and not her lover. "Escape? Charlotte, why would you think that?"

"I saw the way you eyed the shore. It wasn't hard to know what went through your mind."

"I was not thinking of escape, only the challenge that is waiting when we land. The time has come to plead my case. I am home again, and instead of feeling relieved I am," he paused and then decided to be honest, "I am all but frozen with fear."

"Papa!" Pierre called to him, waving to him from a sickening distance up the ratlines. The boy must have found his sea legs. Today he was playing the part of powder monkey, obeying commands as if he had been at sea all his short life.

"I will face what is coming, Charlotte. I want to see my family again even if it means no more than pity and disgust." Underneath it all would be love. He was sure of that. Not quite sure enough to say it aloud, though.

He watched Pierre as he spoke, seeing the child in a different light. The boy might not have had the mother or father he once knew, but he seemed to believe that all would be well. Would he trade places with the boy if he could?

"And, as you have reminded me more than once, madame, you will be paid a bonus if I am returned whole. Now that I know why the money is so important to you, I would never betray you or these children for my own ends."

The rest of the morning was entertaining enough as long as he repressed the idea that a hangman might be in his future. The prospect seemed no more real than it had all those months in a cell. Less actually. Here the wind meant action and the open sea freedom. It was another prison nonetheless. Someday he would make a list. Could it be that a sense of honor was the greatest prison of all?

By the time the captain came on deck and gave orders for the boat to be lowered, he had been asked at least a dozen times to "step aside, please, sir." Charlotte had retreated to the cabin with Claire after the third such request. When he declined her suggestion that he join them, she simply nodded.

Captain Wilton came to him. "Come to the quarterdeck. You will be out of the way there."

Gabriel followed him to a place in front of the wheel and stayed where Wilton pointed. The captain stood with his arms folded. A critical eye was all the command he gave. It was enough. The crew moved sharply. The Diplomats behaved as the team they were trained to be.

Gabriel had seen enough of the ship's maneuverings. He concentrated his attention on the man who was his brother. He looked like a Pennistan. He had that same inclination to command. It was compounded in him as well as in the duke by the roles life bequeathed them.

He wondered what parts of his father they both shared. Temper? He supposed if Wilton had one, he had learned to curb it early in his naval career.

Stubbornness. Not that Gabriel considered himself obstinate. Even if Jess had called him implacable often enough. He preferred to think of it as single-minded.

The captain turned to him, watched him for a long minute and then spoke. "Lord Gabriel, there is something I want to make clear to you." He waited until Gabriel finally encouraged him with a "Yes, sir?"

"The Pennistans left my mother to live in poverty. She died before her time because she had the misfortune to catch your father's eye and succumb to his seduction."

"Our father did that, Captain Wilton. Lynford was twelve when your mother died. You were ten. There was nothing either one of you could do. My mother? Well, she was his wife. She had no power of her own no matter how hard she would try."

"I do not care, my lord. I have a wife and a family and a career that has served me well. I have no need of the support of the Pennistans; as a matter of fact, I reject it totally and completely."

Before Gabriel could reply, the captain turned and walked to the railing to call something to his first lieutenant.

The day dragged on as had the day before. This time they were in more company than yesterday's trip from Le Havre and with less tension for everyone. Except him. He was vastly relieved when Charlotte came back on deck.

"How much longer, do you think?" he asked her.

"The captain is in charge. And he is awaiting word from shore. I think that is called the chain of command. I am at the end of the chain and you are not on it at all."

Anxiety chilled his blood so that he was not sure he would ever be warm again. It also served to keep him alert. "You are at the head of my chain of command. When we reach land, what will we do?"

"It depends on who is waiting for you."

He strongly suspected that she was not telling the whole truth. She who planned her moves to the smallest detail would hardly leave this last to chance. What if he lost her? What if he never saw her again?

He did not ask, simply did his best to memorize everything about her. How often she used her hand to smooth her dress, or Claire's hair, or a wrinkle from a table cover. A sensual gesture that he imagined she was not even aware of. How short and neat her fingernails were. How hairs slipped from her cap and curled on her neck. He kept up the mental catalog until she looked at him.

"My lord," she said with some irritation. "You said yourself that I would not leave before I have the money from your brother."

"Not unless it would endanger the children," he agreed.

"Precisely."

"So you will wait in Portsmouth until he comes? I can hardly imagine he will be waiting there for us."

She gave him her Gallic shrug, which was explained this time. "Someone will be there. Your brother Lord Jessup, perhaps."

"Yes, I suppose that could be."

"Is the story now scripted to your satisfaction?"

"Yes, thank you, madame," he said with a bow.

The gig was back. It nudged the side of the ship and the second lieutenant scrambled aboard. He did his best not to acknowledge them and headed directly for the captain.

Not a minute later they were being prepared for departure. Wilton called Charlotte over and discussed something with her. To the crew it would appear that he was reassuring her about the short trip to shore. Gabriel knew better. He stood with Claire and Pierre and tried to decipher what Wilton and Charlotte were saying. Their brief exchange and nods were not much to interpret.

They boarded as they had left the fishing boat. He watched Charlotte. She concentrated on nothing more than soothing Claire's fears.

The water was calmer here. Still, Pierre began to groan the moment they were in the jolly boat. "Shall we count the number of boats in the harbor?" Gabriel asked.

"Please be quiet, Papa," Pierre said with pained disinterest. "I am going to watch the dock we are headed for and think of nothing but arriving there. If I am sick on the way, then I can tell myself we will be on land soon."

Better for the boy to worry about this trip than what was coming next. Where would they go until she could take them home? Or was her home in Portsmouth? How long would the money from Lynford support them? He knew Charlotte would have a plan. Two thousand pounds could last a very long time. As much as he wanted to help them, there was nothing he could do until he had helped himself.

As the boat made its way through the maze of larger vessels, Portsmouth came into view, and with it the smells and activity of a busy port city. So unlike home, but one step closer.

When the boat came alongside the dock the seamen shipped the oars. One jumped out ahead of them and extended a hand for the lady and children. The tide was low and Charlotte had to make a great and rather unladylike step up to the wharf.

Gabriel helped from his end, lifting the children to waiting hands. As he was about to join them, one of the seamen called down, "Beg pardon, sir; would you toss me the dispatch bag at your feet there?"

He would never know if that request for help was plan or accident. He reached for the bag, handed it to the seaman. When he took his giant step up onto the dock he saw that Charlotte was almost to the street, the children in hand.

"Wait," he called. Where was she going? Damnation. She had lied to him. No one was here to meet him.

There were not many women in the crowd, but she would be easy enough to lose. He was about to run after her when a man—no, two men—came up on either side of him.

"Lord Gabriel Pennistan?"

"Yes," he said with some distraction, craning his head to keep her in sight. She too had been stopped. He could see a lively discussion ensuing and began to walk toward them, followed by the two men who had approached him. There was still no sign of his family.

"You are to come with us. There are some gentlemen from London who want to speak with you." They had not taken his arms when he began to move away, but the one who had not spoken held up a stick to block his progress.

"First I would see if the lady I traveled with needs help."

He pushed the cane aside and continued walking toward her. Not running. He avoided movement that would be construed as an attempt to escape.

"There is no need to go to her. She will be coming with us."

"But she has children."

"They will be kept safe while she is detained."

When they were within earshot of her, almost upon them, he could hear Charlotte having the same discussion with her captors.

"I will not leave my children. They have been separated from their father for years, and now you would deny them their mother?"

"We want to know your relationship with Lord Gabriel Pennistan—" the man began.

"Lord Gabriel Pennistan?" She cut him off and laughed. "If I knew a lord, do you think I would be walking to the posting house? No, there would be a carriage waiting here for me, and servants to care for us. My husband was supposed to be here to meet us. Pah."

They seemed at an impasse, when the man with the cane stepped forward. "Lord Gabriel, do you know this woman?"

When he hesitated, the man cast him a murderous look. "Be aware, sir, your life depends on the truth."

"You mistake my hesitation," Gabriel said with a calm that was no sham. "Look at what you are doing to the children. The girl is terrified. The boy will defend his mother with his life. I ask you, what value is there if you win by sacrificing the most innocent?"

He held Charlotte's eyes with his own. If he lied for her, it would help the children, but they would be separated. It would be the same as good-bye, for now and possibly forever.

Yes, he had insisted he was done with lying. But only a fool or a desperate man would swear "never." Looking her in the eyes, those lovely eyes, he spoke for the children.

"I did no more than travel from France with this woman. I can only assume she was rescued as I was. She said her husband would be waiting for her, and I am surprised he is not here."

It was quite a speech. Gabriel was proud of it. As he had hoped, a small crowd had gathered around them. They were clearly on the side of the woman and her children.

"Let 'em go, you fools."

"What harm could one woman and two tykes do?"

As if on cue, a man in an officer's uniform made his way through the crowd. Charlotte's relief was evident. Gabriel was not at all sure it was an act.

"Here I am! Here I am!" The man, an army major, stumbled as he reached them. "The colonel would not stop talking." He grabbed Charlotte and hugged her, unmindful of the public display. "Thank God, thank God, you are safe, you are safe."

"No thanks to you, Major," his wife said. "That is the last time I will follow you anywhere. It is home to Devon. You are on your own until this benighted war ends."

"Yes, yes, yes," the major said, laughing at her annoyance. "Just as you wish, as you wish."

He bent down to pick up Claire, but the little girl cringed and wrapped her mama's cloak around her face.

"I suppose she does not remember me. I suppose not," he said, clearly wounded by the rejection.

What a performance, Gabriel thought. He let himself smile. Everyone would think it was happiness at the reunion. Indeed, the crowd broke out in applause and cheers. Charlotte accepted the compliment with a nod and then gave the major a kiss on the cheek. The crowd cheered even louder.

As the crowd began to drift off, Charlotte left Pierre with the officer and came up to Gabriel.

"Thank you for your support." She curtsied to him and he returned the gesture with a bow.

"You are most welcome. My apologies for forcing this situation on you." What else could he say with an audience? *Tell me where I can find you? We cannot let it end like this?* That was absurd. This was the end. For a dozen reasons.

She shook her head as if she had heard each of the unspoken words. "This is good-bye."

Gabriel watched as she took her supposed husband's arm and, holding Pierre by the hand, showed Gabriel her back as she was lost in the crowd.

"MAMA, MAMA, YOU ARE hurting my hand."

Without speaking to the boy, Charlotte eased her grip. She did not, would not, turn around. The major was ahead of her now, holding Claire. The child watched her as though a blink would cause her to vanish.

Gabriel had come to their rescue, every bit as much as

Major Shelby had. More, for if he had told the truth, nothing Shelby could have done would have kept her from being separated from the children.

Shelby fell back and in step beside her.

"Did you know the officials would be waiting for him?"

"Yes, Wilton warned me." She reached up with her free hand and smoothed Claire's hair. The little girl smiled at her and closed her eyes. "Thank God he did. It gave me time to prepare the children. If you had been there, we would have been away before Pennistan was out of the boat."

"Yes, I am sorry, Charlotte. But it would have caused worse problems than what we faced if I had not reported to my superior officer as ordered."

What could she say to that? Men would insist on their chain of command. There was discipline, yes, but from her perspective it was too closely akin to pride and power.

"Why would Pennistan do that for you?"

"Lie?"

He nodded.

"What good would detaining me have done? Nothing more than slow us down. Sidmouth's office knows precisely who I am and what I am doing. Those two buffoons were no more than petty tyrants."

"You are counting on a man most consider a spy and a traitor telling the truth. He could have complicated the situation mightily, compromised your work. It was no small thing allowing you to leave." He looked back. "Why would Pennistan protect you that way?"

"He was protecting the children, not me."

"Hmm" was the only comment he made. He stopped to shift Claire higher against his chest. Charlotte moved on.

"Mama, are we lost?" Pierre pulled her to a stop as he asked the question.

"No, dearest, I know exactly where we are going."

He nodded.

They walked on, and she tried to see the streets through his eyes. Not totally unlike Le Havre; but then, they had not lived there but in Grenoble, inland and much quieter. This world was as alien as the ship had been.

She could feel the boy's uncertainty and waited for him to speak. It did not take long.

"Did the man who pretended to be our papa, did he save us?" Pierre stared back down the way they had come.

"Yes, he did."

"They took him to jail anyway."

"Yes, they did."

"Can we save him?"

"Pierre, that is noble of you, but I think the best way to help him is to pray for him."

"All right, madame. I will pray for him every night." They walked on for a few more steps. "If you please, Mama, my name is Peter now."

He still held on to her hand, but drew himself up as straight as he could. And so it began. A new life. Shelby's wife would take her in, welcome the children until they were ready to move north and home. The money from the duke would arrive within days. She would have time to fortify herself and prepare the children.

All that it would cost her was a tiny bit of her soul, a hole in her heart. Once she was home, she could wait for the wound to heal, distract herself with her work and hope that the next trip would be the last. And pray that this trip had done more than deliver a man to his death.

22

GABRIEL'S DETENTION BY THE government authorities had turned into weeks, then months of questioning, observation.

The men who had met him at the dock took him to a house in the country. The accommodations were better than a French prison. There was no physical torture, but there was no contact with his family. No word from Charlotte. That he had hoped for word from her surprised him. Nothing could have been more final than that last rejection. Still, she haunted him, even as the days passed and winter edged toward spring.

He'd worried that this was his trial, any optimism he had squashed by day after day of being held in secret. Then a letter from Lynford assured him he was using all his influence to spare him "the indignity." Indignity of what? Gabriel wondered. A trial? Death by hanging? Prison for life?

Finally there was action. The questioning began. It was civil enough, but the two men doubted every word he said by gesture and glance. They twisted his answers until even he was confused. He'd raged in private, doing his best to be calm with his questioners.

"I was recruited by Wellington himself. I reported to a senior aide."

When he protested that "Surely you know all of this as well as I do," he was told to cooperate or "It will not go well for you, my lord."

So he cooperated, recounting how often he reported, even the details of what he had learned, feeling compelled to add, "It is ancient history by now."

"Yes. We know." The two men looked at each other and a secretary wrote down notes, if not every word. "Could you identify the men you met?"

"Possibly." He wondered if that would count against him.

Had he taken written notes? they asked.

"Of course not. Though once or twice I wrote some things down, using a cipher that I developed. Those notes were destroyed as soon as I had no use for them."

"Were you paid for your information?"

"No," he said, adding to himself, *only in detention, beatings, and this pointless interrogation.*

By far the worst was the detailed telling of that last night. How he had arrived at the tavern to see the men under guard. His denial of spying. His refusal to name any as his colleagues. Their death. The fire that destroyed the evidence. Sleep was difficult after those questions. He wondered if his questioners had nightmares as vivid as his.

The next day he had his most memorable visitor of all. "Seven are dead because of you, you son of a bitch." The man, who introduced himself as Doncaster, made Gabriel sit in a chair in the middle of the room, circling him as he railed on and on, ending with a demand, which he yelled to the ceiling: "Admit you are a traitor!"

Gabriel said nothing, watching and waiting for the man to pull out a knife and end Gabriel's life right there.

Doncaster came to face him, bending close so they could look eye to eye. "It hardly matters, you worthless spawn of the aristocracy. You do nothing but take, and even when you try to give back you are a failure. For that alone you deserve to die."

He sounded more French than English.

"Studying the stars." His face was as filled with disdain as his words. "What a useless way to spend a life."

Gabriel had an answer for that. He doubted this man wanted to hear it.

"The life will be squeezed out of you, my lord, while you beg for mercy, for breath, for life, and then finally you will beg for death. I will see to it, I promise you."

Gabriel believed him. From that meeting on, his most constant dreams were the dozen variations of his own death. Sometimes his whole family watched, crying. Sometimes they were cheering. Sometimes he was alone except for the hooded executioner. Once Charlotte had been there, her vague curiosity the last of this life he saw. He would wake up from the dreams in the dark, once or twice sure he had died. Once or twice wishing that he had.

The process continued, covering the period following his

detention. He told them all he could, but was careful to tell them only what he had experienced then. He did not mention the story that Charlotte had relayed to him, the suggestion that he was being taken to Paris to be offered a bribe.

It went on day after day for weeks. During all that time, not once did they ask how he escaped and came to be on the *Diplomat*. Did they know about Charlotte? Had they been advised not to ask? Odd, he thought. Very odd.

One morning, while the fog was still low to the ground, they woke him, told him to dress and hurried him into a coach. They would not tell him what awaited him.

He had only the vague reassurance of his brother's one letter that there was a chance he could cheat death. Doncaster's wrath made Lyn's efforts seem insignificant. Once he was dead, all his brother's letters would be useless.

It was less than a day's travel from the house in Sussex to London. He wished for more time before he was forced to be inside again, and not only because he did not know what awaited him. The flowers were in bloom. Spring was a reminder of what he most treasured about the land, the physical beauty, "the charm of nature's embrace," as one of his sister-in-law's poems described it. The promise of life that each spring brought. He concentrated on two birds chasing an interloper and did his best not to think beyond the moment.

They took him to London. His cell there was as comfortable as any inn he had ever visited. He was staring out the window, watching nothing more than the tradesmen moving up and down the street, wondering if Charlotte was settled and if the children were comfortable, when the ringing of keys the jailer carried announced a caller.

Gabriel stayed with his back to the window quite deliberately. It gave him the advantage. He could see the caller quite clearly, and the caller saw only a shadow framed by light.

It was his brother. Now the Duke of Meryon.

Gabriel waited to see how he would be received.

It seemed that Lyn was waiting for the same thing. They watched each other for a moment. Had he aged as much as his brother? There was silver in Lynford's hair now, lines around his eyes, though the rest of him looked as fit as it ever had. It did not appear as though his new duties kept him from his daily riding and fencing.

"Whoever thought that I would be so happy to see you that the fact you are in prison does not matter at all."

Lynford came to him, and with a hug that was as surprising as it was welcome. Gabriel swallowed the lump in his throat. "I am so sorry, Lyn. So sorry for all of it."

"Yes, I am sure you are." He stepped away, as though the show of affection had taken all the emotion from him. "I will see that you spend your life making up for it."

That was more like his brother. One could not tell if it was meant as humor or threat.

"Sit down, Gabriel, we must find a way out of this mire." He took a seat at the table near the other window. Gabe followed him.

"Directly to business." Gabriel bowed to his brother. "It is one of the things I admire most about you, brother. But first," he went down on one knee, "you have my fealty and support, Lynford Pennistan, Duke of Meryon."

"How medieval," Lynford said with a smile. "Stand up, Gabe, I never doubted it."

"With you in the Meryon seat, the House of Lords might actually find themselves doing something." He sat down opposite his brother. "Please, Lyn, tell me how everyone does. How father died. I heard there was word that David has been found. My God, Lyn, that is amazing."

"Yes, it was. I will tell you it is difficult as well. Your return has accomplished the impossible. He has not yet been to London, but I had word that he will be arriving today. To see you."

Gabriel nodded, feeling as excited as a child at news of an unexpected treat.

"Olivia is as she always has been, perhaps even more so since father died. She and cook spend days concocting new receipts. Some are wonderful and some are good only for the dogs. We are vastly entertained."

"Jessup?"

Lynford shook his head and turned away. "He is staying at his club in town and I have not seen him since Christmas. Though I am sure he too will be here to see you. I believe you owe him some money."

Not good, and best left alone for now. "How is the duchess?" Odd that Lyn had not mentioned his wife, that Gabriel had to ask after her.

"She is well, and with me here in London. The ladies will wait to see you at your welcome, though I expect Olivia will be sending you treats guaranteed to sustain life."

"I imagine she could even make bread and cheese appealing." They both smiled. Would she remember that lemon tarts were his absolute favorite?

"As for your other question, we are not sure how father died. We found his body and that of his horse at the bottom of Pencey Gorge. There had been a storm the day before, and we assume the track was muddy. He was missing for near a week."

"It must have been a difficult time for all of you."

Lynford gave a vague nod.

They were both silent a moment.

"We will be out of mourning in another two months."

The silence settled again. Were they mourning the man who was their father or the man who had been such a power in the world? Both, he supposed.

"You will not face this alone, Gabriel," his brother said. "I and the full force of our name will be with you every step of the way. We know you are innocent and will, by our presence, make that known. If it comes to a trial, you will be as well defended as money will allow. While these preliminary proceedings go forward you will be in my custody. You will still have to stay in your quarters here but will not be taken to the hearings in restraints or accompanied by a guard."

"Thank you," Gabriel said with a relief so profound it made his brother laugh. "But would it not be wise to have counsel now?"

"You are innocent. To have someone representing you might imply otherwise. One thing Father taught us well is that appearance is as great an ally as wealth and power."

"Sometimes more important," Gabriel agreed, thinking

of Charlotte Parnell in all her disguises. As much as he wanted to ask Lyn about her, he held his questions and let his brother take the lead. At least he had learned patience in some things.

THE DAYS PLAYED OUT much as Meryon had predicted. Their first meeting was with Lord Hasseldine. Lynford described him as "the buffoon in charge of prisoner exchange."

Any sensible man would have been chastened or at least apologetic for his failure to negotiate an exchange. Instead, Hasseldine began by implying that hiring Charlotte Parnell had been a waste of money. Lynford withstood the insults for all of a minute, then held up his hand.

"Madame Parnell came to us highly recommended," Meryon said. "We hired her, Lord Hasseldine, when it became clear to us that your primary goal was to make use of my brother's imprisonment to further your own ends."

Hasseldine blustered and stumbled, but found few words sufficient to express his outrage at the insult.

"You, sir," the duke began, rising from the chair, "are the kind of man who stays as far from the front as possible, while insisting that you are as dedicated as any soldier in his majesty's army."

It was clear Meryon considered the discussion finished. It had better be. If they stayed much longer, one of them would wind up challenging the other's honor. Gabriel could see that Lyn had a touch of the Pennistan temper after all.

Gabriel opened the door for his brother and they left without exchanging any courtesies with Lord Hasseldine.

Once out of his company Meryon's mood lightened considerably. "Would you like something to eat or drink before we take on the viscount and his people?"

"No, I do not want food," he said with a burst of temper. He tried for calm. "Hunger is not my primary concern at the moment."

"Yes, I can understand that," Lynford said with a composure Gabriel envied. His brother raised his cane to point in the direction they should walk. "Why are you expecting the worst?"

"That I will ruin the Pennistan name?"

"No, you sod, that is not the worst. You are a fool to think that our name means more to us than you do. Trial and death are ahead of it by a good distance."

"Thank you, Lynford, but a blight on the family honor is not how I would choose to be remembered. We have yet to meet with the man who threatened me in Sussex."

"I think we are about to."

For the first time Gabriel saw worry in his brother's eyes. "It may be beyond the influence of the Duke of Meryon, Lyn. Men are dead because of my intrigue. Some are rotting in prison. Heaven forbid they are awaiting a prisoner exchange."

They started walking again, moving down the crowded hallway. The building that housed the business of war was as big as a palace, white marble walls and columns, wooden floors, with endless hallways to the left and right. The sound of footsteps was as constant as a troop of soldiers on parade, everyone moving with purpose and direction. Like the rest, Lyn seemed to know exactly where he was going.

Gabriel saw people part like the Red Sea to let them pass.

They might not know who Gabriel Pennistan was, but the Duke of Meryon did not need his title announced for people to recognize he was a force. No one actually groveled, though a few did turn to stare after they passed.

Meryon did not even notice. He kept on talking. Those who watched were probably wondering why Gabriel was not taking notes.

"Gabriel, you have only to ask him and Jessup will take you north and out of the country on the first means available." Meryon made the suggestion casually, as if he was discussing an outing and not a crime.

"No," Gabriel said, with enough vehemence that two men stopped talking to watch them as they passed. "No," he said more quietly. "Thank you and Jess both, but I will face what is coming. I will not ruin the entire family to live a coward's life."

Meryon nodded as though that was what he had expected his brother to say.

They went up a flight of steps and were halfway down the next hall when the duke spoke again.

"Charlotte Parnell is an amazing woman."

"Yes, she is." At last, here was the subject he most wanted to talk about. "I assume you paid her the bonus she insisted on."

"Yes, I did."

"Then you have seen her since we returned?"

"No, I have not. Her man of business contacted me and I sent the promised payment." He shrugged. "That was directly after we received notice of your return. I expect that is the last I will hear from her."

"You met her in person, Lynford. What did you think of her?"

Lynford stopped and gave his brother a speaking glance. "Rowena and I met with her here in town. After she left us, my dear wife said that Charlotte Parnell was an amazing woman. Then she added, and I quote her, 'Please, your grace, never meet with her alone.'"

Gabriel's burst of laughter made several people jump. Lynford's answering smile was worth the embarrassment.

"It is not hard to see what is on Madame Parnell's mind. Or do you need spectacles, brother?"

"No, no, not at all."

"She appeared to be a wellborn widow of modest means and no morals, which I suppose is the best role to play if you want to convince someone that you will do anything to gain your ends. My source had complete faith in her."

"Who was your source, Lyn?" Gabriel asked, wondering exactly who Lynford was willing to trust that much.

"Wilton."

"Ah," Gabriel said as he considered whether that bit would prove useful or not. "Do you suppose that means Wilton is in the spy business as well?"

"I would assume so," Lynford said, as though he never thought about it and did not care. "He wears a naval uniform, but I imagine that is as good a masquerade as any."

"Have you met with him since I returned?"

"No, I have not. He has avoided me at every opportunity. Deliberately, I think. He refuses to acknowledge the connection, even though he met with me more than once when we were arranging for your rescue."

"Yes, rescued by a woman. Please let that be a story no one will hear. I could not live it down."

The duke laughed and tapped his brother's arm with his cane. "Women come to our rescue constantly, though usually not in such a dramatic way. I am sure it was Mrs. Wilton who talked our brother into helping us."

"He did help in the end."

"Yes." Meryon stopped and turned to him. "It proves to us that he is a Pennistan by blood regardless of his mother and his name. It gives us some hope for the future."

23

THEY ARRIVED AT THE ROOM that Lynford had pointed out before. The door porter bowed. "I beg your pardon, my lord. They are not quite ready for you."

The duke nodded his acceptance.

"When was the last time someone made you cool your heels?" Gabriel asked.

"For you, brother, I will wait with patience. I have waited more than once these last few months."

"Waiting on a woman like Charlotte Parnell must have tested you."

"That was hardly the worst of the waiting. Months and months waiting for a letter that never came. Weeks of waiting for word from the man I sent to Wellington's camp." Meryon stopped the list abruptly. "But nothing compared to what you went through."

"We can compare battle scars when this is truly over. I am not sure our waiting is all in the past tense."

The duke put his hand on Gabriel's arm. "This is not a trial, but when we are finished here we will know your fate. These people are the ones most closely involved."

The door was opened from the other side and the porter moved to hold it for them. Meryon raised his hand to stay the man and turned to Gabriel, who almost laughed. "Now you are going to make *them* wait?"

"Only for a moment." Lynford took his brother's arm. The humor left his eyes. "Listen to me, Gabriel. Do not say a word. Do you hear me? Keep quiet," he urged.

It was his familiar way of saying, "Do not lose your temper." Gabriel nodded. They stepped into a room considerably less pretentious than the one they had just left. There were six men seated around a large table and they all rose as Gabriel and the Duke of Meryon approached.

Introductions were made and Gabriel recognized one of the two men who had questioned him in Portsmouth. He cringed at the sight of Doncaster, the man who had sworn his death. There was another in uniform. This man was also familiar, though his presence was a surprise.

It was the officer, now introduced as Major Shelby, who had come to Charlotte's aid in Portsmouth. Gabriel let his gaze pass over him as if he did not remember him. He counted the rest around the table.

The most interesting man was a civilian who was clearly the veteran of some atrocious action that had left him scarred about the face and neck, with an eye patch as well. He wore a kind of cap, covering what looked like a misshapen head.

All in all, the kind of injuries that made one wonder if death would not be more welcome than such a misery of a life.

Viscount Sidmouth was flanked by another man, who had the look of an aide. He invited them to sit as the viscount continued reading some papers. The aide picked up a thicker stack and handed a few to his superior.

Gabriel waited, drawing deep breaths, trying for calm. He looked at each of the men who were to judge him. The wounded man did not raise his head. The others met his gaze, their expression as impassive as he was trying to be. He hoped this was not some kind of contest. His anxiety was much too close to the surface for him to have any chance of winning, no matter how many times Lyn told him to "be quiet."

He had hoped that Charlotte might be here. He smiled a little at the mix of curiosity, anger, lust, concern that accompanied the very thought of her.

For the hundredth time he wondered how she was. *Where* she was. Would the major know? Was she far away? In Cornwall? In some quiet London neighborhood? In this building? Right on the other side of the door?

If this did not go well, would she come to his execution?

His speculation was cut short when the man shuffling papers finally stopped and the silence was complete. The viscount folded his hands on the table. He cleared his throat. It must have been a call to order, as the others all straightened in their seats.

"First, your grace, I thank you both for your willingness to come here today. Your support of your brother is commendable. I apologize for keeping you waiting. Events in

Europe are coming to a head and it is imperative that we be available every minute."

"Lord Sidmouth." Meryon acknowledged the greeting, nodding slowly as though his waiting attendance on this group was a gesture to King and country.

"Lord Gabriel Pennistan," the viscount began, watching him steadily as he spoke. "We thank you for the months you spent in Portsmouth talking to our people about your experience before and after you were detained by the French. I know that you are as anxious to see your family as they are to see you." Sidmouth nodded at the duke, who said nothing.

He didn't have to. His narrowed eyes and unsmiling mouth spoke volumes. Gabriel worried that Meryon was the one about to lose patience.

"I hope you consider that a form of service to your country, my lord," Sidmouth said. "Which brings me to the reason we asked to see you today. When you went to Portugal and offered your services, there were several who thought it a good idea to have you work as a civilian instead of wearing a uniform, which I understand was your preference."

"Yes, my lord," Gabriel answered, as neutrally as he could manage.

"It is true that most of the staff did not have much confidence in an amateur's ability to gather meaningful information. But to their surprise you proved a great resource. In fact, your work in Portugal was quite valuable. Your efforts saved hundreds by undermining and leading to the dissolution of one of the most malignant and persistent of the enemy secret-agent groups."

Gabriel nodded. *What the hell are they talking about? Are*

they calling me a hero? What happened to traitor? He did not ask, holding his tongue. His temper was beginning to stir.

Gabriel could see that not everyone was delighted with the commendation and, indeed, when the viscount nodded, Doncaster ended the paean of praise.

"That does not relieve you of the responsibility for the deaths of your colleagues and the innocent in the tavern, your last known action before disappearing. Those of us in service in Portugal believe that you were giving the French information in exchange for the information you gave us."

"In other words, you thought I was spying for both sides?" He saw his brother wince. So much for staying quiet.

"Yes."

So he was both hero and traitor. How was that for an epitaph? He sat back in the chair, waiting for the next blow.

"How else do you account for the success of an inexperienced and untrained agent?" The man who'd called him a "son of a bitch" was on center stage. "It became apparent that you were trading information so that you and your enemy contacts would both appear to be doing well."

"To what end?"

"For the opportunity Fouché offered you. To join Napoleon's physicians to pursue your interest in science." Doncaster leaned forward, vengeance in his eyes. "Those men were murdered as a ruse to cover your desertion. You were to be assumed dead until an announcement could be made that you had joined Napoleon's court. To study anatomy." He spoke that last as though it were the trump card.

"Why could you not study anatomy in England?" Sidmouth asked.

"I gave it up when my father asked that I choose another field of study."

"Come, come, my lord," Doncaster said, "that is much too simple an explanation of a major rift. You were *forced* to give it up because the duke insisted. He said he would provide you no more support if you continued."

"My father is dead, sir."

One of the others interrupted. "Under questioning in Sussex you admitted that you did not know that he was dead until Madame Parnell told you."

Doncaster nodded and continued, "You were following the work of John Hunter. Some considered him a great man of science, but, in fact, he was no more than a reprobate, hiring body snatchers to bring him the dead so he could study them." He turned to face the men seated near him. "The duke stated publicly, and rightly so, that God and salvation were more important than science."

"I know this has happened before, gentlemen," Gabriel said, pleased that he sounded so calm. "Lord Richard Selwick went with Napoleon to Egypt. He insisted that science claimed no national loyalty. But for once, I agree with my father. There are some things more important than science."

"Did it not occur to you," his brother asked, leaning forward in his seat, "that my brother was effective because he is untrained in your ways, but as a man of science, a natural observer of detail?"

"Yes, yes, it did," Doncaster agreed. "Until the incident that resulted in his disappearance. When we could find nothing of him among the dead, we began to ask our contacts. Eventually word surfaced that it had been a plan all along for

Pennistan to sever all ties with Britain and join the French cause. Among Napoleon's physicians and in the French court he would be welcome and valued far more than he had been in England."

"Does no one understand that it is about science and not about personal recognition?" Gabriel asked, frustrated as usual by the constant misunderstanding.

"That is not the issue right now," the duke said.

"Yes, it is. I study subjects of interest to gain knowledge, not to impress people." He looked directly at Doncaster and continued, "I do it to help man understand his world. It is not as straightforward a contribution as a soldier makes, or as my brother does seated in the House of Lords, but it is something I have the talent for and an interest in."

The group nodded, though not all of them were convinced.

"I study the sciences and am also a loyal British subject, willing to serve my country in any way I can. I did what was asked of me." He turned to the viscount. "By your own admission I was successful until the end. Do you actually have any proof I was colluding with the enemy? Or do we not need proof in wartime?" He sat back, shaking his head. "Do you realize that you are considering sending me to prison or even the gallows because I was *too good* at the task you assigned?"

"We were impressed," Sidmouth said, nodding, "until the information reached us that you were being taken to Paris to meet with Fouché."

Major Shelby spoke up. "Is it not possible that Lord Gabriel was a pawn in a game of revenge? All of us know that Fouché and the second duke, Lord Gabriel's father, were personal enemies. Could it be that the brutal murders in the tavern and the detention of Lord Gabriel were orchestrated by Fouché for the sole purpose of embarrassing the duke? It would have had the added benefit of discrediting the family name of one of Fouché's most outspoken critics."

Doncaster waved off the suggestion. "It is too contrived."

"Precisely the way Fouché likes things done," the viscount said, nodding at Shelby, who continued.

"Fouché would then bring Lord Gabriel to Paris and offer him the bribe, with the added threat that Fouché's men have let it be known that Lord Gabriel conspired with them in the deaths of seven men. Should he refuse the offer Fouché presented, he would be sent back to England to face the hangman. Either way, the Pennistan name would be sullied."

Gabriel surveyed the group, trying to decide who, besides Shelby, was on his side. The scarred man sat with his eyes closed as though in pain, or perhaps so people could stare at him without embarrassment. The others appeared intrigued by Shelby's comments, except for Doncaster.

"The plot was abandoned when Fouché fell out of favor with Napoleon and was shipped off to Rome on some pretext."

"Naples," Viscount Sidmouth corrected.

"How can you prove this ridiculous idea?" Doncaster asked, though Gabriel was wondering the same thing.

"It would help if we knew what Lord Gabriel said the night of the massacre." This from Lord Sidmouth's deputy.

The group began talking among themselves with shakes and nods, just short of raised voices.

It was Sidmouth who ended the discussion by simply raising his hand. "We have new information that enables us to conclude that while the suggestion exists that Fouché was going to offer him a position, Lord Gabriel had no idea that he was about to so used."

The last whispers died completely and everyone gave the viscount their full attention.

"New information?" Doncaster echoed.

"Yes," Shelby said. The major turned to the viscount. "My lord, thank you for your consideration. Mr. McNulty is still recovering from his burns and wounds. Even now it is an effort for him to be here." McNulty, his eyes open, nodded slightly, acknowledging the attention.

"McNulty!" Doncaster said, turning to look at the man whom they had all been wondering about.

"Since speaking is difficult for him, he has prepared a statement, which I will read, with my lord's permission."

"Is that your wish, Mr. McNulty?" the viscount asked.

"Yes, my lord, it is."

His voice sounded as damaged as his face. It made Gabriel's throat hurt in sympathy. One of the others coughed. Not one person wanted him to say any more.

"Then you may proceed, Major."

Shelby read the date and place and then cleared his throat and began. "I was to meet my contact, a young man, Lord Gabriel Pennistan, who was, at that time, unknown to me. He would come to the bar in the tavern and order a brandy. I was to approach him and ask if he was the man who had recently read a paper at a meeting of astronomers. We would then exchange information."

Gabriel nodded. It was not precisely how it worked, but he assumed McNulty meant to protect others who used the same codes. He did not recognize the name, and the damage to McNulty's face was such that he could not tell if they had actually met.

"None of what I expected came to pass. While I was waiting for Lord Gabriel a group of men came into the tavern, sent most of the men and prostitutes away and then lined up the chosen few along the back wall."

This part, before he had arrived on the scene, was new to Gabriel. He listened with interest and a sickening sense of impending disaster.

"They did not so much as question us. There was no torture. They said they would use us as an example to all who would betray French interests. To this there was much objection, by both the innocent and the guilty."

Gabriel could imagine the fear. Could almost smell it.

"When Pennistan entered, they accosted him and demanded he name his fellow spies. Pennistan refused to do so. He could speak honestly, since he had no idea who I was or who else might be there as support for me. In the end, his attempt to defend us failed.

"Pennistan protested with some violence. He managed to overcome one of his assailants. Two others restrained him while they used guns and knives to dispatch the lot of us, guilty or innocent. I fell before they could attack me, and was bathed in the blood of the others. I found myself beneath one of the victims, thus able to escape murder. All the while, Pennistan protested with the shock and horror anyone would expect of an honorable man."

Screamed and begged was the way Gabriel recalled it. He swallowed against the bile that rose in his throat.

"They did not kill Pennistan, but told him that they were taking him to Paris. The Minister of Police himself would speak with him before he was sent to his death."

The group looked at Gabriel.

"As they left the tavern, two of the men stayed and began to pour spirits on the floor and the bodies. They set the tavern afire and I was not able to escape immediately. That is how I sustained the injuries that mark me today."

Shelby paused in his reading, as though McNulty himself was an exhibit of Gabriel's innocence.

"I am writing this on Lord Gabriel's behalf. He was not the one who betrayed the group gathered there. Further, he was not trained as a spy but acquitted himself with distinction. For that he is to be honored and not vilified."

Major Shelby finished and handed the paper back to the aide, who set it aside for the viscount's further perusal.

"Comments, gentlemen?" the viscount's aide asked.

"How does this prove he is innocent?" Doncaster did not stand up, but spoke in a loud voice. "It was an act, as proof of his innocence."

"His audience was dead, Doncaster," Shelby reminded him. "Or so the French thought."

No one else had a comment, and Doncaster seemed to shrink visibly.

"Doncaster, we understand your bitterness over the organization's failure in Portugal. You are no more to blame than Lord Gabriel is. Someone compromised the organization. We will find out who. Not today, but we will make it a priority, I promise you."

Doncaster nodded. "I will remind you of that promise, my lord." He had the look of a man defeated in spirit and will.

The aide drew everyone's attention back to Gabriel.

"Is that accounting commensurate with your experience, my lord?" the aide asked him directly.

"Yes," Gabriel said. "When I saw that they intended a fire I begged them to stop, to allow the men a decent burial. They pulled me out and ended any discussion by rendering me unconscious. That is all I remember until I woke up in a local prison." He had not seen the actual fire. It was one of the small graces of that horrible day.

"Thank you, Mr. McNulty," the viscount said. "Your account solves a puzzle for me, a puzzle for all of us, which you can see from the varying opinions expressed today."

Several others nodded as the viscount went on, addressing McNulty directly. "The information Lord Gabriel has given us since his return is going to be just as useful as the observations he made while in Portugal."

Now the viscount turned to Gabriel. "Your description of the state of the countryside, your mode of travel, what you saw along the way, your skill in physically describing them was most useful, your clarity of expression impressive. It is as refined as your brother suggested earlier."

The man who had questioned him spoke next. "Most important, my lord, is that never once in the last three months did you attempt to bargain for your life or for any gain. We kept waiting for you to do so, and you never did."

Had he come that close to prison? In the end, had McNulty's testimony been the only thing between him and the gallows?

The questioning appeared to be over and general comments began. Gabriel glanced at McNulty, who seemed calm enough, if somewhat uncomfortable. One hand rested on the table.

McNulty was wearing gloves, Gabriel noticed. To protect or hide his disfigured hands? Perhaps both.

McNulty was looking down at the table. Even with the gloves on, he was running one hand along the fine wood as though he could feel its texture.

As he did so, Gabriel remembered Charlotte's way of running her fingers over fabric, along his body as though any tactile contact entertained her as much as a good book would entertain her mind.

He raised his eyes slowly and looked into the one eye he could see.

The color was hard to decipher, as it had always been with her. The expression was not. She might as well have shouted it. *Control yourself. Do not ruin this.*

24

GABRIEL LOOKED AWAY from her. With great effort he kept his seat, mightily resisting the impulse to jump up, grab her and smother that well-disguised face with kisses. Betray her? Never. Not in ten thousand years.

He stood up. Lyn straightened and Gabriel shot him a reassuring smile.

"The great disadvantage in being an untrained spy is the amount of time I have spent heartsick at the memory of the men who died while I watched." He stopped so he could steady his voice. "There are men who will not see home again because of me. Men were murdered in front of me and McNulty scarred for life. Because the French wanted me to know that I was at their mercy."

"Please, sit down, my lord," the viscount spoke. "I know you will find it hard to believe, but all of us here live with those same nightmares. Our experience is less immediate than yours, but our responsibility far greater."

Gabriel eyed each one of them and wondered if that was the truth. With McNulty in their midst, how could they sleep, much less eat dinner or read a book?

"There is only one thing I need to know from you," Gabriel said as he sat down again, slowly. "I want to hear you say out loud and in words I can understand that there is no court or hangman's noose awaiting me."

The silence was complete. Was it not as obvious as he thought?

"My lord, gentlemen," he said, prepared now to plead his own case. "I have given service to my country. Not as long or as meaningful as yours, but we have well established that this is not where my talents are best exercised."

There was a choke of a sound from McNulty. Was it a laugh? Shelby popped up from his chair. "Viscount Sidmouth, with your permission I am going to escort Mr. McNulty out. I do believe his business is complete."

That interrupted Gabriel's thought process and diverted everyone's attention. With praise and thanks, the man was allowed to leave.

Gabriel stepped out and blocked the way. He waited until he could see her eyes and then spoke. "Thank you." *For believing me. For defending me. For saving me.*

"You're welcome." The rusty voice was a whisper.

"I trust we will meet again."

She said nothing to that and began the slow, apparently painful process of leaving the room, leaning heavily on

Shelby's arm. When the door closed behind them, Gabriel turned back to the table. He repeated his question.

"I want to know when I will be free to return to my home, to resume study in those areas where I can make a contribution more suited to my training."

"You are free when you walk out of this room, my lord. There can be no doubt of that." The viscount gave his verdict and the rest nodded, though with various degrees of enthusiasm.

The viscount's aide leaned forward. "We would ask you to explain your absence in a more innocent way."

"I do not wear the title 'spy' with pride. I too would prefer no one know of this."

"The discussion has not gone beyond this room," the aide said.

Viscount Sidmouth nodded a little. "If you refer them here, we will say we have never heard of you and have never met you."

Thank you, Gabe said with a nod. That was one way of dealing with painful memories. Pretend they never existed. He wondered how many of the men in this room did that, with or without the help of brandy.

Gabriel considered how long it would take for McNulty to work his way down the hall. "I do have one more brief question, gentlemen. Have you met Mrs. Parnell?"

They all looked at the viscount, who nodded to his aide.

"Yes, we have," the aide said. "We know little about her, but we have met her. She might be an older woman, but it is precisely her grandmotherly demeanor that gives her freedom of movement in France."

Did he truly think Charlotte an older woman? Gabriel looked at each of them. Several of the men were staring at the tabletop. The viscount was reading yet another dispatch.

"Thank you, my lord, gentlemen." He bowed to them. "Good day to all of you. I trust we will never meet again."

No one had an answer for him; but then, he did not wait for one. He left the room, anxious to speak with McNulty. He would let his brother clean up the bits.

He saw Shelby and his crippled friend farther down the hall, almost to the front entrance. McNulty was not walking as slowly as he had in the conference room. Gabriel went after them, trying his best not to attract too much attention.

"Major," he called out. "Mr. McNulty." They appeared not to hear him. Odd that everyone else turned but neither one of them reacted. The twosome was already out the door. Major Shelby was handing McNulty into a coach as Gabriel caught up to them.

The major turned as if he would block contact, when a woman's voice discouraged him. "I will speak with him, Shelby."

Shelby moved aside, walked to the coachman and turned his back to them.

"Charlotte," Gabriel began.

"Listen to me," she said, shaking her head. The eye patch was gone; otherwise, she looked as she had before. "This is good-bye, my lord." Her words were firm. "My work as Charlotte Parnell is complete. I owed you this for saving the children in Portsmouth. This was my last masquerade."

He reached into the coach, took her gloved hand and pulled off the bit of cotton. "You've rescued the last child?"

Her reluctant nod made it clear that was more information than she wished to give. She pulled her hand away and raised it to knock on the roof of the coach.

"Wait, there is so much more I need to know. Tell me where I can find you. I need to see you again. We cannot let it end like this."

She was watching him with strained patience. As if he were an actor and she were the audience. Not the other way around.

"At least tell me your true name, Charlotte."

"No." The one word was a vow. "You saved me in Portsmouth and I have saved you here. We are even." Now she did knock on the roof. As she did, she gave her parting shot. "This part of my life is over forever. I never want to see you again."

"Liar," he said as Shelby pulled him away from the moving coach and slammed the door.

Gabriel and Shelby made their way back to the building. "At least the true major does not feel the need to speak every thought twice."

"You do remember me!" Shelby said. "You gave no sign of it, my lord." He stood back and looked him up and down. "You pay amazing attention to the finest details. I imagine you were good at your work. If the war were not about to end, I would try to persuade you to give it another try."

"I do believe I have done my part," Gabriel said as they started walking again. "Tell me, was there really a McNulty?" he asked, with no expectation of an answer.

"Yes," Shelby said. "I knew him and called him friend. He died two months ago after he came back from Portugal.

He told me the story that basically corroborates the version you told.

"After the incident in Portsmouth, Charlotte asked if there was a way she could help you. I told her that the government did not see you as innocent. I could repeat McNulty's version but was not sure they would accept it if he was not present.

"She was the one who suggested that she pretend to be McNulty. It took us weeks to make it work. She could never disguise her voice enough and then we thought of having me read the testimony, with McNulty present."

Gabriel could see Lyn coming down the hall, hurrying toward them as though he feared a fight would break out.

"A fine last performance, Major. Deceiving the deceivers."

"But we did not fool the amateur, my lord. Tell me," Shelby urged in a voice suggesting a secret, "how did you recognize her?"

"As you said, I notice details."

"And that was?" Shelby prompted.

Did he ask the question as a confidence between equals? Gabriel was not about to answer without bargaining. "Major, I will tell you, if you tell me where to find her."

Shelby actually considered it for a minute, then smiled and shook his head. "No, I will not. Let it be your final test. You can tell her personally what detail gave her away."

By the time Gabriel and the duke were in the coach and headed through the busy London streets, Gabriel had calmed down enough to explain the whole to Lyn.

"That was her, sitting right in the room? How did you know? How could you tell?"

It took a great deal to impress his brother. He wished he could take more satisfaction from it. "I know her," he said, not interested in the past, trying to determine what the next step would be. "What does it matter? I found her and now she is gone again."

"Answer me one more question before you sink into a puddle of self-pity."

That drew his attention.

"How can the government trust someone to work for them when they do not know anything about her?"

"It is not about trust, Lyn. It's about finding someone who will bring you what you need as quickly as possible. You thought she could do the job, but did you trust her?"

"Point taken," the duke said as he reached under the seat and produced a bottle of brandy. He pulled out the cork and handed it to Gabriel. "I forgot to bring glasses, but a swig of this might help your mood."

They each took a drink straight from the bottle. It reminded Gabriel of his first London Season. In those days Lyn had seemed so much more worldly than he was. What was it about years that lessened that sort of gap?

They settled back as the traffic slowed to let the crested coach pass.

"Do you think anyone else knew she was McNulty? Except Shelby, of course."

Gabriel thought about it and shook his head.

Lyn answered his own question. "I think the viscount knew. I tried several times to see him over the last week or so and he always said he was too busy. Which may well have been true. At the time I thought it was a bad sign; now I think he knew there was nothing to worry about."

"It would have taken no more than a minute to tell you."

"He wanted to preserve the air of uncertainty," Lyn said, nodding with perfect understanding. "The House of Lords is a fine training place for intrigue."

"You seem to have learned very quickly. Politics would not suit me at all." Gabriel dismissed it with barely a moment's thought. "Do you think Sidmouth allowed the ruse to accommodate you or because he believes me innocent?"

"Of course he believes you. The whole trap stinks to heaven of Fouché's machinations. Do you remember father's endless tirades about how he was a madman?"

"A little. I was not beside him all the time the way you were."

They sat quietly for a moment, watching London life pass by. *I am free,* Gabriel thought. *I can climb from this carriage and run all the way home, or stop at my club and pretend I have been in Canada for the last two years, or tell the truth, to hell with what the ton will think.*

What did *he* want? To see his family. To visit Rhys Braedon and his wife. One more thing, at least as important as the other two: "I am determined to find Charlotte again, Lyn."

"How will you do it if she does not want to be found? How do you think the government found her?"

"I think Major Shelby is the go-between."

"Yet he does not know where she lives?"

"So he said. I would not bet on his honesty." Gabriel took another drink from the bottle. "It's amazing. Those few days in France seem simple compared to life now. I never thought I would say that."

"So how does he contact her?"

It was not often that Gabriel was the expert. It was so rare, he was positive his brother was trying to keep him from falling into the well-phrased "puddle of self-pity."

"I expect he sends a message through some reliable party with no interests in the war effort."

"Like her man of business or a physician or someone with whom both might have contact?"

"Yes, then they meet somewhere in town, most likely at a bordello." Madame Rostine's came to mind. "You see, Lyn, the magic of doing it thus is that no one has to trust anyone."

"So you need only to find a contact willing to talk about a woman who has most likely confused them as completely as she has confused you."

"Yes, but at least I know where to start. Did you tell me that you knew her man of business?"

25

THE BUTLER SERVED the last soup. The duchess picked up her spoon and everyone else followed.

"Gabriel still has a temper," Lynford said, before taking a spoonful, "but he has learned how to control it so that it may be used as an advantage."

Olivia nodded. Jess laughed. Rowena watched Lynford as though each word he spoke was gold.

Gabriel tasted the turtle soup and then put his spoon down. Here he was in the townhouse in Mayfair, in the midst of a celebration dinner. How completely his life had turned around in one single day.

"Gabriel, you do not like the turtle soup? Would you prefer something else?" Rowena asked as if it was a rejection that would break her heart.

"It tastes wonderful. Only, the food is so much richer than I am used to."

"Spreen," she called to the butler, "please bring some of today's chicken broth."

"Yes, your grace," the butler said, and left the room.

"It is not necessary, Rowena," the duke told his wife. "He is not interested in this excellent soup, because he went to the kitchen and Olivia gave samples of everything she and cook were planning for dinner." The duke nodded at Gabriel as he spoke.

"Yes," Gabriel admitted, "and besides, it is not as though you keep chicken broth on hand all the time."

"Of course we do," she said with affront. "With a staff this size, someone is always ill. Just yesterday morning, Magda drank some chocolate, and chicken broth was all that she could stomach after that. Olivia is determined to devise a receipt for the best chicken broth possible."

"Gabriel," David said, "Magda is her new puppy."

They all laughed, and not only because Rowena's attachment to her pets was amusing. David spoke so rarely. He had not been like that before. It was as though he was not a part of the family yet. Even after almost a year among them again. He watched them as though they were some foreign sort that he had yet to fully understand. David did not make them uncomfortable so much as sad. Gabriel knew that their laughter was relief that the old David was still with them.

Gabriel felt his eyes fill. He bent his head and took some of the chicken broth Spreen placed in front of him. He nodded to his sister. "I think you may have reached perfection."

Olivia tried to look blasé but failed. "The secret is to slowly boil a whole chicken and then let the broth return to room temperature before you remove the chicken." She watched him take another spoonful. "When you are a little stronger," she teased, "maybe Rowena will allow some chicken in the broth. It is even better that way."

Before Rowena could send Spreen off for some chicken, Gabriel spoke up. "I am delighted to be here. I must tell you that without the help of Charlotte Parnell it may never have happened."

Gabriel looked at all of them and could not help but smile at their various expressions of concern. "She is one of the most amazing women I have ever met, and I am going to find her."

"How?" Jess asked.

"Why?" This from Olivia.

Rowena nodded. Lynford did not react at all.

Gabriel ignored Olivia's question and took a sip of his wine before answering Jess. "I will go to her man of business and see what he will tell me. I will talk to Shelby, the man who is her contact with the government. If neither of them will help me, I will go to Robert Wilton. Lyn told me his home is south of here, less than a day's ride."

"I thought you said that he was barely civil to you?" Olivia asked, and then answered her own question. "I suppose you can tolerate some incivility to find her."

"More than incivility, dear girl."

"But why?" she asked again.

"She is as fascinated by the night sky as Gabriel is," Jess joked as he elbowed his brother in the ribs.

"He wants to find out what kind of woman she truly is," the duchess said with certainty.

"Yes, exactly, Rowena," Olivia agreed.

"Oh, I think there is a little more to it than that," Jess said, picking up his wineglass and taking a sip before he spoke again. "I'll wager that part of the reason is that he wants to prove that he is a man even though he was rescued by a woman."

"Nonsense," Rowena said, coming to Gabriel's "rescue" by ringing the bell for the next course.

The rest of the meal was taken up with family details and news of friends who had married or had children. When Jessup began to tell him of the last boxing match he had attended, Rowena interrupted him in mid-sentence, "Shall we move to the drawing room, Olivia?"

"Of course, if you wish, Rowena." Before she stood up, Olivia leaned across the table. "Do not make us wait too long. I want to hear of your adventures before you met Mrs. Parnell."

Gabriel shook his head. "You will hear nothing but stories of nights watching the sky and looking at stars and then long evenings in smoky taverns trading information and not knowing whether it was truth or lies. Not a story I ever want to tell."

Olivia stood up and went around the end of the table to kiss him. "If that is what you wish, brother, then I shall not ask again. I am so happy you are with us again." She popped over and gave David a kiss. "You too."

David looked down and did not seem happy with the attention.

Rowena stood up too. For the first time, Gabriel noticed that Rowena was thickening around the middle. Was she increasing again? The two previous miscarriages that Olivia had told him about could well be the reason that Rowena and Lyn had yet to announce it.

He was almost sure of it when Lynford stood up to escort her to the door. "We will join you shortly. I know how easily you tire."

She nodded and kissed his cheek. She and Olivia left the room.

"So, are you in love, Gabriel?" Jess asked.

"Jess," the duke said. "Why don't you join the ladies?"

"No, thank you, your grace, but I do wonder what else Gabriel has to tell us about his time with the mysterious Charlotte Parnell."

"Love does not enter into it," Gabriel insisted. "Curiosity is my besetting sin. I want to solve the endless mysteries surrounding Mrs. Parnell. I will find her, Lyn."

"You can make your escape tomorrow," he said, nodding at the window even though the drapes were drawn. "There is no moon tonight, so one of your insane night rides is out of the question."

"Bugger it, Lynford. I will leave when I want to leave," he said with a passionate, quiet anger. The rage was so intense and so misplaced that both of them were surprised by it.

"I'm sorry," Gabriel said. *Rage and remorse.* It happened all the time and at the most inopportune moments.

"You will leave when you want to leave, brother," David said with quiet authority. Lyn agreed, though he was looking at David as he did so.

"I will have to wait to speak with her man of business and that major, Shelby." Gabriel gave a jerky nod and was silent a moment more.

"What is it you want to know, besides that she is safe?" David asked.

"I want answers to a hundred questions, David. Beginning with her true name."

LYNETTE GILRAY, I WANT you to tell me the truth. Could you be with child?"

Her mother resumed the warm-water rinse of her daughter's hair as though the question were as commonplace as a bath. Lynette smiled and shook her head. "No, Mama, I am not increasing. It is only that I am tired from travel." She had wondered herself at first and was relieved when she had been spared that embarrassment. She had been fool enough with Gabriel Pennistan and had no need of a constant reminder.

Esther Gilray said nothing but kept on pouring water through her daughter's hair. "I think this will be the final wash. The brown is almost completely gone."

"It feels heavenly. Thank you, Mama." Lynette closed her eyes and hoped that her tears would blend in with the water that escaped to trickle down her neck.

"I am only too happy to wash all of Charlotte Parnell away."

"Yes, I know you worried." It was an old and endless complaint. "It was not dangerous or even very exciting." *Except for the adventure with Gabriel Pennistan.* "The orphanages were always happy to have a child taken. Especially if a donation was made. The biggest challenge was remembering what part I was playing."

"Hmph" was all her mother said.

Lynette was on the verge of sleep when her mother began again. "You have been home a month since your last trip.

I am happy to note it was your very last trip. You should be celebrating, but you are spending all your time in your studio, and you do not eat enough. What happened in London that has you so upset?"

Mama might not understand the first thing about surviving in an enemy camp, but Lynette knew her mother could see the toll it took on her. She was always exhausted and nervy for the first few days. This time it lasted much longer than usual.

"It has been a difficult year. The work I did this winter did not go smoothly, and then I had to hurry back for the last child."

"That I do not understand. Once Napoleon accepts defeat, will it not be easier?"

"No, Mama, because France will change. Yes, it was dangerous, but Georges and I both thought that it was better to move quickly than to wait. It all turned out as we hoped."

"Then you rushed up to London."

"One last bit of acting, Mama. You would have been impressed. Rather like the time you played a boy in that romp where you met Papa." If Mama would tell that story again, she would forget about the last few months.

Her mama leaned down and kissed Lynette's wet head. "We are finished. The children will hardly recognize you."

Once she was in her nightgown and robe, she sat with her back to the fire, stroking the cat on her lap, while her mother combed out her hair. Now she *would* fall asleep, comfortable under a lap robe, the fire warming her back.

"You have to tell me, Lynette. You know you do. I failed as a mother before because I did not insist on the truth."

The purring cat and the long gentle pull of the comb through her hair was as mesmerizing as the warmth from the fire. She was right, Lynette thought. Mama would nag her to death. That much had not changed. Her eyes flew open. She had not said that aloud, had she? Mama tried so hard.

"How can I explain," she said, the tears leaking out, "when I don't understand myself?"

Her mother did not miss a stroke, but Lynette could almost hear her smile. "Is it a man?"

"Yes," her daughter sighed.

"The one you were paid so much money to rescue?"

"Yes." The cat jumped from her lap. She could feel the tears bubbling up; even her horror at the weakness could not stop them. "He was not at all what I expected." She turned to face her mother. "I hate him." She hated him, herself and the world.

"Yes, darling, I know. I hate him too." Mama finished brushing her hair. "Tomorrow I want you to go with the girls to feed the ducks. Spending time with the children is the best cure I know for an aching heart."

Lynette nodded. Was it that obvious? Perhaps only to her mother. She hoped only to her mother.

"Come to bed now, Lynette."

Mama led her to bed and tucked her in. Lynette closed her eyes and pretended she was a child again. Ten years old and waking from a nightmare. Mama was with her and would not leave. She was now closer to thirty and had lived a nightmare, but was home with her family and safe once again.

26

ROBERT WILTON'S HOME was a prosperous place, Gabriel decided as he urged his horse up the drive. The trees that lined the avenue to the house were well established and in full leaf. He slowed his horse and took a moment to enjoy the sound of the breeze rustling the leaves, the light and shadow of the sunlit day. He saw a deer and wondered if it was too early for fawns in this warmer climate. Not for weeks yet in Derbyshire, but Sussex was so much more temperate than home.

The house was not overly large, but the generous windows gave it a welcoming, tranquil air. He had not expected anything this gracious, even if the man was a captain with more than twenty years of prize money to his name.

As Gabriel neared the house, the peacefulness was obliterated by squawking hens racing across the front yard, chased by two boys old enough to know better. He guessed they were both older than twelve. Did they really think the hens would do their bidding? As he watched he realized he was too long from childhood. Chaos was precisely the fun of the exercise.

Gabriel watched them until they were out of sight and then rode to the stable, a well-kept building a short walk from the house. A groom rushed out to take care of his horse. Gabriel handed him a coin and his thanks.

"Would you be wishing for me to show you to the house, sir?"

"No, thank you."

"Mrs. Wilton will be pleased to have a caller."

Gabriel nodded and was about to walk on when the man added, "Too bad the cap'n's not about."

Gabriel stopped and gave the man what he wanted more than coin. His attention.

"Yes, sir. He went off to Edinburgh two days ago to attend his business." His conversation was artless and friendly. "He travels by land," he made a sound of disgust, "and will be gone only a few weeks, so Mrs. Wilton will not worry overmuch."

"Have you been with the Wiltons long?" The Pennistan servants were loyal, but did not act as a member of the family the way this man did.

"I been with the cap'n since his first command. When I near drowned I decided it was time to leave the sea. The cap'n gave me work here. My father was a groom, so learning this job's been easy enough."

Oh, so this man *was* part of the family. Gabriel thanked him more formally and walked toward the house. The yard was quiet again. Before he could knock, the door was opened by a properly clad butler. Gabriel had been expecting a man with a peg leg or maybe an eye patch.

When he met Madeline Wilton a few minutes later he could see why the staff might wish for the captain's quick return. His wife was surely only a short time from her lying in.

She was a lovely woman, in both looks and manner.

"I am so sorry that the captain is not here," she began once they were seated. That was after she sent her maid for tea, and then asked her butler to check on the progress of painting in the nursery. "Then, Yancy, would you please find the boys and tell them they will do without eggs if the hens are too upset to lay."

Now she gave Gabriel her full attention, regarding him intently. They spoke of the weather in the nearby village and in London. Of the family and their health, the precociousness of boys when they were on their own. Their tutor, she explained, was away on urgent family business and would be gone for at least three weeks.

Yancy came with the tea and a large plate with a variety of sweets. Madeline Wilton poured and handed him a cup, then offered him the plate. He took one cream cake, proud of his restraint. He wanted one of each kind.

"Your letter came after the captain had left for Edinburgh, though I have no doubt he would have refused to see you even if he had still been at home. We both know that is nonsense."

Gabriel almost choked on his tea. He had not expected such plain speaking.

"I wish he would consider meeting with us," Gabriel answered, trying for equal openness, wondering how he could work the conversation around to Charlotte Parnell. "He has the Pennistan stubbornness."

"Yes." She dropped her gaze to her hands, hiding a smile. "Though I have found there are ways around that."

"What wife does not?"

She gave him a conspirator's smile and Gabriel fell half in love with her himself. Wilton had best be as enamored as Charlotte had said and as faithful. This woman deserved nothing less.

A silence settled as Gabriel tried to decide what to do. Did Mrs. Wilton even know of Mrs. Parnell?

Madeline did not seem to mind the quiet. She poured more tea. She offered him another biscuit, but she ate little herself.

He decided to take the leap. "Mrs. Wilton, I was wondering if you were acquainted with Mrs. Parnell, Charlotte Parnell."

She replied with a cautious "Yes."

"Do you know where she lives?"

"I do."

He slapped his knee and started laughing. Triumph and relief jumbled together to make him feel as though his heart would explode. He stood up and walked to the window. What was that odd feeling? Ah, yes. It was what being free felt like.

"I would very much like to speak with her," he said, turning to face Madeline Wilton again. Her expression made him wonder if he had rejoiced too soon. "Will you tell me where I can find her?"

"You wish to call on her?"

"Yes." He moved closer to where she was sitting.

She looked away this time, as she considered his request. He was not nearly as comfortable with this silence as she had been with the previous one.

"I think you should wait until Robert returns," she said, her eyes filled with apology. "He is the one who should decide."

"Can I say nothing to convince you otherwise?"

"I am so sorry, my lord." Madeline Wilton rose and curtsied. "In this I agree with my husband. She has a right to her privacy. And I will not violate it without first discussing it with him."

Gabriel did no more than nod and try to wait out the silence, but could see he was embarrassing her. No woman in her condition needed that. "Your loyalty is admirable, ma'am."

That said, there was nothing he could do but wait for Wilton's return, or come back when he knew the captain was again in residence.

Before Madeline could accompany him to the door, there was a great crashing sound from overhead. She pressed a hand to her stomach as if to calm her baby but did not look more than slightly startled herself. For his part, the burst of anxiety he felt at the unexpected noise was as familiar as it was frightening.

He hurried into the hall, Mrs. Wilton following at a more decorous pace, only to hear bellowing calls for help from a floor or two above.

"Those boys will not taste a tart for a week," she exclaimed as she began to make her way up the stairs.

"May I, Mrs. Wilton?" Gabriel asked, pointing up.

"Oh yes, would you, please? There is the chance that someone is truly hurt, and I do not move as quickly as I did a few months ago."

It was not hard to find his way to the room where the accident had happened. One had only to follow the commotion. Well-chosen swear words. Yells of "Hurry!" and the final "I'm stuck. We'll not have tarts for a week. You had better run."

"I'll sneak some to you," the other called as he, by the sound of his fading voice, ran away as directed.

Gabriel slowed his run and pushed carefully through the door. It was the nursery, in the process of being painted. That project was now in ruins. Two ladders were knocked down. A tin of paint lay half-tipped. Not yet spilled. Gabriel righted it, then moved it to a corner. Away from the jumble of ladders and boards.

It appeared to him that one of the boys had been trying to walk a board that connected the ladders. It had given way, taking the circus clown with it. The boy was not so much stuck as trapped in the broken boards and ladder steps. When he saw that Gabriel was not his mother, he brightened.

"Oh, sir, if you will help me up, I can escape."

Gabriel folded his arms. "Then who would be blamed for this? Me?"

"Oh no, sir. We can blame the rabbit. If you let him out of the cage he will make an amazing mess."

Heaven help Madeline Wilton. She lived surrounded by a domestic battlefield with the two boys about. He helped the trapped one stand and let him run. Gabriel opened the door of the rabbit cage and scooped up the white bundle just as Mrs. Wilton came to the door.

"No one is here," he said.

"If you are going to make a habit of lying, then I will refuse to give *you* any more tarts."

"I am sorry," he said, trying not to laugh and failing. "He told me to tell you that the rabbit must have gotten out."

She raised her eyes to heaven and then nodded. "How old are you, Lord Gabriel?"

"Old enough to understand that no tarts for a week is a terrible punishment."

"If they had spilled the paint, I truly would enforce it." She went through a connecting door. Gabriel trusted that the boys were long gone. Putting the rabbit back in the cage, Gabriel followed her into what he saw was the schoolroom.

There was a large table and chairs. Maps on the wall. Books tidily arranged on the shelf. A table in the corner where someone was designing and cutting out the pattern for a wooden puzzle. The scent of slates, chalk and paint was part of the ambience. Even the way the light came through the window reminded him of his schoolroom days.

He turned to the window, where Madeline was checking inside a large chest. As he moved Gabriel saw something that slowed his world to a stop.

It was a dawn view of Le Havre. He recognized the first light coming up behind the city, casting the buildings into shadow. The church spires were black arrows against the gray sky. The water was a mirror broken into pieces, reflecting no more than the colorless dawn. It was the same sight he had seen the morning he, Charlotte and the children had finally left France.

He walked closer. It was not a drawing or charcoal, but rather done in paper, layers and layers of paper, some fine, some heavier, a few bright white, others more cream and even gray, cut in amazing and intricate detail, each sheet then pressed on top of another so that varying degrees of light shone through when it was put up against a window. It was the size of a pane of glass, and a work of art.

He remembered Charlotte's intent gaze that morning. How he had turned around because he was afraid someone was following them. It was this scene she had been studying. Memorizing. Charlotte Parnell was an artist.

"I do not think they climbed out the window," Madeline said. "Oh, that is an amazing piece, is it not?" she said when she looked back to see what he was studying so intently.

"Yes, it is."

"It's called a cut-paper transparency, a kind of silhouette. This is a sophisticated form of it, actually."

"It is far more complex than the portrait silhouettes I've seen." As he spoke he considered how to find out the name of the artist. "Does he do portrait silhouettes as well?"

"Yes, she does, for the artist is a woman, you see."

"Yes, of course," he said, doing his best to hide his elation. "There is a delicacy about this work that few men would have the patience for." Nonsense, but his whole goal was to keep her talking about it.

"She is a truly talented woman."

"Where does she live? I imagine that Meryon would love to have one done of his wife."

Madeline had walked toward the door. She stopped her progress and straightened. That was the moment she realized that she was about to give away Charlotte's secret.

She turned to face him, speaking slowly, as though she were talking her way through a word maze.

"She only works for friends, my lord. I can contact her and find out if she will consider a commission for the duke."

Now who is lying? He did not say it, accepting this setback, settling for the conventional "Thank you, I would appreciate it."

If she was surprised by his lack of persistence, she did not show it. "My lord, I must find the boys. Tying them to a chair may be the only way to quiet them. I had forgotten how much I depend on their tutor to keep them occupied."

"Let me take a moment to right the ladder. It could be that they will come back. If they do, I will bring them down to you."

Now she did look tired. Not in the eyes, but in the way she drew a deep breath and her shoulders sagged a little. "Thank you."

"You are welcome," he said as he headed toward the connecting door and she for the stairs. Gabriel righted the first ladder and considered the rabbit.

He picked up the rabbit cage and walked back into the schoolroom, scanning the walls as he passed through, thinking of himself at thirteen or fourteen and wondering where they could hide.

Really, there was only one place their mother had not looked. He went to a cupboard built into the wall and pulled the door open. The boys fell out amid sneezing and groans.

How had they managed to fit in such a small space? No matter, he was the one who appeared a genius.

"How did you know where we were, sir?"

"Yes, we must find a way to make it more secure."

"I was twelve once too, you know."

"I'm fourteen," the taller one said, insult edging his words.

"Are you?" Gabriel asked, pretending shock. "Your behavior is not what I would expect from a boy so old."

The two looked at each other and shrugged.

"Surely there are things that interest you more than chasing hens and ruining the nursery."

"We want to go to the lake, but mother says we may not. We have nothing to do."

"What is at the lake this time of year?"

"Nothing," one answered.

"Ducks, we like to look at the ducks," the other said.

"Girl ducks?" he asked.

They could not tell if he was joking, which was exactly the way he wanted it. He'd bet the rabbit he was holding that girls came down to feed the ducks every day. "If you are not permitted to go to the lake, why not practice your fencing?"

"We do not know how to fence. Our tutor wears spectacles," the shorter one said, as though that was an explanation.

Gabriel was only half attending, which was never wise when dealing with children. How could he work his way to the silhouette of Le Havre? And what did it say about him that he did not have a qualm about using the boys this way?

"Have you tried your hand at cutting silhouettes?" he asked as he put the rabbit back in its hutch.

They shook their heads as though held by the same puppet master, eyeing him as though he were crazed. He turned to look at the view of Le Havre again, unable to hold back a smile. "Do you know who did that one? It is quite impressive." Gabriel heard movement. "Do not touch that latch," he said and then turned around. He saw Burgess—he was fairly certain that was his name—step away from the rabbit cage, his hands behind his back. He and his brother exchanged a glance that would warm a tutor's heart. Yes, Gabriel thought, let them think that I have eyes that see everywhere.

"What was your mother thinking to allow your tutor to leave? She was right, you do not deserve tarts. For a week at least," he said in his best imitation of an adult. "Tell me," he said without stopping for a breath, "who did that city silhouette?"

"Miss Gilray," they answered promptly.

Charlotte, I have found you.

27

ONE HUGE STEP in the right direction. How many more steps would it take before he could see her again? "Does she live nearby?"

"Yes, sir. Her brothers come here to share lessons with our tutor."

The other spoke at the same time. "She lives near the village, in the cottage Mama grew up in. We have this house now, so we do not need it. This one is much closer to the lake. Miss Gilray lives on the other side."

He could see water out the window, a short walk even by city standards. "That close?"

"Yes, sir. You have to go around the lake to reach it."

"Do you know if Miss Gilray is in residence?"

"Yes, sir, she is. Mama went to call on her yesterday. Or was it two days ago?"

He wanted to leave the boys behind, race down the

stairs, find the lake and Charlotte. Guilt for his betrayal of Madeline weighed him down just enough that he found himself offering to teach the boys the basics of fencing. It would give him an excuse to be in the neighborhood for a while. The basics could take a day or two years.

When they reacted with crazed excitement he promised he would speak to their mother on the way out. In the meantime, they were to clean up the rest of the nursery or he would run them through with the sword.

He found Madeline at her husband's desk, half-asleep, her neck at such an awkward angle that he picked up a pillow from a chair.

The movement must have awakened her, for she jerked upright and smiled a tired apology. Before she could beg his pardon, he handed her the pillow.

He made his good-byes as quickly as he could. Madeline seemed appreciative of his order for the cleanup, but sent one of the servants to surpervise. His offer to tutor the boys while their regular teacher was away brightened her tired eyes considerably.

"Do you have any idea what you will be taking on, my lord? Honesty compels me to ask."

"Boyhood is not so far in my past that I cannot recall what works and what does not. I think I will start with fencing lessons."

When her eyes widened in alarm, he raised his hand to stall her dismay.

"With blunted tips. I will have them fashion head gear and protective vests. They will not come to any more harm than they do chasing hens."

Madeline not only welcomed him as a tutor, but offered him a room with them. If he would spend one night in the inn in the village, she would have a room ready for him on the morrow.

Her genuine relief at his promise to return the next day eased his conscience for using the boys to further his own ends. How would the captain react? Gabriel was sure that his wife had considered that.

He rode out the drive and headed south.

Less than a quarter mile away he passed the lake. He kept on and at the end of short path saw a tidy house with a tightly thatched roof, set back from the road. It was two stories, with a tower to one side.

There were flowering bushes along the lane and trees that had been planted long ago and randomly on the grass. The house itself was surrounded by more greenery, looking almost as though it had sprouted on the spot just as the plants had. There was a settled feeling about it. Not elegant, but welcoming in the way his nurse's lap had been in childhood.

He stopped when the house was fully in sight, and drew a long, uneasy breath. What was he going to say? He had been so focused on finding her that he had not paused to consider what he would do when he did.

Was this, as Jess had suggested, about nothing more than his masculine pride? Or was he afraid of what he would find when he saw her again?

His horse danced, sensing his unease. Gabriel settled him, wondering if he should wait until tomorrow to call. It was close to evening now, the sun moving more deeply into the west. It would give him time to sort through his reasoning. *To hell with that,* he thought. He wasn't some boy longing for a romantic liaison. He was, in fact, a man who wanted some answers.

"CLAIRE, DEAR, THE KITTY MUST go to its mama now." Lynette stooped down so that she could see the child's face. "Let her go, please."

Claire was sitting on the front step, cuddling the kitten despite its inclination to leave. She released it with a pout. "I love her, and Peter said that we have to give some of the kittens away. Not this one. I named her Marie. I want to keep her. I will not let her go to an orphanage!"

"We will ask Mama, but I am sure it will be all right to keep one and, of course, we will find good homes for the others." Then everyone in the village would think they were daft. Who needed more cats?

The orphanage was Claire's constant refrain. Lynette understood perfectly, and not only because they had been through various versions of this with the others.

Last night Claire had cried because she could not eat all her peas and was afraid they would have to "go to the orphanage." Mama's solution had been to feed them to the dog. That had satisfied Claire for almost an entire day. Was the little thing tired? Or was it hunger that reminded her of the past?

Claire pulled on Lynette's skirt.

"Is that Monsieur Papa coming to call?"

"Who?" Lynette looked down the drive, now in deep shadow. She could see nothing.

"Monsieur Papa. The man who was with us on the boat from France."

Gabriel Pennistan? Now she could see a man on a horse at the far end of the drive. No one's eyes were so good that they could make out who it was from this distance. He was not moving, going so far as to still his restive horse rather than come closer.

A man has been asking for Mrs. Strauss. Wilton's warning words came back to her, as well as her mother's mention of another incident that occurred a few days before she returned from France. This time it was a letter addressed to her mother asking if she could please advise the writer of her daughter's—Mrs. Strauss's—whereabouts for a "business suggestion of mutual benefit."

Mama had burned the letter. Now all she could recall was that the name was unpronounceable. So typical of Mama to think and still do the wrong thing. Lynette was sure if she could have seen the letter, she would have been able to find some clue as to who had sent it and why.

Even as the memories flitted through her head, she patted Claire on the back. "Mama is in the sitting room. Would you ask her to come here? Then you go to Cook and tell her I said to give you an apple. It is still a long time until supper."

Lynette watched the motionless rider while she waited, stepping to a shaded part of the entry, where she could not be easily seen. It was the first time she had felt the need for protection at home.

Mama came quickly enough.

"Where are the boys?" Lynette asked, still watching the man on horseback.

"Marcus took them to the old Norman watchtower. They have a picnic with them and will be back before dark."

"They walked?" she asked, still watching the man watch them.

"Yes. It is not more than three miles."

Lynette could feel her mother move closer to her.

"My eyes are not as good as yours, Lynette." Her mother stepped down into the drive as if that would improve her vision. "Do you see someone?"

"Yes, a man. I am not sure if he is lost. Or, Mama, could it be someone looking for Mrs. Strauss?"

Her mother burst into action. "Come with me now, Lynette," she said, turning so quickly her cap would have fallen off if it had not been pinned securely. "I've thought about what to do if this happened when we are home alone. Let's go inside and close the door and have the maid tell him no one is home."

Lynette almost laughed, would have if there had been anything funny about her mother's fear. "No, Mama, we will wait right here and see what he wants. And exactly why are we afraid of someone looking for me as Mrs. Strauss? I broke no laws as Charles's wife. No laws of man, at least."

"He broke enough to taint everyone near him, Lynette. I fear that some would blame you for his behavior."

Even as she spoke, the rider began to move up the drive, toward the two women, standing alone. The mother moved in front of her daughter. Lynette honored the gesture by allowing it. "Go inside, Lynette. I will take care of this."

"I will be right back, Mama. Do not do anything foolish. Talk to him." She hurried into the house. She knew exactly where her gun was.

GABRIEL SAW ONLY one woman by the front door and saw that Charlotte was in yet another costume. Was Gilray even her real name? This time she was dressed and made up as an older woman. Padding made her look a welcoming mother, or would have if she were smiling.

How did she change her hair from the brown it had been in France to the blond streaked with gray? Not becoming so much as comfortable. She did not welcome him, but she did not look angry either. Suspicious. Wary. Uncertain. Not qualities he had seen before. He felt awkward, as though confronting a complete stranger. How odd. He had thought some sense of who she was and what they had shared would transcend any costume she wore.

He jumped from the horse, still watching her.

"Who are you and what do you want?" she asked.

"That game will not work, Miss Gilray. You may be in costume again, but I am sure your memory and eyesight are as good as they were in France."

She raised a hand to her throat as if she had just recognized him. "But . . ."

"I told you I would find you. I told you I wanted answers."

A woman came from the house. She was the one who spoke. "You also said 'I will see beyond the costume you wear to the true woman you are.'" The woman came forward, a gun in her hand. "Apparently not, my lord."

Oh yes, he thought with relief, there she is. He knew he should be at least a little worried about the gun in her hand, but the sense of triumph brought its own euphoria. He drank in the sight of her and stepped closer so he could recognize her scent. Not the spicy perfume Charlotte favored but a clean sweetness that was unmistakable. The simple hairstyle, the odd apron she wore made her look not much more than twenty when, by her own admission, she was closer to thirty.

She waved the gun under his nose.

"Lynette," he said with feigned patience, "put the gun away. You are not going to shoot me."

"Do not tempt me." As she spoke she did lower the gun and then set it on the ledge of the potted profusion of flowers beside the door.

"Do you know this man?" the older woman—aha, her mother—asked.

"Yes."

"Oh," her mother said with keen new interest. She leaned forward as though a few inches less between them would give her all the answers she was looking for.

"I am Gabriel Pennistan, madame," he said, giving an answer to one of them. He accompanied the self-introduction with a generous bow.

"Esther Gilray, Lynette's mother," she returned, bobbing a curtsy.

"As beautiful as your daughter, madame."

Lynette shook her head. He was sure she was about to say something like "Stop acting, you are terrible at it," but her mother was so clearly flattered by the compliment that her daughter settled for shooting him a nasty look.

"Lynette Gilray?" he asked, taking a step closer. Her mother matched the step as if to protect her daughter.

He stayed where he was, mentally trying the name out. He gave his attention to her mother once again. "Before I begin to think of her that way, madame, would you swear to me that she was born Lynette Gilray?"

"Isn't that what I said, young man?"

"Yes, but you did not swear to it."

"Swear, Mama. Or this farce will never end." Lynette had folded her arms across her waist. She meant it to show disdain. It did. But it also emphasized her lovely breasts.

"All right," Mrs. Gilray said with a puzzled shrug. "I swear that on her birth her father and I named her Lynette. I know it is not a conventional name, but she was named for my mother and my husband's mother. It seemed to please them. To my mind it suits someone with her sort of artistic temperament. I will tell you, though, that by the time she was ready for her come-out I was not at all sure that it had been a good idea."

"Mama does not need a weapon. There are times when she can talk people to death." Lynette then turned to her mother. "You do not have to give him my life history."

"Oh, but I wish she would. I can see you as a little girl with braids, and a paintbrush in your hand." When Lynette looked surprised, he nodded to her smock. "I saw some of your work at my brother's home."

"What do you want, young man?"

"I want to talk with your daughter." *I want to lie with her. I want to know why she feels such guilt, such pain. I want to see her art and hear her dreams.*

He spoke the first to her mother and told Lynette the rest with his eyes.

"I do not know what you hope to learn from her after all these years." Her mother came closer, brandishing her finger as if it were a weapon. "Strauss was a devil in human form. He made her his wife and then ruined her."

"Mama!" Lynette almost shouted. "No, Mama. Lord Gabriel is the man I rescued in France. He only knew me as Charlotte Parnell. That is why he wanted you to swear to my name."

If Lynette and her mother had not both looked so distressed, Gabriel might have announced that the farce was complete. Instead he bowed to Mrs. Gilray. "My apologies for confusing you, ma'am. There is so much left unsaid between your daughter and me, it would ease my mind considerably if I could speak with her for a few moments."

"No."

It was not her mother but Lynette who spoke. Her tone made him glad that she had put the gun down.

"Aha, now I can see a bit of Charlotte in you. In the hardness in your eyes."

"There is more than a bit of Charlotte in me, my lord. You would do well to remember it."

"Happily," he said with a smile that was as sincere as his words.

"I have no desire to see you," she said, this time with desperate earnestness. She picked up the gun. "I do not wish to speak with you. And I am telling you to leave now."

"As you wish," he said, knowing it would surprise her. "I am staying with Mrs. Wilton and will be teaching the boys while their tutor is away. I am sure we will have a chance to speak often." He raised his hat in farewell. "Until we meet again, ladies."

They made no response, so he turned his horse and cantered down the lane, pleased if not elated by his success. He knew her name. He knew where she lived. It was enough for one day.

HE HAD FOUND HER. She wanted to be angry, tried to find a reason to be frightened. Something more than surprised. Even more worrisome was the little thrill of pleasure that she was doing her best to ignore.

Did he say he was staying with the Wiltons? What was Madeline thinking? What would the captain say? Once he was home Gabriel would be sent on his way. All she had to do was steel herself for a few days. He would not be there long enough to upset her life. Though if she were honest with herself she would admit that he already had.

28

MRS. GILRAY'S DAUGHTER is home."

The three men at the rail looked up.

Gabriel sat at his corner table watching the reaction to the piece of news while ostensibly scribbling in his notebook.

"She brought another boy with her."

"How many by-blows can one woman have?" This from a man well into his cups.

"Not hers, you dolt. She rescues them from whore-houses." His friend eyed the others with a firm nod.

"Could be. Could be she is going to start a school."

"For what?"

"For artists," one of the others said. "Remember the harvest fair? She did those paper pictures of my boys. She is going to teach them how to earn a wage."

"You can't earn enough to live on with that rubbish unless you pick pockets on the side."

There were nods and silence, as if the idea of a school for thieves was taking root.

"Now you're all daft." The barkeep shined the wood counter. "Her mum, Mrs. Gilray, would not be bound to anyone unlawful. She is a good mother to those little ones, a regular churchgoer, and brings my mother soup whenever she is too poorly to come to work for her."

The others nodded and the barkeep continued, "The only odd thing is that there's never been the sign of a gent around there. You think someone like her daughter, that Miss Lynette, would have a hard time keeping them away."

One of the others laughed. The barkeep didn't give him time to open his mouth. "You keep them thoughts to yourself, or I'll not pour you another."

"Aww, come on, Adams, she could have five men in her bed and you would find an excuse. All your women work for the Gilrays."

The barkeep did not take offense. "As good a reason as any to keep a civil tongue in your head. And I'd be the first to know if anything was being done wrong there. She's a strange one, I'll give you that. Never know when she will take it in her head to go on a trip, but she never give us any reason to think her wild."

No one had an argument for that fact. Gabriel sat back and closed his eyes. Only in England could you find a village where the barkeep kept gossip to a minimum.

When the group was well into an enthusiastic discussion of a horse race three towns over, Gabriel left the tavern. It was a beautiful evening, warmer than spring ever was in

Derbyshire. As dark settled, he walked the middle of the road, heading for the Gilray residence. It was as good a place as any to watch the stars and make sure that Lynette did not "take it into her head" to leave before he had a chance to talk with her.

Once there, he sat on the ground, his back to a tree, and noticed for the first time that it was too cloudy to watch the stars. It was only an excuse anyway. Gabriel waited as his eyes became accustomed to the night. Within twenty minutes he could see the house in some detail, as more than a shadow darker than the sky behind it.

His greatcoat was perfect for an evening cooler than the day, with a touch of damp. He wondered if it would rain. Even as he had the thought, the clouds scudded away from the waxing moon and the alley to the house was bathed in shadow and light. At that same moment, he saw someone come around from the side of the house. She moved to the front step and sat down there. He saw her reach for something and pull it into her lap and knew that it was Lynette, with a cat for company.

She did not look his way but rather raised her eyes to the moon and the stars glistening nearby.

He should leave now. It was clear that she had no intention of running away from him. At least not tonight. He did not move, but watched her, like a boy watched a woman he could not have, or a man watched a goddess who was beyond his reach.

All his questions faded. He had wanted to see her again, he realized. *See* her again. Sitting here watching her might be enough. Even though his leg was all pins and needles, he held himself still and wished he could tell if she was content or troubled. If she had missed him or was relieved to be done with the Pennistans.

He stood up, shook his leg and waited until he would not limp before moving toward the front door, down the center of the alley of trees so she could see him coming, thinking as he walked that freedom was an amazing gift.

LYNETTE *KNEW* HE WOULD be here tonight. Setting the cat on the cushion near the door, she stood up and walked out to meet him.

"I thought that I would be content to sit under that tree and watch you all night."

"Apparently not." She watched him rub his thigh and worried that he had exposed himself to more of the night air than was healthy.

"Freedom is an interesting concept, Lynette. When we are not constrained by a prison, we are still only as free as we allow ourselves to be."

The absolute truth of his thought made her heart hitch. She might have nodded a little, because he kept on.

"I expect, my dear, that it is something we have both learned in the course of our unconventional lives. I could have stayed out of sight, but I *chose* to approach you. You chose to stand and greet me, not to turn your back on me and go into the house." He came closer and held out his hand. "Now we have another choice to make."

She stiffened. There was no pretending she did not know what he meant, what he wanted.

Instead of taking her hand he held his up. "I can see what you are thinking, but that is not what I am referring to. Not yet anyway. That choice will come, but the first of the choices is whether to be honest. Whether to tell the truth or pretend that we do not both want and wonder."

"I've told you the truth," she said, expecting him to scoff at her. He did not.

"When you explained about your cur of a husband?" He did not wait for confirmation. "I trust you did. Do you hear that? I trust that you told me the truth. That is the other half of honesty. Trusting in the answer."

"You should have studied philosophy instead of science." Even as she spoke, she considered what he said and realized that she had trusted him since that night in the tavern. When he did not take what he wanted but gave her what she needed.

"I know Charlotte Parnell, but I am honest enough to admit that is not enough. Now I want to know Lynette Gilray."

Oh no, she thought. "That is asking too much, my lord." She took a step back.

"At the moment, perhaps, but I am not asking for your soul, only some idea of your life here. Your family."

He was not asking for her soul, yet.

"Will you tell me about your art while we walk?" He held out his arm. "Also, I must know what has become of Georges."

"Do you think it is mid-afternoon and we are free to walk in the garden together?" She laughed a little.

"We are free to walk whenever we want. You can only imagine how happy that makes me."

She took his arm and led him to a path of crushed white stone that led to a summer house. Lynette knew she was giving in too easily, but she was curious to see what kind of man Gabriel Pennistan was when his life was once again his to command. What did it mean that the first thing he did was find her?

It was either very romantic or absolutely terrifying. She patted her pocket, relieved that she had her small pistol with her. "Georges came back with me to England this last time. He went up to London, determined to find someone who needed a valet. He thinks he can resume his life as though the last four years can be put in some box and never examined."

"Some men can do that. I think women must, or how could they ever have more than one child. Some try to make sense of it by talking about it," he bowed to her, "and some, like my brother David, seem to want to solve all the mysteries of life on their own."

"I want to ignore it, distract myself with my work and hope someday it will be forgotten." She shook her head. It wasn't working. "Georges wrote that he has found employment and gave me his direction should I ever need help. I think he has done quite enough. I almost wish he did not know where I lived." That brought to mind a question of her own. "How did you find me?"

"The marvelous cut-paper transparency in the schoolroom at the Wiltons'," he answered promptly. "I remember that last sunrise in Le Havre as clearly as you do."

She nodded, wondering at the oddity of chance that led him to that room and led her to give the boys that scene.

"I started drawing when I was old enough to hold a pencil," she began. "First on the walls and then on paper after Mama gave me a sound spanking. By the time I was fourteen I was doing small watercolors of family life." Where were they? Did Mama still have them? "After I married Strauss, I needed to find something that used less space and was easier to move or to leave for long periods of time. The silhouettes and cut-paper transparencies were what I decided on. It helped that I love doing them."

They had reached the folly, a small hipped-roof building with columns on one side and walls on two others so that it was protected from the prevailing wind.

There was only a chaise lounge for sitting. There was an easel as well. She had tried to paint here more than once, but could not, simply could not. They stood in silence. A not entirely comfortable one, she thought as she ran her hands up and down her arms. The fine cloth of her shawl was comforting. "How did you recognize me at the hearing?"

He nodded toward her arms. "Your hands are not still when you are nervous or worried."

She clasped them in front of her immediately and he shook his head.

"Too late," he said with a smile. "I assure you that you have nothing to be worried or nervous about. This visit is by way of making an end to one of the saddest chapters of my life."

"If that was all, then you would have waited until tomorrow to call again."

"There you see, Lynette," he said, nodding thoughtfully.

"You are honest for me. Perhaps what I am looking for is a beginning as well as an ending."

"I am not interested in a beginning. I enjoy solitude, or as much as you can have with a houseful of children." They were watching the clouds hurry across the sky. At least she was. When she turned to him she saw he was considering her as carefully as she studied a work of art.

"Could that be another reason that your art is all shades and shadows? You do not want to share too much of yourself."

She had never thought of that before.

"One kiss is all it will take to prove there is nothing left for us to explore."

"You will not catch me with that. I am not an untried girl, my lord," she said, trying to sound as blasé as Charlotte would.

He nodded. Was he admitting the loss before he even debated the issue?

"One touch, then." As he spoke he stepped closer, so close that they were not an inch apart.

She did not need the touch to know. This was enough. She could feel his warmth, his breath in her hair, see the line of his neck, dark against the white of his neckcloth. Her body was drawn to him, longing to fit herself in the curve of his shoulder, raise her mouth to his and brave the kiss. Though he blocked the moonlight, she saw pleasure in his eyes.

"You see," he whispered, his words echoing her thoughts, "we do not even need to touch, much less kiss."

He waited, which was her undoing. If he had moved to kiss her she would have stepped back, she was sure she would have, but he waited, watching her with an expression that made her feel cherished.

She laughed at the thought, though it came out more like a rather inelegant grunt. And still he did not move, his expression did not harden. "Gabriel, it is impossible."

Then he did move. He framed her face with his hands, holding her as though she were as delicate as a paper silhouette. "As one who studies science, I can swear to you that nothing is impossible. As a man, I truly believe that what is behind us is not all we have to live by. As Gabriel Pennistan, I know that you and I are meant to be together. Tell me the truth, Lynette."

"A night with you would be paradise."

Finally he kissed her. At last. Or did she kiss him? No matter, it was the touch of paradise she knew it would be and together they explored it fully.

The chaise served them well and she wondered if it was put here by the same magician who had put her transparency where Gabriel would see it.

The last of her reluctance faded away. As he kissed her neck and mouth and helped her with her stays, she considered the chance of it all. That he should be left in Le Havre, a city she knew, that Wilton should be his brother, that he was still alive when she found him, and on and on and on, to this moment.

When they were both undressed, or undressed enough, he settled beside her on the chaise and pulled his greatcoat over them for protection against the night air.

He was a man of few words, his actions speaking for him. His control amazed her, her lack of it was equally surprising.

When he would have drawn out their joining, she urged him to her.

It was as though half was made whole. If he could read her mind he would hear her begging him to hold her forever. To give her his coat when it rained, to undress her when she was cold, to warm her feet with his hands, to give her brandy to make her just dizzy enough to take what he offered, to dim the beast of conscience that declared her forever unworthy of this kind of caring.

THEY MIGHT HAVE SLEPT a bit, or at least he did. When he woke, she was starting at the ceiling.

"This is the end, Gabriel, not a beginning."

"Not now, Lynette. There is no need to make a decision this moment. We can—"

"There is nothing good in me." She cut him off with an angry gesture and raised her voice. "Nothing, do you hear?"

She stood up and pulled on her shift. He handed her the greatcoat and began to pull on his breeches.

"Yes, I hear, my dear, but you are wrong."

"No, I am not. Let me tell you how wrong you are, you fool."

She waited a moment until he had his shirt over his head and was buttoning it.

"Charles Strauss seduced me before I was twenty. He showed me the pleasure of sex until I wanted it more than I wanted my art, more than I wanted honor."

"You are not the first woman to be enthralled by a man. Though it is rarely one's husband." Exactly why was she angry at him? "I do not mean to make light of your distress, but Lynette, your past does not matter to me." A different thought occurred to him. "Unless you mean that no other man can equal his skill." He could not help but smile. "I could happily die trying."

"You would not make a joke if you understood what it was like."

"Tell me. We have time, we are alone. I want to understand."

She stepped back from him. She closed her eyes for a moment. When she began she looked him in the eye with anguish that tore at his heart.

"We went to a masquerade. They were quite popular in Le Havre. He had given me an amazing domino, a silk material that in itself was the most wonderful fabric I had ever felt against my skin. It was as exciting as a man's touch."

Ah, thought Gabriel, so Strauss had understood the way she loved the feel of things.

Lynette turned her head. "He suggested that I go to the party naked under my domino. I wore a mask so no one would know me. I was depraved enough that I agreed. We drank champagne on the way to the fete, and when I had had just enough he told me that I could have sex with one particular man, a man he wanted to impress and his beautiful wife was the most valuable gift he could give. He would watch to make sure I was not harmed."

She swallowed as though trying not to be ill. His own feelings were a mixture of disgust at the man and pity for the girl she had been. "Lynette, you do not have to go through this again."

"I did it." Her voice was laced with challenge. "I had sex with the man as Charles suggested. A man who was at least as debauched as he was."

"That's enough—"

She cut him off again. "No, it is not. When we went home he was so aroused he wanted to have his turn. I let him, I pretended that it was what I wanted, or else he would have used the sex to punish me."

She drew a breath and a small moan escaped. His silence was a great act of will.

"Some years before, when we had been married for almost a year, I refused him. I suspected he had been with another woman. I was in a jealous rage. We fought. I mean physically, not just with words."

He remembered the night in Le Havre when she had been afraid of him and understood why.

"Charles insisted that he loved women he called 'spirited' and that I had become too docile. In the end he tied me to the bed, blindfolded me and told me that if I did not pleasure him as he wished, whenever he wished, he would have one of the footmen come and enjoy himself. Then I would wonder which one it was and who he had told."

That made Gabriel feel sick in heart and body.

"Oh, I learned to do what he wanted, even if I was sick for days afterward. In time I learned to use sex as effectively as he had."

Gabriel was beyond disgust. Anger took its place. Didn't she know that Charles Strauss had taken more than her innocence?

She put her hands around his arms above his elbows and

shook him. "Do you not see that I am wanton, ruined, a whore of the worst kind?"

He let her keep him prisoner. "What I see is that your husband, who vowed before God to care for you, did exactly the opposite." He spoke with a quiet fury. "He taught you all there is to know about sex and nothing about love. You deserve so much more than that."

She pushed him away, only because he allowed it.

"I do not care what you think I deserve, my lord. I will never put myself in that situation again."

"What you had with him was not marriage. It was slavery, or bondage, and not what marriage should be."

"I do not want your pity!" If one could scream in a whisper, Lynette did.

"I cannot think of anyone less in need of pity," he said, surprised that she would even think it. "No pity, Lynette, only patience. It has, until recently, been a virtue I lack, and now I see why I was made to practice it these last years. So I would be ready to wait for you."

With a frustrated cry, almost a scream, Lynette grabbed her shoes and ran down the path, away from him.

He started after her. Then stopped, accepting the test of patience.

29

WORD OF NAPOLEON'S abdication swept through
the village a few days after the event. Captain Wilton brought
the news on a gallop from London. He relayed the story with
uncharacteristic excitement. He had stopped in town to discuss some matters with his man of business and left that gentleman's office to a benign riot at the good news.

The certainty of the war's end and the perfect spring
weather were just the excuse needed for a celebration in the
village, one that would include an impromptu fair and food
and dancing.

That was why Lynette was standing next to Gabriel at the
back of a crowd of people gathered near the church steps. He
had not seen her for a week, but who could carry ill will into
a celebration that marked the end of more than ten years of
war?

No matter her feelings about him, today she was smiling.

He had even heard her laugh once. It was the first time since the war began that Gabriel had reason to be grateful to Napoleon for anything.

Could it be that war's end would mean an end to other experiences best forgotten? His time in prison was fading from his mind. He might even be able to forget it if not for the everyday events that brought it back so forcefully.

Claire was a deadweight, asleep against his shoulder. There was no chance for privacy here, which may well have been the real reason Lynette was willing to have him so near. Or was it because she was playing the role of demure lady? Doing her best to discourage the one or two interested men who had been watching her all afternoon?

He cast about for something innocuous to discuss. "This is quite a crowd, is it not? Do you think there is anyone left at home?" he asked.

She did not answer at first.

"You know, Miss Gilray, if you talk to me then those two might think that the three of us are a family and go away."

"I imagine no one is home for miles around," she said. "A few servants left behind to discourage anyone dishonest enough to take advantage of this gathering."

"Why would they? The pickings are too good here." Even as he spoke a man took off after a boy who was either his son or a pickpocket.

They were all waiting for Captain Wilton to speak. He was the most senior officer living in the village and someone had to give a speech honoring the occasion. He was chosen, despite his suggestion that a retired colonel do the honors.

"Doesn't it look as though Robert would rather be facing a fleet of French ships?" Gabriel said.

"I imagine he would." Lynette kept her eyes on the boys, who were doing various acrobatic maneuvers on the green, conspicuously close to some girls from the local young ladies' seminary.

She gave Gabriel a quick glance. "What did he say when he came home to find you in residence?"

"He was surprised."

Before he could say anything else Lynette laughed. He loved that sound and vowed he would hear it again today.

"Yes, well, Madeline is ready to deliver and he is not about to deny her anything."

He thought about his brother and how aloof he was. "He has been quite civil, in fact very generous."

"He is a generous man," she said, as though he were being sarcastic and she hoped to start an argument.

"He never says no," Gabriel continued, delighted that they had found something else on which they agreed. "He never says no, but explains how this will further his own plans or can be used to his advantage."

"I've decided that it his way of trying to appear selfish when he is anything but," Lynette said.

"How long have you known him?" he asked, even though he knew it was the sort of question that would annoy her.

"I met him while I was still married, and he terrified me." She spoke frankly, as though the memory was an amusing one. "He was such a bastion of moral superiority. I tempted him, oh I tried," she said, with a curve of the lips that reminded him of

Charlotte at her most sultry. "He was a naval officer and unattached," she said as if that was reason enough. "He never, not once to this day, has treated me as anything but a lady."

The mayor was calling the crowd to order, and Lynette leaned closer to finish. "I hated him almost as much as I hate you."

She faced the speakers and let him chew on that bit of food for thought. Robert Wilton was at least two minutes into his oration before Gabriel realized the man was speaking.

Not the most eloquent speaker, Gabriel decided, but his uniform added power to his speech and his last two thoughts were worth hearing.

"Those who sacrificed for this victory number many who did not wear uniforms." He spoke to the crowd, but his eyes rested on Lynette more often than not. "Men of all ages and stations, and even women, were part of this effort to preserve our country and our King. I honor them in the same voice with which I praise the men who served under Wellington and in the memory of Lord Nelson." There were cheers after each of those names.

Then finally, "The war has ended. Let us not obstruct the peace with ill will and bad feeling. English children and French children will call one another friend. Let it begin here. God save the King!"

There were thunderous cheers of "Huzza!" and applause as the crowd converged on him with their congratulations. Gabriel and Lynette moved away. He, at least, was ready to find the captain's carriage, fill it with children and return home.

"Perhaps you should let me take Claire," Lynette said when a woman gave them a look of curiosity and disapproval. "People will be wondering who you are."

"Tell them the truth," he said as though it were a novel idea. "I am the boys' tutor and living with the Wiltons."

"The truth, but a carefully tailored truth," she said with approval. "I see you have learned something from Charlotte Parnell."

"Or Mrs. Charles Strauss," he suggested.

"I would appreciate it if you would never refer to me by that name," she said coldly. "Our hold on gentility is precarious at best. We have few servants and do not own a coach. There are no disguises here and my life before was nothing but pretense."

"I beg to differ, Miss Gilray. Most people live with disguises, just not on the outside, though I must admit the color of that lady's hair does challenge credulity."

Lynette turned her laugh into a cough as Gabriel bowed to the lady under discussion. The coquettish smile she sent his way was totally inappropriate, given her age.

"For instance, the smith is not well, but will admit it to no one, including himself. The vicar's daughter is going mad with boredom. She can hardly wait to escape to a town, even if it is only Bath as companion to her godmother, and the captain would much rather be at home with his wife."

"You sound like my mother after she has spent the day at the drapers."

"A smart woman, your mother," he said. "She has seen how the smith's hands shake, and that the vicar's daughter will sit for hours staring off into space, and that my brother Robert is letting those boys run riot through the streets."

That was the sign from the heavens that it was time to gather the family. Wilton rode with the coachman to supervise the two older boys, who wanted to play tiger and hang on to the straps. That left Lynette with Gabriel in the coach. Alone. Almost. If you did not count a grumpy Claire, and the other children, who were vexed at not being allowed the adventure of riding outside.

The only thing their ride home proved was that they shared the same inclination to swat the boys if they did not stop teasing the girls. It was something, Gabriel decided.

It was a very short ride to the Gilray residence, and Lynette climbed out of the carriage with a chorus of farewells. He said good night once again, reminding himself it was not good-bye.

The last leg of the trip was even shorter. Robert let his boys sit with the coachman while he claimed the seat opposite Gabriel. They sat in silence for a few moments.

"Fine speech, Robert."

"Thank you."

"There was a thought in it that struck me as notably valuable."

"Was there?"

"Are you surprised that I listened?" Gabriel asked. He did not so much as wait for a nod before he continued. "That last part where you encouraged the crowd not to hold a grudge against the French. That their children and ours would be friends."

"Yes."

"True, and surprisingly diplomatic for a naval officer. Then I realized that you must have learned diplomacy at an early age. *Compromise* might be a better word."

Wilton nodded, his eyes narrowed, and Gabriel was sure he had his attention.

"Lynette told me tonight that you knew her when she was married to that animal, Strauss."

"She told you about Strauss?"

Robert's surprise was gratifying. "Yes," Gabriel said and would have loved to leave it at that, a long see-how-you-like-terse-answers moment, but the coach had already turned into the drive and Gabriel knew he did not have much time left.

"She also told me that you are one of the most generous men she knows. That you have never once blamed her for what happened to those children or their parents."

"Lynette was as much a victim of that filthy bastard as those children trapped in the orphanages."

"We are agreed on that and so I have told her. Charlotte has her way of making some use of what she learned from him, of turning it to the good. Of expiation for her imagined sins."

"Yes, I suppose so."

"The point is this, Robert." Gabriel leaned forward. "My brother Lynford and the rest of us are just as innocent of our father's perfidy. Lyn was not the reason your mother had less than she needed, that she died unnecessarily."

"You think not?"

"You were Father's responsibility," Gabriel went on, relieved that Robert had not shown him his back, "one he denied. It was a disgrace for a man who was always harping on how important honor is."

Wilton looked at his hands.

"Robert, what you said today applies to families as well as countries. Continuing to label Lynford with the same disgust as you did Father is the only thing that will keep your children and his from being friends."

There was a long silence. Wilton shifted in his seat, but that was the only comment he made.

"Think on it, brother." His timing was perfect. The carriage rolled to a stop in front of the house and Gabriel opened the door before the coachman and the boys were off the box.

IT WAS HARD to believe it was still several hours until dark. Lynette felt as though she had not slept for days. She envied Claire's ability to doze off instantly wherever there was a convenient resting place for her head.

It was Lynette's shoulder now and she was glad the six-year-old was such a little thing. Carrying the sleeping child made it impossible for her to give the boys as much attention as she should, so she was relieved and then surprised when it was the Wiltons' butler, and not her mother, who came to greet them at the door.

"Miss Gilray," he explained, "your mother is at the Wiltons'. Mrs. Wilton is in labor and she will be asking the captain to go for the midwife. Mrs. Gilray wants you to come to them. I will watch the children." He related all this information as he took Claire from Lynette and they made their way into the front hall. He sounded concerned. And relieved to be handing off the responsibility.

A surge of energy displaced her fatigue. Lynette gave him some help and then took the cart he had left at the kitchen gate.

"THANK YOU FOR COMING, dear," her mother said, meeting her at the front door. She covered her face with her hands as though a brief respite from the late-day sun would help her see better. "The captain is in charge now, but Madeline needs some company and you know how useless men are."

Lynette nodded, although it had occurred to her that men were never given a chance to be anything but useless during a birth.

"I've thought about it, dear heart, and it would be better not to upset the children. You stay with Madeline and I will go home."

"Mama! I know nothing about a woman's confinement."

"And I have had only one experience. I am sorry to say, it was so awful, the thought of watching someone else go through it makes me feel quite ill. No, my dear, it must be you. One thing I do remember is that it will be hours before anything happens."

Mama would not budge from her decision and ten minutes later was hurrying down the path. As Lynette watched her, she prayed that someone here knew more than she did.

Madeline was already in her nightgown and in bed. Propped high on pillows, she was directing her maid and the others so efficiently that Lynette decided, if the baby was born before the midwife arrived, Madeline would tell them exactly how to proceed. She was, after all, the most experienced among them.

Her pains were about ten minutes apart. "It could be quite a long wait," Madeline assured Lynette, who began to wonder who was comforting whom.

"It is a relief to have someone near. The staff are wonderful, but they try to do too much, when all I really want is someone to sit with me."

"That I can do," Lynette assured her with relief. She claimed a chair placed near her bed and waited while Madeline finished giving instructions. There was one long pause as a contraction came and went. Lynette noticed that she was not the only one holding her breath for the duration.

"There," Madeline said, sounding more satisfied than relieved. "I think all is in readiness. If you would leave me with Miss Gilray, I would have you come back in an hour or so."

When her maid demurred, Madeline insisted. "You must rest now. The midwife will need you later." That seemed to please the woman, and she left with a self-satisfied air.

"She has a son away at school and has been telling me the most awful stories of women in labors. I have heard them all before and need no reminder."

There must be a dozen subjects the two of them could talk about and all Lynette could think of was stories about children. Not the best topic at the moment.

"Lynette, tell me what the captain is like at sea. I have never seen him in command and I'm curious." Madeline pushed the top cover back, as though she was hot.

"Give me a moment to think," Lynette said, hopping

from the chair to move the covering to the foot of the bed so that it was folded and still within easy reach. "Captain Wilton is completely in charge. He is curt, quiet, and authoritative. He is alone but not at all lonely. A man comfortable with his position, even though it costs him the camaraderie of his fellow officers."

She stopped as Madeline concentrated on the next pain. Lynette walked to the window and stared out.

"There," Madeline said again, though this time it was with some annoyance. "Is his brother anything like him?"

"Gabriel?" she asked, then could have kicked herself for calling him anything but Lord Gabriel.

"Yes. I know they have different mothers, but I am amazed at the small things that Robert and his brother Lynford have in common. Of course, Jessup is as different as can be from those two. I was wondering what you think of Gabriel."

What did she think of Gabriel? If she were being honest she would have to think about that answer for a day or two. "He is a charming man with too much faith in the essential goodness of his fellows, but not blind to their failings."

"Yes, exactly."

It was the truth, she thought. She did not have to think about it at all. As easy to say as it would be to recite the letters of the alphabet. Was that good or bad?

"He is convinced man can overcome his failings," Madeline added. "Just as he is convinced that Robert will one day see the light and accept his place in the family. It is something we have talked about a number of times these last weeks. He is an optimist."

Yes, that was Gabriel Pennistan in a single word. She was about to answer when Madeline's expression changed. Closing her eyes, she put her hand on her stomach and let the pain overwhelm her. Lynette came close to the bed and took Madeline's other hand. Madeline squeezed her fingers, more tightly than Lynette thought possible, and let go as soon as the pain ended.

"Oh my," she said, reaching for the damp cloth in the bowl nearby and wiping her face. "Lynette, do you think it is the mother who has the greater influence over the child even before it is born? James and Robert have the same autocratic way about them. They have the same father but different mothers.

"I worry about it," Madeline confessed. "I want our children to have Robert's strength, his generosity, his fairness, his sense of commitment."

"You, my dear Mrs. Wilton, are calm, patient, sensible, too sensible sometimes. They are all admirable qualities as well. If you are lucky, your children will have the best parts of both of you."

"A lovely thought," she said, patting Lynette's hand. "I hope that you find a man as fine as Robert."

She already had. She was the one who was not "fine" enough.

As another pain ended, Madeline went on. "I hope that by the time you have children they will have invented a way to eliminate this part of the birthing process."

30

IT WAS FOUR HOURS BEFORE the midwife arrived. Madeline's pains were much closer now and the midwife muttered a word or two and waved everyone out of the room while she "took a look at the missus."

Lynette went to the parlor and was directed to the dinning room, where a cold dinner had been set out. The captain was in his study and not at all interested in food or company, according to Yancy, who was back from the Gilray home with the assurance that all was well there.

Lynette helped herself at the butler's urging and then could not resist asking where Gabriel was.

"He's with the boys, to make sure they do not make trouble."

"They wouldn't. Not tonight!"

"Boys don't think about much but what they want, miss," he said, as though he were the father of a dozen.

"Could be Lord Gabriel would like some of that ham and a bit of that bread with it. If you put some butter on it, there be nothing as good as cook's supper bread." As he spoke he made up a plate and added some spring vegetables. "Why not take it up to him. I'm sure the boys would like a bit of news even if you have to make it up. The captain is struggling with his own fears and is better off alone."

She made her way to the nursery wing, where she could hear nothing but a man's voice. Tiptoeing into the schoolroom, she put the plate down and walked to the door that led into the bedchamber the boys shared.

"Is there anything else that you wish to know?"

Gabriel sounded every bit the man of science.

"No, sir." The response was like a chorus.

"Shall I wake you when you have a brother? Or sister?" he added quickly. "Of course, the baby may not come until tomorrow."

"Mama won't die, will she?"

Had they been discussing childbirth?

"I cannot promise that nothing will go wrong, boys, but your mama is a strong, sensible woman. She has been through this before. You two are proof of that."

As if that makes a difference, Lynette thought, but what else could you say to children when you were as unfailingly honest as Gabriel Pennistan?

"The best way you can help is to be quiet and behave like you have halos. I know it will be difficult. I think you are up to it, though. If you are able to control your baser urges, I will take you to Astley's Amphitheatre as soon as the captain gives permission. If you do not behave, I suspect that your father may ask me to sell you to the circus."

"Yes, sir," they said with a crispness that meant they understood it was not an idle threat.

"It is early for bed. I will leave one candle and you may play a quiet game if you wish. But if I hear a giggle from this room I will be back."

"We do not giggle, sir," one of them protested in an injured voice.

"Yes, I know, that is why if I hear a giggle I will know there is a girl in here."

The boys laughed at the joke and Gabriel came out of the room without waiting for any more of an answer than that. He did that often, she realized.

"What about girls in here, Lord Gabriel?" Lynette asked.

"I have never heard you giggle. Do you even know how?"

"When the need arises," she said, and then decided it would be wise to change the subject. "Astley's Amphitheatre? You are going to take them to the circus? It will give them ideas that will haunt the Wiltons for years."

"I think Astley *finds* his acts by watching young boys. They will learn nothing new, Lynette. If the bribery works, I will gladly take them to London at my own expense and without a thought for what a fool I will look with two scapegrace boys in tow." He saw the plate and walked straight to the table. "Of course, if you were to come with us, then no one would even notice the boys. Or me." He took a bite of the bread and hurried to swallow, as he apparently had something else important to say. "How odd, we have not seen each other for weeks. Now we are together twice in one day."

"Odd? No, it is the way of village life."

"I think you are avoiding me."

"The sun does not revolve around you, Lord Gabriel. I have children to help with, and my art is what feeds us."

That did give him pause, but not for long.

"You see," he said, waving an empty fork as if he were taking lessons from badly mannered schoolboys, "I think you realize that the more time we spend in each other's company, the more you will see that we are meant to be together."

She had no answer for that other than to repeat what she had said before. She settled for a shrug.

"I know this is an important decision for you, Lynette, and I am willing to wait for as long as it will take for you to accept me."

That made her laugh, when it should have made her angry.

He sat down and finished the food and seemed disappointed that there was not more. She tidied up the room, though it really did not need it, then, when he started to talk again, she wondered why she had not left.

"During the day the light of nature gives life to a cut-paper silhouette. Does the moon give enough light to see the details at night?"

"I suppose a full moon might," she said, wondering where that question had come from. "Especially in April and May before the trees are fully leafed. If the sky is clear."

"You sound like you are humoring a madman." He raised his hand toward the window. "The transparency of Le Havre is truly a lovely piece of art. I am only disappointed that I cannot admire it right now. During the day I am too busy trying to control the chaos." He pointed to a cracked window. "That is what happens if I dare take my eyes off the boys during the day."

"The captain and Madeline insist they love the silhouettes and the transparencies." She walked over to trace the crack and shook her head. "I have done some for the boys' tutor too. Famous mountain peaks, a volcano erupting, the insides of a fish. Now, that was an odorous project. If I could find the right commission, I could support my family doing it and truly be an independent woman."

"Your fondest wish," he agreed as though it were a sword through his heart. "Do you play chess?"

So he wanted to change the subject. Or was he reading her mind again? She played chess badly and said yes with the delightful idea of making him work so hard to lose to her that he would go completely mad.

Only, he played almost as badly as she did.

"Distracted. We are both distracted," he insisted as they began their second game. "I don't know if I want to hear screams or if the quiet makes me more nervous. This is almost as bad as waiting for that damn French colonel to decide whether he was going to shoot my head off or not."

He took one of her pawns with his queen and sat back awaiting her move. "Does that happen to you? You are going about your day quite as usual and then all of a sudden the simplest thing will happen and you are reminded of the worst parts of your days in France? Or, even more frightening, you cannot remember where you are?"

"Or who you are." She picked up the pawn, moved her bishop and took one of his pawns. "Yes. Now it happens most often when I wake up. After the first two trips and some awful nightmares I began to sleep on the window seat in my studio. Then I would know I was home when I woke up. And that my name is Lynette Gilray."

He picked up his pawn and gave up any pretense of playing the game. "I show the boys how to fence and pray they will never have to use it for more than sport."

"I show the girls how to paint and hope that they will never face any choice more difficult than what color to choose."

"And the oddest thing of all," he said, "is that life went on here at home in England, as though there were no war."

He *could* read her mind, she realized, but only because it was his experience as well. "Sometimes," she said, "I wonder which of the two worlds is more real."

Gabriel nodded, but before he could answer they were interrupted by a tap at the door. He raced to open it and found Yancy, who shook his head at Gabriel's expression. "There is no news yet, sir. The captain would like to see you." He took in the chess game and Lynette and added, "If you are available."

Yancy behaved as though it were perfectly normal for an unmarried lady and an unmarried gentleman to be alone together in a room with only one candle lit.

"Of course, I will come right now."

With a bow to Lynette, he started out the door and then realized he had responsibilities on the other side of the wall. Judging by the sounds, the boys were nowhere near close to sleep. "Lynette, would you mind acting as governess for a few minutes?"

"Surprisingly enough, it's a character I have never played. I would be happy to help," she said with a small curtsy.

Wilton was at his desk, working steadily on a letter. Gabriel took a seat opposite him and thought he might go out for a look at the night when they were finished here.

"Thank you for your patience, Pennistan." Wilton put the pen down and sanded the letter. "I am better at writing than speaking and I did not want to lose the thought."

Gabriel nodded. He understood that well enough.

"This last week has been amazing," the captain said, leaning forward, folding his hands over the paper. "A war is over. One that has spanned most of my lifetime and more of yours. Within the day, hopefully within the hour, I will have another child." He shook his head. "It is an overwhelming thought. That my blood will continue long after I am gone."

Gabriel decided that was as sentimental as Robert Wilton could be and was astounded when the captain handed him the letter.

"I have written a letter to the duke asking if I could call in Derbyshire. It seems to me that this is the month, if not the year, for new beginnings. I understand his wife is increasing." He stopped and waved a hand at the letter. "Would you please read it and tell me if it will be met with approval or find offense?"

What a gesture, Gabriel thought. He read the letter, which was as eloquent as Wilton's speech had been prosaic. He *was* a skilled writer. Gabriel told him so. "It is especially thoughtful of you to mention Rowena's condition."

"I was afraid that it might be too personal."

"No. We are family, Robert. I am sure she will be more than delighted to have you two meet. As I am."

"I will tell you that it's what's happened all around me, plus my own words that you tossed back to me. It's the future we have to think about and not the past."

Gabriel felt his eyes fill and blinked the emotion away. He stood up and held out his hand. "Welcome to the family, Robert."

"Thank you, thank you," Robert said, and cleared his throat, standing to shake hands. "I will have one of the men take it tomorrow." He hesitated. "Or as soon as we can make our own announcement." His try at a smile was not entirely successful.

"The waiting is hard enough for me," Gabriel said, "it must be so much more difficult for you."

"I am more used to action" was all he would admit.

"I can only imagine." Worse than difficult, Gabriel thought, more like a refined kind of torture.

They sat again, talking a little, listening to the quiet of night settle on the house. They heard a door close occasionally, and once Madeline's maid came to tell them that the confinement was progressing quite normally.

"Whatever normal is," Robert muttered as the door closed.

Gabriel was nodding off, considering ways he could induce Lynette to come watch the stars with him, when the sound of a key being turned in a lock filled him with such panic that he jumped from the chair. "If you lock that door, I will break it down and kill you with my bare hands."

The man standing by the desk stepped back in surprise.

He held up his hand, from which a key dangled. "Gabriel, it's Robert Wilton. I was locking my desk, that's all."

"That hideous sound was the key?" Gabriel shuddered as Robert finished the job. It made the smallest grating sound.

Gabriel sank into the chair again, covering his face with his hands. Finally, he looked up at his brother. "How long? How much longer will the most common sound awaken a nightmare?"

"That I cannot tell you." Robert walked to the sideboard and poured some brandy into two glasses. He handed one to Gabriel and tasted his own, sitting down heavily. "I can only assure you that you are not mad. Or alone in this."

"It is not just the panic. Lynette and I were just talking about it."

Robert nodded encouragement.

"Until today, at the celebration, I would have sworn that the people here had no idea we have been at war. Do you ever feel like you are only watching and not truly a part of the world around you?"

"Not when I am at sea. But ashore, I felt that way all my life until I met Madeline."

Now, there was a bit of honesty he had not expected. "Parts of Spain and Portugal are a shambles," Gabriel went on, "tens of thousands are dead, and here their biggest concern is why the Gilray ladies have no butler. Is it worth it? If no one appreciates the pain, the death, the loss, why do we do it?"

"We do it for that very reason," Wilton said, pausing to sip his brandy. "We do it so that our countrymen can live in comfort and security, with nothing more to worry about than their neighbors' propriety." They heard someone come down the stairs. They waited, but no one came to their door. Wilton closed his eyes for a minute and then went on. "We do it so that our families will never have to face what we have."

"Oh yes, I see," Gabriel said. "I have been considering this selfishly."

"The work you and Lynette did was the most unselfish gesture possible. You were not in uniform. You worked in secret with no expectation of appreciation, much less reward. Now you are home again, and where do you put the fear, the heartache? You are entitled to some confusion."

"All right," Gabriel said. Calling it confusion sounded much better than *selfishness*.

"My consolation comes when I see the boys laugh, when Madeline smiles at me, while I wait to hear a child's cry. Believe me, Gabriel; all of this is worth fighting for."

"Yes, I see." He allowed the memories now and remembered. "Who did I think of when the beatings were unbearable, when even the rats would not come to visit, when I thought that the French colonel would kill me just for sport?" He stopped the catalog though there were a dozen more he could add. "I thought of the people I love, the ones who love me, my brothers and my sister, of the children they have not yet had, of the men who died." He stared into the brandy and tried not to count the enormous cost of this peace.

"That is as it should be."

"Lynette would say that she did it for the children."

"Yes, she would. Do you know how she thinks?" Wilton asked, as though it might be possible.

"Sometimes I think I know what she wants, but perhaps it is really what I think she needs. I am rarely able to convince her to accept it."

"When you figure out how to do that," Robert said with a laugh, "please do tell me."

"You will be the first to know." They raised their glasses and toasted their camaraderie. One thing this day had proved was that they were brothers in so many more ways than blood.

A few moments later there was a true commotion on the stairs. They could hear someone running down and across the hallway, no pause to knock on the door. Yancy threw it open and announced, "It's a girl, Captain. You have a daughter!"

31

IT WAS CLOSE TO DAWN before the household was ready to sleep again. The newest member of the family had to be introduced, first to her papa and then to her brothers.

Lynette and Gabriel were included as if they were family, and both professed amazement at the beauty of the alternately crying or sleeping babe. Madeline was radiant, declaring that the euphoria of the moment had erased all memory of pain and that the midwife was truly gifted. It was praise the woman accepted with a nod of satisfaction.

Finally, with a chorus of good nights, Gabriel went down the stairs with Lynette. He took her hand.

"We have a few moments before the carriage is brought round. Come with me to the lake house, we can sit on the terrace and count the stars."

"I have never been propositioned in quite that way before."

"No, I truly do mean look at the stars," he said, shaking his head. "I told you before that we will do the rest on your terms and when you wish."

"I think never, Gabriel," she said, veering away from the front door and walking into the salon that Madeline used to receive those who called.

He followed her. "Never is not one of the choices. Surely someday you will have room in your life for me."

"Listen to me, Gabriel. I had a letter ten days ago from a man named Adam Schotzko. Mama had told me that someone was looking for Mrs. Strauss. I never for a minute thought it could be for something I wanted."

She stopped walking and looked at him. "His wife, Ann, had seen my transparencies and brought them to his attention. Dr. Schotzko inquired about offering me work. As an artist," she said, as if it were the most amazing miracle in the world. "He wants to know if it would be possible to make paper transparencies of the human body based on Vesalius's drawings. Do you know the book?"

"*De Humani Corporis Fabrica*? Yes, of course I do. Yes."

"He wants me to test the idea of making transparencies from the drawings. Layering the muscles over the skeleton with a transparency of the skin over all, so that lit from behind they will be easily visible. He will pay me for that. And if it is possible and the results are satisfactory, he will commission me to do several of them." She shook her head.

"That is marvelous. *De Humani Corporis* is one of my most treasured books." He hoped his father had not sold it. "The art is such a far cry from anything done before. Vesalius actually commissioned artists to do the drawings. He does misrepresent some things, but I can show you the mistakes."

"I am sure Dr. Schotzko will give me all the information I need. I am to meet with him tomorrow—or actually, today."

"He is here already?"

"I assume so. And even if the whole project is not commissioned I will be able to support the family for years with this first attempt, thanks to Dr. Schotzko's work along with Robert's generous gift of the house rent-free and the money your brother paid me. Why, we will even be able to hire a butler."

"So it is the ideal combination of doing work you love for a reasonable wage." He could feel her slipping away from him.

"Yes," she said, with satisfaction.

Hearing the crunch of the carriage wheels outside, Gabriel stayed her with a hand on her arm.

"So your work will engross you. Financial security will guarantee your independence. Was my only hope that you would need a patron to support you? Have I not touched your heart at all?"

She laughed a little, not unkindly. "Oh, Gabriel, I am sorry, but my heart was hardened too many years ago for anything or anyone to touch it."

"I was hoping that it had melted a bit now that your private war has ended."

"It may be over, Gabriel, but all the goodness was bled from me long before that. All that is left are ugly scars."

For her this was the truth and he could think of no way to disabuse her of it. A huge roiling burst of anger overwhelmed him. "I want to kill that bastard Strauss with my own bare hands. My only consolation is that he is burning in the worst circle of Dante's hell for all eternity."

When she shook her head, he went on.

"You are so much more than good, Lynette. You are generous, loyal, trustworthy, determined, inventive—"

"Gabriel, do not talk like a besotted fool," she said, curtly interrupting the list of virtues he had only just started.

"Tell me, how long has *fool* been an endearment?" he asked, still angry, but the worst of it was easing as her annoyance showed. "Do you know what that word really means, Lynette?"

"Whatever it is, it has meaning only for you."

"It means 'I want you here beside me so you can give me back all the love that was taken from me.'"

He smiled at her and she looked away, but he glimpsed the longing in her eyes.

"You are wrong. It is only when I am around the children that I see any hope for my future."

He raised both hands to frame her face and was encouraged when she did not swat them away. "I think I must love you." He said it as a matter of fact, as though discovering something of vague interest. "I love every prickly, angry bit of you. Love is not a prison, Lynette. I want to show you that. I am willing to wait. Until I am convinced there is no hope."

She reached up and took his wrists, pulling his hands away from her face. "I will not change my mind." She said it with a sadness that hurt him more than her words.

*   *   *

320 MARY BLAYNEY

L YNETTE LOST HERSELF in her work for the next few days.
Her mother made her join them for dinner, Claire would
come and invite her to play and the carter came regularly
with the supplies she had ordered for her project. Her plan
was to bury herself in her art, with only her cat for company
and evenings with the children. That way she was able to dispel thoughts of Gabriel Pennistan, at least during the daylight
hours. That worked quite well. Then word came that he had
left the Wiltons.

Left? Without seeing her? Without saying good-bye? *Do
not be a twit*, she scolded herself. *You told him it was hopeless,
pointless, and he finally listened.* Only it was so unlike him to
admit defeat so quietly that she felt let down out of all proportion to the news. It was so quiet without him in the neighborhood, as though he had taken all the excitement with
him.

Schotzko had allowed her two days with his copy of
Vesalius's book. Working until her hands cramped, she had
come up with an overall design and began ordering the supplies she would need.

Schotzko had promised to answer all her questions, but
there were dozens, and now she wished the man had been
willing to leave the book with her. The fact that the cat had
spilled a vase of flowers and water onto her worktable surely
could not have anything to do with Schotzko's hesitancy to
leave so precious a volume in her hands?

She was in the midst of composing a letter to the doctor
when someone tapped hurriedly on the studio door and
came in without waiting for permission.

"Lynette, I do not know what to do about the butler."

Her mother closed the door firmly and sat down in the nearest chair, rubbing her eyes as if the effort would help her see better.

"I thought you had found someone for the position?" Lynette wiped the nib and put a cap on the bottle of ink.

"Yes, I do have one that I think will suit us perfectly. His wife will come and act as governess for the children as well. She is increasing, but another child is always welcome."

"Then what is the problem?" She did her best to be patient, but she really wanted to write down the questions before she forgot them.

"He cannot start for another two weeks."

"Mama, we have not had a butler for the two years we have lived here. What is another few days, less than a month?"

"It seems forever now that I know we can afford one. Gabriel is coming back before he goes to London and offered to help until the new man can start. I thought about it before I wrote back to him. He is going to start as soon as he returns."

"Mama! He is Lord Gabriel Pennistan, brother of the Duke of Meryon. He is not a butler."

"Of course he is not a butler. He is just going to help with the things I cannot manage myself."

"Mama, it will not do." The cat escaped with a silent leap from her arms. "Have you ever 'thought something through,' as you say, and made the *right* decision?"

Esther Gilray looked more annoyed than hurt. "Yes, my dear, when I agreed to help you with your wild scheme to save the children."

That put an end to Lynette's annoyance. "I know, Mama, and I am so sorry I said that."

"I'm not. I know I am far from perfect, Lynette. I made a terrible mistake with Strauss, but I have tried to make amends here, tried to be the mother I failed to be before."

"You have been wonderful."

"So you say, and yet there are times when I feel as though you have never forgiven me, that I could go on and on and a part of you would forever hate me for encouraging you to make that match. I may ramble on, I cannot see to read unless the print is large, I am not that fond of cats and I—"

"Oh, Mama, stop." Lynette hurried to kneel in front of her. "You were willing to take me in when I had cursed and swore at you. Since then you have never once made me feel anything but loved. I am so grateful to you."

"Thank you, dear." Esther dabbed a tear from her eye. "I will tell you this: I did not make the decision to help you lightly. Even before I knew it would be more than a temporary arrangement. I went to talk to the vicar. We talked, or perhaps I was the one who talked, but in the end I was convinced that anything can be made right with love. There is not a crime so heinous that God will not forgive it. Why, even on the cross, Jesus asked his Father to forgive the ones who were crucifying him.

"Now, I ask you, Lynette, if Jesus could do that, how could I not forgive my daughter for mere words and, perhaps even more important, let my daughter forgive me?"

This was her mother at her rambling best. Lynette kissed her on the cheek and stood up. "That is lovely, Mama," she said, following it with a sigh of resignation. "Lord Gabriel can play at butler if he wishes, but while he is here I will continue to spend most of my time in my studio and he may not come to visit me. Do you understand?"

"Yes, darling, I do. But sometimes I wonder if you listen to me at all."

MADELINE WILTON'S HOME WAS as quiet as an abbey if one compared it to Esther Gilray's. The Gilray home was smaller and was home to twice as many children. When the children were not having lessons, there was always someone begging for attention, or yelling, or insisting they were starving. Doors slammed as often as they were shut quietly, and by noon the hall was littered with balls and toys despite the fact they were picked up and put away each evening.

The staff took it all in stride, and despite the occasional tears and constant chaos not a one—staff, child or either of the Gilray ladies—wanted to be anywhere else.

Gabriel learned the routine of the house quickly and began to make the kind of contribution that Mrs. Gilray needed: someone with eyes good enough to do her books for her, to read to the children and to be sure the clock was wound so that, as the days grew longer, she would know by its striking that it was time for the children to prepare for bed.

It was fun. It would have been a lot more fun if Lynette had been anywhere in sight. She did indeed sleep in her studio and she ate there as well. He saw her exactly once in his first two days in residence.

"Lynette was a stubborn child," Mrs. Gilray said as she watched Gabriel. "I thought Strauss had beaten that out of her, but apparently not. I think it is a good sign that she is obstinate with you. A very good sign."

Esther Gilray was a romantic. It might be a good sign, but how was he to win her interest if he never saw her? He *was* able to find out the answers to all the rest of his questions. Mrs. Gilray's eyesight might be poor, but her memory was excellent.

When he asked her why she and Lynette had chosen to raise some of the children, she explained in detail. It had not started out that way. She was only to care for them until the parents were located. Then, as it happened, they discovered one boy's parents had emigrated to Canada. They could hardly send him to an orphanage, could they? The parents of the twin boy and girl had died. They simply could not find Claire and Peter's parents. They could be dead, they could be in the next town. And the child who had just arrived, his father had died and his mother had remarried and had two children. "That heartless woman told Lynette that she wants no reminder of that time. I suspect she has never told her second husband about it. I do believe that is all of them, and our unique family is complete."

Then there were her stories. "Did you know I was an actress? My husband was the son of a wealthy country family who were anxious to have him find a place in society. Instead he married me. Neither one of us regretted the choice, and once Lynette was born his parents relented and were kind enough. One thing I know, Lord Gabriel, is that a true match is about more than money and rank in society. I lost sight of that when she met Strauss. I will never make that mistake again. So allow me this advice: Do not tolerate her stubbornness for too long."

The evening of that second day he went up to the studio with the one item he thought might make him welcome. The door looked like all the others in the house: brutally clean, closed tight against drafts. For Gabriel, opening it would be like stepping into a room filled with treasure.

He tapped twice, and when there was no answer he opened the door and looked in. He closed the door quietly behind him.

She was asleep on the window seat.

Hardly breathing, Gabe stepped into the room, intending to put his package on her worktable and then leave. Her head was leaning against the window, exposing that one sweet spot. It distracted him so completely he tripped over something—the cat—and almost fell. She woke with a start and jumped up.

"I didn't mean to scare you."

"Yes you did. Yes you did." She raised a hand as if to still her heart and then bent over to pick up the pad that had fallen to the floor.

"Did not," he said with a laugh. "I am not fourteen and you are not a young girl. But we can bicker about it if you wish."

"What was my mother thinking to hire you? She is hopeless." Her expression was pure exasperation.

"No, I do believe she is just the opposite, always hopeful."

"Perhaps you should be flirting with her."

"I do, all the time. If you refuse me, we are planning a torrid affair under this very roof."

She did not even smile at his joke. "What do you want?"

"I brought you something that I thought might prove useful." He nodded toward the package on her desk. "The one gift a man of science might give an artist and both would appreciate."

"I hate riddles."

He almost laughed. She sounded like Claire when she was tired or hungry. "Then open it, Lynette."

She did, untying it carefully as though the boys had wrapped it and a hundred beetles would pop out. When she saw what it was, she stopped and looked at him.

"Oh, Gabriel. Thank you."

"You're welcome." His heart skittered with pleasure. He had finally found something that would make her world a better place.

"You are exactly right, *De Humani Corporis Fabrica* is something both of us treasure, for entirely different reasons."

"I all but begged Schotzko to hire me to advise you. He thought my credentials adequate but said that it was your decision. I knew what that answer would be." Gabriel went over and pulled the last of the paper and string from under the volume and left the book in the middle of her desk.

"I saw him the day after he first called here. He told me that he could not, in good conscience, leave his volume here. He is a bit of an old maid, is he not? His wife must be very patient. I offered to allow you the use of my copy."

She nodded and touched the leather binding, ran her fingers along the gilt edges of the closed book.

"He did warn me that you have cats as pets and they were nothing but trouble."

She was not looking at him, but staring at the book. Gabriel wandered around the space, trying to make sense of it. He decided she might know where each little item was, but she was most likely the only one who did.

A cat was sunning itself on the window seat and Gabriel walked to it. The window faced east, overlooking the side yard and stable. He stood at the window, wondering if this room was not both prison and sanctuary.

He saw Claire chasing her kitten, Marie, across the yard and waited, expecting to see the young maid who cared for the girls close behind. When she did not appear, he decided he should go after the little girl himself and tell her to be careful.

"Thank you, Gabriel. It is the perfect gift. I shall treasure it, and return it when the work is done."

She was standing close to him, and when he turned around, she stood on tiptoe and kissed him on the cheek He left the studio to find Claire, more encouraged than he had been in days.

That was as close as he was to come to Lynette for the rest of the week. Hopeful or not, his time was running out. The new butler would be with them in two days.

Robert had gone to Derbyshire at Meryon's invitation and had insisted that Gabriel was welcome at his home until he returned, or for as long as he wished.

It was tempting, but Gabriel would give Lynette what she wanted. He would leave.

32

THOUGH HE WAS LEAVING, Gabriel had an ally in Esther Gilray and knew he could keep track of Lynette through her. As painful as it was, it did not appear that the end of the war and the birth of a child would have the same softening effect on Lynette as it had had on the captain.

Gabriel was walking back after making a call on the baby and her mother. A noisy spring storm had delayed his return and he was hurrying when he saw Lynette and her mama in the front garden. Lynette was holding her mother's hands. It was clear that Esther was upset and Lynette was trying to understand the problem. He reached them in time to hear the pertinent details.

"She is not in the nursery and two of the kittens are gone. You know how upset she was about not being able to keep them all. I think she has run away with them."

"Nonsense, Mama." Lynette started as Gabriel came up to them. She gave him a pleading look and he nodded.

"It is almost dark, Mrs. Gilray," he said. "I know you are worried and I would share it with you if it were one of the boys. Claire will not have gone far. Does she have a favorite hiding place?"

Esther put her hands to her head as though it would help her think. Lynette began to move off to the stable before her mother answered. "Yes, yes, Lynette! The stable. She used to love to go up in the loft and watch the kittens with their mother.

"You go there with Lynette, Lord Gabriel. I will see if any of the others know what she had in mind."

Esther ran with surprising speed back to the house. Gabriel caught up with Lynette at the barn door just as the plaintive sound of a scared child reached them.

"Mama! Mama! Help me!"

They broke through the stable doors at the same time and stopped short. The length of the room was as black as night. There was the sound of a scuffling, restless horse and the hiccoughing crying of a child.

Since there was no groom, Gabriel had been here daily to care for his horse. He knew the layout well enough. Starlight was the only horse in residence. "Claire is in the back." Gabriel grabbed Lynette's hand to slow her.

The thud and crack of a horse kicking the side of the stall ratcheted up his fear and Claire's pleas for help. Lynette pulled at his hand.

"Let me go, Gabriel. She needs me!"

"He is *my* horse," he said, holding tight. "Starlight is not bad-tempered, but he is upset by storms and he hates cats."

"Stop talking and let me go, Gabriel. I have to help her."

He took both of Lynette's hands and leaned closer to her. "Let me handle this." He looked her in the eyes and asked the impossible. "Stay here and let me do it."

Claire began whimpering, and Lynette closed her eyes. "All right. Only hurry, she is so afraid. Please."

Nodding, he kissed her hands and pushed her behind him, wondering if she was telling the truth or if she would bash him on the head and take charge herself.

She did not try to take charge, but she did follow him, despite his insistence that she stay back. He moved slowly, letting his night vision grow as he stepped deeper into the shadows. He found the baton he needed and then stepped around the corner.

Claire had pressed herself under the grain bin in Starlight's stall, a spot the horse could not quite reach. She would be safe enough as long as she did not move.

The white dress she was wearing made her easy to see, and as Esther had predicted, she held on to one of the kittens with all the commitment of a savior.

"Monsieur Papa!" Claire began to crawl out and would have run to him. As she moved, the horse stretched his neck and bared his teeth.

"Stay right where you are, Claire. Let me come to help you and the kitten."

"All right." She sniffed and then drew a long wavering breath. "I do not like that horse."

"Starlight feels the same way about little girls who scare him."

"I wanted to help my kitten. He is the one who scared us!" the girl said, as though Starlight were one of the boys.

Gabriel could feel Lynette literally breathing down his neck. Thank the heavens, she did not say a word, did not natter with useless advice, beg him to be careful or cry her own tears.

He took the baton and moved steadily down the side of the stall. When Starlight sensed the movement, Gabriel led with the baton, and the horse nipped it.

Good, exactly the way it was supposed to work. He faced Starlight and worked his way to the corner. The horse lunged. Starlight took a bite that most likely ruined Gabriel's jacket, but Gabriel had Claire in his arms. He ran now, all pretense of calm gone. He had made it almost out of range when he felt a kick to his back. It was enough of a stretch by the horse that it only pushed him rather than knocked him down.

He handed Claire to Lynette and turned to make sure that Starlight was not going to join them. With his stall to himself again, the horse gave Gabriel an evil eye, twitched his tail and ignored them.

"That was what I was going to do," Lynette said as she cuddled the crying child.

"I was there first," he said, "and I know how to use the baton."

"Why do you have such a nasty horse?" she asked as she smoothed Claire's hair.

"He's not nasty, only upset by storms and cats. Perhaps I should add bellowing children to the list."

"She was not bellowing."

"Not to you, but Starlight has sensitive ears."

They were walking out of the stable when Wilton's groom came running down the road with Pierre-now-called-Peter. Esther and the rest of the family were holding on to one another, a good distance from the stable.

"Everyone is fine," Gabriel said. "You can all go back to the house."

He knew that was no more than wishful thinking. He was right. The waning moon was well risen before everyone was settled again. Lynette had disappeared into her studio. Finally there was nothing to do but go to the kitchen to see if there were any tidbits left from dinner or maybe a piece of pie. He would find a spot to watch the stars and think about how to fill his life until Lynette's trust was something given freely and not reserved only for emergencies.

LYNETTE SAT IN HER darkened studio, on the window seat, with her cat for company, and watched Gabriel make his way from the side yard to the stable. Checking on his horse again, no doubt.

Esther tapped at the door as she did each night and came in without waiting for permission. Putting her candle on the table near the door, she made her way to the window seat. And as was her custom, she sat next to her daughter to talk over the events of the day and plan the morrow.

"It was a little more of an uproar than usual, wasn't it, daughter?"

Lynette laughed a little. "You do not see chaos as a natural part of our life?"

"With this many children it is unavoidable, I suppose. I am hoping the butler and his wife will help calm things."

"Our current butler certainly has not," Lynette said, solely because she wanted to talk about him.

"How can you say that? Lord Gabriel found Claire and kept her from harm." Her mother leaned closer for a moment as if she would have a better chance to see if Lynette was teasing.

"Mama, need I remind you that there would have been no horse to harm Claire if Gabriel had not been staying with us?"

"Oh yes," she said, hesitating, "I see what you mean."

They were both looking out the window as they talked and both of them saw Gabriel come out of the stable. He headed toward the path to the lake house, looking up at her window as he passed. There was no light directly behind them, so there was nothing for him to see.

He disappeared into the dark quickly enough. Mother and daughter sat in silence. Esther was unusually quiet. Finally Lynette asked the question her mother was longing to answer.

"What do I do about him, Mama? He might love the night, but it is the only dark thing about him. For me to marry him, or even be his mistress, would be to corrupt him the way Strauss ruined me."

"Do not be ridiculous, Lynette. That is not true at all. You will give him the one thing that Strauss never gave and it will make all the difference. Love him, dear girl, love him and all things will be new."

"Are you not being a little bit theatrical, Mama?"

"No, I am not, and your cynicism offends me."

"I'm sorry, but not all things can be 'made new' with love. I wish it were that easy."

"Easy? You think love is easy? My dear child, it is the biggest risk one can take. As you know too well."

"I never loved Strauss."

"No, but you love these children. You were willing to love me again. They are all steps along the way to a greater love."

"Where did all this wisdom come from, Mama?"

"Lord Gabriel and I have been talking lately. I have gone to watch the stars with him once or twice. He has a nice spot established at the crest of the hill just beyond the turn in the road. You know, where that copse of trees is?"

God help her, she prayed, he must know every detail of her life by now.

"We talked mostly of his parents and his brother's reconciliation with Captain Wilton. We agree that love for one's family is at the heart of true happiness."

Oh, Lynette thought. *Not about me.*

"I am to bed now, my love." Esther pushed herself off the seat with a huff, kissed her daughter's cheek, found her candle and left the room.

Lynette sat a few moments longer, wondering how honest Esther had been with her. And how hard she had been trying to influence her to go to Gabriel. *Mama need not have tried so hard,* Lynette thought, standing up, finding her shoes and her heavy cloak.

It did not take as long to find him as she thought it might. He was on the hillside her mother had described, lying on his back watching the sky—or maybe sleeping, for all she knew. As she drew closer, he sat up and turned in her direction.

"Good evening."

She was walking slowly but stopped short at his greeting.

"If you will assure me that you have no weapons, we can easily share the hill."

"It's Lynette, Gabriel."

"Yes, I know." He stood up and brushed his clothes. "Good evening and welcome to my observatory, primitive as it is." He waved at what she thought was a blanket spread on the ground, with another as a headrest.

"How did you know I was here?" she asked.

"In the years I have been watching the sky I have learned a great deal about the ground as well. When one is lying still, I can feel the footsteps. I knew you were coming long before I could see you."

"What makes this spot so ideal?" Moving closer, she made a turn, feeling decidedly small beneath the expanse of night. "It looks like every other hill on the Downs."

"This spot is a little higher," he said, gesturing for her to sit beside him. "It has unobstructed views in all directions and no buildings that I can see. There is that small copse of trees below our sight line for shelter if the weather should turn."

"If the weather should turn?" Was he serious? "You could

see it coming from here and run back to the house in less than five minutes."

"Yes, well then, if one needed to rest one's eyes, it would be an ideal spot."

"Oh, I see, you can watch the stars with your eyes closed?"

"Why would I want to close my eyes when I can look at you *and* the stars?"

That made her heart melt a little. *Change the subject, you have some important things to cover first.* Instead they sat in silence. "Are you asleep?" she asked.

"No, my darling, I am listening to you very carefully. Even without words you are speaking volumes."

How did he know that she needed time, that "I think I love you" would be the most difficult sentence she had ever spoken? "When I first came back to England and could not support myself as an artist, I took a lover."

"What did you call yourself then?"

"Marie LeSeur." What did that have to do with anything?

"You do seem to favor French."

"It was my mother's stage name."

"Ah, I see." He propped his head on his elbow and gave up all pretense of looking at the stars. "Lynette, I love you. No matter what you had to do to survive. No matter what your name is, or was. One day I do hope you will consider changing your name one last time. I love you." He did not seem to expect an answer, but lay on his back again.

She sighed and did the same. They were side by side, the only sound their breathing.

"Thank you for rescuing Claire."

"It was hardly a rescue. I know my horse and what to expect from him. There was not nearly as much danger to me as there would have been for you." He turned his head to her. "Thank you for trusting me, for trusting me to care for someone so important to you."

"I hated you so much, Gabriel." She sat up and he did too. "Almost from the beginning. When you asked me what would happen to Georges not five minutes after we left the prison. When you offered me your coat in the rain. Even when we had sex, you were such a gentleman." She laughed through tears. "You promised me tomorrow. I have not wanted tomorrow with any man, for a long, long time."

He reached over and wiped away a tear that was trickling down her cheek.

"I have known more gentlemen than you can count and you are the first that I would trust with my life." Drawing in a deep breath, Lynette let go of despair. It felt wonderful.

She shifted slightly so that he could put his arm around her. She relaxed against him and he pulled her cloak around them both as they lay back down again, this time in each other's arms.

"The stars really are lovely," she said. "I do not need to know anything about them to feel one with them."

"They are nowhere near as lovely as you are." She raised her head so she could see into his eyes, and kissed him. "You shine so brightly that you are all I can see." He kissed her.

HER LIPS WERE LIKE the rest of Lynette Gilray, soft and welcoming with a touch of spice that came to him in the way she pressed herself to him and the soft sounds of pleasure she made.

"Thank you," she said when they were both almost breathless.

For what? he thought. "I will be happy to do it again." Even as he gathered her close she whispered against his lips, "For giving me tomorrow." This kiss was sweeter, and made perfect when she said, "I love you."

They lay for a long time. Just holding each other, for his part wishing for a bed. No, not yet. He had to tell her what he had been thinking about before she came.

"Lynette, I do not think I want to study astronomy any longer. I cannot see it as a way to honor Dr. Borgos's wish, even if it was his field."

"You have come up with another idea."

"Yes. I want to study anatomy again, human physiology. To make a contribution as significant as Vesalius. Much has changed since Vesalius wrote his masterpiece. In his studies William Harvey learned immense amounts about how the heart functions, facts that make some of Vesalius's drawings obsolete."

"Yes, Dr. Schotzko pointed them out to me."

"I was thinking that, if you would like to, we could work together to prepare a new set of drawings, with the latest information available. I know several publishers who would be interested."

She pulled away from him. "You are not saying this to humor me?"

"God, no, most certainly not. Ask Jessup, my interest in physiology far surpasses my interest in astronomy. The stars were a hobby I indulged in until my father could come to his senses. He never did, but his passing ends the wait." He propped himself up on his elbow.

"Do I sound unfeeling?" Before she could answer he went on. "He was so much more concerned about how the world would see my actions. Making a contribution to science meant nothing to him. I am sad he is gone, but my life will be the fuller for it."

"If you are serious, I will do it," she said, nodding enthusiastically. "It will fulfill Dr. Borgos's urging you to make the world a better place, will it not?"

"I hope so." That story had been one of the first he had told her. Did she realize that even then her heart had been touched?

"First though, Gabriel, I must fulfill my commission for Dr. Schotzko and the other work if he wishes. It will be good practice for our own project."

He did not want to diminish the enthusiasm radiating from her, but felt compelled to be honest. "Our project will be nothing like his, but it will give both of us knowledge about what the other knows."

"I suppose you could assist me on Dr. Schotzko's project." She considered it a moment longer then nodded. "That is, if you accept that you are only in charge of the science."

"It seems to me I learned to follow your lead in a very hard school." He laughed. "Now I see that even that will prove useful."

They kissed, but the air had cooled so much that anything more than kisses was something only a fool would consider. "It is a very good thing that there is no bed in your studio and your window seat is only big enough for one."

"Gabriel, surely you realize that a bed is hardly a requirement. I will be delighted to educate you."

That she would tease him with her past was the finest gift she could give. He kissed her and in one fluid motion stood up, took her hand and pulled her to her feet and into his arms.

"I knew that I was not a true astronomer when I realized that this next moment means more to me than all the stars in the sky." As he spoke, Gabriel put his hands on her shoulders and turned her to face the first light of day. Lynette leaned against him. The sky warmed from gray to rose to gold. They stayed in that one place until the sun blinded them.

In the smallest of movements Lynette turned her head to him. "This is tomorrow," she said, her face lit with a smile that could easily be called laughter. "And it is all ours."

"This moment is blessing and commitment." Gabriel kissed her temple, kissed her smile. "Someday I would like the church's blessing, when you are ready and our children insist." That made her giggle, a sound that bewitched him. "Until then, Lynette, love is enough."

Author's Note

Illuminated transparent images were a popular art form from the middle of the eighteenth century to the middle of the nineteenth century. They were created in different mediums, among them glass, paper and cloth by artists like Gainsborough, Daguerre and Turner.

My heroine, Lynette, explored the form in cut-paper as did many of her amateur contemporaries. Most of their efforts were done in the form of silhouettes that were pasted into albums. Landscape views, like the Le Havre harbor scene, represent a talent beyond the average.

My first experience with cut-paper transparencies was at the Metropolitan Museum of Art in New York. Several visits later I am even more impressed with the talent of the unknown artist who made the cut-paper silhouettes that comprise the forty-two pieces in the Met collection. Known only as "Aunt Sophy," she probably lived in East Yorkshire during the first quarter of the nineteenth century.

My thanks to Dr. Elizabeth Barker for introducing me to the work, sharing her knowledge and sparking a significant part of Lynette's story.

The work *De Humani Corporis Fabrica* by Vesalius is one of those amazing bits of science that are equally incredible work of art. If you would like a good look at Vesalius's work, it is available online, including a turn-the-page version, a project developed by the National Library of Medicine. I first discovered *De Humani Corporis Fabrica* at the National Library of Medicine at the National Institutes of Health. Thank you to Betsy Tunis for making that possible.

Thanks also to Dr. Meg Grasselli at the National Gallery of Art for her assistance with French translation. I knew the simpler phrases, but "English pig" and "filthy traitor" were not covered in my high school French class.

As always, endless thanks to the Beau Monde Chapter of Romance Writers of America and to my writing group, Marsha Nuccio, Elaine Fox and Lavinia Klein.

One last note. Gradsbourg is a fictitious European country and Lord Richard Selwick, the man who went to Egypt with Napoleon in the name of science, is the creation of Lauren Willing in her charming book *The Secret History of the Pink Carnation*. We both agreed it would be fun to have our versions of the Regency mingle. In that world, I trust Gabriel will eventually find out that Lord Richard was a spy. In every other respect, I have done my best to accurately reflect the history of the time.

Lover's Kiss

To Ann and Deanie
The best of sisters
and
my best friends.

THE PEAK DISTRICT
DERBYSHIRE
APRIL 1816

MICHAEL GARRETT SLOWED HIS HORSE to a stop. Pulling off his gloves he put a hand on his pistol, his eyes fixed on the drift of snow twenty yards ahead.

A last touch of winter, mottled shades of white, banked against a fallen tree. Yes, spring had been slow in coming. God knew it was cold enough for patches of snow to outlast the calendar.

But snow did not move.

There were no bears or wolves, not in England. As he watched, his gun at the ready, something struggled to rise from the sheltered spot.

The bank of snow became a woman.

A naked woman. Michael holstered his gun as the ghostly figure glided away deeper into the morning mist rising through the copse of trees.

"Dear God in heaven," he prayed, urging his horse

forward. She was no vision or ghost. The woman was as solid as the branches that slapped her face as she moved deeper into the trees.

She was in trouble. Terrible trouble. Her white flesh was covered with dirt as if she'd spent days wandering the forest. Five minutes ago he had been on his way to Manchester. It appeared that his plans had just changed.

"Are you lost?" he called out.

With a sound that was not human, she tried to run. After no more than ten feet she staggered and collapsed, falling to the ground with brutal momentum.

She could be running from him. Or from someone else. Michael stopped his horse again. With the fog wet against his face, he concentrated, listening for sight or sound of another person. The heavy quiet added to the mystery, but he heard nothing, sensed nothing.

To hell with caution. She was a woman in distress, not a French agent. He dismounted and ran the last few feet as though three seconds would make a difference.

Michael came upon her sprawled facedown in the dirt. She was not quite naked but wearing a thin shift. Despite her very short hair there was no doubt of her sex. The linen was wet and clung to the curve of her back, the robust shape of her hips.

Squatting down, Michael turned her over. She felt brittle, like a fallen leaf that had lost all its color. Despite the steady movement of her chest Michael wondered if nature had already won. If she was so cold that it would be impossible to warm her enough to save her life.

Helping her could well bring him the kind of trouble he

was doing his best to avoid. Even as he lifted her, he considered the idea.

If she was mad, she would not thank him for the rescue. If she was lost, she might be grateful. If she was worse than lost, thrown like rubbish and left for dead, someone might take issue with his efforts. Rescuers were not always heroes. A hard-learned truth, courtesy of Napoleon's war.

He swore halfheartedly, disgusted that he gave any thought to leaving her. Even if she was facing death she deserved better than to be left to the animals.

As he held her, she moved. Michael hoped that she was waking up, but her eyes remained closed. The movement was no more than a convulsive shudder. It was a perverse relief that she still could shiver, that her body was not so cold it was shutting down completely.

Energy replaced confusion. Action suited him better than uncertainty. He stood up, looking about for a way to warm her quickly.

The fallen tree would do. The side facing south would give them shelter and sun. The spring sun, though weak, would be better than clouds and rain. He would wrap her in his greatcoat and build a fire.

He could wish it was warmer, but if he wished for that why not wish for a house to appear with help at hand? He would deal with what he had; improvising had been a way of life for years.

Sliding his arm under her shoulders and his other arm under her knees, Michael lifted her. As he did, her head lolled back, exposing her neck to the morning light. He stood up abruptly when he saw the nasty, purpling bruises on her throat. It made his own ache in sympathy.

"I am in England," he whispered, closing his eyes. This woman was not much more than a girl. He knew well that youth did not guarantee innocence, but he did not want to consider what she had done to earn such vengeance and be left for dead.

Michael set her down on the ground in the shelter of the fallen tree, then spread his coat in the hollow.

Bending over her he watched her short shivering breaths. Keep breathing, he begged.

He was about to lift her into his arms again when he realized that the wet shift was adding to her chill. Thinking only of her survival, he ripped the fabric away. Her sweet body was not a girl's, but a woman's. Ignoring the rush of awareness, he looked for bruises or evidence of brutality. There were none, only the bruises on her neck. Nor was there any blood.

It was awkward but he settled her on his coat in the recess, wrapping the voluminous wool around her, covering her feet and tucking the fabric tightly. He watched her as he gathered wood. One thing was for sure; he would not know any more until she told him.

A naked woman didn't give many clues to her identity.

An *unconscious* naked woman even fewer.

He hoped that the memories hinted at by her bruised throat were not as sordid as the injury, that she wouldn't hate him for saving her life.

It didn't matter what she thought. Helping her was a purely selfish act. A way to convince himself that he had some humanity left. Saving a life was a good place to begin. He let out a breath of laughter. Saving someone who would rather be dead would be an ironic quirk of fate.

He built the fire with the efficiency of long practice. When he was done, he came close and crouched beside her. She would warm more quickly if his body was next to hers. It would be even more effective if his naked body was next to hers, but there was more than one reason that was a bad idea. If someone were to find them, nudity would leave him at a decided disadvantage.

Even if no one found them, the two of them naked was an invitation to trouble which was as far as he would allow his imagination to go. She was at death's door. Had been brutalized in ways he had yet to learn. He was not going to add to that even in his thoughts.

Unwrapping her and rewrapping both of them in his greatcoat was a clumsy process. She was completely limp, her fingers and toes blue with cold. He arranged her body as if she were a life-sized doll and cradled her head in the crook of his shoulder. Her hair smelled like cinnamon and spices, an odd perfume but as comforting as it was appealing.

The next step would have to wait until she was conscious. He would take her home, of course. But if home wasn't an option he was at a loss.

He could hear his colonel's voice deep in his memory, damn him, insisting that preparation was pointless unless you had some sense of the enemy's purpose. The colonel had been a gross caricature of an officer, but in this one thing the man had been right. Before anything else, Michael would need to know who was friend and who was foe and where they were.

Not here, he was sure of that. There were no sounds of humans in the area, no twigs broken or leaves crunched. He'd been watching before and seen no sign of anyone else on horseback.

Pulling his hand out from under their covering, he found his gun deep in the pocket of the greatcoat. He laid it on the ground behind her where he could reach it easily, but it would not alarm her.

Michael began to pick away the small pieces of leaf and bark on her face. Her long eyelashes lay heavily on her pale, almost blue cheeks. Her lips were full, her nose short and determined, her ears—. Oh hell, the woman was freezing to death and he was trying to find a word to describe her ears. "Fragile shells" popped into his head and he swore out loud.

Despite the fragile shells and long eyelashes, someone wanted her to be lost and never found. She could be a prostitute who'd irritated a customer, a thief who had stolen from the wrong person or a lady's maid who had asked for more than her wellborn lover was willing to give.

He could see where she would be well nigh irresistible. Youth and lush curves would draw male attention whether she spent her time in the servant's quarters or the salon.

Distract yourself, Michael. She is more a wounded animal than a woman. He shifted her so that she was not pressing against him so suggestively.

She stirred a little and did nothing to ease that discomfort when she moved closer, pressing her face into his neck, her soft brown curls tickling his chin.

Leaning back, he raised his head and watched the breeze stir the budding branches as the sun rose completely. There was no moment but this one. In the slanting rays of dawn he could see flittering insects he never would have noticed. Sitting so still he could hear his horse nibbling grass, some small animal chittering a message. A bird flew by carrying a twig to its nest.

He shouldn't have fallen asleep but he did, dreaming an odd assortment of scenes, most of them erotic, involving a wood nymph who claimed his heart and shared her world of pleasure, light, happiness. She shared her body and her mind without hesitation and at last offered him her heart. He took it and dropped it, by accident or on purpose, he was not sure. It broke nonetheless and all she could do was stare at him as she began to fade away.

A rusty whisper roused him from his half-sleep. He guessed it was midday. It was cloudy now and there was no sun to use as a timepiece.

Michael could see that she was waking. Good. He was chilled through. He needed to add more wood to the fire.

She began to struggle, pressing her hands into his chest, trying to push her body away from his. That she had any strength at all amazed him. The panic he felt in her struggles made him realize that the rusty whisper was all the screaming she was capable of.

He held her still, hoping he was not bruising her more. "You're safe. I have you safe," he spoke softly. "I rescued you." She would not listen or could not hear through her terror. That she would not surrender to him, seemed intent on escape, made him rethink what had happened to her. Very possibly something worse than the bruises on her throat.

He repeated his words in a stronger voice. She paused for a moment and he thought he had reached her. As he relaxed his grip, she raised her foot and tried to unman him. Her aim was off and she only bruised his thigh. Pushing his greatcoat off her shoulders she aimed for his eyes with her hand curled into a claw. He grabbed her fingers and held them with his one free hand. Her other hand was pressed against him and he held her as tightly as he could, in a mockery of an embrace.

All in silence now, the only sound her ragged breathing and rusty screams.

"I will not let you go. You have no clothes. It is cold; you will die before you find safety."

As she raised her eyes to his, he saw the promise that he would die with her. God help him, he had to convince her.

It was Troy who calmed her. His horse came toward them and nudged the girl's head with her nose. Why it worked Michael had no idea, but the girl stilled her breathless struggles.

"I found you here in the woods," he explained. "You needed help."

She made no answer. The shivers were gone but fear had her as tense as a bowstring.

"I found you . . ." he said again. Before he said more she made a noise that was close to "Yes," and raised a hand to her throat.

"It looks like someone tried to strangle you. You will have bruises for awhile."

She nodded, her eyes glistening with tears.

"Did you escape?"

"I woke up." Her voice was as much a whisper as her screams had been.

"You woke up. You mean you were asleep?" That argued for a prostitute at odds with her customer or a lover tired of her demands.

"Not asleep. Drugged." She drew in a deep breath that became a quivering sob.

Were you raped? Why ask. It hardly mattered. She had been grossly violated in some way. He did not need to add to her torment. Instead he asked the most pressing question of all.

"Were you followed? Will they be trying to find you?"

2

THE GIRL SHUDDERED at his question, shook her head and stretched away from him so she could see down the path. "No." Then, "I hope not."

"Was it one man or more?" he asked. If they were on her trail he would be prepared.

She held up her hand with two fingers extended.

"There were only two? Good. Two I can handle."

She gave a nod that was more of a shiver.

"We need warmth more than we need to hide. I am going to add more wood to the fire."

"My shift?" she asked in that rusty hard-used voice.

"I'm sorry. I had to take it off."

Tears began trickling down her cheeks. "Why?"

"I don't know why they took your clothes, miss, but your shift was filthy and soaked through. Ruined. You can have my coat while I start the fire." He wiped her tears with his finger. "I have an extra shirt I can give you as well, but there is no way around what must happen next."

She nodded with more resignation than embarrassment.

Michael moved quickly so that neither one of them had time to think about it. He stood up. The coat fell around them. She turned her body into his and shut her eyes as if what she did not see could not embarrass her.

Keeping her pressed close, he grabbed his coat from the ground and wrapped it around her naked body. Not a prostitute, he decided. Too modest. That left about a dozen other unsavory possibilities. He lowered her back into the hollowed tree, and began to stand.

The sound of a branch cracking caught both their attention. With a gesture for her to stay hidden he stood up, but saw no sign of life other than his horse, grazing on what little the ground had to offer. Troy would not be so disinterested if there were strangers nearby.

When he stepped away, the girl grabbed his boot.

"Stay." The word held fear and command at once. "Do not leave me."

"I will not leave." He crouched down so that she could see his face. "I am staying. Right now I am only going to find more wood to add to the fire." He took both her hands and pressed them together, his hands covering hers easily. "I promise. I will see you to safety."

She nodded and leaned back against the fallen tree, never taking her eyes from him.

"There are plenty of small branches from the winter," he said as he stood up and began to collect them. "And an endless supply of twigs." He looked back to where she sat.

She had her eyes closed now, so he stopped talking, but the moment the silence stretched out longer than one would need to take a breath, she opened her eyes and looked for him. That was just as well. If she went to sleep now, she would probably never wake up. It was not his usual style, but he would keep on talking if that's what it took to keep her awake and alive.

"I'm on my way to Manchester. Word on this side of the Peak is that the town is growing. The roads and canals are filled with goods." He dumped the wood onto a spot about three feet from the hungry fire. "The factories are always looking for help. Straightforward, honest work. It will kill me in a fortnight."

She did not react to his joke, but he kept on talking.

"It's incredible the number of factories that are springing up all over the Midlands. No matter how hard the Luddites fight it, the towns will change and grow in spite of their opposition. That, of course, will increase the need for coal. I'm counting on there being work for all the able-bodied. I know there are too many retired soldiers and not enough work. If there are no positions in the city, I will look in the mines."

He glanced up from the wood he was stacking to make sure she was awake. She was wide-eyed, from shock most likely, but she nodded and he blathered on.

"I'd thought to look for work in Pennsford or at the castle itself." As he sorted the wood he kept an unwieldy pile of small branches in case the fire faded again. "Do you know Pennsford?"

A single nod was all she gave him, but she had answered his question.

"How typically English that the town is called Pennsford and the castle, not a quarter mile away, is Pennford."

He stood up and warmed himself front and back before heading off to collect more wood.

"I've been three weeks traveling there from Sussex. After no more than a day in Pennsford I find that it will not suit me at all. The world revolves around the Duke of Meryon. Pennsford is even named after the family, the Pennistans."

She was watching him over the back of the fallen tree, her eyes all that he could see. He had all her attention.

"Do I sound like a revolutionary?" He tried for an apologetic tone but he was feeling more righteous than diffident. "I've had enough of men who think a title makes them smarter or better than the rest. Years fighting Napoleon has cured me of idol worship. I know he's on St. Helena now, but not before he started a war that killed thousands and left even more lives disrupted."

He came back to their campsite with an ambitious armful of wood and dropped it with a grunt. He brushed off his jacket and pants.

"The Duke of Meryon may not want to take over the world, but even Derbyshire is more than I can stand. I wonder what kind of dictators I'll find in Manchester."

Her expression was more cautious than trusting. *End the rant, Garrett,* he commanded himself. *You'll have her thinking you are ready to do murder and she's come close enough to that for a lifetime.*

As the flames grew more greedy, Michael added more wood. "The fire doesn't have to be big. The tree will capture the heat and we will be as warm as a . . . cat sunning itself."

He'd almost used a much more crude analogy. He was not in the army, and for all he knew she could be the local squire's innocent daughter. That was his best guess.

She was no daughter of the ton. Her hands were used to work, though well cared for. Her hair was too short for fashion, not cut with any sense of style. Her sweet compact body was of sturdy yeoman stock, not the delicate constitution of a girl about to make her bow.

He brushed off his hands and came to her.

She leaned away from him, actually held up her hands as though that could stop him. He had become a villain again.

"What is it? I told you that I would see you to safety and I mean it." As he spoke he stood up and backed away from her. Never mind that he had held her in his arms for hours. She did not want him close now. "You need to be warm first, and rested enough to go however far we must go. It is imperative or you will die. Do you understand me?"

She nodded.

"As soon as you are ready to travel we will find a way to your family."

She did not respond. He hoped it was from the pain in her throat and not because she was taking ill.

"Will you tell me your name and where you live?"

Closing her eyes, she made a little sound that was something between a moan and a word. He watched her swallow very carefully and after a very long pause she opened her eyes and spoke. "Big Sam?"

"Your name is Big Sam?" He could not help the smile. "I think not. You are a lovely armful but hardly big and much too pretty to be called Sam."

She narrowed her eyes as though the compliment was a threat.

"Spare your voice and tell me your name."

"Lollie." When he didn't answer she straightened and said it again. "Lollie," this time with an expression that dared him to deny it.

"Lollie and Big Sam make an interesting combination, a yeoman farmer and his bride or fiancée?"

She shook her head.

"It does not matter who Big Sam is. I wish he was here too. He could lend a hand and fill me in on a few of the missing details."

A nod this time.

"Miss Lollie-the-cautious, I would much prefer your full name. There is no reason to lie to me unless you are the one in the wrong here, or Big Sam will beat you for disobeying him." Any life was worth saving but his heroics were cheapened if this was no more than a lover's spat.

Her eyes flashed with anger as he'd hoped. "Sam would never hurt me." She raised her hand to her throat, and finished. "Or leave me."

She lay back again and closed her eyes. It was those eyes that gave her face such life. With them closed she had the air of a cherub. It was not an entirely misplaced description, though her efforts to hit him where it would hurt most were proof enough that there were moments when spitfire was more appropriate.

So his woodland maid was married to Big Sam. Or he was her beau. Hopefully Big Sam *was* big and they would hear him coming. If he was trying to find her. If he was not, if

Big Sam was home in his bed sound asleep, the man deserved to be beaten to a pulp, and Michael would be happy to be the one to do it. He could not think of a punishment bad enough for a man who would leave a woman like this.

Pushing the image of a bloody Big Sam to the back of his mind, Michael bowed to her.

"Do Lollie and Big Sam have a last name?"

She was confused for a minute, then uncertain and finally resolved. Her eyes spoke for her. She shook her head, unwilling or afraid to share any more.

"It will be Lollie for now." He could do better than the made-up "Lollie" without even thinking about it: *Captain Raoul Desseau, French guard captain. Now retired.*

He was done with lies, Michael reminded himself, and Raoul was part of his past. He was going to speak only the truth now, though it might well kill him in a week if work did not.

"How do you do, Miss Lollie? My name is Michael Garrett."

HE _SAID_ HIS NAME was Michael Garrett and he was here to rescue her. How very convenient.

Olivia bit her lip to keep from crying. In her worst nightmare she had never conjured an experience this humiliating. To be found in the woods, naked. By a man. Was it better that he was a complete stranger? She wiped away the tears trickling down her cheek.

They were somewhere in the Peak, she was sure of that. No one came this way before June. The hills were treacherous until the last of the snow. Everyone knew that.

Olivia curled up inside his coat, pushing herself farther into the corner where the fallen tree lay close to the stump. Would someone need to rescue her from her rescuer?

Her throbbing throat was a reminder that she could take care of herself. She had escaped once. She would do it again if she had to.

The men who took her had insisted that her near strangling was a mistake. If she had not fought them it never
would have happened. Anger trumped fear.

Of course she fought. What did they expect her to do?
Wait to be raped and murdered? When they had forced the
laudanum on her she almost wished she would not wake up.

Michael Garrett could not be his true name. There was
an air of authority about him that was at odds with such a
simple name and the way he was dressed.

He had the look of a gentleman fallen on hard times. His
greatcoat was nothing more than practical, his horse well
formed, but the ugliest piebald mare Olivia had ever seen,
with coloring that was a nauseating puzzle of orange-brown
and white pieces fitted against each other.

In spite of his ugly horse and his worn clothes, he was
most definitely in charge of the situation. When he had held
her, she felt as though escape was hopeless. She was not even
sure she wanted to escape. What kind of magic was that?

Even nature was cooperating with him. There was no
rain for the first time in days and the wet wood was burning
bright and hot as if responding to his orders.

The heat was a small piece of heaven, reminding her of
cold mornings when the kitchen was the only comfortable
spot in the house. Her toes and hands were warm for the first
time since she was taken; she wiggled them without fear that
they were frozen and would break off. For this heat alone she
would be grateful to him, even if Michael Garrett was not as
innocent as he said he was.

It was not long before her feet were actually too warm so
she pulled them under the coat and rubbed them up and

down her calf, sitting in a tight little ball, doing her best not to shiver.

How was she to be sure he wasn't one of them? If he was, he was surely their leader.

Fear sharpened her anger, fueling her wits.

His accent was not at all like her captors'. She heard no hint of where he was from in his English, as though he had learned from someone who insisted that he speak the language perfectly.

That was a sign that he was more than he pretended to be. Who spoke that way unless he was from another country or had spent so many years away, speaking another language, that English had become the foreign one?

He worked the saddlebag open, and she watched him pull out a flask. He uncorked it as he walked back to her. "This is brandy. It will burn but I think the liquid will help ease your throat."

With a vigorous shake of her head Olivia refused it.

"It will help warm you," he insisted.

Drug her, more likely.

She had not spoken aloud but he heard her nonetheless. "Ahh. You're worried that I slipped something into it. That I am going to drug you again." He took a good long drink himself, then lifted her hand and slapped the flask into her palm. "It is harmless. That is, as harmless as brandy can be. Since I am not a wealthy man I have watered it some."

Desperate to soothe her throat, Olivia accepted it. Lifting the leather-covered bottle, she wiped the mouth with the cuff of his coat and tasted the brandy. It went down with welcome ease, the warmth spreading through her instantly, aided by the intimacy of drinking from the same bottle.

"You've had brandy before?" he asked.

She nodded, though it was hardly any of his concern.

"Hold on to it, but use it sparingly. I'll find my shirt." He rummaged through his bag again.

Staring at the fire, Olivia did her best to ignore a simmering panic, to convince herself that he did not mean her harm.

Could he be a soldier? He wasn't wearing a Waterloo medal or even a uniform and looked nothing like the troops that had been stationed in Derby.

But somehow he had the look of one. She watched him move around his horse and closed her eyes. He wore his clothes with pride, as if he had worn a uniform and not because he was a dandy. If he was one of those stupid London fops he would be complaining about the dirt or how she was treating his greatcoat. Instead he was working steadily to find ways to warm her, to keep her alive. Why?

Or had he been a spy? That would account for the too-perfect English. He was a Frenchman who had spent years in England and was afraid of prosecution if he was caught.

That was absurd. Blame that on the brandy. Drinking it always brought her imagination to life. Though it was wonderful for cooking.

Oh dear, everyone would be worried. Her brothers would pretend all was well but everyone would know that something was wrong. Like when Papa had died. Missing for those two days before they found him at the bottom of Pensey Gorge. A horrible accident. Would they think something like that had happened to her? It was bad enough she wasn't there to cook for them but even worse to cause such upset.

Low-voiced words shocked her from her thoughts. Olivia jerked her head around to see who else was with them. It was only Mr. Garrett whispering to his horse. She took a good long look at him as he continued searching through his belongings.

There were other clues that he had once been in uniform. He appeared to have spent a lot of time in the open. His face was tanned, his body hard-muscled.

He talked to his horse. That didn't count. She talked to hers. As she had the thought, his horse gave a soft snort and nodded. Olivia might talk to Medina but she had never answered.

Mr. Garrett lifted his head at the sound of a bird call and watched as a linnet swooped by. He was aware of movement around him as if he suspected that attack or discovery was imminent.

With his extra shirt in hand he came to her. He wasn't threatening. Not really. His presence was overwhelming. Even when doing something as simple as handing her his shirt she felt his power.

She knew how to handle men like that. She had four brothers, all of them tall and strong. Even before they spoke they were intimidating.

All that she had to do was look him straight in the eye and insist on her own way as often as possible. If she were at home she would find out his favorite foods and make them often enough to win him over.

But looking this man straight in the eye was not as easy

as it should be. He did not look away or shift his gaze. Indeed it felt as though there was some sort of contest going on, and the victor would win something more important than a fruit tart. When he realized what she was doing, he smiled a little. Not a patronizing smile, a sweet one as though he thought she was pretty and could look into her eyes forever.

She let him win and studied his face. Not perfectly handsome, but very—um—attractive was the word. There was a small scar on his cheek and a tiny bit of his earlobe was gone. The injury made him look seasoned, as though he had seen more of the world than was healthy. His eyes were hard, which made him more compelling, not less.

"I saw some more pieces of wood behind the fall. I won't be far away." Putting his shirt into her outstretched hand, he disappeared around the stump, whistling a little.

She did not take off his coat but struggled into the shirt under its cover. He could smile and speak noble words forever, but how did she really know that he was not one of them?

Should she try to escape? She had no shoes and no more than his greatcoat. Home was due south. At least she thought it was.

No matter how close home was, her kidnappers could still be between her and safety. The swoop of dread that came with that possibility made the company of Mr. Michael Garrett a risk worth taking at least for a little while longer.

Olivia forgot escape as she pulled his shirt over her head and realized her hair had been cut. Feeling the blunt, ragged ends along her neckline, she pulled again and again as if tugging would make it grow. Her hair, please not her hair. She began to cry in earnest.

"What is it?" He was beside her again in a moment.

Olivia put her head on her raised knees and pretended he could not see her.

"What is it, Lollie?" He sounded confused and angry.

"My hair," she rasped. "It's been cut."

If her throat did not hurt so much she could tell him that it was her one great beauty. She was short and stocky, her breasts were too big, her face too round, but her hair had been lovely and thick and long, her one joy. "Why?"

"Ah, not something life-threatening." He spoke as if calming himself and stood up. "It will grow back."

"Grow back?" She struggled to her feet. "It will take years." She threw off his greatcoat and leaped on him, wrapping her legs around his waist as she screeched the last words. She tried to scratch his face, all the while yelling in what was no more than a hoarse whisper, "If you are one of them, I will kill you!"

She hated him. Hated all men.

4

LOLLIE WAS A WHIRLWIND OF RAGE. Using as little force as possible, Michael tried, for the second time today, to avoid her kicks and subdue her.

He grabbed his greatcoat from the ground and swaddled her in it, trapping her arms and legs. She did her best to push him down and trample him. He pulled her down with him and rolled on top of her. He was annoyed that he was panting, almost out of breath.

She was gasping, too, and he moved off her a little.

"Rape me and I will kill myself and haunt you forever." She started coughing and he saw the desperation in her eyes.

He stood up as fast as he could. She tried to stand but fell to her knees, her head down as a coughing fit ended her tantrum. Michael thought she would hack her insides out, but he waited it out, hoping that it did not make her sick.

When she could finally draw a breath without consequence she sat back on her heels, scrabbled for the brandy flask and took a sip, only a sip. When it went down smoothly, she took another. Finally she found the strength to stand up.

"Listen to me." As he spoke Michael backed away from her. "Listen to me, Lollie. No one has ever accused me of rape. No one ever will. Do you hear me?"

She gathered his coat around her and pulled it up in front so that she could walk without tripping over it.

"I am leaving, Mr. Garrett."

"We are both leaving. Later," he corrected.

Without comment, Lollie headed for the path. She had gone about three yards when Michael realized that she might actually walk off. He could tell by her careful pace that her feet were paining her and he knew that in less than an hour she would be shivering again.

"Miss Lollie, come back!"

"Why?" She looked over her shoulder as she spoke.

"Because you will not survive by yourself."

She shrugged as though that did not matter anymore, and kept on walking.

"Please, wait a minute," he called, letting the distance between them lengthen.

She stopped but kept her back to him.

"Tell me, why in the world do you think I mean you harm?" he asked.

"Finding me was not an accident."

He waited. Finally she turned around. "No one comes this way so early in the spring." She sipped some more of the brandy and slid the bottle into the pocket. "Unless they are running away or determined to hide somewhere."

His throat hurt just listening to the rasp but he let her talk. He would not force her to do anything until he had to.

"Higher up there are drifts you could die in." She began collecting stones and sliding them into the other pocket. When she looked at him her expression was so challenging that Michael wondered if she understood that she was the one in grave danger. Not him.

"I didn't know about that. I'm from Sussex." He kicked a branch lying in the path. "This looks dry enough here."

"If you are not one of them, why is there no one else searching?"

"I wonder the same. Since you know more about the men who did this, why don't you tell me?" He took a few steps toward her.

She turned and began walking again.

"Can you tell me, how far away is the place where you were held?" He ran up beside her.

"I have no idea. The drug would not leave me." She stopped and turned, put her hand on her throat and shook her head at her body's weakness. Obviously she was not done speaking even if her voice protested the abuse. "You could be their leader. Angry because I escaped."

"Do you read the novels of Mrs. Radcliffe?" He wanted to laugh, but reminded himself that she had good reason to be suspicious of strangers.

"You were a soldier, were you not?"

He was going to deny it when he recalled his vow of honesty. "What makes you say that?"

"I can tell. You are disillusioned because you cannot find work. You have kidnapped me as a kind of revenge and to make money."

She began to cough and pulled out the brandy. She opened the cap and took the smallest sip.

"The brandy seems to have made you fantastical. That is absurd." Michael came a few steps closer and sat on a fallen log, pretending to relax. "You are not completely wrong about me. I am a retired soldier, but I was disillusioned long before I came home, in fact before I even went to France. I have learned to live with it. It is not something for which I seek revenge. Not at all. I have skills. I have prospects. I do not need to rely on kidnapping to support myself."

Lollie began to collect bigger stones.

"If you truly thought I was one of the fiends that took you, why would you confront me with it? It would be far wiser to keep it to yourself."

"What does it matter, if you intend to kill me?" She did not look up from the stones she was gathering and he wondered how she could seem so calm discussing her own death.

"Why do you think I would do such a thing?" He was appalled all over again.

"I've seen your face." She raised her eyes to his and stared at him as though once again committing his features to memory so she could accuse him when he faced God.

"I have the look of a murderer, do I? Now there is an insult." He waited. Soldiers killed. It could well be etched in the lines in his face.

"Not your looks," she said as though the idea was

something an idiot would think. "Once you have the money, you will not allow me to live, because I can identify you. Mind you, they will not pay a ransom. Someone will rescue me and Big Sam will kill you by breaking every bone in your body. It will be a slow horrible death." The whisper gave out with the last of her diatribe and she raised a hand to wipe her eyes.

She looked and sounded all of fourteen and he made a note to try to recover his flask and keep it away from her. "I assure you, Miss Lollie, I am not a kidnapper and am not courting death." She continued to collect stones, ignoring him and weighing each one in her hand before adding it to her collection. "Do you understand me, madame? I am your rescuer."

He stood up and was about to say it again, louder, in case she was going deaf, when something else she had said struck him. "You did not see your abductors?"

"I was blindfolded the entire time." Her confidence faded away as she spoke.

"Lollie of Derbyshire." He took a step toward her, one step, and stopped when she held up her hand. He stayed where he was and held out his hands instead. "Please believe that it is my only goal to see you safe and home with your family. I swear this on my mother's grave. If I meant you ill, why would I rescue you, give you my coat, build you a fire and share my brandy? If I was trying to show my confederates how to deal with you, where are they?" He looked around. "I am doing my best to treat you with the care and respect a woman deserves."

The ground fascinated her. She stared at it for a long time, until he thought she must see something more than dirt and dead leaves. Without looking at him, she finally whispered, "All right." Her chin quivered. "All right," she said again. "It's that stupid brandy," she muttered. She wiped her eyes. "My feet are so cold."

Not waiting for any more of a concession, Michael walked back to the fire. "Come back to your little nest. I will leave the fire between you and me. I can even give you my pistol if it will make you feel safer. Have you ever shot one?"

"I have brothers." Despite the tear-swollen eyes she walked gingerly back toward the fire. "Of course I've used a pistol." She sniffed and shifted her eyes from his just before she spoke.

He could tell she was lying. She had never held a pistol in her life. She might have brothers though. Lollie was part pampered princess and part tomboy.

"With brothers, I imagine you are adept at defending yourself." He came closer to give his pistol to her, then stepped back. "It is not loaded, but I will hand it over to you so you know that it cannot be used against you."

She took it with both hands, lowered herself to the ground and, without a thought for modesty, stuck her feet out toward the fire. *How much of the discoloring was dirt and how much was bruising?*

He watched as she began to pull out the stones she'd collected and pile them up within easy reach. They wouldn't kill anyone, but they would hurt.

"Do you think that the men who took me have not even

tried to find me?" She looked up, her eyes confused and dis-believing. "Do you think that they have left me for dead?"

His heart ached at the question. "No, I do not. I think any moment they could come upon us. And you are an odd one if that comforts you."

"It is only that before today my biggest worry was when the strawberries would be ripe." She smiled a little.

It was such a sad smile that Michael wondered if all her innocence had been destroyed.

"Lollie, I will hear them before they are within sight and my horse will know before that."

She nodded slowly.

"Good. That is one less thing you have to worry about." He put more wood on the fire and broke some of the branches into more manageable pieces. Just when he thought that she might have drifted off to sleep again, she spoke.

"No one will recognize me with my hair so short."

Michael was not sure this was a worry he had an answer for. "Your new curls are very charming."

She did no more than nod.

"I thought it was some new style."

"New style?" She gave an unladylike sniff which he was sure was meant as an insult to his understanding of the latest fashion.

Maybe he could provoke her out of her misery. "I beg your pardon, Miss Lollie-the-condescending, I may not be Beau Brummell, but I do have eyes. The way women look is one thing a man will always notice."

"Men only look at the dress to gauge the body it covers."

Lollie did not blush, though she did pull the brandy out again.

"I think you should give me that." He gestured to the flask. "It would seem that spirits make you irritable."

The huff of temper she let out made her cough. "I have been taken by force, near strangled and had my hair cut off. I have no idea what is happening in the kitchen or if Cook has one of her headaches." She kept on, even though her voice was wearing out. "I don't know how I am going to escape ruin. I assure you, Mr. Garrett, watered brandy has only a little to do with why I am irritable." Leaning back, Lollie closed her eyes. He waited while she did her best to control a spate of coughing. When she had finished she added, "And I don't know if I will ever be able to speak normally again."

"I stand chastened. Clearly brandy is the least of it." He bowed a little and sat down with the blanket he had found in his pack. "Please do not test your voice anymore. Rest is in order. We will wait until late afternoon to travel. There will be fewer people about and more shadow to hide in. For now I will stay on this side of the fire and keep watch."

He added two more pieces of wood to the blaze and sat cross-legged. "I will find a way to save you from ruin and preserve your reputation as well. I promise that I will not abandon you. Soldiers keep their word."

"I already have a plan." She raised her hand to cover a yawn. It must have hurt her throat because he watched her stop and do her best to swallow the yawn instead. She closed her eyes and was asleep.

Watching her breathing deepen and her body relax

he sorted through the parts that made up Miss Lollie-the-secretive. The cultured accent he could hear even though she whispered, her worry for her reputation told him she was more wellborn than he originally thought. He could only guess at her age. At least seventeen. Her concern for the kitchen suggested lady of the house. She wore no ring. Of course that could have been stolen but still there was no mark where a ring would have been. She was too young to be a housekeeper.

Being taken for ransom seemed the most likely explanation for her abduction. If there was enough wealth in her family to make the risk worthwhile.

Her hands were used to work but felt well cared for, which did not argue for great wealth. Were her brothers all bachelors and she no more than a glorified servant? Most of all he wanted to know how Big Sam fit into her life. He could be the villain or the hero of the piece.

Lollie of Derbyshire was a puzzle. He would defend her, but he would need more of the puzzle before he could guarantee her reputation could be salvaged.

He kept his promises. His years of spying had challenged his honor and compromised his self-respect, but he had kept his promises, obeyed orders passed from both of his commands.

When the colonel told him what ships were coming into the port at Le Havre and what the cargo was, he would pass the information on to his contact. That task complete he would turn around and do everything in his power to see that the ship and what it carried was protected.

For five years he had lived the tangled lie that was Raoul

Desseau, but beneath it all Michael Garrett had stayed sane by demanding Raoul share his sense of right and wrong, of honor and honesty.

Now he had no one to please but himself. He swore Lollie would not suffer for it.

LOLLIE, LOLLIE, WAKE UP. We have to move, find shelter."

She came awake with a start and pulled the gun from her pocket in the same instant, her dark green eyes wide with panic. "Do not come near me or I will shoot."

"You have no bullets." He could take the gun from her, but that would only confirm her worst fears.

"I will brain you with it. Move away." She blinked twice. The panic ebbed, replaced by resolve. Lollie did not have to use her wounded voice; he knew what she felt by reading her oh-so-expressive eyes.

"I will not make you surrender it, Lollie, but there is wind and I suspect weather coming with it. Look." He gestured to the sky. As they watched, a gust whipped the empty branches into a devil-driven dance.

"The wind makes the fire ineffective, if not dangerous.

We should find a place that is more protected. If it settles into a gale it can freeze us as quickly as rain or snow."

"What time is it?" She lowered the gun, her eyes confused and a little worried.

"I don't have a timepiece but it is not as late as it looks. You have been asleep for perhaps an hour." As he spoke another gust of wind came and went.

"We have an hour or so until dark comes on. Let me help you up on Troy and we will find a cave or a cabin—there must be something around here for the shepherds."

The sound of a tree falling somewhere in the distance seemed to convince her as thoroughly as anything he had to say. Lollie grabbed a handful of her stones and dumped them into her pocket as she scrambled to her feet.

"You had best ride astride. It will not be very comfortable but it will be safer on this uneven ground."

She nodded and hurried towards Troy, his greatcoat trailing behind her like an unwieldy train.

With a glance at Troy's ears, Lollie stood on her tiptoes and spoke to Michael in a whisper, this time a deliberate one. "This is a very ugly horse."

Michael smiled at her. It was not news to him. Actually he was relieved that she could notice something beyond her own misery.

"Troy is beautiful in every way except for coloring, which we think is simply a style that is not yet appreciated. She is the finest horse you will ever ride." He drew Troy closer to introduce them to each other. "She was a gift from a friend who died at Waterloo."

"Oh, I'm sorry," Her regret was so sincere that he felt his

eyes sting. "I hope you tell people that when they first meet Troy. It will keep your friend alive in many more hearts than yours. What was his name? Your friend."

"Jackson. Major Thomas Needham Jackson." Michael raised his hand to his forehead, covering one eye, his thumb resting on his cheek.

"My—" She coughed and started again. "Matilda Elderton. Tildy. She is the reason I know brandy better than I should. Even for that she was the finest person I have ever known. Ever."

"Please stop taxing your voice."

"It sounds worse than it feels," she said as though that meant using it would cause no further damage. Maybe she was right.

Lollie approached the horse, giving Troy her palm. The horse nuzzled her fingers and bowed her head, as if in a polite greeting. Lollie curtseyed back and started a laugh which turned into a cough. Even while she coughed her eyes were alight with pleased surprise. When she recovered Lollie asked, "Did you train her to do that?"

"No. She is a genius, as I said."

"The same way people can appear one way and be something else entirely."

Oh, the truth of that, Michael thought. She had the lush and inviting curves of a farm girl or a dairymaid and he was almost sure she was neither. Any more than he was the knight rescuer he wanted her to believe he was. A gust of wind so strong it whistled reminded them that this was not the time for conversation.

"There is no mounting block. I will have to help you with a leg-up."

Lollie did not answer, but came up to Troy and laid her head on the horse's neck. Troy whinnied encouragement.

"I wish people were as honest as horses." Sad eyes now. Defeated.

"Yes," he had to agree. "Even with the mean horses you know where you stand."

Lollie abruptly abandoned the comfort of Troy's neck. Michael linked his hands together and stooped so that she could step into the lift. Her foot was small and as cold as a piece of marble. That was all he would allow himself to notice.

Lollie grabbed the saddle and pulled herself up and over with surprising strength. It took her a few moments to settle into the saddle with his coat under her. It was so long that it covered her feet. He hoped that would keep her warm enough.

She straightened and ignored the way the wind was ruffling her hair. "If she is a mare why do you call her Troy?"

"It is short for Helen of Troy. I will explain later." He could already feel the cold in his feet. Time was the enemy. "I came up through the woods, Miss Lollie. I have not seen a road since I left Pennsford."

"South." She shook her head. "Only I do not know which way that is."

South made sense. North or east would take them into the Dark Peak. "The weather always comes from the west so we will let the wind be our compass point."

"Oh, very good, Mr. Garrett."

"Old soldiers are good for something."

She did not answer him. Or perhaps she had not heard him. The gusts were strong enough to whip the words from his mouth. Michael kept the wind to his right. His right ear grew numb within the first minutes.

He jumped when he heard a branch crack and plummet down, taking others as it fell, hitting the ground with a resounding thump, not fifty yards from where they were.

As he pushed a tree limb out of their path, he made a list of what he should be grateful for. They did not have to walk into the wind. It was not snowing. Or raining. He moved along hoping they would find a road or, please God, a house with a generous host.

Neither one of them spoke. He watched for falling branches, keeping track of trees and where they came down. It was so constant that after a while he did not even look to see where they fell as long as it was not directly in front of them.

God bless Troy for her steady nerves. Once or twice he turned to see how Lollie was faring. She had her face buried in his coat, her mop of hair all he could see.

The wind was a brutal enemy. Several times there was a gust strong enough to push him sideways. He wanted to move faster but knew it would expend too much energy if they were facing a walk longer than a mile or so. He settled into a slow, steady pace, the way the troops marched when they knew they would be at it for days.

He forged onward, praying that they would find shelter

before the cold claimed them. Surely, God would help her, if not him.

Finding shelter was the first item on his list. Making sure those sweet green eyes did not become clouded with illness or the cough become something more than an irritation. After that she needed something to eat to help settle the brandy.

He did not even want to think about how Lollie would respond to the fact that she would be away from her home for another night, a possible death blow to her reputation. If her world was rigid her standing would not survive this. There were families you could count on and families like his that were more concerned with their status than with one another.

Michael tried to keep his mind on the future and ignored the shivering that was verging on the uncontrollable.

OLIVIA POKED HER HEAD out of the collar of his coat and the wind made her gasp. She braved it long enough to see how Mr. Garrett was managing. The wind whipped his jacket away from his body. It could not be giving him much protection. He was wearing a hat, but it barely covered his ears and he had no scarf to protect his face.

How long could he endure this? She was cold enough with a coat wrapped around her and with Troy's warmth on her legs. Should she suggest he ride with her? She could return the favor and warm him as he had warmed her. Tucking her head back into its cocoon, she debated.

*   *   *

Michael began to second-guess his judgment. They should have stayed where they were. They should have gone in the other direction.

When he could not stop shivering he stopped their progress and stumbled back to Troy and Lollie. She lifted her face, full of worry, and peeked out of the neck of his great-coat.

"I am going to find my blanket. I should have thought to do that before."

Without hesitation, she handed him the brandy flask. He took a long drink and gave it back to her, and began searching through his pack for the blanket. A tree crashed to the ground on the trail in front of them. Lollie gasped. Even Troy shivered with a restless dance.

Michael did not even look, merely wondered if it would have hit them had they not stopped.

As he pulled the blanket out of his pack, Lollie leaned over so he could hear her despite the wind and her need to whisper. "Climb up here with me. We have no choice."

"I'll walk beside Troy. She'll act as a windbreak."

"No."

Her warm breath on his ear burned it. The wind seemed warmer now, his body not as cold.

"You need more than a windbreak. You need warmth."

"If I can rest for a few minutes, curl up somewhere, I will be warm enough." He was having a difficult time forming the words. He began to turn away to find a spot.

She grabbed his shoulder. "You said you would not leave me." Before he could tell her that he was too tired to argue she was off the horse. Grabbing the blanket, she spread it on the saddle.

"We will ride together, Mr. Garrett, with your greatcoat around both of us."

"After I rest."

"No! You cannot lie down. That is the worst thing you can do. Stop arguing and climb up. It will not be a comfortable seat but it will help keep us alive."

God help him, if she would stop badgering him he could close his eyes and rest.

"Listen to Troy. You insist that she is the smartest horse in the world. She will tell you."

Her urgency made Michael wonder why she was so worried, or if what she really wanted was company. His horse betrayed him with a vigorous toss of her head and he decided to give them both what they wanted.

He nodded. She took off his greatcoat and climbed back on Troy, in an amazingly unladylike way. He could see her legs all the way up to her hips and smiled at the unexpected show.

"Hurry, and stop smiling. This is no time for lascivious thoughts."

With his greatcoat slung over his shoulders he climbed up behind her. The first time he tried, he could not stop his shaking long enough to control his legs. With an effort and a hand from Lollie he seated himself on his second try.

She felt so warm and welcoming. He rested his head on her neck, warming his nose as he wrapped the coat around her. By the time he finished, the coat was wrapped around both of them, not actually closing in the front. It was the best they could do, not ideal but already he felt warmer and imagined that she was colder. He gave her his gloves. She put them on without comment and took the reins.

Troy took up the pace again.

Michael wrapped his hands around the shirt she wore and joined his fingers under her breasts. He turned his hands so that the fullness of her breasts rested in them with the material between her flesh and his. Her hips were between his and his body warmed quickly. The sexual pull he felt was so strong that it was all he could do not to put his hands between her legs and burn himself with the pleasure of it.

6

OLIVIA COULD FEEL HIS HANDS warming against her stomach, his cold fingers beneath her breasts. But if he moved his hands any lower she would have to do something even if this was a matter of life and death.

Riding like this had been her idea, she reminded herself. He had even refused. Thinking on it, he must have been half crazed with cold to think that stopping to rest was a reasonable thing to do.

They passed the newly fallen tree and she wondered if Mr. Garrett was too lost in his confusion to see that the tree was healthy, showed no signs of rot. It was a single solid trunk at least fifty feet high.

She turned to remark on it and realized he was asleep, his cheek lying on her neck so that when she turned her head his lips touched the spot just below her ear. Oh! It sent a thrill through her all the way to her belly. Olivia turned her head to face straight ahead and pretended she could not feel his cheek against her neck. Could a man arouse a woman without even trying? Apparently. *Oh my.*

"You know this is the worst time of year for a windstorm." If she talked aloud about something prosaic maybe he would wake up and be the gentleman he was raised to be. She cleared her throat and tried to speak normally. If she turned her head again he might be able to hear her.

She did, and this time his lips found her earlobe. "In the spring the trees soak up water like sponges and they are much more likely to fail in a strong wind."

He took her earlobe between his lips and she gasped. "Are you awake, Mr. Garrett?"

"Hmm," he said and straightened. "So sorry, Miss Lollie, I thought that was a sweet treat for me. It tastes like you smell, of cinnamon and spices."

"Yes, well, I hope you are warmer now." That was exactly like something her governess would say. Tildy had always sounded more proper than she actually was.

"Much." He moved his hands from under her breasts to her hips, which was not altogether an improvement. .

Before she could ask him to move his hands to, say, her shoulders, he wrapped his arms around her and rested his hands on the saddle horn. Somewhat better. But hardly a scene she would want to recount to her brothers.

He must have fallen asleep again, his head lying heavily on her shoulder. Please let him be resting and not giving up the fight. If he died, she could not manage. She would die.

She kept them on a southward track using the wind as a guide as Mr. Garrett had suggested. The gale force had eased to a steady blow. It would have been bearable if it had not so brutally chilled them earlier. Plus night was coming on quickly and she could see lightning in the distance. Was it possible for things to grow worse? She sniffed back the tears that were her last consolation.

Four hours ago she could not have imagined ever letting a man touch her again, much less sit this intimately between his legs.

The will to live had made a number of conventions seem unimportant now. Running nearly naked in the woods, spending time with a man to whom she had not been properly introduced.

To think what a fuss the dowagers made over more than two dances with the same man. They would have apoplexy if they heard about this. She laughed even though the first thing they would say was that it was "not a laughing matter."

Her brothers were anything but models of virtue, except for Lyn who never put a foot out of place. They would stand at her back if her reputation suffered. Lyn would do what he thought best. But that was both reassuring and worrisome. What if he insisted she go to London? Lyn had never understood that all she wanted was her family near and her cooking. It was all she truly cared about.

A streak of lightning and a low rumble reminded her that first they would have to survive the night. How hideous to have come this far and die where no one would ever find them.

"That is not going to happen," she said to herself, then raised her head and shouted. "It will not happen."

Mr. Garrett made a sound and Olivia's mood lifted. They

had come this far. "When we are home we will celebrate with cake and champagne before a blazing fire." She went on in silence debating what kind of cake and thought about closing her eyes for a few minutes. Troy was smart enough to find her way.

Troy must have read her mind. She raised her head, jingling the bridle, and Olivia looked up. Was that something square and solid ahead of them?

"Mr. Garrett. Please, you must wake up."

She felt him raise his head from her shoulder.

"Up ahead. Do you see that?" she whispered.

"YES," Michael whispered back, thanking God for the distraction. Now that he was warm enough to think clearly he was not sure how much longer he could stay this close to Lollie without doing more than kissing the side of her neck and nibbling her ear.

Even in sleep he had not been able to escape the feel of her. His half-waking fantasies were more carnal than erotic. Lollie deserved better than that.

He could only imagine how hard it was for her to let him be this close.

"There are no rock formations that square. Even in the Dark Peak. Could it be a building, Mr. Garrett?"

He fought off lethargy and strained his eyes through the fading light. Taking the reins from her, he urged Troy to the right. "Yes, yes. I think it is. No light, no smell of fire. It's an empty building, Lollie. But that's better than nothing."

He did not like the trees that surrounded it, but they had

no choice and, thank God, it seemed the wind was weakening. By the grace of God and His love for Lollie they had found a refuge.

Troy sensed his interest and picked up her pace. Lollie must have felt it and sat up straighter. "It looks abandoned."

"Yes, it does. Lollie, we cannot afford to be choosy. I know it looks run-down but it has a roof and four walls."

"We have no choice," she agreed.

"Can you stand another few minutes out here? I will go see if it is safe." He supposed a rotten floor or a large dead animal might discourage him. But not much else.

"Yes. Hurry. Go inside out of the cold. Now I am worried you are the one who will die."

He led Troy to the leeward side of the house. Being out of the wind was such a relief that this spot was almost enough, especially when he considered the challenge of disentangling himself from Lollie.

She brushed off his apology for exposing her to the cold so he wasted no time unwrapping his greatcoat and laying it out behind him, draping it over Troy's hindquarters. With his foot in the stirrup and his hand on the front of the saddle, he levered himself off.

Once on the ground he reached up. Lollie bent over and he lifted her from Troy. The horse sidled closer and Lollie was in his arms with her body pressed against his.

Lollie had put her arms on his shoulders and now she slid them down his chest, hugging him as hard as she could, pressing her face into his chest. "Please be careful."

"I will come back as soon as I know it is safe." As he spoke Michael pulled the greatcoat off Troy and wrapped

Lollie in it, pulling her arms away from him. He kissed her on the forehead, reminding himself that all she felt was gratitude.

NO ONE HAD COME to the window or the door as he approached. There was no sign of life of any kind, but there was also no dirt or cobwebs on the door. The windows had been cleaned of the worst of their dirt. Abandoned for awhile but in use fairly recently.

Michael knocked at the door and turned the handle at the same time. No one answered and he stepped inside. The place was well aired, which also argued for recent use.

Without the wind's battering cold Michael felt warmer instantly. As his eyes adjusted to the new kind of dark, he could see a candle on a table with a tinderbox next to it. He wondered who would leave a candle and flint behind. Someone very wealthy or in a great hurry.

It was an effort to control his shivering enough to light it, but he finally succeeded. With the dim light casting uneven shadows Michael turned to face the room and knew what they had stumbled across.

Lollie's prison.

There was no furniture beyond a bed, a table, and two chairs. The bed had rope springs and some kind of straw-stuffed mattress, but the real confirmation that this was the place Lollie had been held were the ropes that trailed from the bedposts.

Rage at the inhumanity man could heap on an innocent girl came with memories. He wanted that kind of cruelty to have ended with the war, to be part of the past, but he knew it would go on as long as man wanted more than he had. A cottage in Derbyshire could be as much a battlefield as the streets of Badajoz.

Michael pulled the ropes from the posts and threw them across the room with all his strength. They hit the wall with the sound of a whip breaking over a back and slid to the floor in a corner. He kicked one of the chairs. It bounced off the wall and fell, still in one piece.

Still breathing heavily but with his temper under control, Michael went to the fireplace. Her kidnappers had left a stack of dry wood next to the fire and even though it was obvious that no one had used it for hours, there were still warm coals in the grate.

The ropes, the candle and now the warm fire. They might not be gone for good. If her kidnappers were to return he and Lollie would face an entirely new set of problems.

He was marshaling arguments to convince her they had no choice but to shelter here, when he realized that if she had been blindfolded for her whole captivity she had never seen the place. If he could act naturally she might never realize it.

If acting was a lie, it was one of those wrongs that was the right thing to do.

He found her huddled next to Troy.

"It's empty. Has been for awhile," he called as he hurried to her side. A streak of lightning and a rumble echoed off the hills. With a nod she patted Troy's neck and followed him.

Before they reached the door she stopped and, with an embarrassed sigh, turned to the woods. "I must . . ."

"Go ahead but stay out of the wind. Troy will stand guard and I will start the fire."

A mark of trust on his part, though only the smallest. Only a fool would run off with rain threatening on top of the wind.

Just as he began to worry that she had decided to try for home, he heard her. He stopped tending the fire and was almost at the door when she came in. Three steps into the room she stopped, her hair wild from the wind, her face a picture of recognition and disbelief.

Before he could say a word she began backing out of the room, shaking her head. "No, no, no. Not here. Not here."

7

NO HYSTERICS, Lollie. I thought we were beyond that." He took her by the shoulders. "This is our only choice."

With her hands against his chest, she pushed and pushed. "I am not hysterical!"

Michael let go of her and went to bar the door so that she could not leave. There was lightning and some thunder, but in her agitation he did not think the threat of the worsening storm would keep her from doing something foolish.

Before he turned around he heard the clink of something thrown with force hit the window, cracking the glass. Three more struck wide of him.

"Your brothers might have taught you to throw but they left out the lesson about aim. Or you were not paying attention."

"Leave, or I will hit you with your pistol." She raised the

gun over her head. "I would rather be on my own than spend any more time with a liar like you."

The gun, even without ammunition, could be a far more damaging weapon than the stones. She was making the most of her pitiful armory.

"To think I believed you, did not want you to die. You are a bastard, do you hear me? I hate you."

A distraction, Michael thought, he needed a distraction, or one of them would end up hurt. Troy! No better diversion than a horse in a cottage. He could count on Troy's cooperation. It wouldn't be the first time she had entered a house.

Michael opened the door, silently thanked whoever built the cottage for making the entrance big enough to fit a grown horse, and whistled for his mare.

Troy came immediately. Michael pushed the door wide open and reached for the reins. Stroking the animal's velvety nose, he pulled softly on the reins and whispered, "Come on, girl, walk on. Remember Spain? The little house?"

Troy nudged her nose against his hand, gingerly took one step forward and stopped. She lowered her head, inspected the threshold with a thorough sniff, before she advanced another step.

"Good girl," Michael praised her in a low voice as he put one hand on the crest of her neck. His fingers played with the horse's thick mane. "Just keep your head down, girl, and you'll be fine." Clicking his tongue, he moved backwards and Troy willingly followed—her withers passing just one inch below the lintel, the saddle's knee rolls scraping along the door frame. What was he thinking? He should have taken her saddle off first.

The hollow clomp of her shod feet on the wood floor matched the drumming of the rain on the roof. The wind and thunder made for a bass symphony he was not in a mood to appreciate. Michael turned, scanning the room in disbelief. Lollie had disappeared.

He would have been afraid if there'd been any other way out of the cottage, but there wasn't. He'd checked that before. She could not have gone far, must be hiding somewhere, waiting to attack.

He was not sure if it was the sight of the horse in what had once been a parlor or the sound of the deluge that had escaped the clouds, but a minute later she came out from behind the door, holding his gun at her side.

"Even the smartest horse in the world has no business in a house."

There was no accommodation in her voice. But she was distracted.

"She will add warmth to the room. We need that more than we need good manners."

"Humph," was as close as Lollie came to admitting he was right. "Will Troy tell us if she needs to go out?"

"Like a dog that is housebroken?" He did not laugh but pretended it was a reasonable question. "No, but I can tell."

"All right." She thought about it for a moment. "Does that make you as smart as Troy?"

Michael did not even bother to answer her. He knew a trick question when he heard one.

When she raised the gun, he thought maybe he should have let her win.

"You knew this place was here. You are one of them. Did you think I would not remember it?"

"Lollie, I swear to you I have never been here before. Yes, I did realize that this is the place where you were held and yes, I was hoping you would not recognize it."

If her thoughts were as pitiless as her eyes it would be a death wish to turn his back.

"We can talk about it. But first let me start the fire. There is plenty of wood here." He tried to sound practical. "I had no time to check the roof but there are no water stains so it may well be watertight." He made sure that Troy was between them and turned from her to finish building the fire, prepared to fend off the attack of a wild-eyed gun-wielding woman.

PLEASE, PLEASE, PLEASE, PLEASE. The word played through Olivia's head like a chant. *Please help me.* She moved to a corner of the room and crouched down, making herself as small as she could. This was only a bad dream. A nightmare. To have escaped her captors only to run into their leader and wind up here again. To have believed him, and now find him the worst liar of all.

Please let me close my eyes and be home. Let there be a miracle that will sweep me home with Big Sam nearby. There will be some chicken soup and my special honey tisane for my throat. She closed her eyes and waited but knew that nothing changed.

If she was going to survive this she would have to save herself.

First she had to find a way out before he could tie her down. If she was tied again she knew she would die. Olivia put her hand out to push herself upright and found the ropes in the corner with her.

Fighting a sick feeling in her stomach, she sat down hard and tried to come up with a way to take control. Holding the gun tight against her chest she knew that if she used it right it could save her life.

She could knock him unconscious using the butt of the gun and tie him up so that she would be the one in charge. Would she be a kidnapper then? It didn't matter. She would call it self-defense.

He was having trouble with the fire. The logs were too big for the faint coals. Olivia watched as he used a knife to shave off some splinters from one of the logs to use as kindling.

Now was the time to act.

She stood up and moved as quietly as she could across the old wood floor, the barrel of the gun in her hand, the butt raised. Just as she prayed for strength enough to hurt him, someone bumped her arm. With a screech, Olivia whirled to confront her second attacker, only to find Troy watching her with woeful eyes.

"You see, she *is* the smartest horse in the world. I will have to add this to the times she has saved my life."

With the horse at her back and Garrett right in front of her, she was trapped. "I was not going to kill you. Only knock you unconscious and tie you up."

"I'm not sure that makes me feel any better."

"Are you joking? Do you think this is funny? You must be

one of them," she said, all doubt erased by his uncaring attitude. Why was he standing there with his arms crossed, not even trying to take the gun from her? "You brought me back here and they will be returning any time now. You will tie me to that bed again."

She turned the gun so that the barrel was pointed at him. "Do you think my womanly sensibilities will keep you safe? I assure you that I am more than willing to take drastic action to save myself."

He said nothing, but watched her, his eyes considering but not at all concerned. What would it take to convince him that she was a force to be reckoned with?

"If this gun was loaded I would not hesitate to use it. With the barrel so close to your chest I could not miss no matter how poor my aim is." She closed her eyes and pulled the trigger to prove that she could do it if she had to.

The sound of a shot echoed through the room. She screamed and dropped the gun. "No! No! No!" What had she done! Reaching for his jacket, she pulled it open, buttons popping off as she did. "Do not die. Do not die." Where was the blood? Had the bullet gone through him?

He grabbed her and shook her, none too gently. "Stop it, Lollie. Stop it! It was thunder. The gun is not loaded."

Another flash and boom convinced her. She dropped to her knees on the floor at his feet; her screams became sobs. "I am no better than they are. I could have murdered you. I would have murdered you. Take the gun. I never want to see it again."

"That is quite enough drama, my girl."

The ice in his voice cut through her despair. She choked

back a sob, sat back on her heels and looked up. His eyes showed the concern that was missing from his voice. That calmed her more than his coolness.

"I am not your enemy, Lollie. Fetch the ropes and we will throw them on the fire. That way neither one of us will be tied up."

Her chin quivered and Olivia bit her lip to keep the tears inside, turning her face away from him.

He had saved her life, held her to warm her and let her ride his horse. It sounded generous. Standing up she closed her eyes and tried to sort out her feelings. Suddenly the significance of her despair struck her.

She was hysterical at the thought she had hurt Michael Garrett.

Was she worried about the men who had kidnapped her? No. She hoped they were dead or, better yet, had been hit by a tree that was felled by a bolt of lightning and were dying slow painful deaths.

She was tired. Her throat hurt. Her feet ached. She could not reason when she was so distracted, but she did not need a reasonable explanation. With life at its most basic all she had to do was listen to her heart. He was her rescuer. She struggled to her feet.

"Listen to me." He would have taken her by the shoulders again, but she stepped back and he dropped his arms. "We are only here by luck or God's grace."

Olivia nodded, too tired to do more; besides, he was angry now. Not the kind of anger that meant fury, the way those men had acted when she tried to fight them off.

"Lollie, I was so cold and windblown I had very little idea where we were going except for direction."

His anger was more like David's when he'd had enough of her chatter. Or Jess when they played partners at whist and she was the reason they lost. Exasperation. That's what it was.

"You recognized this place," he said again, "and yet I still believe that you told me the truth when you said you were blindfolded the whole time."

As she considered his words, Garrett strode to the corner and grabbed the ropes. Walking back he tossed them on the fire. They writhed like snakes, flamed up and disappeared, sending sparks up the chimney and leaving a vastly unpleasant odor behind.

"Sit down and think. Use your head and think," he insisted as though he thought women never used their heads. "I am going up to the loft to see if I can find anything useful."

He stopped on the first rung and put his foot on the floor again and said more gently, "I know this place is full of bad memories. I expect they are the worst that you have ever had to deal with. I hope they are the worst you ever know."

She nodded as she sat in the chair closest to the fire.

"Think about it, Lollie, and if you have any sense at all you will realize this is the best place for you."

8

OLIVIA CLOSED HER EYES, but listened as he carefully tested the rungs of the ladder before he put his full weight on them.

Troy came close and nudged her shoulder and she realized that she was crying. Not the big sobbing kind of tears but a steady stream of water down her cheeks. With a wavering breath she raised a hand, wiped away the tears and whispered, "I wish we could go home."

The horse nodded. Troy was further proof that Mr. Garrett was an honorable man. No animal this smart would be loyal to a villain.

It occurred to Lollie that Troy would be much more comfortable with her saddle and bridle off. Relieved to find something familiar to do, something that would mean she was as much help as burden, Olivia jumped up from her chair and went through the routine, wondering if Garrett had a brush or currycomb to groom her. It did not look like there would be any oats for Troy and the rain would make foraging impossible. How did animals handle hunger?

Lollie undid the girth and pulled at the saddle. It was heavier than she expected, much heavier than the one she had learned on. When she tugged it off, she fell flat on the wood floor, the saddle on top of her.

The ache in her middle paralyzed her. She could not breathe, could not scream. A moment later, Garrett appeared and lifted the saddle off of her, but it did not help. Her lungs were frozen.

"Where are you hurt?"

She shook her head and pressed a hand to her middle. Her heart thundered, her blood rushed in her ears, she tried but there was no breath to catch. It was not her sore throat that kept her from speaking.

"I understand the discomfort. It will pass."

She felt him loosen the greatcoat around her and she knocked his hand away. "It's—all—right . . ." She forced the words out, one at a time, as she exhaled each newly found breath.

He said nothing, but nodded and went back to the fire.

Troy nudged her shoulder and Lollie reached out a hand to pat the horse's cheek.

Lollie lay back on the floor and stared at the ceiling. The pain eased and she was able to breathe more naturally.

The smell of the place filled her nostrils. That was how she had recognized it. It smelled of dust, emptiness and wood smoke. And now Troy. She closed her eyes and breathed again. The smell of the place was forever ingrained in her mind. Even with her eyes closed, *especially* with her eyes closed, she would recognize this spot even ten years from now.

The sooner they left here the better. Once they were within sight of Pennsford it would be best if he left her on her own to make her way home.

Garrett came back and squatted down near her. "Now do you trust me enough to allow me to give you a hand up?"

MICHAEL WOULD NEVER KNOW what convinced her to accept his help, even in this small thing, but she nodded, still very cautious but less tense.

"Good. Good." But not perfect.

"All I want to do right now is drink some more brandy so I do not sound like I swallowed sawdust and sit close to the fire and warm myself. You should, too."

"As soon as I am sure we have enough wood and are secure for the night."

"You will not go outside. It is too dangerous."

"I think I preferred the Lollie who did not care what happened to me."

She drew a deep breath as though breathing was her greatest joy but was not smiling when she spoke again.

"You are worse than my brothers. Much worse." She fumbled in the pocket of the greatcoat, pulled out the brandy and took a sip.

"Any one of them or your Big Sam can try to beat me to a pulp when we are back wherever you call home." He brought a chair close to the fire. "No matter what you command, I am going to take Troy out and draw some water from the well for her and for us."

"It may not be raining but the trees are still dripping." She sounded vastly disapproving. "The wind is still blowing. You will come back wet and cold."

"Such womanly concern is so unlike you, Lollie." He knew how to make her huffy again. "I think it is because you are developing a tenderness for me." He shot her a wry smile.

"Yes, I suppose it would seem that way to someone like you, but it is no more than worry for my own well-being that makes me care what will happen to you."

"I will wager a guinea that all your brothers are older than you."

"What does that have to do with anything?"

"You learned the great art of extremes somewhere, Miss Lollie. You are the most confounding mix of sweetness and willfulness. Something well learned when trying to win out over older brothers."

"You think you know me so well? I will tell you what I know about you. You are too used to being independent and not having to consider what someone else wants. Despite your age, you have never been married, though any number of women have found you irresistible."

"Despite my age? How old do you think I am?"

"Much older than I am," she said, smiling sweetly.

"I asked for that." He shook his head, grinning, which was as close as he would come to admitting defeat in their war of words. "There is some truth to what you say, Lollie, especially the part about the women. What a shame that my good manners will keep me from showing you exactly how irresistible I can be."

With a word, he led Troy through the door as though the horse made calls on a regular basis and before Lollie could think of a retort scathing enough.

OLIVIA WENT TO THE FIRE, added another log before she sat down and realized that Mr. Garrett was a worthy adversary, her brothers, except for Lynford, having given up arguing with her long ago. That was enough to convince her that he was as different from her captors as it was possible to be.

They had been nervous. She realized that now, if only because Mr. Garrett was not.

They had done nothing but tie her up and wait. Mr. Garrett did not wait. He took decisive action. Was that from his war experience?

If Michael Garrett was in charge of an abduction, he would have chosen villains with steadier sensibilities than the men who had almost strangled her and slept on the job, allowing her to escape. He was not in league with her kidnappers, not their mastermind. The reason he frightened her had nothing to do with that.

Her fear grew from the feeling that he was even more dangerous than they were.

It was more than the slight scar on his cheek and the damaged earlobe. No, it was because he insisted he was going to see her home. No matter how difficult it would be to explain, no matter how ruined her reputation, he would make sure she was safe before he abandoned her. He did not seem to understand one critical fact.

He was the kind of man whose mere presence could ruin a woman's reputation.

He would neither understand nor believe her if she tried to explain that. Michael Garrett was intractable. He would do what he thought must be done. If she refused to cooperate he would force her.

The better part of an hour passed before he came back. She looked out the window twice and the door once. He and Troy were in the shelter of the trees, Troy munching at some grass and Garrett picking up and discarding branches of varying size.

He came back without Troy. "There is a better shed on the other side of the house. There is even some hay that I suspect your captors might have left behind. The weather is clearing and Troy will be happier there." Pulling off his jacket, he draped it on a branch he stuffed into the stack of logs. His white shirt was not wet, but very fine. She could see the muscles of his back work as he sat down, pulled off his boots and set them in front of the fire.

She pulled the brandy out again and took a sip, her throat suddenly dry. "Do you think they mean to come back? They left a candle, the ropes, wood for the fire, and now you tell me there is hay."

He took the brandy from her and put the cork in the bottle.

"They will not be back tonight, I promise you that."

She closed her eyes and pretended to accept his words with a nod.

"Lollie, I will keep you safe. I promised and I can."

"All right, Mr. Garrett." She would not ask him how many other women he had been called on to protect, how many others had believed him and if they had survived. "They will not be abroad tonight and we cannot leave here until the morning. But I will be ready, for you see, I have a plan."

He set the second chair on the other side of the fireplace. Before he sat down he took some of the logs and made a small pyramid so she could rest her feet more comfortably. She wished she had some water to wash. Bare feet were even more embarrassing when they were dirty.

Mr. Garrett leaned back in his chair, balancing it on two legs with his feet on the woodpile. "So you have come up with a way to explain your abduction. One that will answer all questions. That is impressive, Miss Lollie."

Oh, she thought with impatience, he had the same tone that Lynford used when she wanted to try something different for dinner. Why did they think it would work to pay her a compliment when it was not sincere? Olivia sat up straight and prepared to fight for what she wanted.

"Yes, I have a plan," she said with as much conviction as she could muster.

Resting his head on the back of the precariously balanced chair, he closed his eyes.

She was not going to discuss it if she did not have his attention. "So, are you sure that Troy is all right outside?"

"She is fine and will call me if there is a problem." He tolerated the silence for another full minute. "Miss Lollie?"

"Yes?" She kept the chill in her voice and her feet on the floor.

"Are you going to keep your plan a secret? Or do you still think me a villain?"

"That is no longer an issue, Mr. Garrett. What you said made sense. I would never have doubted you if we had stumbled onto any other cottage. It is only that I can see you are very stubborn and will be determined to have your own way."

He turned his head and opened one eye. "Men are not stubborn. That is the purview of women only. Men are determined."

"Mulish."

"Resolute," he closed his eyes again.

"Pigheaded."

"Indomitable."

"Oh, that is a fine word. But here is one more: men can be impossibly *obdurate*."

"I do not even know what that means, Lollie, and am impressed with your education. I bow to you." He turned his head, opened his eyes and nodded to her. "You win. You have proved that you are far more stubborn than I."

Olivia opened her mouth to protest, then realized they had been playing a game and she had lost.

9

NOW, DO TELL ME what you have in mind." Michael plunked the chair back on the floor and held his hands out to the warmth, turning his head to watch her.

"I want you to take me to Pennsford." He nodded and she realized that his eyes were warm brown, the color of coffee.

"To Pennsford," he encouraged.

She almost forgot what they were talking about as she debated the color further. Perhaps chocolate.

"I expect there is more to your plan than that, Miss Lollie."

"Yes, I was just trying to organize my thoughts." The color of his eyes did not matter anyway. "We will part there and I will make my way home. I will tell them that I went hunting for mushrooms and lost my way. I had to stay in the woods all night. That I found a place to shelter in the hollow of an old tree and followed the sun toward home."

He did not answer right away. She hoped it was because he was impressed. He turned to face her and leaned forward, his hands folded with his arms resting on his thighs. His eyes were more bronze than brown, she decided, and wondered if he was trying to distract her on purpose.

"Will you walk in the parlor naked, Miss Lollie? If not, how will you explain my greatcoat?"

She leaned closer but kept her hands in her lap. "I will sneak into the castle, hide your greatcoat and dress in my own clothes."

"Altogether a good plan but I do need my greatcoat."

"That is a detail easily handled. I will ask Big Sam to bring it to you."

"He will not be jealous?"

"Of course not." She straightened again.

"And you think all four of your brothers will find that a reasonable explanation?"

"Only two of them are home and Lynford is the only one who matters."

"How will you explain your hair?"

Oh, her hair. She had forgotten it and raised a hand to finger her new curls. "I will wear a cap and later tell them that it is the latest style. You thought it was."

He watched her finger her new curls, and she put her hands together in her lap again. "Is it not an excellent plan?"

"Yes, it seems so."

He stood up and she knew he was going to be difficult.

"The only problem is that I will not let you out of my sight until I am sure you are safe."

"It is exactly as I thought." Olivia slapped her hand on her thigh. "You will insist on your way."

"What if the men who took you are lying in wait for you to waltz up to the door?"

Now she had it. His eyes were the color of dead leaves.

"You have no answer for me. I didn't believe that was possible."

Or maybe the color of dog droppings.

"Your suggestion is an excellent one, Lollie, but here is what we will do. I will take you to a friend's house. A true friend who has your best interests at heart and is not inclined to gossip. We will use most of your story, but we will tell them that you found this place. You stayed the night and I found you as you were beginning to walk home."

"Will I go naked or wear your greatcoat?" she asked, annoyed that she sounded petulant instead of patronizing.

"Very clever," he said, though he did not seem to find it amusing. "You will wear my greatcoat. Your own clothes being too wet and the threat of illness too acute. That is a fact no one would question."

"Why do we not have my clothes with us?"

"Because you ruined your dress and shift when you took them off since you would not allow me to help you."

"Oh, that is very good." She nodded. "I will consider it."

They settled for sleep after a meager meal, sharing Mr. Garrett's apples and cheese, saving some for breakfast, and argued over who would sleep where. Olivia insisted that Mr.

Garrett drink the last of the brandy and, to her surprise, he did not argue.

"If you are not using the bed, Lollie, then I will."

"You may and are welcome to every bug that will share it with you." She wrapped his greatcoat around her and pretended that his travel bag was an adequate pillow as she lay on the floor. She would not think about what insects and small animals might be seeking shelter from the weather. As long as they did not eat any of her she could stand it.

The fire cast the only light, most of it shadowy and not the least bit comforting. She closed her eyes and listened to Mr. Garrett's even breathing.

Now she would have to explain one more night away from home. It was easily done and Lyn would believe her, but she could hardly send a letter to everyone in the village. At least she had a tomorrow to worry about. More than once today she had thought this was to be her last day on earth.

She prayed, thanking the Lord for this day, as awful as it had been. She hoped He appreciated the gesture. By tomorrow her prayers for patience would far exceed her moment of thanks tonight.

Sleep came, a very light sleep, so light that when she heard animals scratching the wood floor she bolted up and shouted, "Rats!"

"Mice," Mr. Garrett mumbled. "Come lie on the bed. It is plenty big enough for two."

"In the same bed with you?"

"Unless another bed has miraculously appeared."

"You could trade places with me. I am sure you have slept on the floor many times."

"Which is precisely why I prefer a bed when I have the choice. I told you before that I would share it with you and it would be our secret forever."

"You are not a gentleman."

"I have my moments, but right now I am an old soldier who needs rest." He patted the bed as if she was a puppy who needed encouragement.

"You are so small you take up hardly any space. I assure you your virtue is safe. I am too tired to do anything but sleep." To prove it, he turned on his side, away from her, and pulled the blanket up around his neck. "Or is it that you do not trust yourself around me?"

"Of course not, you arrogant oaf," she sputtered, even though that was exactly what she was worried about. She stood up, scooped up the greatcoat and sat on the edge of the mattress.

"*Rats* can climb, you know," she said to his back.

"*Mice* can too, but they will not bother us."

"How do you know?"

"Because I put some cheese upstairs, as far away from us as possible."

His voice was slightly muffled by the blanket. She pulled her feet up onto the bed and leaned a little closer to him.

"It will take them all night to work it out of the place I stuffed it. You, Lollie, are the only thing that is keeping us awake."

"Are you warm enough?" She smiled into the dark. "You can have this side of the bed if you prefer." Her toes were cold but she sat still to see if he was going to answer her. He wasn't going to unless a snore counted as an answer. In this case it was. It told her that what she wanted the most he was not going to give. A sheltering arm. A comforting hug. Something more.

How many times had her governess told her that to be too close to a man could awaken needs in him a woman might not be able to deny?

Olivia had listened and been careful but had never before been in a situation as intimate as this. She had never even considered until this moment that needs could be awakened in the woman as well.

Her maid had taken up where her governess had left off. Kendall insisted that Olivia did not know the meaning of self-control.

That was not true. It was just that when she had a good idea she saw no need to equivocate. She was able to control bad ideas, like not hitting one of her brothers when they irritated her beyond reason. Controlling herself was not a problem.

Of course it had never been tested. Everyone treated her like she was their best friend. It would be nice if just once someone, some man, saw her as—she mulled over the choice of words—if a man saw her as desirable. So desirable that despite incredible self-control he could not resist her.

Her eyelids felt like deadweights and she let them close. She drew a deep breath and dropped off to sleep before she could do more than think, "Good night, Mr. Garrett."

The feel of burlap smothering her and hands around her neck came immediately. The memories were as real as the experience. Olivia jerked herself awake, opened her eyes. She turned to face the fire, away from the one thing she wanted. Mr. Garrett's arms around her.

She did not cry out loud, but she could not stop the tears that ran down her cheeks or the deep breaths that sounded like silent sobs.

"Tell me." His voice penetrated the dark even as she felt him turn on his side so he could see her. "Tell me why you are crying."

She turned onto her back. "I cannot close my eyes without remembering."

"Tell me," he said again. "Tell me what you are remembering."

She swiped at her eyes and put her hand down beside her body and his. *Please touch me. I cannot stand feeling so abandoned.* He either understood or read her mind because he reached over, smoothed her hair and took her hand in his. It was their only contact, but it was comforting and caring and as intimate as a kiss.

"They forced a burlap sack over my head and threw me on the floor of a carriage. The burlap was rough and poorly woven. It smelled awful, of mildew and rot. The little threads of it clogged my nose and made it hard to breathe." She drew in a breath and was quiet a moment, determined not to cry. He ran his thumb over her knuckles and waited.

"It made me itch all over. The dark was complete. I could see nothing. Fainting was the only way to escape."

She turned her head and looked him in the eye. "What a pathetic weakling I am. If I had stayed conscious maybe I could have jumped from the carriage."

Mr. Garrett raised himself up on one arm with such suddenness that it frightened her. "You are not a weakling, Lollie." Command replaced comfort. "You are strong and resourceful. You lived through it. You escaped. You are alive."

What he said was what she wanted, what she needed to hear. *She was alive.* Why was it not comfort enough?

"You have the pistol on the floor beside you. Troy will let us know if anyone is coming, and I am between you and whoever would come through that door. I will kill them before I let them near you."

With a deep breath the urge to cry passed. That was better.

She was exhausted but not tired, which made no sense at all. She turned so that they were facing each other with about six inches between their bodies. Olivia could feel his heat. "Would you hold me?"

10

No." He closed his eyes. "That is asking too much of me, dear girl."

"We are miserable. My reputation is in tatters. Is it wrong of me to want to be held, to feel safe?" To feel his warmth against her cheek. Or pressed the length of her body.

"Not wrong, but unwise."

Olivia turned away from him, wounded by his reasonableness, and now she did cry. Great shaking sobs that were as much anger as pain.

His arms came around her and she started to turn to him. "No, stay just as you are. It is temptation enough."

Temptation or not, it was almost perfect to lie like this. She lifted his hand and kissed it and smiled when he kissed her head.

"We can do anything we want," she said, sounding

dreamy and anything but. "It does not matter anymore. Everyone will think I am ruined completely."

He massaged one of her shoulders, which should have made her more relaxed, but even through the wool of his greatcoat she could feel the strength of his fingers. She wanted to move closer but she was afraid he would stop, or worse, move away.

"The truth always matters, Lollie."

"What if no one believes it?"

His gentle massage stopped. "We would know the truth. We would know and I promised I would see you home safely." He kissed the nape of her neck. "I keep my word."

Garrett let go of her and turned on his back. "You have no idea what people are saying. Do not assume the worst and, in the name of all that is holy, we are not going to do anything that would make the worst the truth."

She turned on her back, too. "All right."

"If you cannot sleep pick your favorite memory from childhood and tell me about it."

"Did you do that in the army?"

"No, I would put whatever I wanted to forget in a box and dig a deep hole and bury it. All in my imagination, you understand."

"Was that not too much like burying the dead?" she asked, turning her face so she could see some of his.

"Precisely." He did not turn toward her as he spoke. "Most often that is what I was doing. Taking the memories and the pain and putting them away."

What he must have endured. It twisted her heart so tightly that it was hard to draw a breath. The ceiling was an easier place to put your eyes when you were sharing your soul. Was he looking at the same part of it that she was? Where the beam had a big crack halfway through it?

"Tell me a pleasant story, Lollie. So we can both sleep."

"All right." He made it sound like it would be a gift. "I remember a time when the whole family went on a picnic, with food that I had made with Cook. I was ten. We had such a wonderful time. Papa never laughed but that day he was as silly as my brothers were. They had a juggling contest and we played hide-and-seek."

She smiled at the beam, remembering Gabriel trying to hide by climbing one of the trees.

"Papa kissed Mama in front of us—only on the cheek, but she was as shocked as we were. He said it must have been something in the deviled eggs. That I had a magic touch with food that cast a spell on all of them." Why should that make her eyes tear up? "I was as happy as I have ever been that day."

He was quiet but she could tell he was not asleep. "I can picture you, Lollie. Smiling. I have not seen you smile enough yet. But if I close my eyes I can see your ten-year-old smile. That was what cast the spell."

"How can you know if you have never seen me smile?"

"I have an excellent imagination."

He said it as though he were imagining something else. Olivia bit her lip and smiled at the beam.

"What is your happiest childhood memory, Mr. Garrett?"

"My childhood was much longer ago than yours, Lollie."

She glanced at him. Just a glance. He was staring at the ceiling, his hands folded across his middle.

"I can wait, Mr. Garrett. We have all night."

"Hmmm," was all he said for awhile.

"I suppose one of my happiest memories is the first time I won an argument with my father." He laughed softly. "Not an argument, more like a philosophical debate."

"Will you tell me?" Even as she urged him to continue, Olivia wondered if men considered life nothing more than one contest after another.

"I was home from school, filled with the superiority of a twelve-year-old who has learned one or two things, both in school and after."

She did not even want to imagine what a twelve-year-old boy learned after school.

"It was after dinner when we were at table. My older brother was at Oxford and not home yet. My mother and sisters had gone to the music room. Father and I could hear the hideous sounds coming from there and were in no hurry to join them, so Father asked me to pick a biblical passage and defend the sinner of the piece."

"Was your father very religious?"

"Yes. Very."

There was a long pause, and Olivia hoped he would elaborate. He had a brother and some sisters. He was not the oldest. That was only the bare bones of a family story.

"I chose the parable of the Prodigal Son and, of course, had to defend the son who took his fortune, wasted it and came back home when he realized that his father would forgive him."

"We hear that every year in church. The vicar has given some fine sermons on it."

"My contention was that the real sinner of the piece is the son who stayed with his father, the good and dutiful son who complained when his brother was welcomed back."

"Oh my." That was hardly the usual approach.

Mr. Garrett laughed. "Yes, my father did not like that at all. But when I explained that if the prodigal son was the one who believed in his father even when he had not seen him for years and knew he would be forgiven, was he not the son with the greater gift of faith. It was the son who lived with the father every day and did not understand him at all. That son was at greater fault."

All right, she thought. That made sense. Olivia wondered what the vicar would say about that.

"My father did not say anything for the longest minute of my life. Finally when I thought I could stand it no longer, he said, 'The prodigal had great faith. Good. You have a future in the church if not in the law.' "

She could feel him shake his head.

"I thought I would burst with pride."

"Oh that is lovely. I am going to go to sleep doing my best to envision you as a boy. Bursting with pride."

She turned and kissed his shoulder—it was the closest part of him—and fell asleep.

BIG SAM WAS NOT HER LOVER, Michael decided as he stared out into the dark. He was sure of that. She had no experience with men or sex. She must be years younger than he thought. She was pretty, healthy and well built, and would last approximately two weeks once she was out in county society. Unless she was a demanding shrew or the kind of woman no man could please.

You would think after being so exclusively in her company he would know more about her. It made him realize how much he depended on hearing a person's accent and how they dressed to help him determine who they were.

It worked both ways. The accent he used, the words he spoke, how often he swore, all were used to shade opinion when he was playing a role.

Raoul Desseau had spoken self-consciously educated French, with an occasional slip into a country accent—as though his ambition had pushed him to the rank of captain, and not who he knew or where he was born.

Now that he was back in England it was hardly a matter of life or death, but he had spent so many years assessing people by their appearance and their words that it was second nature now. Not every villain spoke gruffly. Not every girl was as innocent as she looked.

At a guess he would say this girl had been cosseted, spoiled even, rather than taken advantage of. Perhaps she was being raised with the expectation of marrying well, of moving herself and her family into London society. Maybe she had been kidnapped by someone who had wanted to court her and had been refused.

Now *he* was thinking like a Minerva Press novel.

Despite her asking to be held he was positive that she was not trying to seduce him, or even flirt with him. She had been through a hellish experience and it was not quite over.

He should have let her have the whole bed and slept on the floor, but he had given in to every other damn thing she wanted and that had to stop sometime.

As it was now, he did not even need to turn his head to know what she looked like sleeping. But it would be a joy to see her at rest when he was not afraid for her life, when he knew enough about her to know that her face reflected her thoughts with an honesty that would make lies difficult for her.

Her new curls were as willful as she was. He would never say it aloud, but thank God for that trait. It was the only reason she had survived whatever her kidnappers had planned.

If her curls were wild and wonderful, the face they framed showed a sweetness that her smile magnified. Every feature was open and direct: eyes that spoke as clearly as her words, cheeks that blushed or paled depending on her sensibility, lush pink lips that promised passion.

Michael closed his eyes and told himself that if she had a bad dream she would want comfort from him. Yes, he could comfort her, and her soft womanly body would just as surely comfort him.

The step beyond that would be inevitable with someone as forthright as Lollie-the-nameless. They would make love and she would lose faith in men completely, what little faith she had left. Michael turned his back to her and edged over so he was using about twelve inches of the mattress.

He had to think about something else or he would lie here sleepless all night.

*   *   *

OLIVIA WOKE UP the moment he turned away from her. She closed her eyes again and tried to think of something that made her smile. Oddly enough it was her hair. The thought of short hair had made her furious not twelve hours ago.

It was curly. Without the weight of its length her head was covered with curls. Tomorrow she would find a mirror and see how it looked. It felt wonderful.

It would not be so bad if it was like Mama's and Jess's. How nice to have one part of Mama forever and at least one thing in common with Jess.

Thinking of her brother was a mistake.

Now one sentence went round and round in her head. It was not a dream, even if it was the last thing she heard before the laudanum pushed her into oblivion.

"Her brother will give us the land on a silver platter."

Money. Jess owed someone money. Probably a lot of money. That had to be the reason she was kidnapped. How many times had she insisted that gambling would ruin him? He could not give up the land Mama had bequeathed him. Any more than the rest of them could give up theirs.

She could not afford fear or bad memories now. She had to clear her mind and find a way to save Jess without their older brother finding out. How was she going to reach him in London? Olivia knew she had a problem far more important than going home and dealing with gossip.

If Lynford discovered Jess's debts were so great that he could lose his land it would be a disaster at least as bad as her being kidnapped.

She loved both of her brothers, even if they were as different as kippers and salmon. But Lyn deplored Jess's lifestyle and Jess insisted that Lyn was obsessed with appearances. It had been years since there was anything more than an occasional truce between them: when Rexton was born, when Gabriel came back from France, Gabriel's marriage to Lynette Gilray.

If Jess lost the land there was no doubt that Lynford would be every inch the duke and disown Jess. Her youngest brother would be lost to them forever. No matter if she begged and pleaded, the Duke of Meryon would have the last word.

She dozed off finally thinking that if Garrett insisted on seeing her all the way to her door, she had best tell him her whole name.

II

YOUR BROTHER is the Duke of Meryon?" Michael stood up, unable to contain his astonishment. "We've been together for all this time, you've eaten my cheese and apples, drunk my brandy, slept beside me and only now find the courage to tell me who you are?"

"I'm sorry you are upset."

It sounded to him like the most perfunctory of apologies.

"Mr. Garrett, you made it very clear how you feel about the duke. That's only one of the reasons I was not willing to tell you when you first asked."

Michael looked up to the heavens. "So this is how a Good Samaritan is rewarded. I find out that the woman I rescued is related to the one man in Derbyshire that I want nothing to do with? Jesus, Lord, help me."

"Do not swear!"

"That was a prayer and praying is something I have not done in a long, long time." Turning away from her Michael picked his favorite curse word and whispered it with vehemence.

"I heard that."

"No, you did not."

"Why do men think that swearing is the best way to handle a problem?"

"Why do women think that tears are?" He returned to spreading the coals of the fading fire, with a little more force than was necessary. "This changes everything, Lady Olivia."

"Lollie."

"What?"

"I told you I am called Lollie in the kitchen, and sometimes my brothers use it."

"You will be Lady Olivia to me." He could see that she would balk at every word he said. The terrified girl had disappeared after a few hours' sleep. Though come to think on it, she had not been all that accommodating before. He'd thought that was because she was upset, not because she was the daughter and sister of a duke and used to having her own way.

He wiped sweat from his brow and pressed his lips together to keep the curses from erupting again.

"If the thought of helping me is suddenly repugnant I can manage on my own." She tapped her bare foot on the floor, waiting for a decision. As if he had a choice. "As you may recall that was my preference all along."

"You almost died on my watch, my lady. You are now my concern, no matter how much we may wish it otherwise." Michael turned his back on her and collected Troy's saddle and blanket.

What kind of divine game was being played here? He'd decided not to use his letter of introduction to the Duke of Meryon. Jesus, Lord, did it not matter what he wanted? The answer to that was obvious.

"I am going to saddle Troy. Come out when you are ready to leave."

"I will walk."

"You will ride. It will save your feet from more damage."

She had no answer for that. "I know we need to be on our way, but I want to be sure that we have agreed on what we are going to do."

Michael put the tack down and came closer so that he could tower over her. "I am not as considerate as you. There will be no discussion. We have agreed on a plan. Mine, since I am the one in charge. I will take you to safety and I will bring your brother and a carriage to you."

"Absolutely not." She folded her arms as though it would help her stand her ground.

"You are afraid of your brother. He beats you, I'm sure of it."

"Now you are threatening me!"

"No, I am not and you well know it. It is only that I can understand how a man of less even temper than myself could long to throttle you."

"My brother has more self-control than anyone I know. It

is amazing he never loses his temper. I have never seen it happen. Though there is no doubt when he is unhappy with you." She shook her head as if it was a truth she could not understand. "No one has ever throttled me. All right, Tildy, my governess, did, but that was only because I hid from her when she wanted me to practice Mozart at the pianoforte. Have you ever heard Mozart played badly? That was years and years ago."

Her very insistence made it sound as though it had happened yesterday.

"He would never beat me but there are other ways that he could show his displeasure."

"I will most likely have some sympathy with his choice, short of selling you to a white slaver."

"Do you think that is what the kidnappers were going to do? Is that why they were told not to hurt me?"

He had meant it as a joke but once again she found no humor in his humor.

"No, Olivia. I think it was much more personal than that."

"What could be more personal than taking a woman to give as a prize to some man?"

"Not much, I agree." He pressed his lips to keep from saying that in Lady Olivia they would be on the receiving end of a big surprise. "But, Olivia, think about it. There is no reason to take someone as well known as the sister of a duke when there are dozens of girls whose lives are not as sheltered."

She did not answer at first, seemed to be thinking about it and, in the end, only nodded agreement.

"I think it is more likely they were using you to gain the attention of your brother."

The suddenness with which she looked up and the suspicion in her eyes made him curious. There was something she was not telling him.

He folded *his* arms. "Lady Olivia, the less-than-honest, now I am not sure that you told me the whole truth about how you ended up naked in the forest. Was it perhaps some assignation gone awry?"

"I was kidnapped! An assignation? With whom? I do not interest men in that way."

"If not, tell me—who is Big Sam? You do not attract men? That is such obvious nonsense that I am not sure I believe you at all."

She either did not hear his question or ignored it. "The only reason I was not completely honest about who I was is because I was not sure you were being honest with me. I am still not sure. You may not be as terrible as my kidnappers, but how do I know that you do not mean to trap me into marriage or demand a reward?"

"Your reading tastes are showing again." He clenched his fists so that he did not grab her and shake her.

"It does happen. You know it does."

"Yes, and I assure you, my lady, that I want neither your brother's money nor your hand in marriage." He unclenched his fists to prove to himself that he was not really annoyed with her. "Lady Olivia, it could be that your brother will try to trap *me* into marriage to save your reputation."

God help him, she took it as an insult, turning her head

away from him, but not before he could see the hurt in her eyes.

"Why did you save me?" she asked, still not looking at him.

"Because, my dear girl, in a civilized world one human helps another in distress. You would have saved me if the roles were reversed." *Please God, she would never know that the thought of abandoning her had crossed his mind.* "My lady, we must be on our way."

She did not move, but did raise her head and fold her arms again. It was a stance he was beginning to dislike.

"I still want to approve—I mean hear—your plan, first."

"I so appreciate your condescension," he said with a touch to his forelock to emphasize his sarcasm. "How could I have doubted that you are related to a duke?"

"Mr. Garrett, there are still questions I want answers to."

"I can explain the rest as we travel."

"No." The one word questioned his sanity. "You would not start an important dish without all the ingredients. Where do you think to leave me while you go to my brother?"

"When will you stop being a stubborn shrew?"

"When you stop acting like an obnoxious oaf."

Michael decided it was time to walk away. Having reduced their disagreement to tears and childish name-calling was hardly forward progress.

"We can discuss the details of the plan on the road to Pennsford. I will tell you this much. We do not need to be any more devious than necessary." He could hardly believe that those words had come out of his mouth. Devious

had been a way of life while he was posing as a French officer.

"Finish your apple. It is all the food we have left. I am
going to saddle Troy," he said again, this time opening the
door.

HE WAS COMING out of the woods when he heard horses,
two horses, and, by the sound of their voices, two men riding. With a string of words that could either be prayers or
curses he hurried back to Olivia.

"Two men are approaching. I do not know who they are.
Lie on the bed with your back to the door. Pull my greatcoat
up so that they cannot see your hair."

For once she was too afraid to argue. "Could they be the
kidnappers?" Her voice was muffled as she huddled under
his coat.

"I don't know, but we take no chances." Her fear was
painful to tolerate. He smiled at her face, which was all he
could see of her. "I have handled five and lived to brag about
it. Now tell me something about Big Sam."

"What? Why?"

"Just tell me." He could hear the panic and he kissed her
forehead, hoping she could feel his confidence.

"He's big. His name is not a joke."

"Good, what else?"

"He will be worried and looking everywhere for me."

"Good. Believe me, I know what I am doing. They will be
gone in ten minutes." Or he would kill them.

"Your gun. You might need your weapon." She pushed it into his hand.

The girl was either bloodthirsty or clairvoyant. He would have to ask her later. With his pistol, the unloaded pistol, tucked into the waistband at the back of his pants, he opened the door and stepped out to greet his callers.

12

OLIVIA PULLED the greatcoat over her head and waited. A minute ago she had been annoyed with Mr. Garrett for insisting his way was superior. It had felt so blessedly ordinary to be thinking of some way to make him do her bidding. Now she felt as safe as a chicken whose only company was a man with an ax. She was tired, so tired of feeling safe one minute and terrified the next.

Her brain was the only part of her that was not paralyzed with fear, and she knew hiding under his coat was a stupid idea. Why did he not pretend that he was by himself? She could have hidden upstairs. She still could.

If she stayed here she could not hear what was going on. What if Mr. Garrett needed help? On impulse she hopped out of the bed, took off his greatcoat and dragged it up the ladder with her into the loft.

There was a small window. No doubt some wise woman

had insisted it be put here, and how many times had she and others after her watched what was going on below? Had any of them feared for the life of the man protecting them? Feared for their own?

She had not thought to wonder why no one lived here anymore. Looking over her shoulder she half expected to see a ghost, but all that was visible was dust motes dancing in the morning light.

Hearing the men was more important than seeing them. She would know if Mr. Garrett needed help, if she could hear well enough. And she would know if these were the men who had taken her. Olivia crawled along the floor until she was directly below the glass.

She recognized the timbre of Michael's voice, but what was that accent he was using? Yorkshire? Yes, that was it. They exchanged what sounded like conventional pleasantries but she could not hear the other men.

"My wife and I . . ." Michael began in a booming voice, but then he walked toward the men and she could no longer hear him, either.

Edging up the side of the window she risked a look. The three of them were turned away from the cottage, one of the two men gesturing to the south with some enthusiasm. They turned back to face Garrett, and perforce the cottage. She dropped to the floor, her heart in her throat.

Michael's voice reached her again. Were they coming to the door? "I bought it from a man passing through Pennsford. Ugly but she's strong. When my wife's mare threw her in the river and ran off, this one was able to carry both of us. The man said he would buy it back from me as soon as he won enough gaming. That's not likely to happen."

One of the men said something but Olivia could not decipher it. He was much too quiet-spoken. She took a chance and peeked out the window again.

"Yes, and you are right, this is not the way to Yorkshire, but my woman wanted to say she'd been to the Peak so we came on a ride and trouble courted us from the start. Worst of all she insists she saw a ghost. Now I know why no one visits the Peak in the spring. Just not a friendly place."

Was he trying to talk them to death? They asked another question and he began again.

"The only people we've seen was a man called himself Big Sam. He was mad to find a woman named Lollie, but was so upset that he made little sense and we could not help him."

The men nodded. One gave the appearance of a man as guilty as one could be; the other, on edge of an explosion of temper.

Garrett did not seem to notice their discomfort. "Will be good to get home to my own bed after an unplanned night away. You want to come warm yourself. My wife is still asleep. If she wakes up she is like to throw a shoe at you and yell that you are a ghost. She is a shrew but is a hefty cow and does her share of work on the farm."

Why was he inviting them in? The idiot. He was no more one of them than she was. Or did that make her the idiot? He must have something in mind.

There was more mumbling, unintelligible, and finally he pushed the door open.

"She said it looked like a woman in a white gown wandering in the fog, branches whipping her face. Better a ghost than someone lost. Last night's storm would have done her in for sure."

"Where, where did you see her?"

Olivia began to shake as she recognized the voice. It was one of her kidnappers.

"See who?" Michael the farmer asked with confusion coloring his words.

"The ghost, man, the ghost."

She could hear the same well-bred voice yelling at his cohort to stop strangling her.

"Do not tell me you believe in ghosts. We were north of here someways. Been two or three miles toward the Dark Peak."

One of the men moaned and the other cursed. "We have to be going."

"Nonsense. Warm yourself first. Sara! Sara! Where are you, woman?"

Do not say a word, she told herself. *They will know your voice.* She began to cry, loud screeching sobs which were not that difficult to summon.

"What did you go up there for? These gents mean no harm. They been out in that storm most of the night and just need a little bit of warmth before they move on."

Her only answer was more loud sobs.

"Stay up there if you must, you silly goose." He laughed heartily. "If you did come down you could discuss ghosts with Mr. Smith and Mr. Jones. It looks like they are off to see if they can find that woman we saw yesterday." When

Michael spoke again Olivia could tell he had turned his back on the ladder to the loft.

"Here now, warm yourself, Mr. Smith. It is no inconvenience."

Garrett did not stop talking for a solid five minutes.

Olivia lay on her back, then turned to face the wall just in case one of the men decided to climb to the loft. Mr. Garrett's endless prattle had a certain rhythm to it and after a minute or so it was actually a comfort.

When the men announced that they must leave, Garrett followed them outside, talking about the crops he was planting and asking if they had any interest in marrying one of his sisters. He wanted them off his hands. They weren't much in the kitchen "but the village boys like them well enough."

As they rode away he called after them "Enoch Ballthur, gents, if you're ever near to York."

The one with the temper made a gesture somewhere between "Good-bye" and "Shut-your-bleeding-mouth."

"No? G'day to you both. I hope you find who you're looking for, even if it is a ghost."

MICHAEL WATCHED THEM on their way, heading north. Perfect. Smith and Jones might even find the spot where he and Olivia had camped. All the better confusion for them.

If he had botched a kidnapping he would want to know what had become of the girl before reporting back to the man in charge. Having met these two, he was sure that they were minions for someone who did not make a habit of stealing young women.

Smith, at least, was as confused and frustrated as hell. Jones did not look like he had brains enough to do more than follow the simplest orders.

Michael bet Smith was still trying to decide if he wanted to find her dead or alive. Which would be easier: to evade a murder charge or to have someone identify you as a kidnapper? The question that went unanswered was whether Smith was desperate enough to kill and Jones stupid enough to follow the order. Lady Olivia would not be safe until the two of them were brought to justice.

Michael watched long after they were gone from sight, the gun heavy at his side. His first task was to make sure Olivia was safe. After that he would round up these two, whether the duke wished it or not. *Ride on, you bastards,* he thought. *I will find you and you will pay in a very quiet, very painful way.*

Now Michael had to deal with Lady Olivia-the-suspicious. God help him find a way to convince her that they were gone, he was not in league with them and his plan was the wisest course of action.

He opened the door with considerable caution and stepped inside. "Lady Olivia."

"Are they gone for good?"

"Yes." He looked up to the loft where she was still waiting.

"Why did you not apprehend them, Mr. Garrett?"

"For several reasons. One, my first responsibility is to see you home safely. Second, I am not sure that your brother will want to advertise this with a trial. I am sure he has his own ways of seeing that justice is done." Michael walked to the base of the ladder waiting for her next round of questions.

She was quiet. A moment later she leaned over the edge of the loft and looked around the room.

"Did you recognize them, Lady Olivia?"

"One voice. I was blindfolded, remember? Only the one man spoke. The better dressed of the two."

"That would be Mr. Smith."

"His name means nothing to me, but I will never forget that man's voice." She sat back on her heels. "The one with the nasty expression. As if he was too aware of his seat at the servant's table."

"Or too fastidious to talk to a farmer more than was absolutely necessary." Michael walked over to the window. "I could have offered them a king's dinner and they still would have left after I told them about the ghost."

"They went off to find me?"

"Yes. They must have something to report to the man who orchestrated this." He should not have said that. Better not to remind her, when he was sure that Olivia's own memories were so hard to ignore. "Or it could be that they are afraid I will try to catch up with them and explain why I think my uncle's planting methods are superior to his neighbor's."

She made a rusty sound that he realized was laughter. He walked to the bottom of the ladder again so he was sure she could hear him.

"Enoch Ballthur was a deliberate ruse, Olivia. I had the measure of them right away and knew a farmer from the

Riding would be good for information and nothing else. The last thing we want is their company on our trip back."

The possibility wiped the smile from her face. He felt small for doing it, but she needed to remember that the danger was not over.

13

AS OLIVIA LEANED farther from her perch, Michael noticed that she was not wearing his greatcoat. The first two buttons of his shirt were undone and he could see more of her sweet bosom than was modest. He didn't say a word and enjoyed the view.

"How did you know all that about farming? You were in the army. Not only that but you sounded like a Yorkshire farmer. Even the way you stood. If you met them again as Michael Garrett I do not think they would recognize you."

Finally she was impressed with something. His acting ability. Too damn close to lying to suit him. "I made most of it up. But my father had me read Coke's book on farming when he still had hopes that I would stay on in Sussex. I was able to recall some of the terms."

"If you are sure they have left and will never come back, I will come down."

Her girlish words were completely at odds with the marvelous body his shirt was barely covering. His shirt had never known such pleasure.

"Will you catch your greatcoat? I cannot negotiate the ladder in it."

He caught his coat and waited.

"Turn around, Mr. Garrett. I am not about to show you my legs. You have already seen quite enough of me."

"All of you, as a matter of fact, though I was far more inclined to cover you up and save your life than to look my fill."

He felt something hit his ankle as he walked to the side of the room. One of his gloves fell to the floor beside him.

"I was aiming for your head," she explained, "because you are not being a gentleman at the moment."

"Lady Olivia?" He smiled, not at all a gentleman.

"Yes." The one word was full of caution.

"The gentleman in me has won out over the rogue and feels compelled to advise you to fasten the top two buttons of my shirt."

"Oh!"

The word was like a screech and the other glove hit his shoulder.

"Your aim is improving but you will need much more practice."

When the creaks from the ladder stopped he held out the greatcoat with his back still from her, hoping she would not throw anything heavier than a glove at him.

"Did you find out where they were going?"

She was all business now. He turned. Dressed as she was,

it was no wonder he had a hard time thinking of her as an adult. With his greatcoat a dozen sizes too big for her, she had the look of child playing with adult clothes.

"What is the matter?" She looked down as if she had missed a button or her knees were showing.

"Nothing at all. I have just decided that I will keep that greatcoat forever."

She blushed and wrinkled her nose, smiling at the floor. It was just as well he had not felt the full force of it. Even reflected off the wood planks, he was dazzled.

Michael covered his eyes for a minute and tried to recall what they had been talking about. "Those two men will eventually return to Pennsford."

She stiffened. He had her complete attention. He was sorry to see her smile disappear.

"There can be no argument now, Lady Olivia." He gentled his voice. "I will stay with you until I am confident that you are safe."

"All right." She nodded several times.

"I will keep the gun and have it loaded." He patted his pocket. "Those men will die before I let them harm you again."

"All right."

What had he done to earn such easy agreement? Oh, yes, put her in the presence of the two men who had taken her and threatened her life. It was mean-spirited of him, to invite them inside. But it had worked. She understood that he was on her side.

He went outside ahead of her and brought Troy to the

bench near the front door, a convenient enough mounting block.

Lady Olivia patted Troy, giving the horse the last chunk of her apple, which would most likely guarantee friendship for life.

"You did a fine job of acting yourself, Lady Olivia. The crying was very effective." He came to her side in the event she needed help.

"Yes, I tried to cry the way 'a hefty cow' would." She continued to pat Troy and did not look at him.

"What was I supposed to say?" Michael waited until she faced him, her eyes inviting an explanation she could belittle. "What would you have had me tell them? That you were round and soft in all the right places, with an elegant leg and dainty feet, and a face that is as lovely as a Madonna?"

"Now you are talking nonsense." Her cheeks turned more pink but that was the only sign that she was flattered. She stepped back and checked the saddle straps.

"I beg your pardon, my lady." His indignation was half-hearted. He put his hand on the saddle so that she was tucked between him and Troy. "I see that no one ever taught you how to take a compliment."

"Oh yes, they have." She finished her perfunctory check of the tack and gave him her complete attention. "Allow me to show you, Mr. Garrett."

It was her turn to smile. In a way that was not at all girl-ish. She raised her hand, and positioned it as if holding a fan. Her eyes were filled with invitation. She moved as if to curtsy. "Why, thank you, Mr. Garrett. You are irresistible when you are charming."

"And you are irresistible even when you are irritating and stubborn and barefoot." He was the one who took a step back this time. "God knows why."

"That may be nonsense, too, Mr. Garrett." She closed the space between them. "Still it feels amazingly like flirting."

"Tell me, how does flirting feel?" As if he didn't know.

"As though I must step closer." She took another step. "And closer. So that I can look deeply into your eyes and see if you mean what you are saying. Touch your heart"—she raised a hand—"and know what you are feeling."

The touch of her hand was so enticing that he was tempted to show her how irresistible she was. God knew this was not the time or the place. Not that there ever would be one. Instead he shook his head and moved around to the other side of the mounting block. It was as far away as he could go without appearing a complete coward. He raised a hand to his forehead and rubbed it for a moment, with his thumb resting on his cheekbone. "I can tell you this, my lady. You are trouble. It is one word I will always associate with you."

"Now, *that* is a compliment, Mr. Garrett." Her smile grew to a grin. "Thank you for it, sir. Indeed, I live to trouble you. Waking, sleeping and all the moments in between."

She meant it. Her eyes did not lie.

Climbing onto Troy, she began the complicated process of making herself as comfortable as she could, spreading the greatcoat under her and fixing it so that it wrapped around her legs. "I ask you, sir, what woman does not want to complicate a man's life? Even I, with only one London Season, understand that."

"You've already had a London Season?" He swallowed

the next sentence: *No one snapped you up?* And changed it to "Why are you not there now?"

"One was entirely enough, thank you. I enjoyed it, mind you. Viscount Bendasbrook always had something outrageous planned. Lord Ellinger was very attentive. Too attentive."

She fussed with his greatcoat as though it were the most elegant of riding habits. "It is so completely different from Pennsford: the parties and the art exhibits and the chance to observe Lyn in Parliament. My sister-in-law—the duchess—" she explained, "was the perfect chaperone."

"The duke is married?"

"Yes, but Rowena is increasing and the physician insists that she not travel. Her health is very delicate. She agreed to stay in London when Lyn had to come back here, but then she insisted that Rexton, their son, stay with her. So Lyn is without them and, I think, misses them so much."

"So Her Grace was the perfect chaperone?"

"Oh yes, though we did spend more time than I would like at poetry readings."

"If you enjoyed it so much why was one enough?"

"It was too long away from the kitchen."

Lady Olivia Pennistan spoke as though all the young women making their bow would deplore time away from the kitchen.

"All right," she continued, "I *was* able to talk with Monsieur Carême, the Regent's chef. But for the most part Rowena would not allow me to speak to any of the others. It hardly mattered. Most of the food was conventional or not catered properly. Some of it was completely unpalatable."

"You certainly appear to be fascinated with the kitchen. Not the usual salon for a lady."

He could see she took offense at his statement, and he had not even meant to bait her.

"Everyone says that I 'spend too much time in the kitchen.'" She spoke the phrase in a high-pitched voice. "Mr. Garrett, I tell you what I tell them: I don't give a fig for people who do not understand that food is about more than approving insipid menus." She took up the reins. "Why are we sitting here jabbering? Should we not be on our way?"

"We have time, Lady Olivia. I am happy to let those two travel well ahead of us."

"If that is so, why did you let me mount Troy?" She made a face at him but did not wait for an answer. "Here is what you must understand: Food is the key to peace and contentment, whether it be in Napoleon's court or a Yorkshire farmer's kitchen. Monsieur Carême and I agree on that."

"I thought Carême worked for Talleyrand."

"You know him?" Her didactic look and tone disappeared. Her eyes lit up as though a cook, albeit a famous cook, were the king.

"I met him one or twice when I was in Paris." He could see he had risen seriously in her estimation. He was not about to tell her that her favorite chef was suspected in some circles of being a spy. How strange that these two very distinct aspects of their lives should dovetail in one man.

"Did you ever meet Monsieur Beauvilliers?" Olivia leaned down as if she desperately wanted to hear his answer.

"Is he another chef?"

"Yes." She straightened in the saddle. "Almost as wonderful as Carême, with different skills. Lynford found his *L'Art de Cuisinier* for me last year. It is quite a remarkable book, not only for the recipes. He discusses all aspects of food. How to shop, plan and manage the kitchen."

"I do know that when Carême swore his loyalty to Talleyrand there were those who suggested that kidnapping would be the only way to lure him from Paris. Could that be something you two have in common?"

He meant it as a joke, but when she paled he could tell that it was a subject she did not see any humor in. "I am sorry, Lady Olivia. It was thoughtless of me to bring up that comparison."

"It is just as well, Mr. Garrett. I can only avoid the truth for so long. Once I am home I will have to deal with it." She shifted in the saddle. "Help me down, will you? If we are not yet ready to leave we have time for you to tell me your plan."

He reached up and took her around the middle, swinging her down with her back to him. It was not as compromising as it would have been if she had slid down the front of him, face-to-face, but the very act of touching her was irritating.

He gestured for her to sit on the wooden bench between them. She shook her head.

"I will stand. I will be sitting for hours. Tell me."

What a mystery she was. From sweetly delighted one minute to imperious and condescending the next. Michael saw now what he had missed before when he had called her stubborn. Lady Olivia was very used to having her own way. Not solely a quality of wellborn women.

"But of course, mademoiselle." He set his foot on the

bench and leaned toward her. "Allow me to explain the cornerstone on which I built this house of cards we are calling a plan."

"Do not think that will frighten me. I am fully aware that any plan we have is fragile at best."

Michael nodded. He had to admire her practicality.

"Here it is, Lady Olivia. When you were reported missing your brother would have set about a story that will cover your unexpected disappearance. You became ill, some friend needed your help. It is what anyone would do until they could find out what had happened."

"I had not thought of that." Lady Olivia's smile was like the sun breaking out of fog.

"Your brother is a duke," he reminded her, as if she needed it. "You know as well as I that no one would question the Duke of Meryon. He will not wait for you to come dancing down the drive but would have someone he trusts searching for you."

"Yes." Her face, her whole body relaxed. "Of course he would. I am sure Big Sam is looking everywhere. Why did I not think of that?"

Michael could think of several reasons. She had been close to death, afraid, unable to let go of the horror. Mortified and worried her brother would not understand.

He was about to ask her, one more time, who Big Sam was, when she curtsyed to him. "Excellent, Mr. Garrett. That is explanation enough. I will be ready to leave whenever you think it time."

14

SUDDENLY Lady Olivia Pennistan was all cooperation. It was his turn for confusion. "Please tell me what I said to win your agreement. I want to remember it."

As she leaned close to Troy, he heard Lady Olivia whisper, "Men!" Damn if that horse did not nod with more than her usual vigor. "What you said makes sense, Mr. Garrett. Once you stop trying to dictate to me and say something reasonable, I can be reasonable, too. It took my brothers years to learn that. Take me to the vicarage in Pennsford and we can tell them that I fell into the river while I was searching for mushrooms and you rescued me. Saved my life."

"The vicar? He will support you?"

"Yes. My father and the vicar were friends. Mr. Drummond has known me forever. I have only to ask for him to help us."

"I will trust you in this." Michael nodded even though he had no sense of how good a judge of people Olivia Pennistan was. Though she had thought him a villain and had not been so far from wrong. "I have learned to play most any role with very little rehearsal." He hoped that she could follow his lead if it was necessary.

"Yes, I saw that this morning, Mr. Enoch Ballthur."

Once again she mounted the horse, settling herself more quickly this time. As he led them from the yard, Michael turned back to see if they had left anything behind. The door was closed, the chimney smokeless. The disturbed ground in the yard was the only sign of their time there, and the frequent rain would soon eliminate that.

It had been a strange interlude. He remembered others like it during the war, when the danger was all around them, but he felt the illusion of security in some small pocket of life as it should be.

The time he and Jackson had spent the night in a cave, while on a scouting mission—*reconnaissance,* the French called it. They barely spoke but both of them watched the full moon paint the landscape in black and white, drinking some local wine they had liberated. For that moment life was theirs to command.

If the last hours had been in his control, the next would be in Lady Olivia's. The more information he could have, the less vulnerable he would feel. There was no doubt in his mind that sweet, lost Lollie's world would have been much simpler than Lady Olivia Pennistan's would be.

Given the differences between them, it was intriguing

that there were some consistent elements. Four older brothers. A keen interest in food and the kitchen. And who in the blazes was Big Sam?

"There isn't much color to the sky." With Troy's reins in hand, he led her from the yard.

"I don't think it will rain before evening." Lady Olivia followed his gaze, considering the white-gray sky above them.

He let his eyes linger on her face, the soft curve of her cheek, the long eyelashes framing dark green eyes. Michael jerked away with a silent curse.

At least her voice sounded almost normal now. Even the bruises on her throat had faded some. The resilience she showed could just be another kind of stubbornness. In any case it was a more admirable expression of it than her pointless obstinacy.

"With no rain or wind I would call it a beautiful day. It has been weeks since I've seen sunshine," Michael added. Let them talk about the weather, it was much better than flirting. "It's been raining endlessly in Sussex, too, in the Midlands. My whole way north. I'm surprised I'm not covered with moss."

At least last night's rain had come and gone quickly. The wind had eased from its gale force but had continued strong enough to dry the path so that puddles were all the wet he had to avoid.

For the first little while they counted the number of trees that were downed by the windstorm. Thank God they had found shelter. Michael was not sure they could have survived without a roof and a fire.

As they neared the main road, they had to blaze their own trail, walking around a tree that had fallen across the rough track they were using. No one was going to bring a carriage up here again, at least not before that tree was removed.

"This path was not made for a cart, much less anything bigger." What a rough passage it must have been for her, especially bound and gagged, bouncing all over the floor.

"I remember very little of it." She was watching the ruts as she spoke, had determined as easily as he had what they had been caused by. "I must have stayed unconscious the whole time. Which is just as well. Waking up to a rough journey in the dark to an unknown place would surely have made me sick."

He turned away from her and smiled. There was that practical streak again. What other lady would admit something so vulgar?

There were so many signs of the storm's damage that they stopped counting the trees. Hopefully the main road was not as filled with obstructions as this path was.

When the path joined a road, they found that the large limbs and one great tree had already been moved from the road. He turned his attention to tracking the horsemen they had been trailing. As Michael hoped, they had turned to the left, to the north, back into the Peak. Off to find the ghost that they must hope and pray was their missing captive.

Marks of carriage wheels were everywhere now, and he had no way of knowing which conveyance had carried Olivia.

If he could convince her to tell him what had happened he would not need to investigate the carriage ruts any further.

"Oh, I know where we are!" She studied the trees, the path and the road. "There is a wonderful patch of blackberries not far from here." She waved off the left. "Big Sam and I pick them every year."

He raised his hand for silence, attuned to another sound requiring his concentration. Without a word he turned them back down the trail, far enough so the driver of the heavily laden wagon would not suspect they were there.

Olivia watched him, her face tense, as the wagon passed. A few minutes later he led Troy back out of the woods.

"I suspect this trip will take twice as long as it might. It being wisest to avoid company."

"It's good that we are not five miles from Pennsford," she told him. "Even less from the castle."

"With any luck we can be there before dark. And luck is something we are due." He turned to her. "Which way to the vicarage, my lady?"

They headed south and within a half mile found much less evidence of the storm.

"It's almost as though the wind spared Pennsford."

"I saw that in Spain. There were certain places that rain seemed to favor and others that seemed to be cursed."

They both looked back and could see signs, even at this distance, that the storm had been disastrous there and far more benign here.

"Where do we go from here, my lady?" Michael had a good idea but he wanted to distract her from what was making her bite her lip and appear so worried. Big Sam, he would wager. Any moment she was going to tell him that she had to search for him, even as Big Sam was searching for her.

He had experience in Spain on that score as well. It almost never worked. If he had to force her he would. His order, self-declared, was to see Lady Olivia safely home.

"Where we go depends on where we want to wind up."

She was stating the obvious but he held on to his patience and listened.

"If we stay on this road we can go to either the village or the castle. There is a split after a mile or so. The left path takes us to the main thoroughfare into the village in a couple of miles, but if we want to avoid people I know a track that will lead to the vicar's house. It is a little longer but rarely used."

Moments later they heard another wagon climbing up the road from Pennsford.

There were not as many trees here and it took some distance before they were hidden. Fortunately the wagon moved slowly. It was a farm wagon, with a man and a woman sharing the seat. The woman was telling a story in such a loud voice that she shared it with them.

"Might be she ran away to cook for the king. Or eloped with one of the footmen. Lucy says she spends more time in the servants' dining room than she does in a ballroom."

"How would you know that, Chloe?" her husband shouted back. Either one or both of them was deaf. "We've never been to a ballroom even to mop the floor."

"And we never will. We own our own land and that is the way it always will be."

"Yes, m'dear. Listen to me, let's not gossip about the girl."

"As you wish, husband, but the gossip is so entertaining."

Her husband answered and the last they heard of Chloe was a boisterous laugh.

Michael waited until they were out of sight before he spoke. It was both useful and a disquieting piece of information.

"To the vicar's it is," he said when the wagon turned a bend in the road and was finally gone. "If I do not see the track, do tell me. I think there is too much chance of discovery on this road."

"Yes, all right." she spoke as though she was thinking about something else entirely. She was. "That was Farmer Kinsel and his wife. Fine and friendly people. I have given her my chicken soup recipe."

That made them allies if not friends, Michael thought.

"The way they talked. That is about what I thought would happen." She turned in the saddle to look at him. "You are completely right, Mr. Garrett. The story will be that I am at the vicarage, and most will at least pretend they believe what the duke says."

She nodded and seemed more matter-of-fact than upset by the gossip.

"And would their passing us not indicate that the storm did not take too great a toll around Pennsford? I have been worrying about them."

"That's generous of you, my lady. A tree through a roof or a road blocked by an old giant would distract most people from your absence."

"Perhaps so, but I would prefer to live the lie we have concocted than have anyone suffer to make my life easier."

Even more generous and just as matter-of-fact. Michael hoped that she did not lose that practical sensibility when she was faced with reality.

15

MICHAEL WALKED beside Troy as they made their way back to the road. Lady Olivia studied the area again. "That place they took me to is so close to home. How did I become so lost?" She patted Troy. "I expect I was confused from the start."

It was good that she was talking about it. From his experience that meant the shock was fading and the mind was trying to make sense of what happened.

"The whole day is very hazy. And I was even more confused by the drug. When I woke up, in the dark, all I can recall thinking was that if I ran into the woods I could hide and, when my head cleared and daylight came, I could come up with a plan."

"When they discovered your escape, they would have gone towards the road and town to look for you."

She nodded.

"Will you tell me what happened, Olivia? I want to be sure that our plan will work." Was that a lie, he wondered. He knew what he was going to do regardless of what she said. Yes, definitely a lie.

"My throat is beginning to hurt again."

"We both know that is not the truth. You sound much better after some rest." He stopped the horse and moved to stand by her. "You will have to tell someone, sometime."

"I wish I did not. I wish I could pretend that it never happened." She gazed off to the side, away from him. "I was on my way to Pennsford to visit the vicar and decided that after the call I would stop by the river for some spring ferns or mushrooms."

She flashed him a quick smile. "You see, that part is true. Does it not seem like a wise idea to put some part of the truth in the story?"

He nodded, wondering where she had learned that.

"It always worked when I was trying to spend time in the kitchen. I would tell my governess that I was concocting some lavender water to ease her headache, which was usually true. What I did not tell her was that I wanted to speak with Cook about the lamb ragout. To tell her that it would be better if she used rosemary with the fennel. The fennel was too strong a flavor; the rosemary would balance it, perhaps with some pepper to tease the tongue."

Had she said "tease the tongue"? It was too vivid an image to ignore. "I believe we are slightly distracted." He spoke with complete honesty.

"I would so prefer to talk of food. I could tell you exactly how to make the perfect chicken soup. It really is something that everyone should know. It is one of the few recipes that I have perfected."

No sooner had she finished speaking when they heard the sound of a lone rider racing toward Pennsford. Olivia turned Troy without prompting and they were not quite out of sight when the man charged past. He looked neither left nor right, but was intent on the road, his speed more important than anything else. Michael watched him, and the red scarf he wore, out of sight and wondered who it was and what message he carried. Did it have anything to do with Olivia?

"Mr. Drummond usually has some greens earlier than anyone else," she continued in a soft voice. "More often than not he forgets to harvest them. He lives with his sister. They are both too old to live alone but they will not have it any other way. I try to visit them three or four times a week—not just for the greens, mind you."

"It's the duke's living?"

"Yes. The vicar is a wonderful man. He was such an eloquent speaker in his day and his sister sang with the voice of an angel. They will have the living until they go to heaven, even if Reverend Drummond must be reminded to wear a coat in the winter and Miss Hope no longer sings."

Lady Olivia stopped talking. Troy stopped, too. Michael urged the horse to keep moving. He knew enough about questioning to understand that this sort of prelude was a victim's way of working up courage for the hard part.

"I was hurrying home with the greens, anxious to try a new way of cooking them, when I noticed a carriage by the side of the road. One I did not recognize. Just as I was wishing that Big Sam had not stayed to help the vicar, someone grabbed me from behind, pulled a burlap sack over my head and stuffed me into the carriage."

"It was not a very discreet kidnapping," Michael said before he could stop himself. "On a well-used road, in plain sight. That stupidity makes it clear that they had not kidnapped anyone before."

"Yes, I think you must be right. They were almost inept. Later on one of them almost strangled me, by accident. Now there is an epitaph."

She did not laugh and neither did he. It was too close to the truth to be funny. Hopefully she could make a joke of it when she told her grandchildren.

"I must have fainted in the carriage." Her words were spoken slowly, as though this was the first time she had reconsidered the event. "When I woke up I thought I was blind, then I realized my eyes were covered. I screamed for Big Sam and someone put their hand on my throat and threatened me."

Olivia covered her mouth with her hand. She lowered her hand and with a sniff went on. "I knew I was not naked, I could feel my shift, but my stays and dress were gone. My hands were tied to the bedpost but my feet were not. When one of the men came and leaned over me, I kicked and fought him with every bit of strength I had. The man grabbed me around the throat but I would not stop because I was sure he was going to kill me. The other man made him stop strangling me. After that they gagged me."

Olivia fell silent. Michael was not looking directly at her

but would wager that she was having a difficult time controlling her tears.

"I was so afraid they were going to rape me and kill
me. Until I heard the other say that they were told not to
harm me."

Troy's steady pace set a rhythm for Lady Olivia's story.
She kept on talking as surely as the mare kept on walking.

"I thought that odd. That they kidnapped me and were
told not to hurt me. It must have meant something but I
could make no sense of it then."

Did that mean she could make sense of it now?

"I prayed for a chance to escape. All the while I could
hear them whispering, arguing, I think. They took the gag off,
made me drink laudanum. I fell asleep, screaming. Or at least
I think I was screaming."

He wanted to reassure her, tell her that it was what he
would have done, but he did not want to interrupt again. As
long as he said nothing it was as though she had no audience.

"When I woke up, it was quiet except for the most un-
believable snoring I have ever heard. The ropes were loose,
whether by accident or on purpose I don't know. I fell asleep
again and woke up a second time. The snoring man was still
asleep. I pulled off the blindfold, but it was dark and I could
not make out much."

Michael heard the sound of the river, swollen with spring
runoff. They were closer to town than he'd expected. Lady
Olivia did not seem aware of it, her thoughts turned inward,
her voice practical in its timbre but her eyes lost and filled
with dread.

"I was not thinking very clearly but all I wanted to do

was escape. So I did. Even when I tripped over something, the man never woke up. Was the other man outside or had he gone somewhere? I never saw him. It never occurred to me to find something to wear besides my shift."

"The laudanum would have left you muzzy."

She looked at him. "When you found me? I think I was almost dead." The realization took her by surprise. She nodded to herself and closed her eyes as she continued. "I had decided I would go to sleep again. I hardly felt the cold and I could hear my mother singing. She's been dead for five years."

Silence filled the space between them. He felt water in his eyes and looked away.

"I think you must have saved my life." There was amazement in her voice. "Thank you, Mr. Garrett. Thank you. I am sure I am not the first life you have saved, but I do not think any could have been more grateful."

"Lady Olivia, I am sure yours is a life most worthy of saving." He could not think of many others who had been as innocent. "You are very welcome."

"Oh do not say I am worthy of it." She raised a hand to her heart, her expression showing more alarm than flattery. "I will feel guilty forever if I do not live up to your hopes."

As if he would ever know.

"To be honest, sir, all I want to do is go home, have some chicken broth and go to sleep. Would it be wrong to pretend it never happened?"

"A question for the ages, my lady. I think you must do whatever will enable you to put the incident behind you. Let your brother worry about finding the perpetrators. He will know a way to keep you safe."

"Yes, by marrying me off to some man or insisting that I never leave Pennford or that I go to London and forget about cooking."

What did cooking have to do with it?

"I want to beat those men to a pulp myself. But I do not and could not have the strength. Perhaps I should learn how to shoot."

"See if you can convince one of your brothers to show you how." As he spoke he prayed that none of them would. A woman seeking revenge was dangerous enough without a weapon.

They walked on in silence, the sound of the river making quiet conversation impossible.

"I am going to wash my feet!" She abruptly turned Troy toward a large rock and used it to dismount.

"Wait, Olivia, the water will be freezing." Michael ran after her. "You will wind up ill."

Either she pretended not to hear him, or the rushing water made it impossible. She put one foot into a pool created by rocks or fairies, the perfect place to wade. Gasping she put her other foot in and sloshed around for a moment, obviously uncomfortable, but equally determined to clean her feet.

Michael fully intended to grab her arm and pull her forcibly from the freezing spring melt, but the moment he was close enough she popped out of the ankle-deep water and grabbed the blanket he had in his hand.

"Dry your feet. Hurry." He nodded at the blanket as he spoke. She was already beginning to shiver.

She stood on the claylike shale with a rock at hip height.

"Sit down." He nodded to the rock behind her.

She did sit, most likely because he was so close to her she had no other choice.

"That was a stupid thing to do."

With a glance of pure irritation she began to dry her feet, the speed of it convincing him she was annoyed that he was right.

As she bent her head over her task, he watched the way the sun glinted off the golden highlights of her hair. Until that moment he had thought it a rather ordinary brown, but now he realized that it was streaked with red and gold and bronze. Even unkempt and ragged, he could see the beauty of it. He reached a hand out to smooth it, but stopped himself.

Securing both his hands behind his back he watched the curls shift as she rubbed her toes with the blanket, trying to warm them. There was a mole near the nape of her neck, exactly the right spot to press a kiss if one was so inclined.

He was not.

16

WHAT WAS HE LOOKING AT? Olivia wondered as she kept on drying her feet. Why was he making her feel so warm when her toes were so cold? "You are not supposed to be watching me dry my feet."

"What etiquette book says that?"

"It *feels* risqué."

He laughed. The throaty sound made her want to laugh too, but she bit her lip instead. She handed him the blanket as she stood up on the rock. It made her almost as tall as he was. "Where is Troy?"

"Right where you left her, my lady. Troy knows to do what she is told."

"Oh, now you are comparing me to a horse."

"The finest horse in the world."

"As well as the ugliest." Olivia leaned close to whisper it so Troy wouldn't hear. As she did, Olivia noticed that

Garrett's face was shadowed with whiskers, his eyes had the tiniest creases at the corner. He must be awfully tired.

She knew she could act like a spoiled child. It was sometimes the only way to win out against her brothers. But Mr. Garrett had saved her life. He did not deny it. Her thanks had been to rail at him without ceasing and insult his eyes and anything else she could think of.

Turning her head a little, so that she could see into his eyes, she began an apology. His eyes really were quite lovely, the color of the iridescent pheasant feathers that she used to garnish her favorite poultry dish. Right now they were more gold than brown. "Mr. Garrett, I am so very sorry if I have not been the ideal companion."

The next words died in her throat at the expression in his eyes. Wild and wonderful at the same time. Before she could respond with more than a smile, he turned and whistled for Troy. Garrett stepped onto the rock, scooped her up and dumped her back into the saddle.

"We will move on, Lady Olivia, or the light will be gone before we reach safety."

"I just wanted to apologize."

He still stood on the rock, so their eyes were even. "That's what you are saying with your lips, Lady Olivia. Your eyes? Well, your eyes are asking for something else entirely."

"Are you flirting with me, Mr. Garrett?"

"No, my lady, *you* are flirting with *me*." He hoped that was not pleased surprise he heard in her voice.

"I am not flirting!" She straightened and moved her gaze from his lips to his eyes.

"If you are not, why were you looking at my mouth as

though you would like to do more than see if I have all my teeth?"

Good, there was the indignation he preferred. Her hand twitched and he leaned back lest she act on her inclination to slap him.

"You, Mr. Garrett, are the one who is making something of a natural curiosity."

He laughed. He could not help it. Would she ever say what he expected?

"Very natural," he agreed, and wished he had disagreed. She leaned closer, her eyes holding his with mesmerizing intensity.

"No." The word was out of his mouth before she could move nearer. "You have been kidnapped, stripped of your clothes, drugged. All you should be worrying about is finding home again."

"When I was kidnapped I thought I was going to die. I could die in the next minute. How awful to leave this life without ever knowing a man's kiss." Her eyes turned her wistful words into a seduction. "One kiss would only take a moment, the barest of moments."

As she spoke she moved so that her mouth was just a little from his. She must have been counting on pure male instinct to close the distance and make him press his lips to hers. *Stop! Stop!* His rational mind screamed and still her sweet pink mouth drew him inexorably closer.

Their kiss was the lightest touch, hardly a kiss at all. He had that much self-control. Still, he tasted the sweet and sharp of her, the untouched passion, the soft supple lips that were such a perfect reflection of the body he had held once already.

Begging God for self-control, he resisted the urge for more and drew away.

"Mr. Garrett, that was not a kiss." It wasn't criticism so much as disappointment. "The reverend's nephew did better than that."

"You told me you'd never been kissed before."

"I said I had never been kissed by a man. He was sixteen years old."

"That is quite enough, my lady." Michael jumped down from the rock, annoyed that he had been tricked into playing her game. "How old are you? You act like a child but behave like a tease. It is not at all becoming."

Michael took the lead and urged Troy into a walk, surprised when she did not answer him. He let the silence linger.

They had gone a good distance before he heard any sound from her. First a deep quivering sigh followed by a sniff. Damnation, he'd hurt her feelings. He reached into his pocket and handed her his handkerchief without looking up.

"Thank you," she whispered.

He would not weaken.

"I said thank you." Her voice had an edge to it.

"You are welcome for the handkerchief."

Another long silence.

"I am twenty."

"You are not."

"It's because I am so short that everyone thinks I am younger. And my brothers. They are always treating me like a child, and sometimes it's easier to act like one."

"Because you are then able to have what you want." Another silence. When it persisted he added, "I told you last night. I have sisters, too."

Her "Humph" was not a very ladylike sound. "Can we not go faster? I am anxious to reach home. All I want to do is drink some of my best tisane for a sore throat, go to sleep. My feet are—" She stopped abruptly.

"Cold." He finished the sentence for her. "I am sure if you think awhile you can find a way to blame me for that." He pulled his gloves off and walked back to Troy. Tugging one foot out from under his greatcoat, he covered her toes with his fur-lined glove.

She tried to pull the foot out of his hand. "What are you doing?"

It wasn't insult he heard but panic. That damn excuse for a kiss had distracted him. She was not his latest flirt, but a woman who had been through hell.

He steadied Troy with a hand to her neck and wished a woman was as easy to comfort. "I apologize, Lady Olivia. I was putting my gloves on your ice cold feet. They may be ill-fitting but they are fur-lined and should help warm them."

"All right." The fear left her voice. "I thought you were mad at me."

"No, my lady, you were mad at me." He looked at her for the first time since he had swung her onto the horse. Her tear-streaked face made her look even more vulnerable. He had not thought that was possible. He wanted to cuddle her close and comfort her. Like a wounded puppy, he insisted to his more libidinous self.

He walked around and put the other glove on her left

foot. It felt like a chunk of ice. He doubted his gloves would do much good, but they were better than nothing. With Troy's lead in hand, Michael forged on.

"Do you know where we are, Mr. Garrett?" Her voice was stronger and without any annoyance. "I thought I knew this road. I recognized where we were before, but this does not look familiar at all. I suppose I am not feeling myself just now."

"I think that's because three of four trees were brought down by the wind." Michael knew an apology when he heard one. He smiled to himself. "We are not on the road now, but on a deer track running roughly parallel to it." He looked back at her and she nodded, the worry fading from her face as she noted the downed trees and began to recognize the landscape.

"We should reach Pennsford and the vicarage soon."

"Exactly." He examined the sky. "It will grow colder quickly. Add the rain brewing and it will make night travel a misery."

By setting a vigorous pace they reached the vicar's home just as the light faded. Still, they were both cold.

Michael worried anew about Olivia's health. She was shivering again. Despite her healthy weight and annoying determination, he knew lungs were fragile. He'd seen more than one well-built man succumb to an inflammation and to his eyes Olivia did not look well.

He helped her from the horse and swept her into his arms. Without complaint, Olivia snuggled as close to him as she could. He was relieved when a woman, dressed in black, answered his knock without delay. He was not sure if she was a maid or the housekeeper, too old for one, too young for the other.

The woman's puzzlement lasted only an instant. "Lollie! What happened?" She did not wait for an answer. "Bring her in immediately. I will light the fire in one of the bedrooms. Was she at the river again?"

"Yes," both he and Olivia chorused. Olivia started to explain but began to cough. The sound struck fear in his heart.

"I beg you, madam, can we save explanations for later?"

The woman nodded and called a younger maid. Her rapid instructions were given to the wide-eyed girl who ran up the stairs even as the housekeeper added her last direction. "Do find a warming pan for the bed."

An old man and an even older woman tottered into the hall, both with shawls wrapped around their shoulders. The man still held a newspaper. Reverend Drummond and his sister, Michael assumed.

The housekeeper began to climb the stairs and as Michael followed, the older two trailed behind him making worrisome noises. Miss Drummond asked a string of questions, not all of them pertinent. "What is it, Mrs. Blackford? Who is it? Should we call the surgeon? Who is this gentleman? Where did that greatcoat come from? Why do you smell like smoke? Did the windstorm cause a fire? What happened to Big Sam?"

"Hush, sister," the old man scolded. "Let Mrs. Blackford do her work. We will have the answers soon enough. For now we should thank this Good Samaritan for rescuing our lost sheep."

It was a mixed metaphor but Michael appreciated an end to the questions and the fact that the vicar had cast him in such a generous light.

The vicar's sister did as she was asked, but only after one last question: "Where are her shoes and stockings?"

17

MRS. BLACKFORD OPENED a door and turned around sharply, taking in Olivia's bare feet and legs. With a suspicious glance his way, she stepped back to allow Michael into the room. The fire was alive. The maid had the covers turned back and was hurrying from the room muttering, "Warming pan and some chicken broth."

When the old woman made to crowd into the room, the vicar stopped her. "Let us wait out here a moment. Mrs. Blackford will have her settled quickly."

Michael had Olivia on her feet but still held her, as she was swaying. Behind him the door snapped shut, and with a rustle of skirts Mrs. Blackford came to them.

"Close your eyes," the housekeeper commanded him.

Michael did as told, neither one of them commenting on what he had already seen.

He'd spied a voluminous nightgown on the bed and

within a minute of removing his greatcoat Olivia was wearing it, the nightgown covering her fully, dragging on the floor the way his greatcoat had dragged on the ground. The oatmeal color did nothing for her wan complexion. The bruises on her throat stood out in contrast.

"Lollie, climb into bed. Or do you want the man to lift you in?"

"No, Annie, I can manage." She slid between the sheets and sighed. "Please, please, where is Big Sam? I am so worried about him."

"He was upset. When he realized that you had been taken he ran to the castle and told the duke."

"Did he tell anyone else?"

"I told him not to. I'm so sorry, Lollie, but I had to slap him. It was an emergency and the only thing I could think of to make him calm down so he would listen."

Olivia nodded and Michael wondered who this poor soul was.

"He understood that it was important that no one but the duke know that you were gone, probably kidnapped. I have not told anyone else. Not even the vicar or Miss Drummond."

"But where is he?"

"Out searching for you. I'm not sure what that means to him but he would not wait and do nothing."

Some kind of companion, Michael surmised. Less than bright, but a lifelong friend of some kind.

"Was he out in that storm, last night? Oh, I hope he found shelter."

"I am sure that he did, dearest." The housekeeper took Michael's greatcoat and handed it to him.

Olivia nodded, not fully convinced. Her nod dissolved into a shiver.

"Some broth and a warming pan are coming as quickly as that girl can make it happen."

"It's all right, Annie. Truly. We both know speed is a word unknown in this house."

Mrs. Blackford laughed and patted Olivia's hair.

These two were friends, despite the disparity in their stations and age. The housekeeper was at least ten years older than Lady Olivia. Big Sam, Mrs. Blackford, the aging vicar, Reverend Drummond, and his addled sister—Lady Olivia collected misfits. He could fit right in.

Before any more questions could be asked or answered, the door was opened without a knock and the maid, Reverend Drummond and his sister pushed into the room, making the small space as crowded as a field tent on a rainy night. Michael backed up against the wall, folded his arms and watched.

It took awhile to warm the bed and to allow Olivia to sip her broth, but before long all were waiting to hear the story.

Olivia told them an interesting version of what they had agreed on. "I was walking down from the castle on my way to see you today." She nodded at the vicar. "I was thinking I would do my own inspection on the way and see what damage the storm had done. I decided to stop by the river to see if there were any mushrooms. I have been thinking of making a soup of varying kinds of mushrooms and am still trying to decide what proportion of each would be best."

"It sounds intriguing, Lollie," Mrs. Blackford patted her hand. "So you were thinking about the ingredients and became distracted as you walked along?"

"Yes." Olivia's sigh was all apology. "I heard someone and looked up to see Mr. Garrett and his horse moving along the path. I took a step without watching where I was going, slipped on a wet rock and fell into the river. I think I could have saved myself but Mr. Garrett insisted on rescuing me."

All four looked at him.

"I could hardly sit my horse and watch while Lady Olivia struggled."

"He held up his greatcoat for privacy while I took my clothes off. Removing my clothes was my idea and not his," she hastened to add. "I was already shivering."

"Where are your clothes?" the reverend asked, scanning the room as though they should be there somewhere.

"Left by the river. I think we both just forgot them in our hurry to find someplace warm."

Michael was satisfied with the improvisation. He thought it likely that her clothes had been taken to be used in some part of the plot she had foiled. Busy mulling over that idea, he did not at first notice the silence.

"The vicar asked why you were on that road. What were you looking for, Mr. Garrett?" The housekeeper seemed more than curious. She had already cast him as part of the plot.

"I was looking for the road to Manchester." Honesty made that answer simple.

They looked skeptical. The housekeeper was fingering her keys, the vicar had his fingers steepled, a searching look in his eye, and Miss Drummond was patting her mouth with her fingers as though trying to keep words inside. The "rescuer of lost sheep" had suddenly become the devil.

The vicar's sister could not keep quiet any longer. "Mrs. Blackford, you commented on a new face in town."

Mrs. Blackford nodded. "Yes, your horse is unmistakable. You spent the last while at The Fox and Hare, did you not?"

"I did."

They waited for more. Very well, he would tell them the truth.

"I had a letter of introduction to the Duke of Meryon and was considering seeking employment. It did not take me long to decide that my temperament is better suited to city life." The truth made him feel uneasy. More vulnerable. He hoped it did not show.

"Aha." Mr. Drummond slapped his knee. "You see that work in Manchester was not meant to be. You understand that, do you not? The good Lord found a way to turn you back to Pennsford."

"So it would appear, sir." He could hardly disagree since he'd had the same thought himself.

Miss Drummond moved closer to Olivia, stopped short and cried out, "Oh no! What happened to your hair, Olivia?"

Olivia's hair! They had forgotten to prepare for that detail. He kept his face bland and realized that honesty was not always found in words.

Tears welled up in Olivia's eyes and she buried her face in her hands.

He would have been annoyed if he thought she was·trying to hide from answering. No, her tears were real.

"It was caught on a branch," he said. "I had to cut it to free her from it." How many lies was that now?

The women nodded without question. The vicar eyed Michael with less conviction. "You stupid Galatian, why did you not simply cut the branch?"

"I did not think of it. My only concern was to get her from the water before she drowned." The priest had just called him a Galatian. The verse from Acts came fully to mind. It was translated as "foolish" not "stupid." Foolish he would readily agree too. He had been foolish in more ways than one.

"It is actually very charming, Lollie." This from Mrs. Blackford. "Those lovely loose curls draw attention to your pretty face."

Olivia wiped her eyes on the bed linen. Though she did not appear convinced, it was clear that she wanted to believe it.

"I do think you are right, Mrs. Blackford. I never noticed how green her eyes were before." The vicar stood up and came closer to Olivia and smiled. "Just lovely. Now you remind me even more of your mother."

That was it. Olivia smiled back at him and then wrinkled her face as if embarrassed that she was so pleased by the comparison.

Miss Drummond nodded. "A blessing in disguise."

"Can Lady Olivia stay with you while I go to her brother and have him send a carriage for her?"

"Of course she will stay. Perhaps she should stay overnight so that she is not exposed to the elements again." Annie Blackford smoothed the covers over her charge.

"That sounds a wise idea," the vicar agreed.

Miss Drummond clapped her hands. "Company. We will be having company."

They nodded, even Olivia. No one bothered to clarify that it was far from company to have an unwell neighbor use a bed.

"I know you must be very tired." Mrs. Blackford moved toward the door purposefully. "We will leave you to rest and bring you some dinner later."

"Before he leaves, could I please speak to Mr. Garrett?" Olivia asked

Reverend Drummond nodded. "Mrs. Blackford will be your chaperone."

With the vicar and his sister gone, Annie hurried back to Olivia's bedside. Olivia watched her, mortified by her loving concern. Annie Blackford, her dearest friend, deserved the truth.

"It is a very credible story, Lollie, and well told. But you were gone for two days and the storm only happened last night. The vicar and Miss Hope are easily satisfied, but others will have questions."

"Yes." Olivia sighed with relief. "To you, Annie, I will tell the truth."

"Why not just announce it to the world, Lady Olivia?" Michael Garrett came closer as he spoke. "I beg your pardon for the insult, Mrs. Blackford, but if one person knows, how long before two or three do, and after that the entire town?"

"I assure you, sir, that I have been trusted with secrets far more damaging than whatever it is Olivia may tell me."

Olivia nodded, wondering if that admission was wise. "I will tell her, Mr. Garrett."

When Garrett did nothing but shake his head in resignation, she began.

She did her best to sound practical but Annie's dismay was obvious, and when Olivia reached the part about her escape and rescue by Mr. Garrett, Annie actually went to him and took his hand.

"Thank you so much, sir. How would she have survived without you? The storm was not so bad here, but most who have come to town today have tales to tell. I do not know what I would have done if something had happened to Lollie. We have been like sisters all our lives."

"Annie's mother was our governess. Matilda Elderton." There was so much more to it than that but Mr. Garrett did not need to know any of it. "Trust me in this, sir, she will be my sole confidante."

"As you wish, my lady." He bent over Annie's hand and Olivia could have kissed him for that generous gesture. Kissed him better than he had kissed her, that was for sure. She finished her story with a yawn.

"I am tired, Annie, but will you stay with me?" She yawned again, a real yawn this time. She *was* tired. Amazingly so.

Mr. Garrett took his leave with a gentlemanly bow. The room felt much emptier when he left. Annie stood up with her knitting.

"Annie, sit down."

"I'm not leaving, Lollie. I was only going to move closer to the fire."

Olivia shook off her fatigue and sat upright in bed. "There is one more thing I need to tell you."

Annie sat back down slowly.

"As I was falling asleep after the dose of laudanum…" She shuddered at the memory of the sickly sweet stuff. Brandy would have worked just as well. "They—the kidnappers, that is—seemed so elated that their plan was going to work." Olivia leaned close to Annie and whispered, even though the door was closed, Mr. Garrett had left and the vicar and Miss Hope could not hear well at all. "One said to the other, 'Her brother will give us the land on a silver platter.'"

Annie's expression was part shock and part dismay. "The land? Your land?"

"Mine? No, not at all. I think they were using me as a threat to Jess. I think they were sent from London by moneylenders to hold me in order to coerce him into paying up. With *his* land."

"Oh no." Annie was obviously appalled but she thought about it for a minute and nodded. "Yes, I see it could easily be that. Your brother plays deep."

Olivia watched Annie's expression soften when she mentioned Jess, and harden as quickly at the mention of his gambling.

"I know it hurts for me to tell you that, Annie, dear; you are so much a part of the family. But I fear it is the truth."

"Did you tell Mr. Garrett? Will you tell your brother?"

"Why should I tell Mr. Garrett? He is not staying. He is going to have someone come for me and be off to Manchester to make his fortune. He is just passing through."

"You will tell the duke."

Olivia heard the command, and it pained her to ignore it. "I know you hate secrets, but I cannot tell him. You know why as well as I do. He will withdraw and be angry and come up with some way to punish Jess that will drive them even further apart."

"You must tell someone." Annie had given up all pretense of knitting.

"I've told you, and I am going to write to Jess and tell him he must come home immediately." Her yawn was part moan and she could not fight the fatigue any longer.

She was asleep before Annie could answer, off into a dreamworld that was surprisingly free of evil. In it she was debating with a cabbage and a cauliflower. If she were to wheedle one more kiss from Mr. Garrett before he left, would that mean she truly was a tease?

18

MICHAEL DID NOT NEED directions to Pennford Castle. It was on a rise north of town, impossible to ignore. The descriptive "castle" suited it perfectly. It had probably been sited on the rise to protect the land that made up the baron's domain. Those barons might have been Pennistans for all he knew.

The castle consisted of two buildings attached to each other but significantly different in age. The original keep, which faced the town, was round, surrounded by a moat that was now more of a lake. A square building was attached to the back of the keep where it met the land. The newer part had the same crenellation on a similar flat roof, with several turrets as opposed to the single one in the old castle. The bricklike stonework was comparable, but the stone of the square building was newer, with many more windows.

While the exterior of both buildings was well maintained

it was easy to see that the original keep was no longer in use. It was dark, with few openings. Those had no glass reflecting the last light of the day.

The newer square building was bold with light on all levels. The duke's flag flew over the castles, an old tradition, and it made Michael decide then and there that the duke valued the old ways and was not inclined to change.

Michael turned from the road that led to the new building. Lady Olivia was safe, but he would still make his own reconnaissance of the area and see what he could find.

He took a trail that led south around the moat, effectively approaching the occupied part of the castle from the blind side. The water in the moat was currently covered with bits of leaves and twigs. He imagined someone would be about to clean it when more important damage had been dealt with.

The trail was littered with small branches, but he could see beneath the storm's mark that someone on horseback had used it. The hoofprints were old and hardened, so they had not been made recently.

Once he rounded the old building and moat he was sure that he was unobserved. Michael passed through a stand of trees that were carefully tended to look as though they had been allowed to grow wild. The hand of an artist was at work here. None of it had been compromised by the storm.

A doe, full with fawn, moved across the path and into the trees, following her own trail.

Nudging Troy off the path, Michael found a huge tree that would hide him and most of Troy. He dismounted and waited to see if anyone else was afoot. Speed was the enemy of a successful reconnaissance. His old colonel's voice echoed in his head. Michael had never agreed with that. To his way of thinking each scouting mission called for its own pace. He was in a hurry, but not such a hurry that he would ignore precautions.

It was not a friendly evening even though the rain held off and the sky was clear. There was a breeze building to a wind. Again. He pulled his gloves from his pocket and remembered who had last used them.

Lady Olivia and Mrs. Blackford made a handsome picture. Olivia's fairer hair and pale complexion were as effective a contrast to Mrs. Blackford's silver-streaked black hair as was the housekeeper's tall thin frame compared to Olivia's small compact body.

Every time he held her he was reminded of the lovely curves he had done his best to ignore as he brushed the dirt from her flesh and folded his greatcoat around her.

That was hardly a memory to be entertaining moments before seeing her brother. It would be wiser to use this time to consider what version of the truth to tell the duke. How to frame it so that it would best serve Olivia.

No matter what kind of brother the Duke of Meryon was, Michael felt certain that his sister's reputation would be a concern. Whether the duke saw her as an asset in his pursuit of alliances, a nuisance to be married off or a half-forgotten sibling, the idea that men would use a woman under his protection in their own game would be seen as a test of his power.

Far down the list was the chance that the duke loved his sister, and cared about her enough to be worried for her well-being solely because of it.

Michael pulled off his glove and did his best to wipe the fatigue from his face. With a pat on Troy's neck and promise of "dinner soon," he mounted.

If no one had found him lost in thought and half into a doze, there was no one about but him.

Michael came up the circle of the drive from the west as it wound around the hill and his mental games were displaced by the scene before him. The castle was lit by the rapidly setting sun.

The old stone was lit golden, the glassed windows reflecting the light like jewels. It was at once welcoming and mysterious, the way he felt when he claimed a lover: At last, at last, this woman could be the one that filled the emptiness, the one that made him forget the others. But it was never true. No woman had ever come close.

The sun slipped behind the peak and Michael Garrett was sure this palace of pleasure and power would be no more his saving grace than the woman he had held in his arms. He pressed his fingers to his mouth and laughed a little at the memory of that smallest of kisses.

There was a gatehouse, but the mammoth stone-supported wrought-iron gates were open so he saw no reason to stop.

At the end of the rising drive the castle loomed. The sunset moment of golden glory was gone, replaced with a forbidding gloom that would convince a nervous man to forgo his business. Michael left his horse and a coin with a groom who came running from one of the outbuildings and went to the door.

The word *door* did not do the opening justice. Like the

gates, the entry was oversized, great wooden panels large enough to admit a man on his horse.

He raised the knocker and let it fall. Immediately a servant came out of a small opening to the right of the ceremonial entrance. This door was made to blend in with the stone and was barely noticeable.

"Michael Garrett to see His Grace the Duke of Meryon."

"Your card?" The fellow was surely no more than a porter but spoke with all the arrogance of the estate steward.

"No card."

"His Grace does not receive callers at this hour." The man stepped back through the door and closed it firmly.

Michael used a few words that Lady Olivia would definitely not approve of and turned away. No point in knocking again. He knew this type, one of those petty tyrants who wielded his power when it did not matter and was too easily overcome when it did.

It did matter now, but Michael was trying to be discreet, to spread as little gossip as possible. To that end, he began to circle the building. The sun was gone but he had grown used to the dark and could find his way easily.

Michael moved slowly, careful not to make a sound, watching for a night guard patrolling the grounds. If there was one, a fact he doubted, the guard's circuit around the buildings would take the better part of an hour and be easy to avoid.

A place this size should have one, but there had been no guard at the gatehouse, so it was possible they had only the night porter at the door with some minion to walk the halls inside.

A mistake. If the duke relied on his name and power to protect him, he had not read the papers during the French Revolution. Position gave power, but it also made one a target for thieves, murderers. As well as kidnappers.

With no sign of a guard, Michael moved along the wall of the castle, checking the windows of the darkened rooms. He found one unlatched on his third try. That made the porter lazy as well as arrogant.

Pulling off his greatcoat, Michael leaned through the open window to drop it onto the floor inside. He followed it, pulling himself up on the ledge and working his way through the two-foot opening. The floor was carpeted, and he fell onto it in complete silence. Nice to know that lack of practice had not lessened his skills at entering illegally.

He was in some sort of nondescript parlor, and made his way into the hall without seeing a soul. He was walking purposefully to nowhere when a maid carrying a basket came along. Her screech was understandable. The hallway was lit only every twenty feet or so.

"I thought I was the only one in this wing." She dropped the basket and began backing away from him.

Any second, he thought, she would turn and run.

"I do beg your pardon, miss. I am so ridiculously lost." Michael tried for his most suave voice, while ostensibly ignoring her panic. "I must see the duke and I cannot find my way to him."

"You're to see the duke?" The maid picked up her basket of linens and put it on a nearby chair. "That porter is a fool. He should have accompanied you."

Michael nodded. It was the absolute truth.

"Then again, he is often too busy unless you are some-one the duke knows by name."

So the staff had the measure of the man's failings, too. That would mean he was as ineffective as he was lazy.

"His Grace is in his study with Lord David. It is—" she began and stopped with a shrug. "I had best take you there myself or you will wind up in the old castle with only the ghosts for company." She gave him a wink, and Michael was not sure if she was flirting or showing him that she meant the mention of ghosts as a joke.

Time was he knew by instinct. Not tonight, he realized, thinking back to those moments with Olivia. Lady Olivia. He had been toyed with by an amateur and fallen right into the trap, not thinking with his brain at all.

Sweet-looking though this maid was, Michael was not interested in what she was offering. As she led him down the hall, he was sure she was doing her best to walk with a provocative twist to her step. He followed her and thought only of how much to tell the duke and how much to hold back, trying to decide what would be in Olivia's best interest.

They were crossing the cavernous entry hall, when the night porter caught up with him. "You! Both of you! Stop!"

"Just ignore him," the maid whispered. "The duke's study is up these stairs to the left and down the hall."

She turned back to the porter, leaving Michael to manage on his own. "Really!" Her words carried back up the stairs. "You are the most irritating man. How many times must I tell you that my name is Patsy?"

"That man. Who is that man? Did you let him in?"

Michael did not need to hear any more to know that he

would be followed. As he rounded the corner, two footmen stepped away from a door, clearly the entrance to the study where he would find the duke.

"What is your business, sir? Why are you unaccompanied?"

Before he could answer them the porter came dashing down the hall. "Stop him! That man broke in!"

19

THE FOOTMEN SEIZED HIM by the elbows and held him as the porter ran toward them. The porter paused barely a moment before pummeling Michael with his fists. "You lying, thieving bastard. I told you to leave." He spoke between jabs Michael was able to avoid despite being restrained by the footmen.

Eventually the porter managed to land a couple of punches that hurt. Michael counted that long enough to wait for the duke to take notice of the commotion outside his study. With a twist he broke free of the footmen and tripped the porter. He was reaching for the door handle when it swung open. Michael stepped back and the porter fell, face-first, into the room at the feet of the duke.

The duke ignored the porter and gave Michael his complete attention. Michael sensed a man pushed to the limit of his patience, a man who would like nothing better than to land a few punches of his own.

"Announce the caller," the duke told one of the footmen. His voice belied the tension Michael sensed.

The porter stood up, straightened his clothes.

"He asked to see you, Your Grace. He had no card and was not dressed in a manner that was appropriate. It is late in the day for callers, so I sent him away."

"What is his business?"

"He did not say, Your Grace." The porter's demeanor was so meek that Michael wondered if there could possibly be two men inhabiting one mind and body or if, which was more likely, the porter knew better than to present his superior attitude around his betters.

"He was not asked, Your Grace," Michael volunteered.

They all looked at him. All except the other gentleman in the room. He was well dressed with the same blond hair and blue eyes as the duke. One more of Olivia's brothers, Michael guessed.

That gentleman came out of the room and stood behind Michael, just beyond his line of sight. He was the only one of the five that made Michael at all uncomfortable. He had a feeling this man knew how to fight.

"Your Grace," Michael began with a significant bow, "the vicar asked me to bring you a message."

The duke did not react in any way, though somehow his gaze grew even more intense.

"Your name?"

"Garrett. Michael Garrett."

The duke *did* react to that. His hand curled into a fist.

"You could have given that message to the porter, but since you are here I will have it from you personally."

The duke turned his back on all of them and went into the study, not stopping until he was standing behind his desk.

"The rest of you, be about your business," the duke's brother ordered. He waited as the group scrambled to obey. The footmen straightened their clothes and took their stations again on either side of the door. The porter moved down the hall and Patsy, with another wink at Michael, followed.

"You. Inside." This terse command from the duke's brother.

Michael did not need the direction, but went in ahead of the younger Pennistan, whose ill humor was barely concealed. He reminded Michael of Gabriel, the Pennistan he had met in France, but this one's inclination to hotheadedness had not been cooled by a wife and a ready-made family as Gabriel's had.

The blow to his gut was a complete surprise. Michael stumbled back, doubled over, unable to do more than try to catch his breath and wait for the next clout to knock him unconscious. The dungeon would be next.

"You bastard," Olivia's brother hissed. "Tell me where she is before I beat you to a pulp."

"David, control yourself." The duke's voice came from somewhere over Michael's head. There were no more punches and Michael thanked God for the mercy.

"I am far more even-tempered than my brother," the duke said, his voice even closer now. "When you can speak again, I am inclined to hear your story before I have you drawn and quartered."

This was not the first time Michael's actions had not been appreciated. Once again, England did not appear to be all that different from France. Michael took his time recovering, searching the room for a weapon as he pretended to stumble to a chair. As he straightened his clothes he was relieved to see that the duke's brother was doing the same.

The room was a good size but not so big it needed a fireplace at each end, though it would add to the comfort. There were doors on three walls, five in all, but he had no idea where they led to. He could make his way out the window. Or would he wind up in the lake? He could swim.

As the silence drew out, Michael turned his attention to the duke. He was dressed in black, his white shirt and cravat a stark contrast to the dark wool of his jacket.

He wore the medal of some order. Was he expecting someone he thought to impress or did he wear it all the time? As controlled as he appeared to be there was enough rage, helplessness and mistrust in the air to be shared by all three of them.

"She is safe, my lord." Michael bowed ever so slightly to the man who had hit him. He turned to the duke and spoke, with another, more profound, bow. His last. "Lady Olivia is quite safe and is indeed at the vicarage, Your Grace."

"Why did she send you as her emissary?"

"Mrs. Blackford and Reverend Drummond think it best that she stay with them overnight. She is tired and was coughing when I left."

"Tell me what you know," the duke commanded, still not sitting down, but standing alert behind his desk.

"I will, Your Grace, but I hope that in return you will share what information you have." Michael knew better than to wait for an answer and recounted his meeting with Olivia, his efforts to save her life. He avoided the more personal moments and looked the duke straight in the eye as he spoke.

"I found her wandering in the woods. She was on the verge of death by freezing."

Despite the duke's nod, Michael could not tell if he was convinced. Meryon raised his hand and turned to his brother. "David, I know you were calling on a friend but I ask you to delay that and find Olivia's maid. Have her gather a change of clothes and a warm cloak, but do not let her accompany you. Take the carriage and bring Olivia home. If Annie objects tell her that we both know that Olivia will be safer here."

Interesting, Michael thought. The least important item of interest was that Lord David had any friends at all. Of more passing interest was the duke's reference to Mrs. Blackford as Annie, and most interesting of all was that the duke wanted his sister home so that she would "be safer." Meryon did not think her entirely free from danger any more than he did.

Another fact struck him: The duke knew she needed clothes. Michael had deliberately not described how she was dressed when he had found her.

The duke did not speak even when they were alone in the room. With a silent stare the duke took stock of one Michael Garrett. It was a full minute or more before he spoke again.

The duke pulled a basket out from under his desk and

spread the contents on his desk: a dark blue cloak streaked with dirt and a bonnet with its velvet brim crushed. "You neglected to mention what she was wearing when you apparently found her in the woods."

"Someone brought you this." Michael stepped close enough to touch the cloak. Wool, a fine wool with trim that was an intricate braid in shades of blue. Not sophisticated, rather simple and very well made. It told him as much about Lady Olivia as her brother had. At the bottom of the basket was a long, brown length of hair tied with a blue ribbon stripped from the bonnet. More than the dirty cloak and ruined bonnet it brought a knot of fear to Michael's gut and then anger at the violation. He could easily imagine how the duke must have felt. To not know if she was dead or alive. One more example of hell on earth.

Michael looked at the duke, who was watching him.

"Yes, Your Grace, they cut her hair. It upset her greatly. More than any other aspect of her captivity, I would say."

The duke barely nodded and poked at the basket with his finger.

"This basket was on the seat of my chair. I have no idea who put it here or when."

Michael could hear the anger in the quiet words and wondered how the footmen had escaped with their lives. He wanted more details but reminded himself that Michael Garrett was not in charge here, nor likely to be. He would tell the truth, though it was possible he would not leave with all his body parts working.

"Lady Olivia was in her shift when I found her, Your

Grace. And she was barefoot." *Tell the truth, Michael,* he lectured himself, *and have it over with.* "I had to undress her completely. The shift was wet and was adding to the chill."

He tried to speak as matter-of-factly as possible, but when he looked from the duke's unrevealing eyes to his fist, the knuckles were white with the effort to control his anger.

Michael realized why the duke had given Lord David an errand. The mere discussion of his sister's state of undress would certainly have earned him another punch.

"She was near strangled, but the bruises around her throat were the only injury I could see." He did not add "or feel." That would be asking for trouble.

"I believe you, Mr. Garrett, though I do question your motive for being honest."

There was a scratch at the door and someone opened it without waiting for permission. One of the footmen came in with a satchel.

"The courier has only just arrived, Your Grace."

The duke accepted the bag with a nod and opened it without comment. There were newspapers, magazines and a flood of letters. He sifted through them until he found the one he was looking for. The duke unfolded it and sat down to read. His expression did not change but he seemed to relax. The man was worried about more than his sister.

Michael sat in the nearest chair, though he had not been invited to, and watched.

The duke picked up another letter and read it through. Was it a letter from the duchess? His mistress? Minutes passed as he read it and another. The tension radiating from him built again until the duke closed his eyes and rested his head in his hands, his elbows on the desktop.

One set of papers floated to the floor and Michael stood and picked it up. It was a child's painstaking effort at a letter. "Dear sir," it began, and told Michael all he needed to know about the relationship between the two. Formal at best. Strained at worst.

Michael set it back on the desk.

"I should be in London." The duke spoke out loud before he remembered there was someone else in the room with him.

Not that Michael needed a reminder he was of less account than the footmen at the door.

Pushing the satchel and papers to the side of his desk the duke resumed their conversation as if there had been no interruption.

"Mr. Garrett, the fact that Olivia was injured at all is both insult and worry. Whether she was raped or not hardly matters. No one will believe she was left untouched."

If he was upset, the duke did not show it in his face or his eyes or his voice, only in the way he held his hand. As though he could keep all his sensibilities in his fist and crush them there.

"Surely, Your Grace, you came up with a credible explanation for her absence." Michael stepped back from the desk.

"I let it be known that she had gone to the vicar's and been taken ill and was staying with him until she was fully recovered. Something she ate. It would not be the first time. I was vague about what it was and how long she would be there."

"I can see that I will have to stand in line behind Lady Olivia, you, and your brother when the men who did this are apprehended."

"Once David is finished with them, you will have only to head the burial detail," the duke said.

"Lady Olivia guessed the story that you would spread. That is why she insisted that she be taken to the vicar's and not brought directly home."

The duke nodded. "Now I do not see how that explanation will work. Not if she has bruises on her throat and her hair is shorn. No illness causes those symptoms."

"The bruises are already fading." Michael turned away, not wanting the duke to see the anger he could not hide. "Her maid will have some explanation for the new hairstyle."

Michael rubbed his face with his hand. "You are talking about her as if she was some sort of rarefied legal problem." He wheeled back around. "She is a woman. Your sister."

"What is she to you?" The duke's question was laced with suspicion.

20

THE QUESTION TOOK HIM aback but Michael was saved from answering by another perfunctory scratch at the door. The same footman came in.

"The land manager is here, Your Grace. With the report on the storm damage. Lord David said that you would want to hear it."

Michael noted that the last was added with a note of apology. For interrupting the duke or perhaps for adding more to his long day.

The man who came in looked as though he lived out of doors. His face was colored by the sun, his hair had a perpetually windblown look and his hands, now holding tight to his hat, were the hands of a man who was willing to work.

"Your Grace," the man said as he bowed. He began a list of woods and trees and crops and animals. Meryon held property all over Derbyshire and into the Peak as well.

Michael followed the detailed account for the first few minutes, then his mind began to play with the answer to the duke's question: "What is Lady Olivia to you?"

The true answer to that could take a lifetime to explain. Or perhaps his lifetime would illustrate it. The girl he had found in the woods was his next step toward redemption. His next step toward creating a life that would free him of the war years and the memories that plagued him.

Not that all of his dreams were nightmares. And that was the crux of it. There were times when he wanted to stay Raoul Desseau forever. When he thought it would be easier to play a role that freed him from truth and allowed, even welcomed, lies.

That temptation not to return to face the life he had abandoned weighed on him as much as the crimes he had committed. Those were done for a greater good and God would forgive them. But could He forgive the weaknesses that made honesty such a challenge: pride, stubbornness, selfishness.

That was what Michael had been thinking about when a naked woman had wandered into his life. Facing her, he knew he had a choice, and that choice would define the rest of his days as ones filled with honor or defined by self-interest.

Michael did not know how long he considered the question but eventually he realized the room was quiet and the duke was watching him with cynical interest. "Have you been able to come up with an answer to my question?"

"I will tell you the truth, Your Grace." Michael felt virtue ease his conscience at that decision. "I gave thought to leaving her there, sure as I was that her story was not a happy one and that death was more reward than punishment. But that would have been a coward's way. Instead I chose to try to save her, not knowing anything about her. I did it because all life has value. Even life that others deem worthless."

If the duke thought that last was directed at him, he ignored it. "So if she had been a murderer you would not have regretted the effort?"

"Not for one minute, Your Grace. Murder is not the worst crime a man or woman can commit."

"I imagine you can speak about that with insight." As he spoke, the duke opened the long desk drawer in front of him and drew out a letter.

Michael was standing just on the other side of the desk and he could see the handwriting. He recognized the impatient scrawl as that of Lord Gabriel Pennistan.

"I have been expecting you for the better part of a week, Major Michael Garrett."

The duke dropped the letter on the desktop and leaned across it. "It is much too convenient that you are the one who rescued Lady Olivia." Meryon's eyes pinned Michael to the spot as surely as if he'd used nails.

"Of course. It would be a plot to you." Michael would have laughed if his desire to live had not been so strong. The duke was murderously angry.

As it was Michael could not keep the cynicism from his voice. "If you will allow it, Your, Grace, your story tells like this: I learned all I could from your brother while I was visiting his bride and their children in Sussex. Based on that information you think that I arranged to have your sister kidnapped and her reputation ruined. After that I became her rescuer." There were a couple of other ways to present it, but Michael had made his point. "How clever of me."

"Not clever enough." The duke seemed to relax, but that was after he pulled a pistol from his desk drawer and laid it on the desk.

"Now you have the advantage of me, Your Grace. I left my gun at the stable, thinking I was among allies."

"So my brother reported. That and a knife tucked into your blanket."

"I see you have your own network of spies." Obviously storm damage was not all the land manager had reported.

"Perhaps. But I call them friends, Mr. Garrett."

"Confusing the two is a civilian's greatest mistake, Your Grace."

"Both you and Gabriel call each other friend." The duke's expression finally showed something. Curiosity.

"Yes, but he was never a true spy. Nor was his wife. Lord Gabriel was not at all suited to the life and Lynette did it for her own reasons, which had nothing to do with whether Napoleon was winning or losing. The distinction is quite clear."

"You were a spy, though. In name and in deed. Do you deny that?"

"No, but if you have heard from Gabriel you already know that. And this: It is part of my past. Two years now. Raoul Desseau is gone, not quite buried, but a part of my past." The pure truth of that sentence was a relief, such a relief that he smiled. "I know that I am not welcome in society even if that life is behind me, so it is just as well that I never found much satisfaction in the balls and routs of the London Season."

The duke nodded, otherwise unmoved by his candor. "So you left London and stopped in Sussex, and after that you came north planning to extort money from us to protect Olivia's reputation. So much easier than gainful employment."

"In the name of God, what did your brother say about me in that letter? I counted him a friend."

"Gabriel praised you to the heavens. He says that your cleverness," he paused over the word, "saved his life, as well as Lynette's, when their escape was on the verge of discovery. He owes you for every moment he is alive. I do believe those were his exact words."

"I do not understand your suspicion. Your money funded that adventure, sir. More important than that, Gabriel is a Pennistan. If you do not believe your brother will always put his family first, you do not believe in anyone."

The duke glanced at the letter, otherwise unmoved by Michael's accusation. "I believe every word Gabriel wrote and all the stories he told me. But I know him. As you said he is my brother. His judgment of character is often influenced by his sensibilities. It is enough that you saved his life."

"I hardly saved his life, Your Grace." Honest or not, Michael was compelled to clarify the story. "I lied for him. It was a rather clever ruse, but my colonel was not inclined to use his brain or we might not have been so lucky."

"As I was saying." The duke spoke over Michael's last

words, making his lack of interest quite clear. "Gabriel thinks you saved his life and that of his wife and two of the children that they now call their own. That is sufficient to cloud his judgment."

"So I am to feel the brand of spy and its consequences for the first time." Honesty might make things simpler but it did not make life seem any more fair.

"If you were not part of her kidnapping or an effort at blackmail, it is also possible that you are using this rescue so you can marry Olivia and ally yourself with this family. Again so much easier than employment. The son of an Anglican bishop would be at least marginally acceptable as a husband for someone with the blood of the Duke of Meryon in her veins."

Disgust made short work of any attempt at civility. "You may be a duke but you are also a fool." Michael reached for his greatcoat and hat, relieved that this was one time when he could make his true opinion known.

"No matter what Gabriel told you, here is the truth. I have spent the last five years living a lie, posing as a French officer to extort money and betraying trust to fuel a war we won with dishonor as an ally. For me that ended when I came back to England.

"My family did not want the truth so I left Sussex. Not only do you not want the truth either, you continue to see anyone outside your sacred circle as a threat. I've lived that life and want no more of it." Michael turned to the door, sure, almost sure, that the duke would not shoot him in the back.

But beneath the lofty words was a genuine ache for the

sweet innocent he had rescued. He turned at the door and gave the duke a last scathing look. "No wonder Lady Olivia spends all her time in the kitchen. I'll wager it's the only place she can find any warmth, human or otherwise."

The duke did not try to stop him. As Michael reached for the door handle, it was opened from the other side. A velvet-clad cannonball burst into the room and flew across the floor to the duke. "Lyn! Oh, Lynford, I am so sorry."

The duke pushed the basket of clothes onto the floor and kicked it under his desk.

Then he opened his arms to his sister. The two stood in a bruising embrace, Olivia's face pressed against her brother's heart, Meryon's chin resting on her new curls.

Michael watched the two rock back and forth, each comforting the other, and had the answer to his question. He had been as wrong as he could be.

The Duke of Meryon loved his sister, loved her so much that even now there was a tear on his cheek as he held her tight, as if keeping her close would protect her from the world's dark moments.

"What do you have to be sorry for?" Meryon smoothed Olivia's hair and whispered. "You are safe, dear heart, which is what matters most." The duke leaned back and ruffled her new curls. "I shall have to call you Petite Mama. You look even more like our mother now."

Olivia pressed her face against her brother's chest.

Michael left the room, feeling an interloper. His cynicism faded to regret. Though he had never once experienced it, he knew that familial love existed.

Lynette and her mother shared it with their cobbled family that now had Gabriel Pennistan to head it. Mrs. Blackford and Lady Olivia shared it without the bonds of blood. It existed in the best army units, brothers all. He had never known it. Not firsthand. Not for himself.

Lady Olivia was safe now and he was free. He could make his way to Manchester or wherever he could find work suited to his unique talents.

The footmen did not escort him to the front door, which surprised him. He supposed they were more interested in the story being told in the duke's inner sanctum.

If the duke and his sister loved each other so dearly, Olivia would tell the truth, Meryon would believe her and Michael Garrett would be absolved of trying to extort money or force a marriage. They certainly did have an obsession with the two. There was a story there, one of a hundred he would never know and would not miss.

That was a lie. The image of Olivia's eager face and pursed lips came to mind. He would miss the possibility of another kiss. He could still feel her mouth touching his. Whether that persistent memory was the devil's work or the gift of an angel, he would remember it always.

With a last gesture of ill will, Michael left the castle the way he had entered it, through the salon window. Let the ass of a porter make what he would of that.

Convincing himself it was no more than curiosity, Michael took the long way around the castle again, back toward the stable. There were fewer lighted windows at this hour, but the waning moon was bright, and he let it show him the way.

He tested a few more of the sashes, the ones that were within easy reach, and found them fastened tight.

Where the old building met the land, there were only a few openings. Years ago, the narrow openings that the archers used had been enlarged and made into windows. They were now without glass and covered from the inside. If the panels could be loosened, a limber man could easily climb through.

You are no longer responsible for her safety, Michael reminded himself. He would not be able to explore the ruin in the daylight. That could be labeled his penance for trespassing in the first place.

Thinking of Olivia again, he considered the idea of sending the duke a letter suggesting that he have a trusted servant investigate the abandoned part of the castle.

The wind gathered strength. Last night's storm was still a part of him and Michael looked about even as he walked faster. The bigger trees were barely moving; the smaller trees would cause no harm if they gave way.

Pulling his greatcoat more tightly around him he let himself inhale deeply, the last of the cinnamon and spice that would always remind him of Lollie-the-lost. Lady Olivia Pennistan was far above his reach, but sweet, prickly Lollie had been his dream come true. And like a dream, the fantasy had disappeared with daylight.

Michael sat down on the wall of the moat, the wind blocked by the castle, and let that bit of honesty sink into his soul. He could have done more than see Lollie to safety. Under a dozen other circumstances he could have been more than her rescuer.

The wind changed direction and was brisk enough to make Michael stand and walk on to the stable. What a game life was, to tempt him with Lollie-the-ghost and taunt him with Olivia-who-had-never-been-kissed. They might be one in the same, but her title changed everything.

21

THAT DEBATE WAS ECLIPSED by the immediate need for self-preservation when he saw the duke's brother leaning against the stable wall, smoking, as he passed time with the head groom.

When Lord David saw Michael he pinched out the glowing end of his smoke. "The duke wants to see you." He tucked what was left into his pocket.

"Well, I do not want to see him."

The groom turned a gasp into a cough and Michael smiled at him.

"But, my lord," Michael continued, "to show the great egalitarian goodwill I learned in the army and in France, I will come with you now so that I can be on my way tomorrow."

With no more than a nod, Lord David set out for the castle. They walked in silence, which Michael tolerated for as long as he could. "You did not wonder where I was?"

"You were either dead or asleep somewhere. Or perhaps something in between." Lord David turned up his collar against the growing chill. "I would have searched if you had not shown up by morning."

Michael liked him. In spite of his distinctly unfriendly manner, he was as straightforward as only a taciturn man could be. Lord David was not about to waste words on lies. Not when each syllable he spoke was so carefully weighed.

"I'll tell you what I found if the duke is not interested."

Lord David nodded and let the conversation die.

Oh for God's sake, Michael thought, surely the man had not used up his quota of words for the day. "Was Lady Olivia amenable to coming home?"

"Yes." He hesitated and added, "Mrs. Blackford was not. She wanted her to stay for the night."

"That must have been interesting."

"The vicar is still head of the house. He insisted that they do as the duke wanted."

"No one with any sense says no to the duke." Michael stopped and, perforce, so did Lord David.

"More often than you can imagine."

"Because he thinks he is always right and has no use for counsel."

"No, the opposite." Lord David resumed walking and considered his answer as though he had to build it carefully and test it for stability. "Too many people are distracted by his rank, and make choices based on a coat of arms and not what is the right course of action."

Michael felt the pinch of that pointed comment. It was aimed right at him.

Lord David stopped just out of hearing distance of the porter who was waiting by the door. "I was away in the Americas for almost ten years. I have been back for two. I see things differently now. You must as well."

"Yes. I do. I have seen the best and worst of leaders. The truth is not always apparent, but quickly learned in the first battle."

"You will see soon enough." He started walking again, ignoring the fact that Michael was not following him.

God save him, he hated cryptic comments like that. Another distaste Michael could thank the war for. He kicked at a clump of grass and caught up with Lord David, giving up on the effort to draw any more information from him.

They swept by the porter who bowed them in. Or at least bowed Lord David into the castle. Michael ignored him even though he could feel a malevolent stare that made his back itch.

The study door was ajar, the footmen away from their posts.

"Where are they?" Michael asked with a wave to the doorway.

"Scouring the place for you," Lord David answered. "The porter told us that you did not leave, at least not by the front door."

Michael's smile was his only reply. Let the porter earn his pay. Michael went into the room and was surprised that Lord David did not follow him. The story was hardly over.

He could see Lady Olivia sitting in the duke's chair, behind his desk, looking very much the proper young lady even if her dress was somewhat dated, missing the abundant ruffles and detail that were popular in London and Paris.

The simpler style suited her; the high fichu hid her bruises and the pink helped to add color to her cheeks. A band of pink braid inset with flowers ran around the neckline and then down the middle of the dress, which drew the eye from her magnificent bosom. In his case it was only a momentary distraction. But he could see that someone, if not the lady herself, had given significant thought to her dress.

Lady Olivia was talking with some animation. The duke half sat on the desk, listening.

"Why? I promised one Season. It's not as though marriage—" she saw Michael and cut herself off. "Good evening, Mr. Garrett. I am so glad that you came back. I have not had a chance for a proper good-bye."

God only knew what she would consider a "proper good-bye."

"Lyn, my throat hurts from talking so much. Could I please have some brandy?"

"No, you may not." The duke appeared shocked at the request. "Brandy, Olivia? You are not to drink brandy. What in the world are you thinking to ask for it?"

"Yes, well, Mr. Garrett gave me some with water in it and it is very soothing to my throat."

"That may be, but you may not have any more." His impatience was replaced by something that sounded more like worry. "What if I have some of your tea brought to you?"

Olivia jumped up from the chair, and made for the door. "Better yet, what if I go to the kitchen and make it myself?"

The duke moved to stop her. Michael forestalled her exit by closing the door before she reached it.

"You are not to wander around this place, sister, especially not tonight. It is too drafty."

"Oh nonsense, Lynford." She reached for the door handle but stopped, raising her hands to her throat. "Do you think my abductors are still about? Will they come again?"

The fear in her words made Michael want to take her in his arms. He took two steps toward her before he realized how ill-advised that was. He bowed to her instead, took her hand and held it with both of his. "My lady, those cowards are nowhere near. Do you hear the wind? It is not like the gale but it will make for a miserable night for anyone out of doors. Let us hope they're still searching in the Peak while you are safe with your family."

She nodded slowly at first, then more firmly as if considering his words and agreeing with them. He smiled at her. Her eyes answered and they both remembered the last time they had been this close.

22

GARRETT," the duke interrupted, "ask the footman to bring some of Lady Olivia's sore throat tea."

"Honey and lavender tisane." Olivia pulled her hand from Michael's as she corrected the duke, with a superior tone only a man's valet was allowed to use.

"Honey and lavender tisane," repeated her brother, for all appearances as tame as the kitchen cat.

"I'll tell the footman." Olivia had the door open before she finished speaking.

Michael turned to the duke to see how he would react to this casual usurpation of his order. The duke took his seat, pulled a pair of candles closer and began to read a newspaper. He looked up before he could have read more than a sentence. "Sit down, Major. She will be awhile."

Michael usurped some power of his own and stayed near the door. The footmen were back in place, the same ones who had accosted when he had arrived earlier. They appeared not to recognize him at all.

"Oh it is you, Rawley," Lady Olivia said with real pleasure. "Good evening, and how are you? I am so sorry to have missed your wife's churching. How is the babe?"

"The boy and the missus are doing well. And you, my lady? Are you feeling better?"

"Well, yes, but my throat still hurts quite dreadfully. Could you ask my maid to bring me some of my special tea to ease throat discomfort, the honey and lavender tisane?"

"Happily, my lady."

He moved off briskly and Michael thought it a timely exchange. But Lady Olivia was not through.

"Good evening to you, too, Lester. Do tell me which was your favorite of the buns I made last week? I have been wondering the whole time I was at the vicarage."

"The cinnamon, my lady," the other footman answered promptly.

"Truly?" she said with disappointment. The footman nodded.

"You insist we be honest."

"All right. I thought that the berry and orange buns would equal them in taste."

"My lady, there is nothing that can equal your cinnamon buns."

"Nevertheless I will keep trying."

She spoke as though it was a challenge she would spend her life to achieve.

"We are all willing to sample, if it will please you," the footman said and actually laughed.

"I am thinking that next I will try some with corn and cheese. Not sweet at all."

Lester looked doubtful.

"Trust me, with butter they will be the savory equivalent of cinnamon buns."

"I am a willing tester, my lady, if you think you will be well enough to spend so much time in the kitchen."

"It is just what I need. You see, if you use the cheese that the dairymaid—"

"Olivia." The duke's one word was more than a hint that he had waited long enough.

"I will tell you tomorrow when you come for breakfast. If you will excuse me, Lester?"

"Of course, my lady." The footman spoke hastily and stood as straight as a soldier, resuming his place by the door.

Olivia came back into the room. Lester closed the door behind. "You see, Lyn, I have this idea that savory buns could be as wonderful as sweet."

"I, too, am a willing tester, and I, too, preferred the cinnamon." The duke stood up and refolded the paper carefully. "You see, sir," the duke said to Michael, "this place does have some egalitarian aspects. We are all testers for the finest baker in Derbyshire."

Olivia smiled, lowered her head and wrinkled her nose, a sign Michael already recognized as pleasure and embarrassment. It added to the sweetness he found so endearing. He was not the only one who did. Apparently Lady Olivia Pennistan had managed to charm them all. With cinnamon buns, no less.

*   *   *

OLIVIA WISHED SHE could handle praise with more grace. How many times had her governess told her to "smile, curtsy and say, 'Thank you.'" Instead, embarrassed by the praise, she would blush and hide her face so no one would see how pleased she was. She felt all of twelve when she did that. Maybe Lyn was right. There were times when she did not act her age.

"Olivia, listen to me. Stop thinking about the kitchen."

Lyn's voice was tinged with impatience and she gave him her full attention.

"It is time for you to go to your room. I want to speak with Major Garrett. In private."

"Major? It is Major Garrett? You are in the army." Olivia clapped her hands. She loved it when she was right. "I knew it! Tell me, how were the cooks able to serve hot meals when you were constantly on the march?"

"They didn't."

"I am so sorry. It must have been awful. But it's true, how could they have a fire when you were on the move? Unless they went ahead and set up their fires where you planned to end the day."

"Sometimes they would do that, but too often we did not—"

Lyn cleared his throat.

With a smile the major stopped mid-sentence and bowed to her. "Good night, my lady."

"Olivia, go to your room."

"Lyn, I wish you would not order me about as if I were a child. I am an adult. I will be of age in less than six months."

"If that is true will you please be a sensible adult and go to bed?"

"I would think tonight is one night when I could be excused from sensible behavior." She looked at Major Garrett hoping for support. His sympathy showed but he said nothing. "What about my tea?"

"The maid will find you if you go to your room. Take no detours, Olivia. Not one."

"Please, Lyn. I do not want be left by myself yet." Her heart hitched as she realized who she had forgotten. How could she? "Where is Big Sam?"

The major took a step closer, as though he wanted the answer, too.

"David has gone to find him."

"Is he still out there? Oh poor Sam. He must have been so upset. He will come back all wet and cold and act as though it is what he deserves for not being with me. I should have gone with David." Olivia reached out for the door handle.

"No, Olivia. You cannot join the search. I will not hesitate to order the major to restrain you if you are so foolish."

"I am not an idiot, Your Grace." She could be as chilling as he could. "Big Sam is very dear to me, but I was only going to ask Lester to be sure to let me know when he is back."

"They have been so ordered."

She held her tongue so he would know how annoyed she was. It was an effort.

"If you must stay, Lollie, go sit by the fire."

"All right." She tried to be as gracious as the queen, but it was compromised by a yawn that escaped without warning. Olivia dragged her cloak with her to her favorite spot near the fireplace. How many times had she sat here while Lyn worked, those long cold evenings after her governess left? Poor Tildy.

She made a little nest for herself in the great wing-backed chair closest to the warmth. "Thank you, Lyn. I will feel much safer here."

When her brother did not answer she pulled her cloak around her like a blanket. There was no point trying to hear what they were talking about. The room was too big and they would whisper.

With one last glance at Major Garrett, she closed her eyes and concentrated on her favorite bedtime ritual. The one she fantasized about when the candle was spent but she was not ready for sleep.

She would plan the perfect dinner for him. Not every dish, just the ones that would be set closest to him. Ones that would suit him the best.

With the murmur of their voices for comfort, she considered the options. She did not know that much about him. He had apples, cheese, bread and watered brandy with him. So nothing elaborate. He had lived on army food forever.

Fresh Derwent trout to start. She would cook it, whole, in onion sauce. She would serve her new four-mushroom soup and lamb cutlets with rosemary. For something with color she would serve asparagus in pastry pockets.

The end was easy: the finest strawberries and cream. She

would whip the cream herself. Or perhaps the berries would be better dipped in champagne, with a sweet cake for substance.

She yawned and wondered what a strawberry kiss would taste like.

"Olivia, before you doze off I have one more question for you." The duke walked the length of the room as he spoke. Michael stayed where he was, but he could see that she did not open her eyes. Her "What is it, Lyn?" was filled with sleep.

"Tell me what you think of Major Garrett."

That was not a question Michael wanted her to answer when she was half asleep. God help him, if that wasn't a deliberate ploy on the duke's part to catch her when her answer would be unguarded. Under other circumstances he might be interested in the answer. Given the intensity of their brief history.

"He is a good man." She spoke through a yawn, said it again and went on. "He is not perfect. He is too stubborn and wants his own way. I cannot see him taking orders from anyone." She opened her eyes and turned her head.

She was awake and, God help him, she was going to tell the truth. "He held me naked and even kissed me, but he never treated me as anything but a lady."

With those bombs bursting in the air, Olivia leaned back, closed her eyes and fell asleep. Michael had never seen anyone go to sleep so easily after condemning another to a slow, painful death. He would wake her up with his shouts if what she said led to further bruising.

He, too, walked the length of the room, to stand beside

the duke and see if she was really asleep. Her head dropped, her body relaxed, her breathing grew deeper.

Forget about her. Forget. Forget. He chanted the phrase a dozen times even though it was an impossible command as long as she was within sight.

"She has done that since childhood." The duke's voice startled him. "Fallen asleep in the space between two words."

"I envy that." Michael smiled at her sweet, delicate face.

"You will never know it, Major. It is a gift only for the pure of heart."

The duke turned away from his sister and waited for Michael to fall in beside him.

"Do tell me about the kiss."

It was not a command. It was more a question from curiosity, the tone a judge would use when he already knew the answer and had decided on the punishment. The duke stepped back behind his desk and Michael was grateful to see that the pistol was no longer on his desktop.

"You want to know about the kiss." He so wanted to ask the duke why he felt the need to live vicariously but restrained the impulse. "No, Your Grace, I will not tell you about it. Not one single detail." Michael glanced back at Olivia's innocent face. He had nothing, *nothing* to be ashamed of. A few errant thoughts but he had not acted on a one of them. "That kiss concerns only the two of us. I will swear on my honor that I did nothing to abuse her innocent heart."

The duke did not question what honor he had, did not

curse him as a libertine, did not insist on more of an answer.
He looked troubled.

"Her heart *was* innocent. I don't know now. There are
some things all of us would prefer not to share."

Michael understood that. The duke was not about to di-
vulge his secrets, anymore than he was. He waited to be dismissed. What else was there left to talk about?

"Come over here." The duke led him to a large table, surrounded by chairs, the surface covered with maps. Meryon
sat down with his back to the room and gestured to a chair
across from him.

This was a command and not an invitation. Michael
wanted to ignore it. He had not done well with commands in
the army, and had been naïve enough to think that those days
were over with the sale of his commission. Amazing there
was any naïveté left in his heart.

The duke waited, still seated but not at all relaxed.

"I want to find these men, Major Garrett." He spoke to
the empty chair across the table, then stood and faced him. It
was not much of a concession but it was a start.

"Olivia said that you saved her life. That makes two
members of my family you have rescued from death. Saving
Pennistans is something you seem to have a talent for."

"It was no more than one sentence, one lie. That is all I
did for Gabriel. Hardly a rescue."

"But it saved him. If you had identified him or Lynette
they would not be alive now."

He was right. Michael shrugged, hoping the duke would
let it end there.

"I am asking for your help, Major, assuming that you

have an interest in keeping Olivia safe. I ask you," he emphasized the word *ask,* "to stay a while longer and tell me everything that you recall about the incident." The duke sat down.
"Olivia has told me as much as she can, but you will have another perspective, possibly more valuable. I am asking you,
Garrett, not ordering you, well aware that, according to my
sister, you do not take orders well."

Not a total victory, but good enough, Michael decided.
Without a word, he walked around the table and took a seat.
With the wall at his back and Olivia within sight, he finally
relaxed.

23

THE DUKE AND MICHAEL spent the next hour poring over the maps. Michael recounted every pertinent detail of their time together. Then the duke asked him to describe the two men he'd met at the cottage the morning after the storm.

"They gave their names as Smith and Jones, which tells me they have no imagination but they were so nondescript that those names suited them perfectly."

Michael looked at the ceiling and pulled at the details. "Smith had an accent. Scottish, I think. He was better dressed but not well-dressed. The other was cast as a servant and probably was. Smith did all the talking."

"And they would not tell you where they were from."

"I asked Smith directly and he gave me a vague answer about traveling the Peak District."

The duke nodded. "Which no one does this time of year."

"Smith sounded as though he had been to school." Michael added, "But even that is a guess."

"Do you think he was pretending to be a gentleman?"

"I think he may have been one, Your Grace." Michael looked at the duke with a rueful smile. "Fallen on hard times."

The duke nodded and Michael was fairly certain that he understood the unspoken truth, that one man living hand-to-mouth could easily recognize another.

"They stayed at the place where they held Olivia. The shed where I put my horse showed signs of other recent occupation. They left hay and water, which made me wonder if they planned to come back or simply left in a rush when they found Lady Olivia missing. The yard was full of ruts from a carriage. That would explain why there have been no new faces in the village."

The duke took it all in before he returned his attention to the maps, and said "What do you think the two of them will do now?"

"Try to find out what happened to Olivia. Report to their employer and follow his orders, or run away and hope never to be found."

The duke considered Michael's suggestions but kept his own counsel. That was his prerogative, but it did not make for much conversation.

Sitting for this long was a mistake. Fatigue pulled at him, and with an apology Michael stood up to add fuel to the fire. When the tea arrived, he took it from the footman, another excuse to walk off exhaustion. He set the tray on the table nearest Olivia and made sure the covering on the pot was adjusted to keep the tea hot.

When he returned to the table the duke was lost in thought, tracing boundaries on the map. Michael remained standing. "I have told you all I can, Your Grace." When the duke nodded Michael went on. "That has earned me an answer to a question of my own."

The duke looked up, obviously not welcoming the suggestion. Michael asked anyway. "Do you know why someone would kidnap her?"

"Yes." Meryon did not hesitate. Or explain even though the silence between them grew tense.

"That annoys the hell out of me, Your Grace. You ask for my help but will not give me pertinent information. I have experience tracking men. I could find the kidnappers far more efficiently than a cosseted nobleman whose best skill is giving orders."

The duke did not rise to the baited insult, but Michael did see his hand fold into a fist, the telltale sign of anger the duke was doing his best to control.

Michael braced his hands on the edge of the table. "You do not have to tell me what you know, much less what you suspect. The moment I told you where you could find Lady Olivia, I was no longer responsible for her safety. I have been reminding myself of that since I was made so unwelcome, first by your porter, then by your brother."

His stomach still hurt from that punch. "In this instance, however, I find it impossible to think of myself first. That is why I am willing to tell you everything I can."

The duke was still silent. Meryon watched him with a puzzled speculation that revealed only a little of some inner debate.

The duke would have made as good a spy as Gabriel was a poor one. "Your Grace, allow me to show you once more how an alliance works." He straightened. "I learned something tonight. I give it to you because I do care. Not about your title or your castle. I care about Lady Olivia's well-being."

Michael stared at the tabletop and when he looked up again, he tried for a tone of voice that was not laced with disgust.

"Your protection of the castle is inadequate. You have to look no further than that excuse for a night porter at your front door. He abuses his power, does not do his work and wins you over with a submissive air that you are unable to see through."

He went on to detail his two uninterruped circuits of the castle and his easy access through an unlocked window.

The duke tried not to show his feelings but his fist was white at the knuckles before Michael finished.

So, he was one of those men who did not want to be made aware of his shortcomings. Not that unusual, but in this case very selfish.

Michael's assessment finished, the duke's continued silence was as good as a shout for him to be gone. Michael made his way to the door. He glanced at Olivia and actually prayed for her safety, though it was hardly a prayer that would be well received in a church.

Silence followed him. Just before he left the room,

Michael looked back to see if the duke had been turned to stone.

Meryon was standing, watching his progress with a small smile that should have made Michael feel more comfortable. It did not. It gave him pause.

"I always thought the army did its best to repress independent thought." The duke leaned back against the table as he spoke, his arms folded across his chest. "I wonder how you, and my brother David, survived without a court-martial." The duke's tone was conversational, almost friendly.

"I was not in a traditional unit after the first two years. There was a reason for that," Michael admitted, letting go of the knob. "I cannot speak for your brother."

"Perhaps he will tell you one day." As he spoke, the duke went over to his sister, stood quietly as if he were a mourner and this was where she had been laid out. He nodded to himself, and followed Michael's path to the door. He approached him, speaking in a low voice.

"I have two goals now, Major Garrett. I want to destroy the men who did this. When I find them I will ruin their lives and what is left of their reputation."

Michael nodded.

"This was an assault on my family honor that I will not tolerate. Even more important I want to keep my sister safe. It may be that her reputation will suffer even though she is the innocent in this."

"I can see I have misread your silence again." Michael allowed a smile. "Your brother was right. Your title does not exempt you from sensibilities."

"David said that?"

"No, but that is what I understood from his comments."

What a refreshing change. The duke's anger was not aimed at him, unless Meryon still thought that Michael was one of the villains.

"Your Grace, you call me a rescuer with one breath and still do not seem convinced I am a hero. Yes, I have committed more crimes than any man in residence here, I am sure. All of it done in the name of king and country. Never once did I rape a woman, nor was I ever cruel for a selfish end. God is a master of irony if your sister's ruin is the wrong I am held responsible for."

The tension around the duke's mouth eased, his eyes softened, his expression a silent acceptance as effective as his words of rage had been.

"Please," the duke said, certainly a rare gesture of courtesy, "come back and let us talk about how to secure the castle, how to protect not just Olivia but all the people who live here. You are right. Her life is worth more than our pride." Meryon held out his hand. "Thank you for saving her. Without Olivia meddling in everyone's life from kitchen to chapel, this would be no more than a place to eat and sleep and mourn. I owe you more than money. I owe you respect and honesty."

Michael accepted his hand, touched but also curious about the duke's relationship with his wife and child. Olivia had said they were not in residence. Perhaps they spent all their time in London, he decided. This family was complex, if not downright secretive. Secrets might have been his specialty once but they were no longer his concern.

More to the point, it seemed that the duke wanted his help. The man's trust might only be given in increments, but this handshake marked the first step.

"Would you wake up Olivia? I think her neck will ache enough to make a real bed appealing." Meryon did not wait for an answer but stepped out the door, leaving it open.

Obviously waking a sister was beneath a duke. Michael retraced his steps. He squatted until he was eye level with Olivia so that when she opened her eyes she would not see a man looming over her. He expected she would have nightmares about that as it was.

"Olivia," he whispered. "Olivia, sweet girl, wake up now." He touched her arm just below the shoulder, where her cloak had slipped down. He felt the softness of her skin, the warmth of it, before she started awake.

Thank God, the minute she recognized him the fear disappeared. She relaxed against the back of the chair. "Oh, you're still here. I'm glad." She smiled sleepily.

"Yes, I'm still here." It was an inane answer, but he could think of nothing else to say. Her sleepy eyes reached into his heart and warmed it. Her scent, cinnamon and spices, distracted him. He answered her smile with his own. "Did you dream?"

"No dreams." She closed her eyes and he felt abandoned. When she opened them again, she seemed more awake. "Maybe one dream. You and I on Troy, riding." She shrugged. "That's all."

"That would be an easy one to make come true." He ran his hand down her arm and squeezed her hand.

The duke was beside them now, watching. Olivia's eyes shifted to him. "He is a good man, Lyn, is he not?"

Michael did not wait for the duke to answer. "Your tea is here." He had to clear his throat and repeat the sentence.

Olivia raised a hand to her throat. "It feels better already." Stretching, she stood, tottered a little and put a hand out for him to steady her. She plopped back down on the chair.

Michael poured some of the special tea. Even though it was not much more than warm when she sipped it, Olivia sighed with relief.

"Tea must be the greatest comfort ever invented." She felt stupid the moment after she said it as it occurred to her that tea did not begin to compare to the comfort of being held in Mr. Garrett's arms. Olivia consoled herself with another sip when she realized he had held her for the last time. "Mr. Garrett, you are not leaving tonight, are you?" She sent a pleading look to her brother who shook his head.

"I trust he will accept our hospitality tonight at least."

"Oh, good. For I should like to prepare something special for him and give him a proper good-bye." She gave him her best smile and a little giggle escaped as a mental image of what she would like that to be. Besides cinnamon buns. His lips twitched but Mr. Garrett did not smile back. The silence lengthened. Finally Lynford cleared his throat.

"Olivia, Samuelson is back." The duke offered her his hand to help her up. "He can go with you to your room and stay as a guard. It is time for all of us to be abed."

"Big Sam? He's back. And safe?" She gulped the last of

her tea, accepted her brother's help and stood up with more confidence. She smoothed her dress and her hair as she rushed to the door. Michael felt a stab of resentment as she threw the door open and clapped her hands together.

"Big Sam! How are you? You did not catch a chill, did you? The weather has turned so nasty."

"Not wet or cold, milady. I should be beaten for leaving you to walk home alone. I am going down to the stable and make the groom take a switch to me."

He was the biggest man Michael had ever seen. Not just tall, but massive in every way, with a head too small for his body and skin as pale as his hair. He had the ageless look of a fairy tale ogre. God forgive him, Michael was relieved.

"If you had the groom beat you that would make me cry, Big Sam. It was not your fault. I was the one who would rush home and not wait for you. It was very kind of you to stay when Reverend Drummond asked."

"The vicar asked me to stay?" It looked as though Big Sam was having a hard time understanding her words. "Yes, milady, I should have known it was wrong. My job is to keep up with you. I don't know much, milady, but I do know that. Lord David said the duke might dismiss me."

"No, he will not. We need only blame it on the horrible men who took me. They deserve a name even worse than stupid Galatians."

Big Sam nodded.

"Peach thieves," Olivia suggested.

"Not my fault?" Sam asked as though the idea was taking root.

"Never, Big Sam."

If Big Sam was an ogre, Olivia was the princess who charmed him.

"Fish poachers, that's what they are," Sam suggested.

"Grape apes," Olivia said.

They both laughed at that.

"Good night, Mr. Garrett. Good night, dear brother. I will see you both tomorrow." She gave her brother a quick curtsy, then turned back to give Big Sam her hand. He took it, not as a gentleman would, but as a child might, and the two of them walked down the hall.

"Cook burned dinner," Sam said with more disappointment than amusement. "She was that upset."

Michael closed the door slowly, recognizing envy as it evaporated. He wished he were the one holding her hand. It would never happen. Lady Olivia Pennistan was not, *could* not, be his. She was as sweet as a new kitten and he was anything but innocent. One kiss had proved that. To take more than that one kiss would undo any of the good he had done since he found her in the woods.

24

THE DUKE NODDED as the door closed on Big Sam's story and began his own. "Samuelson has been her body-guard since she was five. No one else could keep up with her. Even at five Olivia was given to impulse."

"Where did you ever find him? He is a giant, especially beside her."

"I am sure that is one of the reasons my father hired him. If you find Big Sam, you know where Olivia is." The duke walked to the fire and stared at it. "Big Sam was an attraction at a May Day fair. My father stopped his keeper from beating the man. He was being treated like an animal." The duke's expression belied the easiness in his voice. "Samuelson is not a man of learning, he cannot read or write, but he is still a human being and has the most basic right to respect."

It sounded as though the duke was quoting his father.

"Big Sam's loyalty is unquestionable. He would tear a

man limb from limb if he thought Olivia was threatened. That is both good and bad. His idea of what threatens Olivia is very broad in definition."

"A long speech, Your Grace, and it applies to me in what way?"

"Stop trying to irritate me," the duke said with more humor than irritation. "Come sit down, Major Garrett, and I will explain what I have in mind."

The duke went to the two chairs by the fire.

Michael followed, realizing that one handshake and an apology had committed him as surely as his concern for Olivia's safety.

He moved Olivia's cloak and folded it over the arm of the chair. Cinnamon and spices tickled his nose, reminding him that her lips might have something to do with his decision to listen. He'd best not let that be known.

"David has insisted for weeks that the porter is a poser and incompetent." The duke settled comfortably into the chair. "Hackett's family has been with us for a century, serving in that capacity and also at the gatehouse, always reliable. This generation has other ideas."

He stopped speaking for a moment and stared into the fire. Some internal debate was distracting him. Michael waited.

"My father believed that change was inevitable and I'm afraid that he is right."

Michael had been sitting on the edge of his chair but as the duke showed an inclination to philosophy, Michael sat back.

"Yes, Major Garrett, make yourself comfortable." The

duke's small smile appeared again. "My father saw what happens to the wealthy and those who support them. He was in France for the worst of the Terror."

He glanced at the portrait over the mantel. A woman, a beautiful woman with eyes the color of Olivia's and hair the same lustrous brown. No doubt it was her mother.

"I thought that when we escaped our own revolution we had escaped the worst. But I think I may have been wrong. Change is coming. The Hacketts are a good example. The night porter is the last of the family to want the position and I think he did it only because his father insisted. One of his brothers took up the Luddite cause and is lost to the family. Another is a miner in the Dark Peak. The gates have not been closed or the gatehouse occupied since the Luddites were last a problem."

Michael guessed that was more than five years ago, when he was far from home. "When I stopped in Birmingham, on my way here, I saw more looking for work than I expected. I know from the army that idle hours go a long way to destroying morale."

"The war is over, so there are more men for fewer positions. I imagine you saw that, too."

"What I saw were too many who had given up country life for the city, with no improvement in their lives." He leaned forward as he spoke and was surprised when the duke nodded.

"That may be so, but the growth of factories and machines is inevitable, as is the need for coal to fuel them. The Luddites may not be a threat but there are other groups that favor the idea that there are options for protest beyond civil discussion."

Michael waited for the duke to tell him what he had heard in London or in Parliament. He didn't.

"I am not going to start closing the gates." The duke rubbed his eyes again. "At least not yet. Coming so soon after Olivia's disappearance it would only fuel the gossip. What I want to do is offer you a place to live, the gatehouse. Further, I will make it clear to the night porter that you are in charge of protection of the castle, day and night."

"You want to hire me?" It was only one of a hundred questions Michael had. It should be the easiest to answer.

"Yes, Major, I am offering you a position. I should think it is one well suited to your experience. You insist that work is what you came here for. Am I wrong?"

"No, Your Grace, you are right." Michael was surprised and decided not to hide it. "You want to hire me to make sure that the castle is as secure as possible."

"Yes. I do not feel for my own safety, but I want to guarantee Olivia's well-being. The staff will be more comfortable if they know that steps are being taken that they will benefit from as well. I think the staff will welcome you, except for a few like Hackett who do not tolerate newcomers."

"Hackett does not worry me, Your Grace. He is a bully and easy enough to handle. I am more concerned about your estate manager. His support is essential, and he does not appear to be part of this hiring process."

"Lord David is the estate manager these days. The two of you can resolve any differences in the boxing ring he has built in the old castle. I'll take a ringside seat."

With a wry smile, the duke stood up and waited for Michael to do the same. The interview was over.

"You need not make a decision this moment, Major. I will tell Hackett that you will be camping tonight in the gatehouse. You can tell me tomorrow if you wish to stay on. For Olivia's sake I hope your answer is yes."

"Your Grace, I do have some questions."

"Save them for the morning. David can answer them." The duke headed toward his desk. "And if you decide that the gates should be closed, make it clear that it is your decision." He gave a curt nod which Michael knew was meant as dismissal.

"I do not use my rank anymore." It was a small thing, but Michael felt the need to assert himself.

"You have certainly earned the right to the rank." The duke stopped and turned back to face him.

"I am not trained for employment in any area where my rank would be an advantage." It was more than that. More, even, than a way to have a word. The army was his past.

"Yes, I suppose studying for the church and military rank are hardly compatible."

Michael was surprised. He did not show it. That skill he'd mastered before even the army. To be surprised once was part of the game, but more than that was perilously close to a failing on his part.

"Did Gabriel tell you I was to take orders?" He didn't think anyone knew.

"No, I have resources of my own."

For a minute Michael thought that was all the duke would admit. He was tempted to shake it out of him, but restrained himself. If Big Sam was Lady Olivia's bodyguard, he did not want to find out who protected the duke.

"Trust is an interesting concept, Mr. Garrett. In itself it is not even as sturdy as a sheet of parchment. Each piece of shared information fortifies the wall of trust. But it must be fortified from both sides or it will break under the pressure from one."

"Those who led the fight against Napoleon learned that." Michael nodded. He did not ask how one established trust in the first place. Something like it had grown between them in an hour or less, grounded in the determination to keep Olivia safe.

"The Marquis Straemore and I were at school together," the duke explained. "When I saw where you were from, I wrote to him. He told me that you completed the studies for orders, but went into the army instead." The duke lowered his head and looked him straight in the eye. "No one abandons the church that close to ordination. I suppose that should have been my first clue that you are not bound by what others do."

"Straemore's father was a tyrant." There were pitfalls everywhere. If Straemore was the duke's friend, employment here might not last long. *Honest. Be honest.* "I had some distinct, admittedly liberal, ideas on how to run my church. The marquis had me meet with him at Braemoor before ordination to discuss his expectations. He disapproved of my approach and I refused the living. My parents bought me a commission to be sure I was out of his sight." There it was, honest and concise.

"The new marquis is of quite a different stamp. It might

be that you could have the Straemore living on your terms
now."

"Do you not have enough lives to manage here, Your
Grace?"

"But you are here now, Major. You are one of us." The
duke raised his eyebrows as though he was making a joke and
inviting Michael to laugh. "I will honor your request to forgo
your rank, Mr. Garrett, and since I hope you will stay I will
not pursue your call to orders any further."

That should have pleased him, but the duke's sudden af-
fability made Michael wonder if he had read Machiavelli.

Once the majordomo was informed that "Mr. Garrett will
be staying the night at the gatehouse," it took less than
twenty minutes to settle him there.

The place might not have been in use but it had been
kept ready for whoever might have need of it next. Michael
had not expected a bed and waved away the butler's apologies that the bed was not made.

"There are sheets in lavender in this chest. I can call a
maid to make it up."

Michael thanked him and said no again, explaining that
in the army he had made do with much less. Tomorrow
would be soon enough for the maid to set the bed to rights.

He spread his blanket under and over himself and was
almost asleep when he stumbled across a thought that challenged the soft foundation of trust. It woke him up as effectively as a bucket of cold water.

Even though Michael had been entrusted with Olivia's
life, the duke still had not told him who was behind her
kidnapping. As he watched from the window he had left

uncovered, the moon moved slowly across the sky. The rain-making clouds raced away to the west, leaving a few more layers that let through the light of only the boldest stars. Michael counted each one and labeled it with an unanswered question.

The answers to only a few of them mattered, and all of those centered around the woman he had found wandering in the woods. He wanted to know who had taken Olivia and why. If she was still in danger.

He tossed the blanket off and decided he was not being paid to sleep. Nor was he willing to trust Olivia's safety to someone as lackadaisical as Hackett. Not while there was so much uncertainty around her abduction.

Pulling on his boots and pushing back his hair was as much attention as he paid to his appearance. He all but stumbled down the stairs and at first welcomed the cold wind that brought him wide awake.

It wasn't long before he was cursing it. Only an idiot would be out on a night like this. An idiot—or someone with a mission that made weather an inconvenience.

25

THANK YOU, Kendall, this is the most wonderful feeling in the world." Olivia wiggled her way under the covers.

"Do you want another warming pan, my lady?" Her maid smoothed the rumpled sheets at the foot of the bed, stretching out every little wrinkle. "You should not risk a chill."

"No, this is perfect." Olivia drummed her feet up and down to loosen the tight wrap of sheets. Surrounded by the familiar scent of freshly ironed linen, the feel of the down pillow, the pleasure of warmed sheets, bed was her haven tonight. She could see the shadow of Big Sam's feet outside her door. Just for tonight she needed to have him on guard. Home had always been comfortable. Now it made her feel safe.

She adjusted the pillow so she could sit up. Before Kendall could ask "What are your plans for tomorrow, my lady?" Olivia told her.

"First thing in the morning I am going to write a letter to Jess." She had the wording almost perfect. She would not tell him exactly what had happened. There was always the chance the letter would find its way into the wrong hands. "After that, I will go to the kitchen."

"I am delighted that you are writing to your brother, and when you are in the kitchen again everything will be normal, like nothing happened."

Olivia could not see her maid's face clearly; the candle was flickering its last, and Kendall was watching the guttering flame as she spoke.

"What do you think happened, Kendall? I was sick from eating something bad. I ruined my clothes."

"If that is what you wish us to believe, Lady Olivia, I had best cut your hair into something other than that ragged mop. What was the vicar's sister thinking to do that? She should know that cutting hair to prevent a fever is foolishness."

Kendall smiled at Olivia's surprise.

"If you wear one of your gowns with a fichu, no one will see the bruises on your throat. It is fortunate that you are always cold. No one who knows you will think it odd for you to dress that way in the kitchen in April."

"All right. Yes, that would work. You are a genius, Kendall."

"Nonsense. There is a way to explain everything, my dear. I learned at the feet of a master. Your mother was brilliant at it."

"Everyone says I look like Mama with my hair this way."

"Everyone needs spectacles." Kendall took Olivia's chin between her fingers and looked her in the eye. "You are so much more charming than your dear mother ever was. How do you think you were able to convince your father and your brothers that practically living in the kitchen is an acceptable activity? That smile of yours. That's how."

Kendall let go of her chin and stood up, with a hand to support what she called "her aging back."

"You would have to look like a suffering martyr and have the patience of a saint if you wanted to be your mama's twin. Not you. You always look as though each moment is a gift and you cannot wait to see what it will bring. It is so unrefined."

Olivia smiled; she couldn't help it. Kendall could make smiling sound as unsophisticated as salting your food before tasting it. And Kendall was wrong. It was not her smile that won people over. It was her cooking.

"The short hair is very becoming on you, Lady Olivia. You know I have wanted to cut your hair for years."

"You are very patient with me. Why do you stay here at Pennford when you know I could care less about what dress I wear or if I have the newest bonnet? You could dress the finest ladies in the land. Your talent is wasted here."

"Now that sounds exactly like your mother's false humility, may the Lord rest her soul." Kendall began to tuck in the sheets that Olivia had just loosened. "There are few ducal families who are as considerate of their staff as your family. Your father observed more than how the guillotine worked while he was in France."

"I know that lesson by heart, Kendall." Olivia erased her smile and did a creditable imitation of her father's quiet voice. "If we do not want a revolution in England we must treat our servants as more than slaves to our whims."

"Do not make fun of your father."

"Yes, ma'am. But I was not. It is how I hear it, as though he is still reminding me."

"Go to sleep, my lady." Kendall tightened the last sheet. "Count your blessings as I will count mine." Kendall took a moment more to replace the spent candle with a new one, but left it unlit. "Good night, Lady Olivia."

"Good night, Kendall," Olivia replied dutifully. She slid under the covers and as soon as Kendall was out of sight she drummed her feet to loosen the sheets again, turned on her side and tucked her arm under her pillow.

Now she had a story every bit as exciting as Mama's. Olivia Pennistan had been rescued from death in the forest by a handsome man on horseback. Did that not have as much drama as living in France during the revolution?

Everyone knew that story. How unfortunate no one would ever know hers. If they did it would mean ruin. If they knew she had been stripped of most of her clothes and tied to a bed they would never believe that she had not been raped. The grip of panic that came with the memory made her short of breath.

It was hideous to be without power, to be at the mercy of people she did not know, could not even see. Her heart began to race and each time she closed her eyes she was afraid that when she opened them she would be back on that bed.

Turning onto her back, Olivia stared at the gatherings of the canopy above her. No matter how hard she tried she could not rid herself of the feeling that she needed to escape, the driving need to run, to hide before they woke up and came after her.

Tears dripped from her eyes and down the side of her face. She would have died if Major Garrett had not found her. As nice as it would be to see Mama and Papa again, she still had too much to do to leave this earth yet, and people who needed her as much as she needed them.

Olivia turned her face into the pillow and prayed that the stupid Galatian peach thieves would die a horrible death. That they would be stripped and tied and left to starve.

If only she had not left the vicar's before Big Sam was ready. But how did they know that he was not with her? How long had they been waiting for a chance? How could they have been in Pennsford and not been recognized for strangers? Annie had recognized Major Garrett as a new-comer. Could it be that her kidnappers were not strangers at all? They could still be watching, waiting for another chance. She glanced at the door again and was reassured by the shadow of Big Sam's feet.

Olivia was half tempted to hold Jess responsible. If it were not for his foolish gambling excesses, this never would have happened. She would write the letter as soon as she was awake and the courier could take it when he left after break-fast. Olivia thought over the wording of her letter one more time. A letter is like a recipe, she decided. Words were the in-gredients and how you put them together was the measure.

Dear Jess, You must come home immediately. There is an emergency that only you can deal with. Do not delay. Leave for Pennford at once. I need you desperately.

She liked it, urgent and personal. She hoped it would work. She hoped Jess was staying at the house on Meryon Place. She hoped the courier was not waylaid.

Guilt pulled at her for not being honest with Lyn. He had been so happy to see her, laughing when she told him that she missed him even more than she missed the kitchen.

He laughed so rarely that she was sure she had made the right decision to keep her suspicions to herself. If she had told Lyn about the threat to Jess's land, he would have gone all cold and solemn. Everyone would have to tiptoe out of his way until David insisted they have a round of boxing. Someone's lip would end up bloodied or worse. She would much rather work on her new corn and cheese roll recipe than on a poultice for a black eye.

Of course the same might happen if Jess came home. The difference was that Jess would deserve it.

Stop thinking about it, she commanded herself. Otherwise she would be awake forever. She sighed, reveling in the fact that she was at home, she was safe here, and fell asleep on the thought that she would see Mr. Garrett tomorrow.

26

IT WAS NOT YET LIGHT as Olivia hurried downstairs. The courier's satchel was on Lyn's desk as always and she pushed the letter way to the bottom. She ran the rest of the way to the kitchen. She could hear Mary talking to someone, sounding much more cheerful than she usually did at this early-morning hour.

Rising before dawn to renew the fire, warm water and begin the bread for the day did not come naturally to Mary. Olivia often wondered why she had opted to be a kitchen maid. She did not have her mother's talent for cooking and was never shown any favoritism, this early-morning task being proof of that. But, Olivia realized, she herself had spent years trying to play the pianoforte as well as her Mama, never winning more than a sad smile and the suggestion that she "practice more."

Olivia loved the early morning, only partly because it was

time to start cooking. She enjoyed the quiet of this little part of the world, her world, with usually nothing but Mary's yawns for company.

It only lasted an hour. By the first light, Cook would be in charge and the kitchen staff would stumble in. The garden boys would bring in their baskets and fruit from the succession houses.

Olivia heard a male voice rumble an answer to Mary's prattle and slid to a halt to listen just outside the kitchen door.

"He is the most proper of valets. Wants the duke's water hot enough to burn. Says he can cool it easier than he can heat it."

"That sounds reasonable."

Delight thrilled through her as she realized who it was. *Reasonable* was one of Mr. Garrett's favorite words. Even more than the words, it was his voice, the friendly quality. Intimate even, so that you wound up telling him more than you ever intended.

What was he doing up at this hour? Her pleased surprise faded as it occurred to her that he was trying to sneak away before she had a chance to see him again. He was already tired of her and flirting with someone else.

"Water that hot may seem reasonable to you, sir. You are not the one carrying boiling water up and up and up. Been many a water boy burned doin' it."

"Good morning, Mary." Olivia breezed into the kitchen with every intention of ignoring Mr. Garrett, until she saw that he was sitting on the table where she usually did her baking.

"That is not a chair, Mr. Whoever-you-are. People prepare food on that table. Stand up and find someplace else to sit. Better yet, go into the servants' hall."

He stood with a nod of apology.

"Miss Lollie!" Mary said.

"Mary, you know better than that. No one is supposed to be in the kitchen unless they have business here."

"It's not even light yet, Miss Lollie. This is Mr. Garrett. He is new to the staff and has had a long night. Besides, I don't mind the company."

"You're working here!" What in the world was this game? Olivia could not decide if she was pleased or put out by his new status. So she gave him a look she hoped duplicated Tildy at her most suspicious.

"Yes, I was offered a position last night." He acted as though they had never met. She could hardly complain about that.

"I am Lollie." She bit back several less appropriate comments, most of them born of pure curiosity. She could wait and talk to Lyn or David. After all, one of them had hired him.

He gave her a perfunctory bow. "How do you do, Miss Lollie."

"What is your position, Mr. Garrett?" After all, Lyn wasn't here right now and Mr. Garrett was.

"I am to provide security for all who need it. To be sure that there is no threat to anyone who lives here. Especially at night."

She nodded, chastened by his gravity. Mary made a swooning sound. "Ooooh, you are? I didn't think Lord David was afraid of anything."

"He does strike one as extremely competent, but he must sleep sometime."

"I don't know when, Mr. Garrett. I see him late at night and early in the morning."

"Obviously he sleeps in between, Mary." Olivia turned her back on Mr. Garrett's smile and Mary's confusion. She did sound like a shrew. Or someone who was jealous. How could she begrudge Mary a few minutes with an attractive man? Mary's world was as filled with sisters as hers was filled with brothers.

Olivia sorted through the basket near the side door, searching for a cap. At least the cap would forestall comments about her hair. Mary was definitely flirting; she had not even noticed that Olivia's hair was gone. Of course, since most days Olivia just piled it on top of her head, it could be that Mary did not really know how long it was. Had been. She heard Mary giggle. Flirting, Olivia decided.

Pulling on the cap and the smock that would protect her dress, Olivia stepped to the table, across from Mary with her back to their morning caller. She pulled away a chunk of dough and began to help with the kneading.

"Mr. Garrett was telling me he started his rounds last night."

Olivia glanced over her shoulder at him. He was sipping from the mug of ale that must be his choice of morning drink. Or was it his bedtime favorite?

"I did not see a soul moving about. Hackett was at the main entrance, Big Sam was at your door and the halls were as empty as the grounds." He spoke directly to her, his eyes reassuring.

"We all feel better knowing that, Mr. Garrett," She kept kneading as she spoke, but she turned her head so he could see that she was as serious as he was. "Thank you." Now that she took a moment to look at him she could see that fatigue accentuated the lines in his face. Olivia turned back to her work torn between feeling sorry at being the cause of his exhaustion and immeasurably relieved that he was still here. To protect her.

"Oh we truly do feel better, Mr. Garrett, sir." Mary spoke with such enthusiasm that Olivia raised her eyebrows at her and felt churlish when the girl blushed.

They worked on for a few moments, but Mr. Garrett did not take the hint and leave.

"How are you, Miss Lollie?" Mary asked loud enough to include Mr. Garrett in the conversation. "Are you feeling well enough to be in the kitchen?"

Olivia heard her curiosity and wondered what the servants' gossip was. "I feel wonderful, Mary. In fact I am well enough to make cinnamon buns."

Before Mary could do anything more than grin with pleasure, Mr. Garrett interrupted. "If you will excuse me, ladies, I am off to the gatehouse."

"You can't leave now, sir. You must wait and have a cinnamon bun."

Mary's distress was flattering, for all that Olivia wished that Mr. Garrett would leave. When he was this close it was too hard to convince herself that her personal safety was the only reason she was happy he was still here.

She did not look him in the eye, but stared at his hands as she rhythmically rolled and folded and pressed the dough.

They were strong and square and very, very clean. As though he had never done a day's work in his life.

MICHAEL COULD NOT TAKE his eyes off her arms. Of all the ridiculous things to find appealing. While the rest of Olivia, every inch, was soft and sweet, her arms were strong, without an ounce of anything soft about them. He watched the muscles flex and relax as she kneaded the dough. Hours and hours of such work would strengthen the weakest arms. He imagined those hands, those arms doing something besides working dough, and decided it was time to leave even if he was going to miss a tasty treat.

"One of Lollie's cinnamon buns is the only proper welcome to Pennford." Mary said with a shy smile that made him smile back.

"I will have one at breakfast." He closed his eyes for a minute and made himself turn away before he opened them. "Did you say that it would be ready by ten?"

"Yes, but sir, no one waits until breakfast if they can have a bun sooner. Even Cook allows it as long as there are some set aside for the duke and his brother. When the garden boys come in with the baskets, and the footmen come, they will smell the cinnamon and sugar and rush through their morning work."

"Waiting for Miss Lollie's cinnamon buns is hardly the way to begin my first day at work here. I will come back later and hope for the best, but perhaps not as late as ten." Michael walked out of the kitchen to the sound of Olivia's and Mary's laughter, as fine a welcome as any cinnamon bun could be.

Fog rose through the trees and off the grass, as the first light seeped into the sky over the fields to the east of the castle. Michael walked along the path toward the gatehouse noting that a friendly smoke was pouring from the chimney at the stables. He could hear horses and grooms moving about, some laughter and a few curses. The day started with the light here. This was a pleasant enough life if you weren't used to the city.

Michael considered taking Troy for a run but realized he needed some sleep before he did anything else.

He lay down on the blanket-covered bed, fully dressed, at the ready in case someone came.

Four hours of sleep refreshed him, even if he dreamt of something that smelled of cinnamon and was always just out of reach.

A sound woke him fully. Not a carriage or a horse at the gate, but the quiet click of a well-oiled door closing. He lay very still. It was not the door to his bedroom, but the sound of the door to the outside, down the narrow round of stairs that led to the small parlor.

Looking out the window he saw the fog had grown more dense, obscuring all but the vague shape of a man as he was swallowed in the mist. Since he was headed toward the castle Michael convinced himself it was one of the footmen delivering a message. Or a cinnamon bun. He took the time to dash some very cold water across his face and slick his hair back. He needed a bath, but that would have to wait.

When he reached the bottom of the stairs he smelled

cinnamon. Ah, the gift-giving fairy had brought him a cinnamon roll. Something between satisfaction and longing made him smile.

Michael came around the high-backed chair by the small fireplace, pretending that his mouth was not watering, but forgot food immediately when he saw, on the chest inside the front door, a basket containing a paper-wrapped parcel. He ripped the paper open and found a blue dress, with two petticoats, both white, of a quality that was obvious.

God help him, someone had left more of Olivia's clothes here. He grabbed the basket by the handle as the distinct smell of Olivia's cinnamon and spice perfume enveloped him.

Racing from the gatehouse he tore up the drive, certain that the man he'd seen was the culprit. It hadn't been more than ten minutes.

He stopped and turned back without even going in the front door. The man would hardly be waiting around to see what his reaction would be. Even as he stepped away from the door, considering what to do next, Lord David came out of the castle, saw him and swore.

"You lying, thieving bastard. I have the note."

"Note? I have no idea what you are talking about, my lord. Someone left these at the gatehouse not ten minutes ago."

Lord David came closer to see what he held and still ready to commit murder.

"It was not me, for God's sake. Not me. Think, man, why would I leave a note and then bring you the basket?"

"Huh," was all that Lord David said for a moment. He

closed his eyes and nodded as Michael's question defused his rage. "Come with me."

Michael followed him back to the castle. The porter eyed them with curiosity, but did not say a word.

Lord David trotted up the stairs and down the hall toward the duke's office. He went into a door nearby, another office, this one filled with papers, endless piles of them, some held down with pieces of odd statuary. Other larger stone figures, equally unusual, sat on the floor and the tables.

Relics of his days in Mexico, Michael guessed. The bizarre, distorted figures were alarming on first glance. The opposite of warm and welcoming. Michael was sure it was deliberate.

"The note." Lord David handed it to him.

It read:

She may be safe now but her reputation is compromised. How many people know? An alliance will put an end to the questions.

"Alliance." Michael decided that was the key word in the note.

"Political. Personal." Lord David tossed out two possible alliances.

"Personal. Marriage." Michael said, imitating Lord David's verbal skills. "There would be no reason to ruin her reputation if it is political."

Her brother nodded.

"We can be easy about Lady Olivia's safety. There will not be another attempt at abduction."

"It is only her reputation that they wanted to ruin." Lord David nodded as he spoke. "And they are going to use her clothes to do it."

"Surely her reputation will survive the subterfuge. Lady Olivia is obviously well loved here. No one would believe ill of her."

"Oh really?" Lord David sounded as curious as a suspicious parent.

"My finely honed skills of observation, my lord. They appear to have a use beyond discerning who is a spy."

Lord David ignored the explanation. "If word of this reaches London there will never be an advantageous marriage."

That did not matter to Olivia. Michael knew that. Surely Lord David did as well. But the duke might want it.

"Lynford told me how you found her. Nearly naked."

Michael could hear the anger in his words. With a temper so short how had the man survived in the Navy without a flogging? Was it up to him to be the voice of reason? Michael wondered.

He might not show the same anger but that did not mean he was immune to it. He was the one who had found Olivia near death. He was the one who had to let the two bastards ride off. He wanted them as much, more, than either of her brothers.

27

"**T**HEY MUST HAVE A CONSPIRATOR on the staff, my lord. Why else would he run back toward the castle?"

Lord David nodded and did not speak for a moment. "Hackett," he suggested. "I dismissed him when he went off duty this morning. Not hard to imagine him with a grudge, even though we gave him a year's wage."

Michael raised his eyebrows. That was unusually generous.

"My father's influence. He once had to dismiss a much-loved servant, a governess. Giving her some financial security was a matter of conscience. He drilled that into all of us."

The old duke. He certainly exerted a strong influence even now.

"It could also be a recent hire," Lord David continued, "someone whose loyalty has not been proven and whose greed won out over his conscience."

"A new member of the household like me." Michael wondered what he had to do to prove himself. "I swear to you again, Lord David, that I came upon this whole incident by the accident of Gabriel's letter of introduction, which I am beginning to heartily regret. Please God, let that be the end of it."

Michael walked over to look at a glass canister filled with dried brown leaves of some kind.

"Mexican tobacco," was all Lord David said.

"As for my conscience," Michael continued with his back to Pennistan, "that has not bothered me since I saw the innocent lives the Spanish and French destroyed in the name of the emperor and the English repaid with the horror of Badajoz."

"Yes," Pennistan said as if he understood man's inhumanity to man just as Michael did.

"Where do the baskets come from? The ones that they delivered the clothes in."

"Those baskets are used for bringing food in from the garden or the succession houses. There are dozens and easy enough to come by."

"We could ask the duke if he knows who is behind this." It seemed the obvious solution to Michael. "He knows. He as much as said so last night but kept the details to himself."

"For obvious reasons." Lord David stood up. "I will speak to him. Burn the clothes, wait until they are thoroughly destroyed, and be about your day. I will find you if I need your help again." He left the room.

Michael stared at the door, growing damn tired of the way the duke and his brother treated him like a thug hired to do their bidding. It could be that that was all he was good for now, and that his next position might not be nearly as straightforward as this one.

He picked up Olivia's dress and ran his hand over the finely woven cotton that was almost as soft as her skin. She was the living proof that this family had love at the heart of their most difficult decisions. He had seen that last night, heard it in the way they spoke with each other. His anger cooled and he realized that he was not so much a convenient pair of fists as a man who was not part of their inner circle. Not part of the family Pennistan.

So Lord David was not going to tell him any more than he needed to know to do his job. God knew he understood the concept of holding information in a tight circle. It would be like the army, where they would fight a battle without knowing why. Or life in Le Havre, where no one told anyone more than the obvious, where secrecy was a fact of life.

Amazing how much life at Pennford was like the army at war. And like the army, when *this* war was over he fully expected he would be sent on his way without the barest of thanks.

He turned his attention to the one thing that Lord David had asked him to do.

Olivia's dress was beautifully made, a fine cotton with satin ribbon threaded through the neckline. But Michael could not imagine Lady Olivia would ever want to wear it again.

Rather the way he felt about Raoul Desseau's uniform. He'd kept one gold epaulette to remind him of all he had lost and what England had won, but the rest of it he'd passed on to a French longshoreman as he boarded a ship for England.

This dress could be handed over to one of the servants, but if Olivia would not want to wear it again he was almost as sure that she would not care to see it again either. Michael unthreaded the blue ribbon trim, stuffed it in his pocket and threw the rest of the dress and the petticoats onto the fire.

Ignoring the sound and the smell of the burning clothes he went to the window, acknowledging to himself that once Olivia's world was safe again, they would not have to dismiss him; he would leave first. It would be too quiet here for him and Olivia would be too much of a distraction.

He would not follow that thought, his imagination being much too vivid right now. Instead he made himself watch as a group of garden boys ran by the window, obviously on their way back from the kitchen to wherever they spent the day.

Three were playing some odd game as they raced along, using their baskets—the exact type of basket Olivia's clothes had been delivered in—to catch something hard that was thrown by hand once it was caught. Loud hoots and jeers insulted anyone of the five who missed his catch. It could be that one of these boys had delivered something other than food this morning.

The two who followed along more slowly were not at all interested in the game, engrossed as they were in eating something that looked like cinnamon buns. Michael wondered if there were any left.

*   *   *

"YOU ALL MISSED the buns more than you missed me."
Olivia laughed. Using her apron as a hot pad, she pulled the
third batch from the baking oven.

The cinnamon and sugar were just right, but the dough
itself was not quite as golden as she liked. When she went to
return them for a few minutes, the universal groans made her
decide that they were done enough for this starving group.
"You must let them cool a little, or you will burn your
tongues."

"It'd be worth it, Miss Lollie." That from the new footman, a cheeky fellow who loved to tease.

Olivia cut one from the pan and set it aside for Big Sam.
When he was awake he would sniff his way from the attic to
the kitchen and she wanted to be sure there was enough for
him. One from each pan. He had an appetite to match his
size.

"Mary, would you please ask the girls to start the clean-
ing up while I finish with the last of the topping."

"Are you feeling well enough to be cooking?" Patsy asked
as she nursed a cup of tea.

"Good morning, Patsy. Are you finished with the bedrooms already?" Olivia deliberately avoided answering her,
noting that Patsy herself was looking a bit pale. She kept that
to herself. Health was not a topic she wanted to discuss.

Olivia began to cut the buns, separating and lifting them
carefully from the pan.

Mary came up beside her with a large serving platter
while Cook directed the other kitchen maid to put some
plates out.

"Ladies and gentlemen." The voice came from the top of the stairs leading into the room.

There were few things that could distract the footmen from cinnamon buns but the sonorous words of Winthrop was one of them.

The voice of the majordomo had the group turning as one. There was a general shuffling of feet, and the stable hand and two of the gardeners drifted up the steps on the opposite side of the room. Olivia blushed furiously, not at Winthrop but at the man accompanying him.

"My lady," Winthrop bowed to her, as did the man with him. "Ladies and gentlemen, this is Mr. Garrett. He will be taking up residence in the gatehouse. The duke himself has asked him to study and improve the security of the residence and the old building, of the entire castle. You are to treat him with the deference shown to a man who has spent his lifetime serving king and country in the army."

Like everyone else Olivia gave Michael her full attention as he came down the steps and into the kitchen. He was not smiling. His eyes were dispassionate and seemed to memorize every face he looked at.

The thin line of his mouth did not look anything like the one she had so wanted to kiss. His even breathing gave no hint of nerves. If he was trying to convince them he was a man to be reckoned with, he succeeded admirably. He would have intimidated the Duke of Wellington himself.

It was smart of him not to use his rank, to pretend that he was not a gentleman by birth. He would fit in better if no one knew he had been a major. All right, Mr. Garrett he would be.

"Welcome to Pennford, Mr. Garrett. Please let me offer you a cinnamon roll. As a gesture of welcome. Winthrop, could I send some to your rooms for you and Mrs. Winthrop?"

"Thank you, my lady, you are all that is kind. It will be the highlight of Mrs. Winthrop's day."

"Help yourself, everyone, and hurry back to work. If you do not, Winthrop will be very annoyed with me."

They all laughed at that absurdity. Half watching the major, she cut the rest of the buns and let Mary and the kitchen maids serve the others.

Winthrop accepted the plate and bowed. "We are happy to see you returned to us in good health."

Patsy had her mouth full but that did not keep her from adding her bit to the conversation.

"Weren't you afraid that you would die, Miss Lollie?"

The laughing and chattering stopped. Olivia heard one or two murmur, "What did she say?" Cook spilled her tea.

Olivia was not sure whether to ignore the question or not. The crowd was not looking at her; their eyes were on each other or the cinnamon buns. She looked at Garrett. At least he was watching her, advising with a wordless communication she understood perfectly. *You cannot ignore this.* Olivia did not know how she could read sympathy in his dispassionate expression but whatever it was, Garrett gave her the boost she needed. Drawing in air as though it was courage she laughed.

"Patsy, why would I die from an upset stomach? I never take sick for long. I think it was one of those greens that looks so delicious but is not at all edible. Yes, perhaps I could have died. Instead I was so sick that I did not even want my own Cure-All Chicken Soup."

They all laughed. Too heartily. It sounded like they were as relieved as she was. There were times when a lie was all that anyone wanted to hear. Everyone returned to the meal with less than the usual enthusiasm. Now she wanted to cry, and tried to think of something that would distract her. Tears would betray her true sensibility: that nothing would save her reputation, not even the best lie told.

What did it matter? She had what she wanted most in life: her work in the kitchen. She turned her back on the others and began dressing the fish she planned to serve at dinner. Salmon pie was one of Lyn's favorites.

The welcome routine calmed her and the need to cry faded even if the heartache did not go away.

"Ohhh, who does he think he is?" Mary said, loud enough for everyone to hear. "There are those who'd give a day's pay for what he's leaving behind."

MICHAEL REALIZED it was a mistake to leave one of Lady Olivia's cinnamon buns half eaten. Yes, it was superb and hard to abandon, but he had not thought it wise to keep Winthrop waiting. Apparently he was wrong.

In less than a day he had committed his first Pennford faux pas.

"The truth is," he began with a bow to Lady Olivia. "I could not stand another bite."

One of the footmen stood up and Michael was sure he was going to challenge him to a fight. Even Olivia turned from her chopping board to give him a curious look. He wanted to wink at her but settled for as bland an expression as he could manage. She smiled, and her eyes shared the joke even though she had not heard it yet.

"I could not have had another bite of this piece of perfection without swooning like a girl. It is superb, Lady Olivia. If I could wrap it up and take it with me, it will be something to look forward to all day."

The crowd laughed and cheered. Olivia nodded with just the right bit of condescension that told him it was exactly what she expected. He came back down the steps as Mary handed him his bun wrapped in a cloth.

Winthrop addressed them all. "We are all pleased to see Lady Olivia back with us, but it is time for work."

In God's good name, Winthrop did not have to bring that up again. Olivia's smile disappeared and with one soulful look at Michael, she turned back to the board.

The footmen stuffed the buns into their mouths. The maids slipped them into their pockets. The household resumed its normal routine. Only Michael had seen the sadness in Olivia's eyes.

28

IT DID NOT TAKE LONG for Michael to understand the routine at Pennford Castle, from observation as well as Lord David's terse explanations.

"The duke is not concerned with the day-to-day details here. He will be returning to London as soon as he is satisfied that Olivia is safe and her reputation intact."

The two men were riding toward the forest cottage where Olivia had been held and where she and Michael had taken shelter in the storm. It was a gloomy day and Lord David had been delayed by a group of tenant farmers who had come to report that their seedlings were flooding or rotting in the fields. Michael thought that this pointless trip was just an excuse to take a break from the endless headaches caused by the rainy weather.

"So, Lord David, you are the overall estate manager.

There is Winthrop as house manager and the land steward who was with the farmers this morning."

Lord David went on to explain that Mrs. Winthrop was the housekeeper, but some undisclosed ailment had kept her in their quarters for the last year. She still ran the castle but now it was through her husband and the maids who came to her with problems.

"Winthrop's voice is his greatest asset."

"Yes, my lord. I can imagine him telling the footmen to jump in the moat and they would only wonder 'With or without our shoes on?'"

To their mutual surprise they did find something at the cottage: definite signs that it had been occupied again. There were new stacks of wood and more hay in the shed.

Lord David poked around the loft and tossed down a chicken bone or two. "Well fed, they were. Which eliminates unemployed mill workers or destitute soldiers. I think our kidnappers might have been in residence." Lord David came down face-first as though it were a ladder onboard a ship, his feet barely touching the rungs. "That means they have not finished their job, or are afraid to report back to their employer."

"Or both," Michael suggested.

"Hmmm." Lord David stirred up the ashes in the fireplace and said no more until they were on their way back to Pennford.

"It means that Olivia may not be as safe as we thought."

"My lord, she is as safe as we can make her. I assure you that no one will harm her while I am a part of the household."

Lord David accepted that with another "Hmmm," and let the conversation end.

Michael was considering the ramifications of that outing one night as he made his first evening round of the castle grounds.

There had been no sign of an interloper and he was beginning to think that he should find someone else to do this night patrol.

Standing along the tree line he scanned the windows, all of them dark. He stepped out from the protection of the tree and pulled his cap lower, burying his chin in the scarf around his neck, and considered how to hire someone when he knew no one.

A rustling sound brought him back to the moment. Some night animal foraging, he decided. Michael stood still and waited, even though he knew it was unlikely it was someone passing a signal. The culprits never fell that easily.

Michael added good hearing to his list of wants for the night guard. Loyal, familiar with the grounds, able to work without supervision. One who could handle routine and still be prepared for trouble. A soldier, ideally one who had been a scout.

He would have to ask if there was anyone recently returned who had been in the army. Besides him. More than anyone, a soldier knew the danger inherent in a job that was for the most part boring—until that one moment when it wasn't. Better not be asleep when that happened.

A snap of a twig broke through the night sounds of the wind in the trees. This was a little sound, one that did not belong with the others, with a human voice accompanying it.

Michael tightened his hand on his hefty walking stick and patted the knife strapped to his arm. He found a tree big enough to hide behind and waited.

There were at least two of them, as one was talking. He could hear the sound of a voice but the wind carried the words down toward the village.

Most likely one was telling the other to move more carefully. They were slow enough, on their hands and knees, and would be impossible to see if one was not so clumsy that each bush rustled as he crept by.

It was night, and unless they were spying on someone else there was no need for such secrecy. Even as he had the thought a man's voice reached him as they finally came close enough to his hiding spot.

"Here, little sheep. Where are you?" A pause and again "Come to me, little sheep, and I will give you rest."

Garrett pulled off his gloves, ready for a fight, before the words registered. A shepherd looking for lost sheep? That was strange. There were thousands of sheep in this part of Derbyshire, but the chance that one had wandered onto the Meryon property was highly unlikely.

"Stupid Galatian. Where are you?" the same voice called, loud with frustration. "I'm tired and want to go to bed."

Michael knew who it was now, and it was even more strange. Unless the biblical phrase "stupid Galatians" was used by all his parishioners, it was the vicar. Reverend Drummond was doing what he had done all his life, looking for the one lost out of the hundred, just as Jesus had. The chance there was a man wandering the grounds in search of spiritual rescue was highly unlikely, so Michael decided on a small lie, God forgive him.

"I can see it, Reverend Drummond."

The vicar stood up. "Where?"

"Over there. Can you see him? He's headed back down toward the village. Come, we can catch him if we hurry." It was more a trick than a lie, and the easiest way to move the old man toward home.

"I cannot run at the best of times and it is so dark that I would most likely fall and break my leg." The reverend proved his point by stumbling in the thirty feet it took to come up beside him. Michael grabbed his arm to keep him from falling.

"Thank you, kind sir. Why, it's Mr. Garrett, is it not? You are a rescuer of lost sheep yourself, are you not? Have you ever considered church work?"

"Yes, Reverend, but I am not suited for some of the more political aspects involved."

"There is a solution to that." Reverend Drummond spoke in a conspiratorial whisper. "Ignore the politics. I warn you, if you make that choice you had better love where you serve because you will never leave it." The vicar pushed his few wisps of hair off his face and went on. "Your true mission as a churchman is simple. Convince people the Creator wants them to be happy and fulfilled and that joy and hope are the surest paths there."

Michael did not answer, though he did spend a spare second wondering when was the last time he had felt happy and fulfilled. The answer came to him as fast. He ignored it.

"Mind you, most will never believe it is that simple. Lady

Olivia is the rare exception. Big Sam, too, though he does not have enough understanding and believes because it comes naturally."

They walked on in near silence, Mr. Drummond humming a tune, one that Michael did not recognize. Some hymn, no doubt. What was it like to spend one's life spreading a message that no one would accept?

To take a page from the vicar, to do it with joy and hope that was all that was needed. The brief personal sermon left Michael wondering at that puzzle.

"Here we are," said the reverend as they reached the path to his house. "I know where I am now."

Mrs. Blackford hurried down the path toward them, wrapped in a long wool cloak.

"There you are." Her relief at seeing the vicar was obvious. "Reverend Drummond, it is too nasty a night to be out looking for lost sheep."

"Yes, the wind is a raw one. But don't you know that I must be about the Father's business. He will protect me."

"Come inside. Now. Please."

"I will. I will. You are too much like the biblical Martha, my dear."

"It is what I am paid for."

Drummond went into the house, and from where he stood outside, Michael could see him climb the stairs.

"Thank you for bringing him home, Mr. Garrett. I was about to send for help." Mrs. Blackford began to walk back up the path. Michael followed her. She was not wearing a cap and her hair was in a braid down her back.

"Does it happen often?"

"No, sir. Only when he is worried about something. I should have guessed it would happen."

"Because of Olivia's kidnapping?"

"I expect so. It has upset all of us and he can sense distress. He went out looking, thinking it was nothing worse than a lost sheep."

"For a vicar committed to the spiritual well-being of his flock a lost sheep might well be the worst failing he could conceive of."

"No, it isn't," she said firmly. "With a lost sheep there is always the hope of salvation. It is a dead sheep, never found, that is the hardest to forgive yourself for."

"That sounds like the voice of experience."

Color rose to her cheeks and Annie Blackford pressed her lips together. He waited.

"You do not strike me as a man who thrives on the pain of others."

He bowed his head. "My apologies. Now that I am staying, I find I am interested in all the details of life in Pennsford. I am entrusted with keeping the residents of the castle safe and I was hoping to count you as an ally."

"Come in for a moment, just inside the door." She stepped back with a gesture for him to follow her. "Reverend Drummond will be our chaperone if you are worried for your reputation."

"Surely you misspoke. It is your reputation that is threatened by a nighttime meeting."

"No, I have no reputation to ruin. I have been married and divorced."

His first reaction was disbelief. Here was another scrap of

honesty: If all were divorced who should be, there would be few who stayed married.

"It's true," she added when the silence had gone on too long. "In fact I am one of the vicar's lost sheep."

"Mrs. Blackford!" the vicar called down from the upper story. "I am going to pray now. Good night, dear lady."

"Good night, sir." She gave Michael her complete attention. "I cannot leave him at his prayers too long or he will not be able to stand."

Surely this is penance enough, Michael thought. He was about to say his own good night but Mrs. Blackford had not finished.

"I do want to warn you, sir."

Michael tilted his head, "About what?"

"Olivia. Be careful of her. She is the sweetest, most generous soul in the world. But she is also spoiled, and used to having her own way even if she must fight for it."

"That was how she lived through her kidnapping. I already know she is stubborn. How does it affect me?"

"You are to keep the castle safe. Both of us know that is a euphemism for keeping Olivia safe. I think that the duke is afraid for her. If not for her safety, but for her reputation. She thinks it does not matter. She will only know how much it matters when she has lost it."

"I have seen that happen, too. Gabriel Pennistan is a friend of mine."

"Oh. I see." She considered that for a moment but was discreet enough not to pursue it. He liked her more and more.

"Big Sam has always been the best of chaperones. But I am not sure he is up to a threat that is not physical."

"Your thoughts mirror my own, Mrs. Blackford. I have an idea on how to handle that."

She seemed satisfied with that assurance, and smiled. "Allies, I do believe." She curtseyed. He bowed good night.

"Do tell Mr. Drummond that I am sorry he did not find his lost sheep."

"Oh, but Mr. Garrett, he did." Mrs. Blackford closed the door on the next sentence. "He found you."

29

MICHAEL CONSIDERED VISITING the tavern. It wasn't too late and it was likely the few who took their drink seriously would still be about. As he had known for years and proved yet again tonight, evening hours were the best time to find out the truth. Dark was the time when men and women were more willing to share the secrets they kept to themselves during the daylight.

He stood at the end of the path to the vicar's house debating the wisdom of leaving the castle unguarded when the smell of a cigar followed by the sight of a man walking up from the village made the decision for him.

"Closed up for the night," Lord David announced, as he pinched out his smoke and tucked it in his pocket.

"Do you ever set your clothes on fire?" Michael asked as he fell into step beside him.

"Not anymore. Years of practice."

They walked on in silence, each testing the other. This time Michael spoke first.

"That was not a social call. I found Mr. Drummond on the Pennford grounds searching for lost sheep."

"Hmmm, yes, that does happen. So your visit to the vicar's house was related to your work?"

Lord David did not seem completely convinced.

"Yes," Michael said firmly, feeling real sympathy for Mrs. Blackford. "My lord, technically, I am supposed to report to you. And I would have mentioned this incident in the morning."

"Technically." Pennistan looked at him and gave a small smile, not unlike the duke's. "That is the most important word in that sentence."

Michael smiled back and waited for what he knew was coming.

"I do not see you as the sort who will report to anyone."

Michael laughed. He could not help it. "And you do not seem the type who will tolerate insubordination."

"We understand each other."

"And will work well together."

Now Lord David did laugh, a short choked sound but it was amusement. "With the occasional time in the boxing ring to clear up any misunderstandings."

Michael let that nominal threat hang in the air while he debated telling Lord David his idea. Michael knew he was as susceptible to the cover of night as anyone around him. But he liked this man, quick temper, ready fists and all. Lord

David made the decision easy with his next question, proving his mind was quick as well.

"What are you going to do about Big Sam?"

"We are agreed that something must be done?"

Lord David answered with a nod.

"If I have observed correctly, my lord, no one patrols the grounds after dark." They had reached the gatehouse but Michael continued up the drive with Lord David.

"There has not been a set patrol for years. I make the circuit when the mood strikes me."

When he could not sleep, Michael translated. "I have taken it on from the first."

"A waste of your talents."

"But a good way to learn the castle, the grounds, who is about or where they should not be." Lord David nodded and Michael continued, feeling like a schoolboy who was afraid to ask for what he wanted. "I am convinced that Lady Olivia is no longer in any physical danger. But there are thousands looking for work and this miserable spring means even worse food shortages. There will be unrest on all levels, and I would not be too confident that even quiet Pennsford will be free of it."

Lord David held up his hand and stopped. With another gesture he walked over to the shed behind the stable and knocked on the door. "Out of there, you two. If I find you again you will have to find new positions."

There was no response and Lord David walked back to him without checking further.

"How did you know someone is there?" Michael asked, embarrassed that he had never thought to check the shed.

"A guess."

They both heard the door open and a man came running up to them calling out, "Sir, my lord!"

They both turned around to find one of the footmen trailing after them. Lester. Michael remembered him as one of the cinnamon bun testers.

"I'm the only one in the shed, my lord. I swear it. Patsy and I are going to do it right and proper. I sleep in the shed, sir, because home is too crowded." He looked distraught and earnest.

"See that you sleep alone." Lord David gave him a curt nod. "I will expect to hear the banns within the month."

"Yes, sir." Lester touched a hand to his forehead in the old gesture of deference. "You see, sir, I come into some money—"

"Within the month." Lord David cut him off with the three words.

"Yes, sir," Lester said. He jerked a bow to them both and went back to his shed.

"Who?" Lord David patted his pocket as he spoke.

Back to the man of few words. Michael tried to recall what they had been talking about before they so rudely interrupted the footman's sleep. Ah, yes, the night guard.

"My current candidate is Big Sam." God help him. That sounded as tentative as a girl asking for a new gown. He hurried on before Lord David could speak. "I want your opinion first but I will ask Lady Olivia, then the duke, if you think asking the duke is necessary."

Lord David gave it some thought. How that was different from a prolonged silence of disapproval, Michael was not sure.

"Samuelson would awaken you constantly. He will sometimes perceive a threat where there is none."

"I am used to that from my army days."

"In many ways Samuelson is a child."

Michael nodded.

"It's a wise idea to present it to Olivia first."

"Lady Olivia made it very clear to me that he is part of her household."

"It's a good idea, for any number of reasons." Lord David kept nodding as if each nod checked off a reason. "Big Sam is a competent guard. No one will question his loyalty. He is scrupulously conscientious. As you will find out."

Michael took the last sentence as approval.

"I would wait a few weeks, Garrett. Otherwise Big Sam and certainly Olivia will take his new position as a criticism of his behavior. Olivia will not be going anywhere for the next bit anyway. And if she does, Meryon will insist she take the carriage or ride, so there will be others with them."

That made sense to Michael. He had already noticed that since he had brought Olivia home she had yet to venture anywhere.

"The question becomes who will guard Olivia?" Lord David asked.

"When she is home there are enough people around her. When she leaves the castle I will accompany her."

Lord David stopped and turned to him. "How wonderfully self-serving, Mr. Garrett. That is like putting a hungry midshipman in a room with a plateful of sweets."

Michael laughed. He could not take offense. It was so accurate a comparison. "I like to think I have more self-control than a midshipman. If not, I shall find my sweets elsewhere."

"Not among the staff." Lord David's sharp words made his sentiment clear.

"No, sir." Now he felt like the footman.

With a curt nod Lord David Pennistan went inside.

"IF YOUR FIRST NIGHT here was hectic, the last few weeks have more than made up for it, have they not, Mr. Garrett?" Mary asked. She had set the bread to rise and was wiping down the table.

Olivia stood nearby. She had told him she was testing a new blend of ingredients for a sauce she was creating, something she was sure would enhance the taste of even the best fresh-caught salmon.

"Oh I have been busy enough, Miss Mary." Michael tore his eyes away from Olivia and smiled at the girl. "Do not be thinking that the only work I do is sitting here watching you two knead bread."

Mary giggled. Olivia was oblivious to the conversation as she stared at the bowl where she was blending this and that from bottles and small dishes in front of her.

"Last night I estimated that I have spent at least ten hours watching you knead dough." With Mary as the unwitting chaperone, this time with Olivia was the one dalliance he allowed himself.

He could not be the only person in the world who found Lollie's movements erotic. It was no wonder that he needed a long walk in the cold morning air before he went to sleep.

Michael had already developed a routine. It would have been anathema in wartime to be so predictable. Last night, when he had counted the hours he spent watching Olivia, he had decided to change his schedule. So, immediately putting the thought into action, Michael decided to stay in the kitchen longer than he usually did of a morning.

If he was lucky he would have a chance to see one more of those quirks of behavior that he would forever associate with Olivia Pennistan. When a taste pleased her, Olivia would close her eyes, lick her lips, draw a deep breath and sigh with a smile as though her lover had just made her the happiest woman on earth.

She was so vastly entertaining. The complete opposite of most of the Frenchwomen he had known. They had been so secretive. It was understandable in a France that had been decimated by men and women only too willing to send neighbors, lovers and friends to the guillotine.

He had come to believe that was what all intimate relationships were like, each one giving only as much as the other.

Lady Olivia had no such thought in her recipe-filled head. She shared everything she had and everything she was. There were times that he wondered if his fascination with Olivia was because she was such a novelty. Reminding himself of that helped him to keep his distance, but every time they were together it proved more and more of a challenge.

When Olivia slapped the table with her hand, Michael knew there would be no sigh of pleasure today. Taking the bowl, she emptied its contents into the bin that would be taken to the pigs.

"Aha, I see there will be no new recipe today but the pigs will have a wonderfully spiced dinner."

Olivia put the bowl on the washboard and came to stand next to him.

"I'll try again tomorrow. I am sure with the right blend of spices I can make a seasoning that will be as easy to store as it will be to use."

"Lady Olivia." Michael raised his hand. In the last few weeks he had also learned that she would talk endlessly about her latest food experiments. "While I take great delight in eating what you cook, in watching you prepare it, I am not at all interested in how you invent it."

"Well!" He could tell she did not know whether to be annoyed or to laugh.

"You must have been told that before."

"Yes, I have, but I was hoping you would be different."

It was the honesty of her sentiment that made him worry about any number of things, from how long he could ignore the way she tugged at his heart, to how long it would be wise for him to keep working here.

"There are times, Miss Lollie, when I would happily

listen, but today I am to finish the circuit of the castle with a tour of the Long Gallery."

"Oh, oh, I want to show you that. Besides the kitchen, the Long Gallery is my favorite room in the castle." She pulled off her cap and smock and smoothed her dress and stopped short. "You have been here this long and still not seen the entire castle?"

"Lord David showed me all that he felt was pertinent to my work, and I have awaited the pleasure of Winthrop for the other rooms."

"It is a busy time of year for him and the weather has not cooperated at all. Did you know that one of the rugs was completely ruined when rain started precisely when it was not supposed to? The sky was clear one minute and rain-filled the next."

"Yes, that is all they were talking about at dinner last week."

"So I am guessing that Winthrop will not mind if I show you the Long Gallery." She stopped one of the footmen to ask him to take the message to the majordomo.

It was moments like these that made Michael realize how spoiled Lady Olivia was. The world ran very much as she ordained it. She had no idea that what she wanted to do was not what others might think was just the thing.

"Do tell him that I will be there this afternoon to read to Mrs. Winthrop. I have the latest fashion magazine as well."

And this time, as with every other time he'd had the thought, Olivia would redeem herself as she had just now.

It did not make her less spoiled but the spoiling hardly mattered when compared with her generosity and genuine caring. He thought back to Mrs. Blackford's description of her friend. Stubborn and sweet. Generous and willful. On most days the sweetness and generosity far outweighed the stubbornness.

30

AS SHE HURRIED HIM down the hall, Olivia chattered on about the treasures in the Long Gallery.

"Why is it that you never walk if you can hop, skip or dance down a hall?"

"I have no idea, but I assure you that I do know how to behave properly." She stopped and slowed to a very decorous walk. "It is only that we know each other"—Olivia stopped, faced him and rose on tiptoes to whisper—"so intimately"—she began to dance down the hall again—"that I feel I can be my most relaxed self when I am with you."

God help him, he prayed, he could feel her breath on his ear and his whole body responded.

She grabbed his hand and pulled him through the giant double doors that were wide open but unattended.

"That is quite enough, my lady." He pulled his hand

from hers. "You are almost twenty-one, and I have told you before that no man likes a tease."

"But I wasn't. I was—" She bit her lip and closed her eyes for a moment. "I'm sorry, Mr. Garrett. I *was* teasing you."

With a small curtsy she drew dignity around her and smiled with such perfect condescension that it convinced Michael she had learned quite a bit in her one London Season.

The room ran the entire length of one side of the castle. The classic Elizabethan version of a way to take some exercise on a rainy day.

"This is my favorite painting in the entire house."

It was rather poorly executed, not a great work of art by any means. "Because it looks exactly like you," he guessed at the risk of insult.

"Precisely, Mr. Garrett." She had her hands folded at her waist and sounded like a very pleased teacher. "My mother showed me this when I was twelve. That was when I asked her where they had found me."

"Found you?" he asked, as she seemed to be waiting for the prompt.

"You see, I do not look like any other Pennistan. Yes, I have my mother's hair and eyes but she is a Lynford. Mama was thin as a waif and only grew more stout after we all were born."

She stepped closer to the picture, and if it were not for the old-fashioned dress and the obvious age of the woman in the portrait he would have thought it was Olivia.

"This is my great-great-great-great-aunt Lucretia. She was born a Pennistan more than a hundred years ago and Mama said that every few generations another version of her makes an appearance. It is the sole reason that this portrait is still here."

"It must have been very reassuring." He did not know what else to say. There were any number of families in England who had siblings that did not bear any resemblance to one another. As a matter of fact he thought that given the rampant infidelity in the ton it might make it the rule rather than the exception.

"Reassuring. Yes, that is a very good word, but I would actually say it was more consoling. Since I so wanted to be tall and blond like my brothers. Consoling." She made the word a challenge he could not resist.

"Comforting."

"Cheering."

"Heartening."

"Oh that is a very fine word, Mr. Garrett. All right, this portrait and my mother's reassurance were heartening." She reached up and touched the frame. "I swear to heaven I had worried since I was at least ten that my parents had found me in the garden and decided that they would keep me so they could have a daughter."

She blew a kiss at Aunt Lucretia and escorted him the length of the hall, identifying the former dukes. There were two. Next she introduced him to their wives' portraits.

"I know you must think Lynford is an unusual name. But you see it is a family tradition that the firstborn son takes his mother's maiden name as his first name."

"Thank you, my lady. I *had* wondered about that." This

was turning out to be a more informative session than most of the time he had spent with Lord David.

"Yes, and Rowena's maiden name was Rexton, so that is their boy's name."

"What would happen if a future duke married someone from Germany or Russia?"

Olivia laughed. "You do not even have to go abroad to run into that problem. There are any number of English names that are unappealing. So far there has not been a problem. But someday."

"If one of the dukes married a widow, that would present a problem."

"Oh, stop being difficult. It is a tradition, hardly a commandment."

"Yes, my lady." Michael bowed to her and she laughed.

He loved that she so rarely held her annoyance and that he had never seen anger. Fear and panic masquerading as anger—but that had been completely understandable, given the circumstances.

They moved on and Olivia waved at several portraits of the Meryon earls who preceded the dukedom. "Does your family have any traditions?"

"Yes, the second son studies for the church."

"Oh, really? Which son are you?"

"The second."

"Oh dear." She bit her lip. "That must have been awkward."

"I see you can be a true diplomat when you wish to be, my lady." He smiled to show her that the memory did not hurt, knowing full well that an expression could lie as truly as words. "When I refused the living I was offered it caused the emotional equivalent of a volcano erupting. The army commission was a way to rid the family of an embarrassment."

"But were they not happy to see you come home from the war?"

"They thought I was dead and preferred it that way." That was all he wanted to remember, much less say, about his family. "Who brought home all the sculpture?" He raised a hand to the parade of pieces in marble that lined the walls at this end of the gallery.

Olivia accepted the change of subject with a small sigh. "Papa brought most of this back from France. Here is Houdon's bust of my father. Houdon is the most amazing talent. Even in marble he has captured the look in Papa's eyes."

It was impressive. Better, even, than the portrait nearby. No wonder the duke's children found their father so hard to forget.

"I have heard so much about the second duke, I almost feel as though I've met him."

"You remind me of him." Olivia smiled and nodded.

Michael could not help but laugh. He should be flattered, but it would be quite a blow to his male pride if she thought of him as a father.

"Stop laughing. You are much too young and your hair is dark, but there is something about the way you command a room, the way people really listen to what you say."

"You think so, Lady Olivia-the-generous? The night I came here to tell the duke you were safe, Hackett would not allow me inside."

"That is precisely my point. Hackett realized, even on first glance, that you are a man to be reckoned with."

He could not disabuse her of the thought and prayed to God that she would not mention it to either of her brothers, to anyone.

"The portrait of your mother is in the duke's study, is it not?"

"Yes," Olivia said, apparently pleased with his powers of observation. "You truly noticed it."

Because it reminds me of you. He bit back that ill-advised sentence. "I am being paid to notice things, my lady."

"Now you sound like Lyn. There is no reason to try to squelch my good spirits. Unless you are afraid of them."

"Absolutely terrified." He said it with a perfectly straight face and her smile faded abruptly. He had no idea how any other woman would have taken God's honest truth, but Olivia Pennistan stood rooted to the ground as she tried to *understand* what he meant. He could show her, was tempted to show her, with a kiss neither one of them would forget. He thanked all the powers of heaven, and hell, when Patsy interrupted them.

"I beg your pardon, my lady. Ruth is supposed to clean in here today. When will you be finished with Mr. Garrett?"

"Thank you, Patsy." Olivia's cheerful voice showed no annoyance. "We are done here."

Good God, did Patsy know what she had implied? Michael stepped away from Lady Olivia and gave the maid a look that would have frozen a hot spring.

"I beg your pardon, sir," Patsy said awkwardly, as though not at all sure for what she was apologizing.

If the servants were beginning to make snide comments, it was definitely time to change his daily routine so that they were less in each other's sight. Or he would be the one who ruined her reputation.

"I **SIMPLY DO NOT** understand him, Annie." Olivia sat across the table from Annie Blackford and concentrated on untangling the skein of wool that one of the vicarage cats had used as a toy. It made her feel better to help Annie while she tried to sort out her sensibilities.

"First, Olivia, there is nothing simple about men." Annie Blackford had her own tangle to unravel and was making much better progress than Olivia was.

Olivia dropped the wool on the table and shooed the cat away when he came towards it. Annie bent over it. "You actually made some progress with that."

"Thank you. I am making no progress at all with Mr. Garrett."

"Progress towards what?" Annie raised her eyes from her work for a moment, her head still bent.

"Knowing him better." Was that not obvious?

"To what end, Lollie?" Annie looked back at the knots on the table and waited.

"Just to know him the way I know most of the staff."

"Olivia."

She recognized that tone of voice. Annie thought she was lying.

"All right, Annie, that's not quite the truth, but he seems

to want the same thing, and just as we are growing closer he backs away."

"He strikes me as a man who is a gentleman at heart. Perhaps he is worried that you are still overset by your experience."

"Do I seem overset?" All right, maybe she did still have nightmares and did not care to be out without someone with her, but with Mr. Garrett she was never afraid.

"No, you do not. But I imagine you are having nightmares, are you not?"

"He said that I terrify him."

"He said that?" Annie looked up from her work.

"Yes."

Annie put her tangle aside, either because it was now untangled, which it was, or because she wanted to give this issue her full attention.

"Olivia, what do you want from him? The truth."

"You know, he is not beneath me in birth. His father is a bishop and his mother the daughter of a baron. If we had met in London during the Season he could have asked to be introduced and we could have danced together as easily as any member of the ton. It's like he is punishing himself by taking a position so far below his birth." She did not go on. She did not have to. The Season was all about courtship and marriage.

"He has to support himself somehow if he is estranged from his family."

"I suppose." Did Annie mean that if they were to marry, she would have to live in the gatehouse on his salary? That was absurd. He would move in with her.

"Olivia, do not tempt him. Your brother wants him at the castle for a reason. I know you are no longer in danger of being kidnapped but the duke must have other concerns." Annie folded her hands and twisted them.

"Have you heard something?"

"The vicar tells me there is *some* real worry that we could face a revolution every bit as devastating as the one in France." Annie spoke in a rush.

"I do not believe that. It could not happen here."

"Yes, it could, my lady. You live in a very protected world and do not know how difficult it has been since the war ended. As a matter of fact, Mr. Garrett is proof that the world is changing. The son of a bishop and a baron's daughter is working for his keep." Annie reached across the table and took her hand. "Dearest, let Mr. Garrett do his work and do not disturb him. It is unbecoming for a woman to pursue a man."

"Now you sound just like Tildy." They were both sad for a moment at the mention of Annie's mother, but Olivia refused to let her be forgotten. "Do you ever hear anything from her?"

"Not for two years now." Annie shook her head as she spoke and Olivia squeezed the hand that was still holding hers, only she was the one giving comfort to Annie now.

"Do you think . . ." Olivia's voice trailed off. She could not speak the words. It was hard enough to even think them.

"I do not know. Sometimes I think it would be a blessing for her misery to be over, and other times I want her here, brandy and all."

Olivia nodded and did her best not to let the tears that

filled her eyes fall. "I am so sorry to bring my stupid, girlish woes to you when you have so much more important things to worry about."

"Nonsense, I am happy to advise you. Sometimes you even listen to what I say." Annie raised her index finger in a gesture they both knew had been one of Tildy's favorites. "Leave Mr. Garrett alone. Do you understand me?"

"Yes," Olivia said, "but it is very difficult when he comes to the kitchen every morning. I am not a saint, you know." Which left Annie laughing, which was exactly what Olivia had intended.

31

THE NEXT DAY, putting action to thought, Michael stopped in the kitchen with the briefest of good mornings, sure that if he simply did not show up someone, someone named Olivia, would come looking for him.

With an intriguingly flavored rosemary and olive savory bun for sustenance he made his way around the castle, a route he knew as well now as the way from the harbor to his favorite tavern in Le Havre. Michael had not thought of Aux Trois Oiseaux in weeks. That must have some significance. He was not going to search it out but let the past stay where it belonged.

He had surveyed the walled windows of the old castle dozens of times on his nightly circuits of the grounds and never seen any sign that any of the panels had been moved. Nothing seemed any different from the way it had looked the first night he had espied the panels, but this morning he was going to see if the old castle could be entered from the outside.

Michael climbed onto the ledge of the most convenient opening, and his heart began to beat faster. On either side of the wood, holes were cut, in the right spot for a man's hands. It could be each panel was like this. The holes could be easily explained, but their existence did not *feel* innocent. He'd learned to respect that sensation in his gut.

Michael bent down to look through one of the holes. It was an awkward effort and a fall would hurt. There was no light. He heard no movement on the other side. Straightening, he put his hands on either side of the covering, carefully setting it inside. He sat on the window ledge and surveyed the room as the morning light, weak though it was, outlined what the room held.

He could see that all was not as it should be. There were signs that someone had been here, though Michael was certain that there was no one else around now. The air around him was flat and empty. It had been for awhile. It was not as though he had frightened anyone away.

He hopped down from the ledge. It was not a large room. Stacks of baskets lined the walls. Lord David had told him that the old castle rooms were used mostly for storage, except for the chapel and the old royal room. This looked to be the space designated for basket storage. But that was not all it had been used for.

There was a straw mattress on the floor, two mugs, candle stubs and what he thought were the ashes of a small fire. No one was spending time here now. The door was locked from the outside, which would explain why the squatters had come through the old window opening.

He raised the panel and left it as secured as he had found it.

Lord David was with the duke. With a nod to the footman who gave him that information, Michael went into Lord David's office to wait. The door was ajar, and Lord David's heated voice reached him without the slightest effort at covert listening.

"You are not going to vote for it, are you, Your Grace?" Lord David was doing his best to control his temper, but Michael could hear the tension in his voice.

"I am going to follow Liverpool's leadership in this. I will use my influence on issues of value." It was obvious that the duke had made his decision. Debate was pointless.

"And half-pay for naval officers is not of value to you?"

"Of interest and of value, but it is not an issue on which I am going to take a stand that will alienate the very people whose support I may need later." He was silent for a long moment. "Habeas corpus is far more important, David."

"But that is about to be expanded and clarified, Lyn. Long overdue, you said."

"Yes, but there are too many who recall the suspension of 1794 and will move to suspend habeas corpus again if they think that the situation calls for it. David, our brother Gabriel suffered under such a suspension. He was in that French prison for months with no idea of the charges, much less if they were justified."

"The French have no habeas corpus."

"It's the principle that matters."

"You think that there is real danger of insurrection?" Lord David sounded skeptical.

"I'm not sure. The air I breathe is too rarified for me to know what most people are thinking. That is one of the reasons I hired Garrett. He knows what to look for. He knows how to keep us safe and I want to be prepared."

"And the other reason you hired him?"

The duke did not answer verbally, or did not speak loud enough for Michael to hear. He would have given a month's pay to know what passed between them. David made a sound that might have been a laugh. "I tell you what Garrett should do. Bed her, wed her and let her stay in the kitchen."

"I think I would reverse the first two, brother."

"You might, Lyn, but few men have your self-control."

Michael had heard quite enough. The two were gossiping like Mary and the scullery maid did when they thought no one else was about. And like them, the duke and his brother made up stories so that the world made sense. He had self-control, damn it. He had been proving it for weeks. He was halfway to furious when Lord David came into the office through the door from the duke's study.

"Well, good morning. Been listening, have you?"

Michael was not going to answer, not if the man bent his finger back until it broke. "I've discovered something that I think you should see immediately, my lord. We will need to go to the room where the baskets are stored."

"In the old castle?"

"Yes."

Without demanding any more of an explanation Lord David led him through the halls and downstairs, into the inner courtyard of the new castle, a space alive with flowers despite this year without a spring. There were even flowering trees and an elegant French garden.

They crossed it and faced a grand entryway.

"The old castle drawbridge."

Michael had to admire how it had been retained as an element of design and wondered if it could still open completely.

He followed Lord David through the small guard door to the left. The old inner ward was as stark as the new castle courtyard was lush. Its only decoration was a very professional boxing ring.

"I am guessing that is a recent addition." He gestured to the ring.

"Yes, my idea. We have matches. Lyn and I, and a couple of the stable lads are good in the ring. One of the footmen worked for a professional and is their coach."

Michael followed Lord David across the courtyard, up a circle of stone stairs and along a corridor with doors on one side and an opening onto the inner ward on the other.

The corridor ran around the castle in a circle, providing air and light when the doors to the rooms were open.

"I told you before that most of these rooms serve as our attic. The chapel is still ready for use and so is the royal bedroom, though no king would ever choose to stay in it.

"The rooms are all locked. I have yet to spend time here unless I need something. I think I must move it up on my list. But, as you can see, each one is labeled."

Lord David found the room designated for basket storage with unerring accuracy. Inside it was just as Michael had left it. He walked over to the window, stepped up on the sill and reached for the handholds, pulling the panel in as he stepped down. A spill of weak sunlight showed the straw pallet, candle stubs and ashes in sharper detail. "My lord, someone has been coming in through this panel to meet here."

"And you have no idea who that someone is." Lord David stood with his hands on his hips looking at the opening.

"No, but whoever it is has not been here for a while."

"How did you find this, Garrett?"

"When I made my first circuit of the grounds," Michael gestured to the panel, "I saw that this opening could be reached from the outside. I finally made time to see if I was right."

"Who is our traitor?" Lord David kicked at an old basket, which produced nothing but dust. He did not seem to expect an answer, but turned and left the room, apparently heading back to the courtyard. Michael followed him, giving an answer anyway.

"As we discussed before, you have to find out who are the most recent hires." *But not as new as I am.* "Who has a grudge." *Hackett or someone else in his family.* "Who needs money." *Surely there were bets on the occasional boxing matches.* "Who is in love with Olivia." *Besides me.*

The two words exploded in his brain, made his heart jump, his stomach clench. It was not love, he insisted, even as Lord David told him to bring him the perpetrators and walked off.

Michael did not move, could not move. All his energy

was focused on denial. He was not in love with her. In lust. Yes, lust he could accept.

It did not take more than one look at her to want all of that warm, lush body. One look into her eyes to want to see the world through them.

That was not love.

It was longing for a life that was as unfamiliar as it was unreachable.

32

I CANNOT COUNT how many times the courier has been here since I wrote and I have had no response from Jess. It has been at least six weeks." Olivia was in bed and Kendall was busy tucking in the covers as though her charge was a baby in swaddling clothes.

"He is a busy man, my lady."

"That is no excuse. It was very, very important. I expected him to come home immediately."

Kendall straightened suddenly. Well-trained maid that she was, Kendall did not ask for details, but Olivia knew she was curious.

"I want him to tell me how Rowena is doing. I want to hear it in person, and I am sure that the duke would like to hear his opinion as well."

It was such a good lie that Kendall nodded approval.

"You should write him again. The courier leaves in the morning."

"I'll do that first thing, Kendall. Then to the kitchen. I have almost perfected the dry spice for the salmon. If it is cooked as slowly as possible, the spices will flavor the entire fillet."

Her maid yawned.

Olivia pretended that was the end of the discussion. She should have asked when they could expect the material they had ordered from London. If that had been the subject, there would have been no yawn. How many times did she have to witness the fact that not everyone was interested in what they ate and how it was cooked? "Good night, Kendall."

"Good night, my lady."

As soon as the door was closed, Olivia drummed her feet to loosen the covers and thought about the letter to Jess. She should write it tonight. That's what she would do, so the letter would be ready in plenty of time for the morning courier.

Olivia tossed the covers back. The sound of the wind beating against the window was a reminder to put on her robe and slippers. Holding an unlit candle in her hand she went into her boudoir.

Her writing desk was as tidy as ever. She lit the candle and reseated the globe. With a piece of paper in front of her and the nib sharpened, she opened the inkwell to find that the ink was no more than a dried lump at the bottom of the well. Oh dear. Should it not last more than six weeks?

All right, that was an easy enough problem to solve.

She would run down to Lyn's office and use his ink, or she could bring the ink up. It would only take five minutes to fetch it.

Olivia dashed out of the room and was halfway down the stairs before she realized that the castle was completely dark at this hour. She was not afraid, but it did not look or feel nearly as comfortable now as it did in the morning.

The shadows were the same, she insisted as a tingle of fear settled next to her bravado. Except for the new statue at the other end of the hall. When had that been put in place? Making a mental note to ask in the morning, she set the candle on the table outside the study.

In the second between placing it there and opening the door someone grabbed her from behind, his hand over her mouth.

Panic gave her strength and she kicked back, aiming for the place between his legs but missing it completely.

"Olivia!"

How did he know who it was? Probably the same way she knew it was Michael Garrett. The way his hand felt on her mouth, the way it made her feel warm all over, the way she wanted to fit her whole body against his.

"Oh for God's sake, Olivia. I'm sorry. Shh. Shh." He smoothed her hair with his hands, turning her into his chest. She was shaking and mad at herself for being so missish, but she could not stop or move away.

Her ear was pressed against his heart and she could feel it beating, steadily but hard, as though he was angry.

What right did he have to be angry? This was her house,

not his. She leaned back to look him in the eye, irritation taking the place of fear.

"What are you doing here? You almost scared me to death."

"You didn't do my heart any good, either, my lady. What are *you* doing here?"

"I asked first." Olivia took a step back, out of his arms. It didn't make any sense to let him hold her if she was going to argue with him. "I came to find some ink so I could write to my brother Jess this evening. There is a courier to London tomorrow and I wanted to be sure that my letter went out as soon as possible."

"What is so urgent that the letter must be written tonight?"

"Nothing," she lied, looking away from him so he would not see it in her eyes. "I could not sleep, and it occurred to me that I should make use of the time by writing to Jess." She was proud of that; it was the complete truth. As long as he did not ask her what she was writing to him about.

"You are one of the worst liars I have ever met."

"Really? But I'm not lying."

"Then you are not telling me the whole truth." He ran a hand through his hair. "You are not going to put anything about what happened in your letter, are you?"

"No, of course not. It's only that I think he should consider coming home to give Lyn support."

"The duke seems to have all the support he needs." Michael folded his arms and considered her from his superior height. "You are telling me that all you will have to do is ask

your brother to come home and he will leave London immediately, make the trip on miserable roads without any idea of
what is so important."

"He will if I ask him."

"Do tell me the magic words, Lady Olivia."

"I am his sister and he loves me. He would die if anything happened to me."

"But you are safe now. Why do you have to tell him anything?" It was a moment before he said, with great certainty,
"You think he had something to do with your abduction."

"No." She hesitated a moment before adding, "Absolutely not." Olivia gave him a quick look from under her
lashes. "I have no idea what worrisome story may make its
way to town. I am going to reassure him and suggest that he
could be of help here. That is all."

"How thoughtful, and what a bag of nonsense." He took
her by the arm and pulled her into Lyn's study. "Tell me what
Lord Jessup has to do with this."

"How do you know that what I said isn't the truth?"

He shook his head.

"You can truly tell when someone is lying?"

"Yes, and do not ask me to teach you how to lie or how
to tell when someone is. Your duke brother would love that.
He would tie me to a cart and drag me in the dirt."

"I was not going to ask you to teach me!"

"That is another lie." Michael rubbed his jaw. "I will not
teach you to lie, but you can keep trying and when I do not
catch you in one you will know you have succeeded."

"It might take forever."

"I devoutly hope it does, Lady Olivia. Telling the truth is so much easier than nursing lies. After a while it is hard to tell truth from story."

"How do you know?"

"Experience."

She wanted to know more about his life before she met him but now he was acting like David. Answering her questions with more of his own. Questions she did not want to answer.

"I must go." She reached around the door and picked up the candle and went to find the ink. He followed her.

She had the inkwell in hand before her annoyance faded enough to let other thoughts take shape in her head. "What are you doing here, Mr. Garrett?"

"Lord David has not found a new night porter yet, so I am making a circuit of the inside as well as the outside to be sure all is as it should be."

He sounded like an officious butler.

"Lady Olivia, you can ask me questions until dawn. I will wait you out and go back to the one you have not answered. Why is it so urgent that you must write to your brother in London?"

Where was the man with whom she had traveled? That man had been kind and only a little autocratic.

Was it because it was just the two of them in the almost dark that his looks were an enticing mix of fascinating and forbidding? If he thought he could intimidate her he was wrong.

"It is none of your business."

"Convince me."

"How am I supposed to do that?"

"Write the letter and show it to me. I will give it to the courier myself to make sure it is the only letter you send."

"That is ridiculous. You are not my father, my brother or my guardian. Go away."

He did not answer her, but stayed right where he was, watching her until she began to be self-conscious. She was wearing only her night robe and while it covered more of her flesh than her gowns did, she was not wearing a corset. The lack of it made her feel indecently dressed. She could feel a blush starting and hated her lack of sophistication.

"You are blushing because it has only now occurred to you how inappropriate this meeting is?"

"Not at all. It is warm in here."

"Tell me why you are writing to your brother."

"Women learned all they know about nagging from men."

"You are going to learn something else in a minute, Lady Olivia."

She made a face at him, picked up the candle and headed for the door. Garrett reached it before she did, blocking her exit. Olivia turned and walked toward the door that led into the library. Garrett stayed where he was. Good. He would learn that he could not treat her like a child.

"Your brother may tolerate it when you act like a child, but I will not."

She slowed a little but did not turn around.

"You are behaving like a selfish chit. It is not only your

safety that is at stake here. There are at least a hundred people in and around the castle every day and God knows how many in the village. Any one of them could be at risk."

She stopped and, still with her back to him, winced at the truth of what he was saying.

"While I am convinced that you are no longer in any physical danger, I still know nothing about the men who took you. Nothing. If someone is hurt because you will not tell me what you know, you will have to live with the guilt. Not to mention my disappointment in you."

"I am so sorry, Garrett. So sorry." Mortified, embarrassed and discomfited. None of those words summed up exactly how she felt. "You are right. There are others to think about. Not the need to protect my reputation or spare Jess from Lyn's anger. I could not live with the guilt. I still feel terrible about Big Sam searching for me that night."

Ashamed was more like it. Ashamed that she had only thought of her brother Jess and not the possibility that others could be in danger.

"Please, let me explain." She put the candle and ink on the table nearest the door, walked toward the fireplace and stood as close to the fading warmth as she could.

SHE REALLY DID LISTEN to reason. Amazing. Michael tried to count. It was the second or third time that she had listened to what he had to say and stopped just as he thought a tantrum was brewing. "Will you be warm enough?"

"Oh, I am almost never warm enough." She waved away

his concern. "But do not add any more fuel to the fire. Not for me."

That was carrying penance too far. He prodded the banked coals and added some more wood. Flames licked up at the new fuel and a heat radiated a few feet from the hearth. She sat in the chair, holding her night robe closed at the neck. Michael moved behind the chair opposite her, hoping to deflect the awareness shimmering around them.

"I did hear one important conversation when I was being held." Her expression was earnest as though she was doing her best to make up for her thoughtlessness. "Not a conversation precisely, more like a brief exchange."

Michael listened as she told him of the comment one of the kidnappers had made and what she'd surmised. He listened not only to the words, "Her brother will give us the land on a silver platter," but to the way she spoke them, the way her body communicated as much as her admission. She was telling the truth, or was a better actress than she was a baker.

"You have four brothers. Why do you think the kidnappers were talking about Lord Jessup?"

"Because he is the only one who is ever in trouble."

"What do you call Gabriel's problems in France? I would call it trouble."

"Not really. At least not the way I mean. Gabriel was there to study science and was caught up in the war, with unfortunate consequences."

"I will pretend I see the distinction because I know Gabriel and cannot see anything in his life now that would lead to such a horror as your kidnapping."

"All right. Thank you. And David is as honest as lemons are tart. He would tell Lyn what the problem was in as few words as possible."

"Yes, he would." Michael sat down in the chair across from her and leaned forward, his elbows on his knees. "So it is your brother who gambles. It could be one other who is at the heart of this. The brother you forgot to mention: the duke."

33

YOU THINK that Lynford knows more about the kidnapping than he has let on? Never." She straightened and took offense for him. "Lyn would not let himself be put in a position like that."

"That is a response based on your sense of his superiority. Or perhaps you have proof." He leaned back in the chair.

"First of all, the land that he owns is his by right of the title." She sounded vaguely annoyed as if she was explaining the obvious and was irritated by the need. "All the land is entailed. He cannot sell it even if it would mean saving the life of his son."

It was an interesting piece of information. "He will have personal wealth. Or perhaps land his wife owns."

"His personal wealth is not in land."

Michael must have shown his surprise at that.

"Yes, it is not the usual, but how many times must I tell

you that our father was profoundly influenced by his time in France? He had interests in any number of ventures, from mines to canals." She threw up her hands. "And a dozen other outlandish ventures for all I know."

"The mind boggles at what those could be." Michael had thought the duke conservative to the point of reactionary. It was hard to imagine what of the newer developments in science and commerce might attract his interest. He caught up with what Olivia was saying too late to understand the details.

"It is a kind of oven that every cook will want—it will make accurate baking accessible to everyone."

It seemed they were now discussing Olivia's idea for improved baking. Food was all the girl thought about. As she chattered on, he wondered if her obsession was a substitute for a lack of other passion in her life. He cleared his throat and forced his mind back to what was important, allowing himself the pleasure of watching her mouth until she stopped for a breath.

"Lady Olivia, the hour grows late and there are still some questions."

She nodded, altogether adorable in her desire to be helpful. He would have been happier if she had been offended by his abrupt change of subject.

"You are sure he said, 'Her brother will give us the land on a silver platter.' Those were the exact words?"

"Yes. Eleven words. Fourteen syllables. I wanted to be sure I would remember it exactly. It seemed an odd sort of ransom until I thought of Jess."

"Is there any land in dispute right now?"

"No, at least I do not think so." She raised her shoulders. "How would I know? I would only hear of it from the servants. That is not the sort of thing discussed at the dinner table." She laughed at the thought and he smiled at her amusement. "Why do you doubt it is Jess? It makes the most sense."

"Lady Olivia, I know you are a valued member of this family. The duke made it clear that losing you would break his heart."

She ducked her head and shook it, touched and embarrassed by what they both knew was the truth.

"But allow me this question, my lady. Why would a London moneylender or any other less-than-honorable man send someone all the way to Derbyshire in order to threaten your brother who lives in London?"

Olivia pressed her lips together as she tried to think of a reason. There was none, so he finished his explanation.

"Lord Jessup has friends, perhaps even a mistress he has affection for. Surely they would be a more likely target and engender a more immediate response."

"Yes, Jess is the most likeable fellow in the world. During my Season he introduced me to an endless stream of gentlemen, not a one of which Rowena would allow me to know better."

"Rowena is the duchess who is in London?"

Olivia nodded, and continued her own line of thought. "What did the kidnappers mean, Mr. Garrett?"

"I don't know yet. But I will find out tomorrow when I ask the duke."

Olivia stood and stalked over to his chair.

"Tell me, Mr. Garrett. Tell me what you suspect. You are not one of my brothers and this has a direct impact on my life."

Olivia might say she was always cold, but her body gave off the sweetest warmth. If he looked, he could see the outline of her breasts, the neat waist belted by her robe. If he looked.

He stared into her eyes and was relieved that what he saw was stubbornness and not seduction.

"In the short time I have known you I have been well introduced to your impulsive behavior, my lady. I will not discuss this with you until I have spoken with your brother."

"I am so tired of being treated like a child. I am not a child."

"I am well aware of that." He glanced down quite deliberately. Only for a second. "But you do have a tendency to act like one when you are denied what you want."

God help him, this was torture. She had no idea what she did to a man. To him. If she did not leave soon he would have to show her.

OLIVIA COULD FEEL where he glanced. Right where her night robe crossed her body. The tingling sensation settled in her breasts and made her smile in spite of her irritation.

This discussion was beginning to sound like one of those bickering matches that she never won. Perhaps she could tease him out of his aggravation. His clothes? No, that would imply poverty. She went through a list of teaseable ideas and found that none of them suited this situation.

"It is time for you to go back to your room, my lady," he said, easing from his chair.

He was right. It would do her still-fragile reputation no good at all to be found here with him at this hour.

"All right. And while I am sleeping you will wander around all night and see if anyone is not where they're supposed to be?"

"Yes. Inside and out."

"I can vouch for the fact you do a wonderful job pretending to be a statue and scaring people." There, that was the tease that would make him smile.

He did not smile or even answer. He stood as still as a stone figure. When she drew close to him he took a step back, raised a hand to his forehead.

Did he have a headache? She was not about to ask, for surely he would blame her for that as well. All right, she would give up trying to make him smile.

Olivia went back to the table by the door, made sure the top was tight on the inkwell. Tomorrow she would win him over with something delicious for breakfast and his pique would fade away.

Garrett moved across the room and came to her. When he put his hand on the door handle, Olivia realized all he was going to do was open the door for her.

She felt as dull as the scullery maid. If he would just look at her when he said good night. If he would smile she could leave knowing he was no longer upset with her.

"Were you a guard in the army? Who did you protect? When did you have time to sleep?"

"I served England, my lady. I slept when the opportunity arose."

"What kind of uniform did you wear?" She eyed him like a work of art. Which he was, in a way. She tried to imagine him wearing something more colorful than his black greatcoat and worn boots. "Whatever you wore I have no doubt women found you irresistible." She reached up, touched the small scar on his cheek and shivered at the tingle that came from him, right through her fingers. "This little scar and your ear, it is just the thing to make people realize that your uniform is more than a fine suit of clothes."

"It is in your best interests to go back to your room, Olivia." As he spoke, through gritted teeth, he pushed her hand from his ear.

She had just picked up the candle, but put it back down, along with the inkwell. She hated that tone of voice, as though she had pushed him to his limits. He did not know what limits were. She was the one who had been pushed enough. "I was going to leave until you commanded me. I think I will stay here and write my letter."

"Oh no, you will not." He came toward her until her back was pressed against the wall next to the door. "Has no one told you that you should play with fire only in the kitchen?"

He kissed her quite ruthlessly. That was the only thought she had. From that moment on it was all feeling. Beyond his mouth crushing her lips, his body pressed into hers, making her feel as though she could never have enough of this fuel that warmed her beyond bearing.

He ended the kiss and pushed her away, leaving her dizzy and abandoned.

"Go back to your room now, Olivia. Unless you do not want to go to bed alone." He reached across her and she was shocked at the way her body responded, a rush of pleasure from her breasts to her belly. She did not want to go to bed alone. Before she could say it, Garrett opened the door and pushed her into the hall.

Olivia stumbled out of the room without her candle or the ink. He closed the door behind her. She stared at it a moment, turned and ran down the hall as if the ghost from the old castle were following her.

She could not begin to sort out her feelings until she was back in bed, the covers pulled up around her neck. She had been playing with fire. It was just that no one flirted with her. No one ever winked at her or teased her or stood too close.

Until now.

Even in London she had been every man's friend—well, except for Viscount Bendasbrook. He was vastly entertaining to be with but would not have suited at all. Oh, and that annoying Lord Ellinger and his silly poems.

Was there not someone between the men who treated her like a sister and the Lord Ellingers of the world? Ellinger tried to sit next to her all the time. Sent a poem or flowers every day and insisted it was love that made him so giddy. Personally, she thought Ellinger was smoking hashish, and Bendasbrook must have been desperate for a wife to court her.

No one had ever looked on her in quite the right way. Never.

Until Michael Garrett, who was yet another type.

He wanted to protect her from a real menace, but also from a supposed menace she was not so sure she wanted protection from. Why could he not let her decide?

That was it! She sat up in bed and hit the mattress with her hands. No man allowed her to make up her own mind, make her own choices. She had to dance to their tune.

All right. That was the way it had been, but her life was about to change.

34

GOOD MORNING! Miss Hope!" Olivia opened the door and leaned in as she called out her hello. Big Sam settled on the bench by the front door. "Miss Hope! I have a basket with me," she announced as the elderly lady came out of the parlor nearest the door much more quickly than usual.

"Oh deary, I saw you coming up the path and thought I might meet you at the door. It does not smell like a cinnamon bun."

"I brought you all a salmon pie. You remember the recipe from the cookery book, the one you gave me as a gift at least five years ago?"

"Not really, Olivia. My memory . . ." Her words trailed off as though she had already forgotten what she was going to say.

"All right. I will remember for both of us." She took Miss

Hope's arm and led her back into the sitting room. "Is the reverend working on his sermon?"

"Yes, and I am working on the songs." She sat at the pianoforte and stared at the keys.

"I will leave you and take this to the kitchen."

Miss Hope may or may not have heard her. Olivia had no idea what she was hearing in her head but Olivia was sure it would not be the hymns they sang on Sunday.

Within five minutes she and Annie were settled in the housekeeper's rooms with a cup of tea and biscuits that were going a trifle stale. She would have to make more for them soon. Maybe the gingerbread cakes that were Miss Hope's favorites, "because they smelled so nice."

"Lollie."

Annie's gentle voice called her back to the moment. It was not nearly as pleasant a place as her imagination.

"The truth is, dearest, that people will think what they want to think," Annie began in that gentle voice that so reminded Olivia of Annie's mother.

"Nothing you can say will disabuse them of it. For example, that awful, awful woman who whores when she needs money tells me to let her know when the duke is bored with me and she will find some other man I can service."

"Annie! That is disgusting. No one believes you are having an affair with Lynford."

"In her head there is no other explanation for why I am allowed to stay here in the vicar's house when I am divorced and disgraced."

"Because you are as much a victim as I am? Why can no one understand that?"

"I am not as innocent as you are." She looked down at the knitting in her lap. "I am not sure anyone is."

"Go ahead and laugh at my naïveté." Olivia saw her try to hide a smile. "*That* I am used to."

"And your joy in the world is one of the loveliest things about you." Annie sobered. "I am so sorry that it has been compromised."

"It has not! I am safe and am sure that I will continue to be safe. I must think of something that will make people forget."

"Let me know when you concoct that recipe. It will not happen until something more titillating comes along." Annie considered the knitting that she had picked up but not started. "The truth is that no matter what you do, the incident is now part of the family lore."

"No matter what I do?" She searched her mind for something impossibly amazing. "Even if I am the first female chef for the king?"

"One is as unlikely as the other." Annie reached over and patted her hand. "I am content here, you know. My divorce was the oddity that we call a blessing in disguise. The vicar and his sister are so grateful for everything I do for them, and your brother is the most generous of employers."

"So you say, Annie." Olivia had often thought that if Lyn was that generous he would have settled money on Annie and let her create her own life, instead of making her stay here where there were constant reminders of her past.

"So," Olivia mused, "if I were to take a lover no one would be surprised." It was more than an idle thought.

"Olivia! I never said that."

"You said that it does not matter what I do now. People will think what they want to think."

"Yes, but that is not permission to live a life of debauchery."

Now Olivia laughed. "I am not going to have a hundred lovers. But if I am never to marry I should like to know what sex is like."

"Who says you will never marry?"

"No one, but I am not going to London again, not when the gossip is likely to follow me. And who marries a woman thought to be ruined?"

"Lollie." Annie leaned forward, her ball of yarn falling to the floor. "Do you have someone in mind for the role of lover?"

Olivia smiled.

"Olivia." Now she sounded exactly like Olivia's governess, or her mother. "You will not seduce Mr. Garrett."

"Never," she said, trying to make her expression as frank as she could even as she thought, *Oh, yes, I will.*

Annie wrung her hands. "I should have lied to you. I should have told you what you wished was the truth."

"Never lie to me, Annie. You are my most loyal friend and I count on you to be the realist." She kissed her friend on the cheek and rose to leave. "Do not worry. He has refused me once, maybe even twice before. I am not sure he even likes me."

It seemed to be small comfort to Annie. Olivia could almost see her friend bow her head in prayer as she closed the door behind her.

Olivia walked home as briskly as her dainty shoes would allow.

"If you are in a hurry, Miss Lollie, I can carry you and run." Big Sam was earnest in his offer. "We would reach home more faster."

"Thank you, Big Sam. It is only that I have this amazing idea and I cannot wait to test it." She sped up. "I can walk more quickly if you are concerned about my safety." For her own part she did feel vaguely uncomfortable in the open even though there was no one else about.

When they reached the castle she hurried up to her room, telling Sam that she would meet him in the kitchen and asking him to tell Cook to have someone prepare a basket of chicken soup and the cheese rolls she had made for the first time that morning.

Olivia went up to her room and surprised Kendall napping on the small bed in the dressing room.

"I am so sorry, Kendall."

"Do not be foolish, my lady. Napping is not what I am paid for. Tell me you want a fresh dress and your hair combed and I will be happy for a week."

"That is exactly what I want." Olivia smiled and wrinkled her noise.

"You do?" Kendall raised a hand to her heart as if palpitations were making her uncomfortable. "How wonderful. You so rarely care."

It took much longer than Olivia had anticipated. Kendall thought the pink dress with the white and pink flounces was too dressy for the time of day and the white dress not at all appropriate for the cool weather even if it was almost June.

She finally allowed that the lovely winter white with the green stripes was perfect. She insisted that Olivia carry a moss green Paisley shawl and wear the beige leather slippers and that she "not walk on the grass."

Finally Kendall did her hair, winding a winter white satin ribbon through the curls. It made her look like a schoolgirl, but Olivia said thank you and did not pull it out until she left the room.

Like the perfect maid she was, Kendall never once asked for whom Olivia was dressing so carefully. If her maid knew, her heart palpitations would not be an affectation.

Olivia found Big Sam waiting for her in the almost-empty kitchen. She took the smaller of the two baskets from him as they walked toward the gatehouse.

"We are taking supper to Mr. Garrett. You can carry the big basket with the soup tureen."

"If that is what you wish, Miss Lollie, but tell me if the one you are carrying is too heavy."

She agreed with a smile and turned her attention to the sky. The sun was doing its best to shine, but she was glad that she had worn the shawl.

Olivia hoped that Michael Garrett did not think this year was typical of Derbyshire spring weather. She would have to explain what Gabriel had told them, though it was hard to believe that a volcano erupting on the other side of the world could ruin their summer.

"Miss Lollie!" Big Sam stopped and pushed her behind him as a man on horseback cantered down the path from the castle.

"It's quite all right, Sam." She waved to the rider who

saluted her with a hand to his cap. "That's the courier, on his way to London. Though he is leaving unusually late today. It's almost four, is it not? He usually leaves after breakfast."

Sam waved at the back of the courier and shrugged off the late departure. "He's the one who brings us poetry from the duchess."

And newspapers for the duke and recipe books for her. His return was one of the high points of her week.

Not a minute later Big Sam suggested that they take a route they had never used before.

"If we do that, Sam, we will have wet feet, and Kendall insisted that I not allow my shoes to touch the wet. Besides, if our feet were wet it would be an invitation to illness." Olivia could never understand why Mary could annoy her so easily and she had endless patience with Big Sam.

"Oh, yes, milady."

On and on. Sam had to be talked out of myriad unrealistic threats to her well-being. By the time they reached the end of the drive and the gatehouse, Olivia wondered if Big Sam was becoming a trifle overprotective.

He knocked on the gatehouse door with all the force of a father coming to confront a wayward beau. Sam's knock was answered promptly by Mr. Garrett. It was, after all, four o'clock and even if he needed sleep she had calculated that he would be awake and dressed by now.

He was wearing different clothes from the ones he had worn last night—a fresh shirt and a waistcoat that was as conservative as his haircut—and had a clean-shaven face. His boots were polished so that, though old, they looked perfectly respectable. She was happy to see him looking so well.

"Good day to you, Mr. Garrett." His smile made her smile back at him, and confusion quickly followed it. She came into his parlor without an invitation, and stumbled, almost dropping the basket.

Garrett grabbed her around the waist and rescued the basket from her. "I'm delighted to see you too," he whispered and proved it by missing the table and letting the basket plop hard on the floor.

They both began laughing as though it was the funniest thing that had ever happened to them.

It might have been. How much cause had they had to laugh about anything until this moment? Olivia was so happy that she turned in his arms to hug him. He dropped his arms from her waist and stepped back.

"My lady." He bowed as formally as if they had met in a ballroom. She gave him a small curtsy and sobered as fast as she had started laughing, more embarrassed than disappointed.

Garrett turned from her and held out his hand to Big Sam. "Samuelson."

Big Sam's confusion was genuine. Most people ignored him, as if pretending he did not exist was possible with a man close to seven feet tall and as white as a ghost.

Big Sam took the hand offered him and smiled when Mr. Garrett gave it a firm shake.

Mr. Garrett pointed at the basket. "I assume that is for me."

"You sleep through dinner most days so I thought I would bring you something. Some of my truly restorative chicken soup and the newest of my attempts at savory rolls.

There is also some ale with which to wash it down, and strawberries and cream."

Stop babbling, Olivia, she commanded herself.

"May I go upstairs?" Big Sam's question was perfunctory as he was already on the first step.

"He wants to be sure that I am safe and that no one is waiting to attack me." She spoke in a normal voice but gave Garrett a look that dared him to refuse the request.

When Big Sam disappeared around the corner of the staircase, Mr. Garrett approached her. For a moment Olivia thought he was going to sweep her into his arms, but instead he took her hand and spoke with some urgency. "While he is gone, Lord David and I discussed something a few nights ago that we both think we should ask you about."

She did her best to ignore the way his eyes crinkled at the corners when he was smiling and focus on what he was saying. Now was not the time for flirting.

He led her to the chair opposite his at the table, apparently unmoved by the feel of her hand in his.

Garrett detailed his plan to promote Samuelson, as he insisted on calling him, to the position of night guard, "second only to the night porter for security of the castle after dark."

"Do you truly think he is ready for such a responsibility?" Olivia folded her hands in front of her on the table and tried to think of more pertinent questions. He was asking her opinion. Amazing.

"I do think he's ready, yes. He will be scrupulous, which is what I want until the miscreants who are responsible for your kidnapping are no longer a threat."

"Why would you think they are still a threat? It has been weeks."

"Admit that you are still nervous when you walk to the vicarage."

He must have seen the surprise on her face at his ability to read her mind because he pressed his advantage.

"Think how much safer you will feel if Samuelson is on patrol and your brother or I go with you when you leave Pennford."

"All right." She nodded and realized that he was right. The very thought that David or Mr. Garrett would be with her made her feel strong enough to do it. Was it that she had lost confidence in Big Sam? No, not really. It was just that David and Mr. Garrett were cast from the same mold. Men who had faced the worst life could bombard them with, and lived.

"Once again, my lady, you impress me with your common sense. Not a compliment I give to many women."

"Thank you." She hoped her dutiful response covered up her longing to hear something a trifle more personal. She could tell him how much she loved the color of his eyes, the way his arms felt wrapped around her.

But if she could not show her affection that way, she would do what she did for all the other men she loved. She would feed him.

35

NOW YOU MUST EAT." Olivia popped up from her chair and lifted the basket onto the table. It took only a minute to set the food before him, on a cream cloth cover, chattering the whole time. "I invented this silverware. It is specifically designed for travel or a picnic. Ideally one would not serve food that requires a knife on a picnic."

He picked up the spoon/fork and put it down again.

"I devised this holder for it, which will also function as a serviette."

She knew she was babbling again. He seemed to have that effect on her. Pressing her lips together she gathered the storage items and the basket, carried them to the door and stayed there to look out the window, so he could eat in peace.

The gatehouse was a charming place, more like a doll-house than a man-sized establishment. When Papa had decided not to staff it after Mr. Hackett retired she had asked

him if she could live here with Tildy and Annie. He had not
even deigned to answer her.

It would have been perfect. There were only two bedrooms, but she and Annie had shared a room for years without telling anyone. Tildy was the most wonderful governess
and mother in the world, even if she had finished off her days
with too much to drink.

When Olivia turned back to Michael he was starting on
the strawberries. He had eaten all the soup but only one of
the two buns. That was all right. They were rather large.

Walking back to the table she sat opposite him, her elbow on the table cradling her chin as she watched him dip
the berry into the cream and take a bite.

He chewed and swallowed, well aware of her eyes on
him. When he had eaten one more she could not stay quiet
any longer.

"Are they not delicious? There is nothing in the world
that tastes better than strawberries and cream."

"They are delectable," he said, nodding, "but I can think
of two or more things that would taste even better."

"Two or more! That is impossible." She could see he was
teasing her, but that she did not understand the joke made it
all the more annoying. "I insist that you tell me what they
are." What could taste better than strawberries in cream, unless it was strawberries in champagne? It occurred to her in
the next second that he was not talking about food, but she
was distracted from that line of thought by Big Sam's voice.

"All is well upstairs."

She blushed but Mr. Garrett looked up at Big Sam with a
blasé expression she wished she could copy.

"Samuelson, would you care to share some strawberries with me? I know for a fact that Lady Olivia would like to take a bit of this roll to my horse, and I would have a few words with you."

"You want to talk to me, sir?" Big Sam asked. Michael knew the request would surprise Big Sam, but he had not realized he would look at Olivia as if something was profoundly wrong.

"Yes." Olivia patted his arm, nodding energetically.

Standing, Michael walked to the window next to the front door. "It is a short walk and we can watch her from here. You can see Troy in the paddock so they will be in sight at all times."

"If it is that simple, I guess it will be all right, sir. But I'd feel even better if we could stand outside and watch. We could feast on the strawberries when we know she is safe."

Michael was impressed again by the big man's dedication to his duty, something a seasoned soldier would never admit out loud.

Olivia happily broke off a good chunk of the bun, wrapped it and with a wave to both of them ran, or was it skipped, down to the stable. Troy came to her without invitation. Even without the proffered treat it would have been a touching reunion.

"Horse likes her," Sam said.

"A mutual admiration." When Sam looked confused Michael tried again. "And she likes Troy."

"Aye, hard not to like a horse as beautiful as that."

Michael knew better than to think Sam was joking, and wondered if the man saw colors normally.

Michael took Samuelson back inside, seated him and set a plate with two strawberries in front of him. After he ate them, in two giant bites, Michael made his proposition with slow and careful wording, so that the man would see he was being promoted and not replaced.

"You know which room is Lollie's and can give special attention to that side of the castle. You know where I live and can come for me should anything seem wrong."

Samuelson was quiet a long time. Then he nodded. "Sir, thank you, sir. No one has ever thought to offer me such a post. I must ask Miss Lollie and Lord David and the major-domo, and I am sure that the duke will have an opinion." It looked like he had thought of two or three other people who he needed permission from but could not recall their names at the moment.

"Ask whomever you must, Samuelson," Michael said, relieved that he had already discussed this at length with Pennistan. "I assure you they will all be pleased with the idea."

"I am not so sure, sir." He looked away. "You see, I have not told the truth about Miss Lollie's kidnapping." When he looked back Michael could see that the giant actually had tears in his eyes.

Michael felt a sinking sensation that had nothing to do with the wonderful meal he had just eaten.

"You see, when I was at the vicar's that day, the day Miss Lollie was taken, a man came up to me and asked if I would stay behind for a few moments so that his master could have some time with her ladyship. That he wanted only a moment to give her a poem and a bunch of flowers and declare his admiration."

Well done, you bastards, Michael thought. Find the weakest point and make it work for you. It was what he had done in France.

"Mr. Garrett, I was so pleased for her. I would be happy to guard her forever, but I am old and will surely die before she does. I thought if she found a husband she would be safe even if I was dead."

Samuelson loved Olivia, Michael realized, in a way most men did not begin to understand.

"Had that ever happened before, Samuelson?"

"No, sir." He hesitated, shifting in the chair. "Once a long time ago I found her in the garden kissing the vicar's nephew. Is that what you mean?"

"Yes." He knew that story. Amazing how much of this woman's life was like a public record.

"That's the only time. I did not go to London with her for her Season. She did tell me that there was no one who was much fun except for Viscount Bendasbrook, but she would never consider a match with him."

Big Sam must have learned his storytelling from Olivia-the-chatty. These were more details than he needed, though now he was curious as to why the viscount was not appealing. Was he not interested in food?

"Finish telling me what happened that day when you let Lollie meet with her new beau."

"He was not her beau." Samuelson spoke as though it was a detail Michael might not be aware of. "It was a lie. I knew it was a lie the moment I saw the carriage racketing up the road. I ran, I ran as fast as I could but I was crying and could not keep pace with them." He stood up. "You may not want me for such a post if I cannot tell an honest man from a liar."

Michael kept his seat. "Samuelson, you must listen to me."

Sam sat back down and Michael looked him in the eye. "There are not many who can tell a lie from the truth when they want to believe something so much."

"Is that so, sir? I thought that one of my weaknesses. I always believe what people tell me." He looked out the window. "I *used* to believe what people tell me. Now I am afraid everyone is lying."

Most of the time they are.

"You will learn who you can believe and who you will always doubt. If you decide to accept this new position you can come to me whenever you are not sure. Even if it is ten times a night."

Big Sam nodded.

"I have one other question, Samuelson."

Big Sam nodded again and tilted forward as if he thought he might miss a word.

"Did you give the men some baskets?"

"No, no sir. I never saw those men before that day."

God help him, he would have to ask Olivia exactly what she was wearing when she was taken so they could determine if all her garments were accounted for.

"Samuelson," Michael stood and waited for Big Sam to do the same. "We all make mistakes, from the Prince Regent to the scullery maid."

"Yes, I know."

The answer was perfunctory. Michael could see that he was not free of guilt. "Go to Lord David and tell him. See what he suggests."

"Do you think that he would take me to the boxing ring, if I asked?"

"I'm not sure. Why?"

"A good thrashing will make me feel so much better."

"If that is so, I will meet you in the ring. With Lord David's permission."

Big Sam looked inordinately pleased at the prospect of being beaten to a pulp. With a bow, he left the gatehouse, stopping for a moment to speak to Olivia.

Michael could tell the moment the man confessed to Olivia the way he had been deceived. Her sympathetic expression changed to disbelief, shock. She put her hand on Samuelson's arm and spoke to him with such earnestness that Michael did not have to hear what she was saying.

Samuelson gave her a profound bow and Olivia accepted it with a pat on his head. Michael watched her watch the big man as he hurried up to the castle, a frown very much in place as she returned to the parlor.

"Did you tell Big Sam that you would meet him in the boxing ring?"

"Yes."

"What were you thinking?" Her frown turned to annoyance.

"I am thinking that I wish it were as easy as that to rid myself of guilt for the wrongs I have committed. I am thinking that the least I can do for the man is ease the awful responsibility he feels for your kidnapping. He will not be hurt above a bruise or two, and he will take on his new position with more confidence and a clear conscience."

"But I do not want either one of you to be hurt. It's barbaric!"

"Perhaps it seems so to you, but Lord David knew exactly what he was doing when he had that boxing ring built."

She folded her arms and turned to stare out the window. Obviously she was not fully appeased.

"How is Troy?" he asked, even though he knew full well that his horse was as happy as a footman with an unexpected day off.

"Troy is settling in quite nicely." She whirled around, apparently delighted to share good news for a change. "The stable lads are so impressed with her and agree that her coloring is all that keeps her from being perfect. I told them what you said. That her coloring will be all the rage soon."

As much as he loved that smile, Michael knew he was going to make it disappear.

"Olivia, there is something I need to talk to you about." At that very moment it occurred to him that he should have asked Mrs. Blackford to have this discussion with her. Too late.

Michael offered her a seat on the settee and sat next to her, not too close.

"I need you to tell me what you were wearing the day you were taken. Every single item."

"Why?" she said, stiffening.

"Some of your clothes were delivered to your brother the day you were kidnapped, and the morning after we returned here some more were dropped here at the gatehouse. It occurred to me that there may be other clothes that could be used to compromise you."

He was afraid of tears, but what he saw was anger. Not at him, he hoped.

"Those stupid Galatians. Those pigs."

Not him, he thought with relief.

"Those grape apes. I cannot think of words bad enough for them."

"I can. Bumbling, bootlicking, backstabbing brutes."

"Buzzards."

"Bullies."

"Bloodsucking fiends."

"That's two words but quite vituperative," he judged, pleased that she was smiling again. "Betrayer."

"Bandits."

"Bad bakers."

"All right." Olivia held up her hand. "I cannot think of anything worse than that." She relaxed a little. "Thank you, Michael, for making me laugh." It came to her that his question was a gift, though probably not from God.

36

WHAT WAS I WEARING?" Olivia mused in a thoughtful pose. Was there a better way to seduce a man than undressing yourself, if only mentally, in front of him?

"Let me start from the outside." She stood up, closed her eyes and mimicked undressing. "My bonnet, and my cloak and my blue half-boots." She opened her eyes. He did not seem particularly moved but she had yet to start on the interesting parts. She sighed. "I loved those boots."

"They can be replaced."

"I suppose so, but they were so well worn and had taken on the shape of my foot so nicely."

He nodded.

She put her hand on her chest, quite deliberately. She loved the cut of this gown. It made her breasts look as though they were much more discreet in size. "I was wearing an old blue gown. I thought I might be collecting greens from Mr. Drummond's garden."

She raised her arms and smoothed her hair and tried not to smile when Michael looked away and back again immediately. She shifted her gaze to the window so he could look at whatever part of her interested him the most, and felt a tingling in her breast. "I had a blue ribbon to tie my hair back. But who would keep that?"

"Uh-huh," was all he said.

She lowered her arms and gave him her complete attention again.

His eyes were hot, with a tinge of suspicion in them. Perfect.

Olivia hoped she was doing this right. She raised her skirt above her ankle and matched it with a look of total innocence.

"Two petticoats, white with white lace at the hem. After that, my stockings." She patted the top of her thigh. "My garters; they match my coloring quite nicely. These were plain, with a bit of lace in case anyone of interest should see them."

Now she gave him what she hoped was a provocative look but spoiled it by wrinkling her nose. Oh, this was stupid. She could no more seduce a man than she could shoe a horse.

With a sound of disgust she finished with as practical a voice as she could manage. "My stays are all that's left. And my shift, but you know that. It was what I was wearing when I escaped."

Michael rose and came very close to her. "I think I like this last look the best."

"What are you talking about?" She had to strain her neck to look up when he was this close. It was as though she was surrounded by him. The aura of power that she felt when he was barely a hand's width away from her was provocative and thrilling and she wanted more.

He cupped her raised chin and let his hand drift down so that it was just above the edge of her dress.

"How many years have you used that guileless look? I bet it works almost all the time."

"But not today." It *was* working. He was going to kiss her. Soon, she hoped.

"No one is that innocent after the age of four, Olivia."

He dropped his hand and took a step back.

Olivia edged closer so her breasts were barely touching his chest, though there were at least five layers of clothes between them. Still she could feel her body warm to his.

She would have to stand on her tiptoes if she wanted to initiate a kiss, and she was still not sure she could reach more than his chin. She sat down on the settee and, thanks be, he sat, too. Before he could rethink the commitment she moved as close to him as she could.

"Innocence is a vastly overrated virtue. I do think I am ready to experience something of the world."

His mouth was on hers before she had finished speaking. Oh, it was wonderful to be given exactly what she wanted. To feel him everywhere, no matter that it was only his lips on hers. She matched his passion and wondered what more there could be than this. It was so intimate—mouth, tongue, arousing every part of her.

When they pulled apart, for breath, for sanity, she could not help but laugh. "That was wonderful. It was so much fun. More than fun."

She started to sit on his lap to kiss him again, but he stood up abruptly.

"That is enough, Lady Olivia."

"Even I know that is not true. It is only the beginning."

"It is enough for you and me. I will not be the one who debauches you. I will not."

It rather sounded like he was trying to convince himself.

"Then can I be the one who seduces you?"

He shook his head, glowering.

"You cannot think of words to describe how much you want me," she teased, ignoring his dark expression.

"I want you. That is the truth, Olivia."

"Really?"

"Truly."

"Honestly?"

"Lustfully."

She laughed again. "I am yours."

"Not now. Not ever." He raised a hand to shield his eyes, his thumb resting on his cheek. "It is one of your more misguided impulses, Olivia."

"It is not. I have been thinking about it all day, for weeks, possibly since we slept in the same bed that first night. Definitely *not* an impulse, and I will not take no for an answer." She looked down and blushed at his arousal. He did want her. No matter how he would deny it. "I am going up to your bedroom. I will stay there all the rest of the day if I must. Dream of me there and come to me."

She stood on the couch, pulled his hand from his brow and kissed him. It was different this time, like unleashing a dragon, desperate with wanting and denial. She relaxed and played the temptress, knowing she had won and willing to let him suffer for a little longer as if it would make it more satisfying later.

When she ended the kiss he looked defeated. She turned away from that look. It made her feel guilty. She jumped off the settee and ran up the stairs.

His bed was neatly made. Was it a habit he had learned in the army or had one of the maids come to do it for him? With a twinge of jealousy she hoped that was all the maid had taken care of.

She heard nothing from downstairs for a few long minutes and could almost feel him fight the temptation. Finally, she heard the sound of the door opening and then being closed.

He had left! She jumped up from the bed and looked out the window. She could open it but someone might see her. She wanted to make love with him but had no need to let the whole world know.

He didn't believe her, she thought, stretching out on the bed. He would discover how true to her word she was. Pulling a spare blanket over her, Olivia determined to stay as long as it took. And fell asleep on that thought.

*   *   *

MICHAEL WAS SURE that God would damn him to hell if he went any further than that kiss. God had made man and must understand, must know that Michael needed that one kiss as a memento, one that he could relive as often as he dared.

He headed toward Pennsford, determined to put some distance between him and Temptation, trying to focus his attention on something other than how provocative innocence could be.

Never, not once in his life, had he wanted a virgin, wanted to be the one to teach and touch for the first time. What was it about this woman with still so much girl in her that made the pull unbearable?

He did not have the answer, and that was rare in itself. As he strode past the vicarage, Reverend Drummond himself opened the front door.

"Mr. Garrett! Could you stop a moment and lend me a hand? I was about to send up to the castle for Big Sam."

Relieved to have a distraction, Michael found himself helping the vicar make room for a new bookcase. The walls were lined with them except for the window wall, which looked out on the glory of sky to the west. The room was filled with as much light as the dank spring day would allow. Altogether a welcoming space, despite stacks of books all over. Not only on the desk and a table and in the bookcases, but also on the floor and on chairs.

First, Michael shoved the desk into the center of the room, closer to the window as directed. The odd placement did allow enough room for the waist-high, glass-fronted bookcase to be placed against the wall.

Mr. Drummond asked him to hang an engraving, or was it an etching, of some confrontation in a classical style.

"It's Hogarth's version of the trial of Saint Paul." The elderly man explained. "I used to have his 'Rake's Progress' hung there until Mrs. Blackford said that too many would think it inspiration rather than admonition."

"No doubt a wise decision," Michael said.

"Pour us some sherry, young man. Mrs. Blackford has gone to the castle to speak with the mason regarding some work needed on the chimney."

Michael tried to make sense of the non sequitur and deduced that Mrs. Blackford would not approve of sherry at this time of day. He poured it, set the glasses on the desk and moved books and papers off one of the chairs.

Michael recognized several editions of *The Edinburgh Review* and wondered what William Hazlitt had to say that would interest the vicar. Or Edmund Burke. He saw two novels and was even more confused.

"You have an interesting collection of reading materials," Michael ventured.

"Mr. Garrett, you would be amazed where I find inspiration. *Pride and Prejudice*. The title itself begs for a sermon."

The books sat on a corner of a Rowlandson cartoon. The drawing was of a gin shop. Not man at his best.

"I have lived a very sheltered life. Rowlandson's more salacious cartoons have made me a far better man of God."

"No doubt," Michael agreed, intrigued by Mr. Drummond's unique view of life.

The vicar seemed inclined to talk and Michael needed the distraction. There was one niggling question to which he wanted an answer. "Tell me, Reverend Drummond, what is the origin of the phrase 'stupid Galatians?' The bible translates it as 'senseless.'"

"Yes, my boy, it does. But if you read the Greek carefully you will see that the word actually translates as stupid. So much more powerful and so like St. Paul. Not a man to mince words, our St. Paul."

Wasn't personal translation some sort of heresy, Michael wondered.

"I have discussed it with the duke and written to the archbishop, but no one in Canterbury seems to think it a valid point. So the translation 'stupid Galatians' is used only in my private life."

Amazing. In his own quiet way this man was amazing. Willing to test the limits of hierarchy for what he believed in. Meryon deserved some credit too, for allowing such free thinking in a living he controlled.

"Come, come, young man, that is not why you came here today. I can only assume that you have come to see me about Lady Olivia."

But he had not come to see him about anything. It was the vicar who had called to him.

"She is a wonder."

"That she is, Reverend."

"Her brothers, except the duke, have a reputation for living life on a grand scale, of making the world bow to their wishes. I do not know why no one sees the same in Olivia."

It was the God's truth, Michael thought, as he nodded.

"She will not allow the rough patches of life to interfere with what she wants from it. I think she could face the grim reaper himself, if such a thing existed, and refuse, just simply refuse to accept that it was her time."

She had come close, Michael thought.

"When I see the results of that stubbornness in the various aspects of her life, I think it must be called a virtue." Mr. Drummond rubbed his chin, as he paused to allow his listener to catch up with him.

Aha. Michael smiled a little. He might be a congregation of one but he knew a sermon when he heard one.

"I have often thought that Olivia would have been better named Martha. For like Martha in the New Testament, Olivia is one who must always be doing for the Lord. She uses her skill in the kitchen to take care of people, no matter their station or age. And it works because in all of her recipes there is a measure of love."

The vicar leaned forward. "She needs you by her side."

God only knew where that came from. They both drank from their glasses.

"She needs you to complete her. You need her to complete you. You have denied your call to God long enough."

Michael stood up. "That is not what I came here to talk to you about." And he remembered, again, that he had not planned to come here at all. "I am no more suited to be a man of God than I am an appropriate husband for Olivia."

"Based on a lifetime of experience," Reverend Drummond stated after he had taken another small sip of his drink, "I can tell you, Mr. Garrett, that men who have seen the world and endured its temptations, those are the men who make the best ministers. Men with my naïveté are not nearly as forgiving of man's failings."

Michael stopped at the door. He understood that. A man who had faced death most fully embraced life.

"Mr. Garrett, you will give her what she needs. What she wants. That is love. That measure of love she has so freely given, but never yet received herself."

"That isn't true, Reverend. They all love her." The man was old and almost as addled as his sister.

"But you see, sir," Drummond said, looking all too lucid, "the difference is that none of them love her like you do."

37

OLIVIA WOKE to the sound of Michael coming up the stairs. She had no idea how long she had been asleep, the gray day making it impossible to judge the time by the sun. It was still light, but this time of year the days lasted longer so it could well be after supper time.

It didn't matter. He had come. Olivia turned her head on the pillow and watched the door open.

"Garrett? Wake up. It's time for you to show Samuelson his rounds."

David! *No, no, no.* One more minute and she could have slid off the bed and under it and he would never have known. But he came into the room before she could do more than have the idea. His shock was at least as extreme as hers.

"What the hell are you doing here?"

"All right, David. Please calm down." She popped out of the bed, pushed the skirt of her dress down around her knees and used one foot to feel under the bed for her shoes. "I fell asleep, but I can explain."

"I will let Garrett explain."

David left the room without another word, leaving Olivia scrabbling on the floor for her shoes.

There was a mirror, not a very big one, but it was large enough for her to see that she looked like she had just finished a very energetic wrestling match. In bed. *Oh dear.*

Her cheeks burned with embarrassment as she tiptoed downstairs, hoping, praying that Michael had gone to Pennsford or at least was in the kitchen or surrounded by others. When David found him there would surely be a fight.

She raced back to the castle and up to her room, thinking to change her dress, but Kendall was not there. At her own supper perhaps. She brushed her hair and grabbed a shawl to cover the wrinkles in her gown.

It took her the better part of an hour to find out that Michael had been to Pennsford, had spoken to her brother the duke, had gone to talk to Big Sam about the details of his new position and was currently in the boxing ring with Lord David.

"The doors are closed." The footman stood in front of the door, emphasizing his point. "No one is to observe them, my lady."

Frantic, Olivia reached around him for the door handle. "I am going in."

What would a footman do to the duke's sister, physically restrain her? Not likely; besides, she would fight him off if he did. She was so afraid that David would hurt Michael or Michael would kill David. She had to do something.

The footman stepped back and Olivia ran into the old courtyard. "Stop! Stop!" she yelled as she reached ringside. The two men circled each other, hands raised, faces intent. "David, nothing happened." She danced down the side of the ring, trying to draw his attention. "David! Listen! Nothing happened! Nothing."

With the doors wide open, Olivia was vaguely aware that people were hurrying through the outer ward into the court-yard, and she knew she would have to stop this quickly or everyone would be here.

Olivia climbed awkwardly into the ring and stumbled toward them. Both had cuts on their cheekbones and David was bleeding from the nose.

Neither of them paid any attention to her. They were lost in a world of frenzied battering and it had to stop.

She stepped between them as they both swung. David's punch caught her in the ear and Michael's in her stomach. Stars exploded as the wind was knocked from her. She went down like a sack of flour and the world went black.

When she came to, Michael was rubbing her back. She could hear David swearing and Michael praying and knew that her hearing had not been ruined even if her ear throbbed.

"What were you thinking, Olivia?"

Even as he chastised her, Michael gathered her up in his arms and held her tight to his chest. Her stomach and ear might hurt but her heart was as light as a feather. He must love her. All right, he must at least want to hold her as though she were a treasure he was afraid to lose.

She leaned back in his arms. "See, if you had come to

me, none of this would have happened." Tears filled her eyes and she buried her face in his chest again. This time her heart was aching.

"Let me take you to your room, Olivia."

"No!" She straightened and pushed herself out of Michael's arms so that she was sitting on the floor of the boxing ring. "You two clean yourselves up. You look disgusting. David, you will stop fighting. Michael, I will be very annoyed if any of your blood is on this dress. It is my very favorite. The material is from a dress that was my mother's."

She looked down at her dress and it seemed blood-free, though there was a small tear in a side seam. That could be easily fixed. "Send Big Sam to me. He can help me upstairs."

They actually obeyed her. Big Sam must have been nearby, for it was only a moment later that he was helping her to her feet. He wanted to carry her to her room but Olivia insisted that she would walk. She would go to bed for the night, and when she woke up in the morning she could pretend that this had not happened.

By the time she was in her room all she wanted was to lie down on her bed. She wished she could fall asleep but could only replay the stupid moment when David had found her in Michael's bed.

When Kendall told her that the duke wished to see her, Olivia felt like she had been punched again.

Her maid made a small sound of disapproval when Olivia suggested she would not be well enough until morning.

"Nonsense, Olivia, you have never kept to your bed a day in your life. Not even with your courses. Besides, your mother would say that it is better to face the problem now than let the duke have all night to think about it."

Kendall helped her change, never once asking what happened. No doubt she had already heard from three other sources some version of why David and Michael were fighting.

Olivia wore her favorite pink slippers even though they did not quite match the pink in her dress, and hurried downstairs to find Lyn in his study. Sitting at his desk.

His face was solemn, not a good sign. She curtseyed when what she really wanted was one of his I-love-you-in-spite-of-everything-hugs.

"Tell me what happened, Olivia." She had not heard him speak in that tone since Jess had bet one of his horses and lost. She could feel her throat fill, and she swallowed.

"Do not start crying."

The way he emphasized the first two words made it a command. As if she had control over her tears. All right, maybe she did sometimes.

"Start with why David and Garrett were in the boxing ring going at each other with no thought to gentlemanly rules or behavior."

She hesitated. Even though she was a terrible liar, Olivia held on to the hope that divine inspiration would come to her. Of course, the divine probably had no idea how to lie. "How do you know that's where David and Mr. Garrett were?"

"Winthrop had it from three different footmen. He came to me. According to Patsy, you stopped them before I could send someone stronger and more capable."

"Patsy saw me?"

"Yes." They both knew that was like making an announcement from the pulpit at church.

"So you are saying everyone knows that they were fighting?"

"Yes. Lovely, is it not?" He meant the opposite. "We spent a ridiculous amount of time and effort trying to save your reputation and it appears it was all for nothing."

"All right." She drew a deep breath. She was going to tell the truth. If she did that she would not have to try to keep her story straight the next five times Lyn asked her to repeat it. "David came to the gatehouse looking for Michael—I mean Mr. Garrett. He was not there but I was in his bed. I was fully dressed, Lyn."

When the duke actually allowed shock to show in his eyes, Olivia tried to quell it with a raised hand and a quick explanation. "When I went to the gatehouse, I went for the express purpose of seducing Michael. He would have none of it and he left. He refused. He said no. He does not want me. Ever. Never. Do you see?"

"What I see is a girl who must have borrowed sheer stupidity from Mary. You have worked beside her too long."

Olivia had to admit that from his point of view her behavior made no sense.

"What were you thinking, Olivia?" He shook his head, "Or was this one of your damned impulsive decisions?"

"It was not an impulse. Michael said the same thing." She was going to call him Michael even if Lyn beat her with a whip. He was Michael to her and would be forever.

"Here is what I was thinking." She folded her arms and

took a stance. "Since my reputation is ruined anyway, I wanted to take a lover and learn what all the fuss is about. When he was done with me I would go back to the kitchen and spend the rest of my life pouring all my love into the food I make."

"But your reputation is not—or was not—ruined."

"Yes, it is, Lyn." She stopped and sniffed. The touch of kindness in his voice brought the tears back. "No one really believes that I was sick at the vicar's."

"But they would have accepted it if you gave them no reason to doubt it." He stood up again. "Now it is too late. There are only so many convincing lies I can tell. You are going to have to marry him."

"Who?"

"Garrett, of course."

"No, no, no." This was a nightmare. "He does not even want to sleep with me, much less marry me. He does not like my cinnamon buns and told me that he could think of at least two or three things that he thinks would taste better than strawberries and cream. And you know that is not possible."

"Your lips being one of them, I'd wager. I will not even guess more than that."

"Oh." She raised a hand to her mouth and felt a blush starting. She wrinkled her nose. "Do you think that is really what he meant?"

"It is worse than inappropriate to be asking your brother to explain the words of your would-be lover." He paused for a moment. "And your future husband."

The duke came around and sat on the edge of his desk.

"Listen to me, Olivia, for I promise you I will have learned my lesson and will never play matchmaker again."

"What does that mean?"

"That means that Gabriel suggested Garrett as a match for you when he wrote the letter of introduction. He said that Garrett needed someone like you to make him realize that there was still sweetness in this world and that it need not be boring to live the life of a civilian. One thing you are not, dear child, is boring."

"So you are saying this was Gabriel's idea?"

"His suggestion, Olivia. I was not very interested in considering it until you had a second London Season but it was like trying to win an argument against coal mining to convince you to consider that. Which is to say, impossible. I watched the way he talked about you, the way he looked at you, the way he touched you, and I thought that Gabriel might be right."

"Do you think so?" She was not convinced but wanted to hear more, as much as Lyn would say.

"I hired him so that he would be around awhile and I could see what developed. But it has been such a disaster that I have learned my lesson and will never try to manipulate Cupid again." He went back behind his desk and sat down again. "Did you know that Garrett's father is a bishop?"

"No." That was a surprise. A bishop? "I do know that they are not close."

"Did you know that he was trained at Oxford to take orders?"

"Yes." How much did Lyn know about Michael that she

did not? This might be a chance to find the answers to at least a dozen questions. "How did he meet Gabriel?"

"That is enough from me. Ask him. I will speak to the major and afterwards I will send him to you. Go to the green salon and wait for him there."

Olivia wanted to be a dutiful sister but she could not bear it. She hurried around to his side of the desk and fell on her knees. "Please, please let me speak to Michael first, Lyn. I would sooner become a lady-in-waiting to Princess Charlotte than have him marry me if the idea disgusts him. Please, please, let me speak to him before you do."

"Off your knees, you silly chit." He raised her by the arm, looking shocked. "You are overdoing it."

"It is my life we are talking about, Lynford!" She had to bite her lip to keep from adding, *I do not want a marriage like yours.*

"Yes, Olivia, you may talk to him first."

Olivia had no idea why he relented, but she grabbed his hand and kissed it.

"You can talk to him, but it will not change what is going to happen."

38

OLIVIA WALKED down to the gatehouse as sedately as she could. It was twilight now and there were few people about, but privacy was a hard-won privilege here.

Her knock was light but not tentative, and when no one answered she tried again. Michael finally opened the door, saw who it was and turned around. He did not invite her in, but he did not close the door in her face, either.

"Say what you have to say and leave."

He sounded more tired than angry and his voice lacked the edge that Lyn used so well. Olivia pretended that was because he cared and did not want to hurt her feelings.

There was a bowl of water and a cloth on the table. She followed him into the room and took his arm to push him into the seat. When she made to dip the cloth in water he pulled it from her hand and nodded his head toward the opposite chair.

It hurt a little to have him reject her tender care, but she was not going to be distracted from what she had to say. She sat across from him and folded her hands in her lap.

"I know you think that I suffered some terrible trauma at the hands of my kidnappers and are afraid that if you make love to me I will be damaged forever."

He rolled his eyes as though they'd had this discussion a hundred times before. "There is some truth to that, my lady, though the way you phrase it is more theatrical than necessary."

"All right. Let me put it this way. You do not think I am being sensible."

"Much better."

"Here is the truth." She raised her folded hands to the table and leaned over them. "I had quite a bit of time to think about it this afternoon while I was in your bed waiting for you to come to me."

He raised the cloth to the cut on his cheek and winced. She tried not to feel any sympathy for him.

"Michael, making love with you and what I was afraid those men would do to me is like the difference between feeding someone and poisoning them. The act is the same but that is all they have in common."

He put the cloth down and raised a bandaged hand to cover his damaged cheek. But he was listening.

"Besides, they did not rape me and I escaped. I saved myself."

He shook his head, and even without words she could see he was not convinced. It was infuriating.

"Why will no one believe I can take care of myself, even

in the face of that? There was no brother to rescue me. I did it. I have done it all my life. Do you think it is easy having four older brothers? Do you think it was easy to have a Season in London when I am so easily mistaken for a milkmaid? Do you think it is easy for the daughter of a duke to make a place for herself in the kitchen? Do you think it is easy to love someone when even he thinks I am too damaged to know what I want?"

"I do not think you are damaged."

She raised her hand to stop his protest and kept on talking. "Michael, there is only one way that you are like those men who abducted me. You are a man."

"I do not want your love. I want that understood." He rose from the table with such force that it shifted. "Besides, love is not what you are feeling. It's gratitude."

"I know the difference." Before she could say more he continued.

"For me, saving your life was the first move toward balancing the wrongs I have committed. There are so many I could live to be a hundred, doing nothing but good works, and still not be finished."

She stood. "Are you trying to make me think badly of you? That is not possible."

He rose from the chair, came close. Taking her by her shoulders he looked into her eyes. She was sure they were tear-swollen and ugly. That did not matter as long as he saw beyond that to the absolute conviction in her heart.

"If I wanted you to think badly of me I would tell you about the time I held a knife at a child's throat so that his mother would tell me what I needed to know."

She did not want to hear this. Her imagination was good enough. She tried to cover her ears with her hands but he would not let go of her shoulders.

"I tell the truth now, to displace the lie I lived for five years. I killed men so that I would not be betrayed, I slept with women so I could find out what they knew and use it against the ones they loved."

It frightened her. He frightened her. It was not a past she could even imagine. That man was not the man she knew now. "Are you sorry for those lies and deceits?"

"Sorry? No, I am not sorry." He let go of her and laughed as though it was the most foolish question he had ever heard. "I wanted Napoleon defeated. I wanted to avenge the lives of the men who died in service to God and king. My skills were to lie and deceive and I used them to the best of my God-given ability."

He took the bottle of brandy off the table and gave it to her with his injured hand.

"You have lived a sheltered life, Olivia. Not all problems can be solved with chicken soup, no matter how perfect the recipe."

"Stop being patronizing." Olivia hoped he heard the anger in her voice. She hated losing her temper and was perilously close.

"If you want to show your gratitude, your love"—he spoke the word as if it was a complete misnomer—"open this for me and leave."

"Of course, I'll open it." If he thought he was going to find the answers in a bottle of brandy he was as wrong as it was possible to be.

She took the bottle and with careful aim threw it at the wall next to the door. It missed the wall but shattered against the door, and the always appealing smell of brandy filled the air.

He raised his bandaged hand to his head and swore very quietly.

"That is quite enough, Michael Garrett. Now you will listen to me."

She pushed him back with an index finger against his chest. He let himself be so handled until they were standing in the middle of the room.

"Brandy is never, ever a solution. I know this from my own experience. My governess abused brandy. I called her Tildy. Her name was Matilda Elderton and she is Annie's mother. I've spoken of her before, do you recall?"

He nodded.

"From my youngest years she would give me a bit when she wanted me to sleep or when I had a loose tooth. When I was twelve she gave me a tablespoon every evening before dinner so that I would not be so nervous joining the adults at table."

Olivia looked away from him so he would not see her tears at the memory of Tildy's hugs and encouragement, of her reminders of appropriate dinner table conversation, of her insistence that her "little lady" was going to grow up to be a beautiful woman.

"That brandy before dinner was how my parents found out. They smelled it on my breath and confronted her one night when she was too intoxicated to deny it."

"This is very touching, my lady—" he began.

"Close your mouth and listen. If you are going to dismiss me from your life, you are going to hear what I have to say first. Sit down."

She poked him with her finger one more time and he sat on the chair right behind him. With him seated, they were almost eye-to-eye.

"Of course she was dismissed. They gave her some money and sent her away within the week. Annie stayed with us.

"When I grew older Jess told me that Tildy had begged my parents to keep Annie, to prepare her for domestic service. They did. Annie and I were both lost for so long and then they sent her to boarding school."

She closed her eyes, remembering that last night when the two of them had planned how they would run away and start a cooking school.

"The new governess was much more interested in finding a husband than teaching me. She would tell me not to go to the kitchen but never actually check to see where I was. By the time my parents understood that I was spending all of my time with Cook, I made it clear I would run away if they made me stop my work there."

He had closed his eyes and she nudged him. "Do not fall asleep on me." When he opened his eyes, she stepped between his legs, took his face in her hands and pressed her lips to his. He did not respond and she dropped her hands, not at all dismayed. "I am coming to the important part.

"Michael." She used his given name and filled the word with all she felt for him. "I learned so many things from Tildy, but she taught me the most important thing without ever saying a word."

Today his eyes were that golden brown that reminded her of brandy. He probably thought they were expressionless, but she knew better.

"Michael." She said it again just for the pleasure of it. "Even the greatest wrong can be outweighed by a generous heart. I learned from her example that love is the greatest gift you can give and receive. I loved Tildy so much and I know she loved me. I pray for her and miss her to this day. I hope she is safe."

She kissed him again, very gently. This time his eyes closed, ever so briefly.

"Tildy shaped my life for this moment, for you. So I would know that no matter what you think you deserve, how bad your life has been, you are entitled to as much happiness as you can find. Love is what will give you the chance to right all the wrongs."

He shook his head and she ignored him.

"And, you lucky, lucky, man, I am here to show you where to find it."

She sat on his lap and this time she kissed him with carnal abandon; at least, she hoped that's what it was. And he responded. Oh the feel of his mouth, his tongue, delighted her. It was not the smell of brandy all around them that made her giddy and eager. It was his hands on her back, pulling her closer.

He kissed her neck below her ear and whispered. "I do not know if you are reward or punishment."

"Both." She pressed a kiss to the corner of his lip and

could taste the sweet and salt there. "And I do love you, besides being ever so grateful it was you who saved my life."

HE WAS TRAPPED. God bless her and her faith in him. That was all they said with words for a long time. He carried her up the angled stairs, pulled off most of the bandage covering his hand and helped her undress.

She returned the favor, taking at least as long as he had without the excuse of sore hands. Still in her shift she had to kiss each part of his body that she uncovered until he turned to her, naked, and showed her where a kiss meant the most. Her lips were soft and warm.

He helped her out of her shift, lifting it over her head, and kissed her forehead, her nose, her mouth, the space between her breasts. She pressed her legs together so he stopped at her stomach, tickling her belly button and finding, he could swear, that it tasted of cinnamon.

He wanted to admire the body he had so carefully ignored the last time he held her naked, but first he looked into those eyes. He saw anticipation mixed with excitement, as though she was waiting for the greatest treat in the world.

"Tell me if you change your mind."

"TELL ME IF YOU CHANGE YOURS," she said as she pressed herself against his arousal. The sensation was overwhelming. Olivia could not stand the feel of it until she let herself abandon control. Surprise changed to a gasp of delight. It was as if a fuse had been set; pleasure arrowed through her, exploding from her core, radiating through her entire body. It must be the way fireworks felt. She shuddered with release and melted into his arms with her eyes closed.

"That is how lovemaking is supposed to end," he said, kissing her eyelids.

It was a moment before she could open her eyes and think clearly enough to see concern mixed with the satisfaction in his.

"I think I have been waiting much too long for that, Michael. Is it your turn now?"

"Oh yes." He kissed her lightly. "How much do you know about sex?"

"The basics." She was feeling restless again. "But I want to learn all the details."

Michael began by kissing every inch of her. She threw out her arms, wanting him to make every inch of her his. She laughed, shivered, gasped and moved so that he knew what she wanted without words.

He pushed into her slowly, as if he was afraid he would hurt her. Not possible. As soon as he began, something primal took over and she wanted him with her, inside her, a part of her. She wondered how she ever thought life in the kitchen would be enough. She wanted this even more, every day, twice a day, for the rest of her life.

When he began to move inside her, the last thing she thought was "Oh!" as another explosion of delight rocked through her. This time he was with her, his body moving urgently, then tensing above her. He made a final thrust and she could feel his seed fill her. Creating as well as fulfilling. Giving. Taking. Sharing.

They fell asleep next to each other, his breath deep and heavy. Olivia watched him as his face grew soft and peaceful and she smiled to herself. She put her head on his chest and drifted off herself, listening to his heartbeat, deciding it would always be her favorite lullaby.

HE SAW HER TO THE CASTLE, in a pouring rain, and into it since he was the interim night porter. She waved good-bye to him and literally danced through the grand hall, leaving small wet footprints that dried almost instantly. She stopped every two or three steps up the grand stairway to turn in a great swirl and blow him kisses.

It was going to be an interesting life. God help him. And that was definitely a prayer.

39

MICHAEL KNEW what the future held. He'd known from the moment that the vicar had said it was time for him to answer his call. He sat in his parlor, sipping a brandy, and considered all the forces that had brought him to this moment.

He did not deserve her. Why would no one believe that? Or was it that Olivia deserved so much better than a man who was a disappointment to his father, whose best work for his country had been as a thief and spy.

Before he'd thought that if he could find out who had kidnapped her, he could leave having started to earn his redemption. But once they had made love he knew that Olivia was the woman that filled the emptiness, the one who made him forget all others.

For the last two days he had avoided her and, to his surprise, she had not sought him out. She had left some berries

and cream and billet-doux last night. He knew she was waiting for him to come to her.

It was a different kind of hell, to have found paradise and
know that you did not deserve it.

Big Sam found him still nursing the glass of brandy as the
sunlight began to fade. Samuelson was dressed in something
that was a cross between an outfit suitable for hunting and a
footman's livery.

"Sir, Mr. Garrett. Excuse me, I do have some news for
you. You know how you left word for the ostler at both inns
and the smithy to let you know if any soldiers or strangers
came through Pennsford? The smith sent a message that a
man came in to have his horse's shoe tended to. He said the
man told him his name was Smith and he would be at the
Fox and Hare."

Giving no explanation for his departure, Michael left orders to call Lord David if anything happened before he returned. Michael hoped that the roof on the henhouse fell in
the minute he was out of shouting range. There was no reason why Lord David should have a good night's sleep if he
wasn't going to have one.

Just as Michael was finishing his interrogation of the
smithy, who worked nights as the ostler at Pennsford Inn,
one last guest rode into the yard. He was well traveled, with
water dripping from his coat, and still in a hurry despite the
fact that he seemed to have arrived at his destination.

Michael was not even sure why the man caught and held
his interest, except perhaps for the red scarf he wore. It tickled some bit of memory and he decided to keep pace with

Mr. Red Scarf since they both seemed to be bound for the same place anyway.

Despite the steady rain, Red Scarf tossed a coin to the ostler and announced his plans to stay if a room was available, all before he swung off his horse. Once his feet hit the ground Michael realized why he gave his commands atop his horse.

If Big Sam was the biggest man he had ever seen, Red Scarf was one of the shortest. Not much taller than Olivia, if he were to guess. Red Scarf took no note of the stares as he made his way to the inn.

Michael followed him into the common room, which was relatively empty. The smell of the rain and the endless damp was relieved by a ferocious fire that burned in a mammoth fireplace, one worthy of a baronial hall.

It did more than burn. It *ate* the wood with voracious flicks of orange and red. A boy sat nearby to feed it from a stack of logs as big as he was.

Any visitor was warmed and dried instantly, but that was still not enough to draw anyone but the few travelers who were in out-of-the-way Pennsford.

Even Red Scarf stopped to admire the fire and look about the room for a familiar face.

Michael found who he was looking for, Smith and his manservant Jones, the two men who had come to the cottage. They were seated at a table as far from the fire as possible. Smith stared at a crack in the wall, physically in Pennsford, but mentally far, far away.

Jones had his back to the newcomers but appeared to be staring morosely into his tankard. Michael had learned self-control but it was sorely tested now. He swallowed against the rage that made him want to scream his fury and confront them in the instant. He stepped back behind a convenient post and waited to see what Red Scarf would do.

Red Scarf arrowed to the table and did not care who was listening. His voice more than compensated for his height.

"You complete and utter idiots."

"My lord!" Smith was surprised one minute and ready to argue the next. Mr. Jones took his cue from his leader. Mr. Smith had half a word out of his mouth, but that was all he managed.

"Close your mouth and listen, you stupid sons of Sodom."

My lord? The addition of those two words was an interesting development. As *Lord* Red Scarf spoke he seemed to grow by inches. It was nothing he did, but a power emanated from him that made the honorific a fact.

"My grandfather is obsessed with one thing: land. Land that will make him money is a double prize. This is not about anything else. And I will tell him that to his face, and my father will be with me on this. It ends now. No piece of land is worth what he had you do."

So the little lord was another of Olivia's champions. Who was he? More important, who was his duke grandfather?

"You will collect your things and leave at once and hope that you are not hunted down, beaten to within an inch of your life and left by the road to rot and on to hell for all eternity."

It was too many words as threats go, but it did manage to convey that Lord Red Scarf was serious.

Smith drew a breath.

"You say one word and I will strip off your cravat and stuff it in your mouth." Red Scarf threw some coins on the table and swore. "Out!" This one had a temper. "Do not keep me waiting. I will see you to the stable and on your way before I find my bed."

"But my lord, the rain." Jones did not seem to realize that Lord Red Scarf had ridden in it himself.

"A nice night ride in the rain is the least of what you deserve. With any luck you will develop an inflammation of the lungs and die before I see you again." The two men moved to obey.

As they hurried up the stairs, Michael wanted to stop them. Even as he took a step forward, he forced himself to think beyond the red haze of anger. Olivia came first. If he caused a scene now, her reputation would take one more blow.

With a prayer for patience Michael approached the now empty table. Lord Red Scarf stepped back and took a seat at another table. The owner grabbed the money and came to the man, who looked most of a normal height when seated.

"I will take their room and pay you for it as well. If the bed has been used have the sheets changed. I will leave shortly after breakfast as I have a meeting with the Duke of Meryon." He handed a coin to the owner, who nodded and left the room as quickly as he could.

Lord Red Scarf tapped his hand on the table, as though he had to rid himself of his energy in some way.

"I beg your pardon, my lord." Michael walked over to Red Scarf, giving a chance to take his measure. The man gave off the aura of someone who would rather fight than discuss.

"And why are you out on such a ghastly night?"

"For the same reason you are. To catch the two bastards who kidnapped Olivia Pennistan."

"Sit down." Lord Red Scarf straightened, thumped the table as he spoke and added, "If you please."

A woman came from the kitchen. Red Scarf turned to her and smiled. A smile that could have charmed the garters off a bishop's wife. The woman smiled back, though she was old enough to be his mother.

"My good woman, I do appreciate your service this evening. Could you bring some ale and bread and cheese or whatever will fill this amazing hole in my stomach."

She nodded, rushed from the room and was back in less than a minute with ale, bread, cheese and a hefty slice of cold ham.

Lord Red Scarf took the mug with a nod of thanks and downed half of it.

"I am Michael Garret, my lord."

"Garrett." He nodded but did not offer his hand. "I am Viscount William Bendasbrook."

Bendasbrook. The name clicked. Olivia's suitor from her Season. The one that had been "fun" but whom she could never marry. Now he knew why.

Lord William eyed Michael and the ham with equal interest, took a great bite of bread with ham on it and proceeded to talk with his mouth full.

"Sorry, hungry as a starving dog." He chewed some more. "So I have no idea how you are involved in this, but I do believe you have just added to the Bendasbrook legend. Thank you. Not that I need any help, but if it comes without strings I accept."

It was an instant decision, but he was bigger than the viscount if this did not go as Michael thought it would. "I came upon Lady Olivia when she escaped the two of them. Now I work for the duke."

He did not add that he was about to marry the lady of the house. Somehow he thought that the viscount might resent that. "I came to the village when I was given word that these two were here. We have been looking for them for weeks." He sat back. "My lord William, they are not leaving until the Duke of Meryon has his say in this."

The viscount had just taken too big a bite of food to even try to talk, so he shrugged as if he might agree to it. He didn't seem to realize that he did not have a choice. He finished the ale and wiped his mouth.

"If you don't want to brain them, my grandfather does. Basically we agree on that. But not on the reason why. My grandfather must think the Tudors are still on the throne. He's old enough to have known Elizabeth at least."

Michael leaned forward. He was going to do something he almost never did: ask a question he did not already know the answer to. "Why did they come back here? Where have they been?"

"The old goat wanted to guarantee Meryon would be willing to talk marriage. So his plan was to ruin dear Lady

Olivia. Smith actually argued that they had not failed, that Lady Olivia's reputation was ruined even if she was not found wandering the Pennsford road naked. There were some of her clothes left here and there, were there not?"

"Yes."

"Damn it! I raced here as soon as I found out his asinine plan. Was delayed by that incredible gale, and arrived too late to forestall them or find anything out without compromising her. Word was she was sick at the vicar's manse. A story that would work as well as any even if it was lacking in imagination."

Michael remembered where he had seen that red scarf before. The day he and Olivia had been making their way to Pennsford, the day after the storm. Lord William had been one of the people who had passed them on the road.

"As to why they came back and where they have been, they have been hiding out at the godforsaken cabin in the Peak."

"I know the place." *Better than I want to,* Michael thought.

"My grandfather told them to wait there until my suit was accepted by Meryon. You will note he did not think to include Lady Olivia in the discussion. He sent me to propose. I told him I was coming to terrorize the two of them and do whatever I could to ensure Lady O's good name. My father backed me in it until we browbeat the old reprobate into doing it our way. I sent word that Smith and Jones were to meet me here."

Michael believed every word he was saying. Only a

complete fool would ride into enemy territory with an explanation so impossible to prove.

"Tell me, do you have a dungeon at the castle?" Lord
William sounded as though it was what he most wanted.

"No, but there is a private boxing ring."

"Boxing! A boxing ring. Capital. That is perfect. A little
punishment and ship them off to my family's sugar plantation in the Barbados."

There would be more than a little punishment if Michael
had anything to do with it. No doubt the duke and Lord
David would feel the same way.

Smith and Jones came down with their kit. Both seemed
to be traveling light. Lord William waved them over and
looked them up and down for a long moment. Smith kept
his eyes on the viscount but Jones looked over at Michael.
Michael gave him a smile that was all Enoch Ballthur.

Jones drew the attention of Smith, who stepped back as
recognition struck.

"The viscount told me you are looking for a place to stay
tonight," Michael began, speaking without his Yorkshire accent. "I explained that the castle has some room available."

"And we will be off," said the viscount as he gobbled up
the last of the cold collation.

Michael saw Jones glance at the door and he stepped
closer to him. "Do not even give a thought to running or I
will track you down and murder you as brutally as an old soldier knows how. If you cooperate you will live."

Jones nodded. Smith was not convinced. He must have
noticed that Michael did not mention what was coming between the cooperation and the rest of their lives.

It took Michael and Lord William a few hours and Lord David's help to settle the two men into one of the old castle's empty rooms. One with a lock. It was not a dungeon, but as Lord William said with real glee in his voice, "Almost as cold, and it's the one that is haunted."

Samuelson insisted on acting as guard, and by the time Michael and the viscount were walking down the drive it was clear that their plan was going to work.

"Don't want it in the courts," the viscount agreed. "That would only make life a misery for Lady Olivia. And the duchess. And the duke. With a duke and a viscount involved, and my father, who is an earl, we should be able to keep this quiet. I'll bring the carriage up in the morning and take them to Bristol. Always wanted to drive a carriage. I'll find a ship headed south and they can recover on their three-week journey to the Caribbean. Could happen that they will be seasick the whole way. Or taken by pirates."

The man had an imagination much bigger than his size.

"Tell me this, Garrett, will you be there when I call on the duke in the morning?"

"Yes, I can promise you I will."

"Good. I'm off to bed. It's a relief that Lord David agreed to allow for the meeting in the morning instead of rousting the duke tonight. Meryon is likely to be in better spirits after a night's rest, and I need sleep more than I need four inches of height. At least the rain has let up. Helluva lousy day to be riding but it would not wait. I will see you in the morning."

Michael nodded and watched Lord William walk down

the road to the village without the slightest sign of fatigue. It was his energy one noticed now, not his height and not his red scarf. Michael could not imagine the man sleeping. He left it at that. His mind was not up to imagining anything more.

40

THE NEXT MORNING, well before noon, found all interested parties gathered in the duke's study. Lord David had briefed the duke, with Michael present to answer questions. While Michael was not actually invited to stay for the interview with the viscount, the duke did not tell him to leave, either, so Michael took a seat at the far end of the room. God help him, he hoped he was about to hear the last act of this play.

Olivia came in, waved to her brothers and came to his end of the room to kiss him good morning. Michael stood and she stopped, giving him a totally inappropriate curtsy. After all, as far as the staff and villagers were concerned, he was a servant. He shook his head and bowed back to her, took her hand and kissed the palm. She widened her eyes and mouthed "Later."

He could hardly wait.

The duke was at his desk, reading a paper, ignoring the rest of them. Neither one of her brothers reacted to Olivia's behavior, and Michael had the feeling that the matter had been settled without consulting him at all.

When the viscount was announced, the duke stood, Olivia brought her hand up to cover her smile and David sat back in his chair.

Lord William came into the room with all the energy he had displayed last night, if not more. He bowed to the duke, turned and hurried to Olivia, bowing to her as he took her hand. "How are you, my lady? I cannot decide if it is more joy or pleasure to see you looking so well."

"Thank you, my lord. How kind of you to come to call."

The viscount shook his head. "I hope you think so when you have heard this sorry tale."

He walked to the other side of the duke's desk. He put his hands behind his back and with a determined effort made himself stand still. "I will not waste your time or belittle your intelligence, Your Grace. It is my grandfather who orchestrated and planned the heinous kidnapping of your sister."

He turned back to Olivia whose expression was shock and dismay. She took a step back when he bowed again.

"I understand your revulsion, my lady. I want to assure you that I knew nothing of this until the day after you were taken, when my grandfather told me what had transpired."

"But why?" Olivia asked.

"First, I want to assure you that until that moment I had no idea Grandfather was so desperate for me to marry you."

"Lord William." She took his hand and squeezed it. "We had some wonderful times in London but that is hardly the basis for a marriage." She hesitated a moment. "My lord, forgive me, but is your grandfather blind?"

"Blind? No," he repeated, apparently not understanding her at all.

"Lord William, I do not wish to hurt your feelings or to say something that will embarrass you, but how tall does your grandfather think you are? If we were to marry, our children would be so short that we would be called leprechauns or something even less kind. I could never marry you. I am so sorry."

"I understand, my lady, and I hasten to tell you that he is so blind that his interest in our connection had nothing to do with your obvious beauty and charm."

"What *did* he want?"

"He wanted your land, Olivia." It was the duke who answered her question. "The acres that Mother left you. The ones rich with coal, to be exploited along with the men who mine it."

"Oh," she said, and Michael could see her mind working out the details. "It was not Jess's land they wanted after all."

"Those acres in the Americas? What good are they to anyone?"

"I thought that . . ." She stopped and bit her lip. "It does not matter now."

"I want to assure you," the viscount went on, never mind that the duke might want to fit in a word or two, "that the evil villains have been caught and will be sent to the Caribbean to a sugar plantation that my father owns there. You will never see them again."

"They've been caught!" Her pleasure made them all smile.

"Yes," David said.

That seemed to be enough for Olivia. Good, Michael thought, relaxing in the chair. He had no idea how she would react to the boxing ring spectacle. She would either compare it to a Roman circus or want to come watch. Better not to give her the choice.

"I will marry you, my lady," the viscount began, "whether your reputation is at stake or not. Just think, we could build a dollhouse just for our family, and whenever someone came to visit they would be as uncomfortable at our table as we are at theirs."

"We are not midgets, Lord William." Olivia seemed to find no humor in his suggestion. "But thank you. I must decline, for my heart is otherwise promised." She must have learned how to handle him while in London, because she barely drew a breath before she smiled and spoke again. "Why do we not have some tea? Do you recall those cinnamon buns you enjoyed so much? I have some freshly made."

"Capital!" The viscount clapped his hands together, apparently fully recovered from her rejection of his suit. He took his leave and followed her from the room.

As soon as the two of them had left, Lord David turned and walked through the door into his office, leaving Michael on his own with the duke.

Michael eyed him shrewdly. "When I confronted you, you mentioned the land and never once said anything about a forced marriage."

"Details you did not need to know before you agreed to become part of the family."

Michael almost stopped him. He had not actually proposed to Olivia yet. He held his tongue. There had been enough talk of boxing rings already today.

"The viscount's grandfather came to call not three months ago, proposing a match between the two of them."

"I thought that kind of arranged marriage was no longer common."

"No, not common, but for someone of the old duke's age, children still exist to do their parents' bidding. Especially girls. The viscount told me that he disinherited one of his daughters when she used the word *no* to one of his musical requests."

"I cannot imagine Olivia surviving in that world."

The duke nodded. "I knew of the viscount's attempts at courtship while Olivia was in London. She had made her feelings known even more bluntly than she did today."

"Is that possible?"

"It is," the duke said but did not elaborate. "I sent the viscount's grandfather away with as kind a refusal as I could word. I never even told Olivia about the offer." He sat down as though he was carrying more weight than was wise.

"No one would think that the old duke would be so desperate that he would resort to ruining her reputation." Michael was sure the duke must realize that.

"I will admit that I think he is also desperate to have his grandson married. Olivia was the ideal partner, whether she was interested or not." The duke rubbed his hand over his face and Michael wondered when he last had a decent night's sleep.

"Your Grace," he began.

The duke stopped him. "Not yet, Garrett. Give me a chance to rid us of one suitor before I deal with the next."

"Not that, Your Grace."

The duke nodded.

"You have a plan for retribution?"

"Dueling is no longer legal, Michael." The duke smiled a little. "But I have a card or two I can play. Parliament. That's where he will find out that no one threatens a Pennistan and does not suffer for it."

From anyone else Michael would have thought this a pathetic gesture, but the hard edge to Meryon's voice and the look in his eye convinced Michael that there would be hell to pay in a way the old duke would never forget.

There was a knock at the door and within a minute the room was once again filled with people. Lord David, Winthrop the majordomo, Lester and Patsy. The three men were as expressionless as Greek statues. Patsy more than made up for it, crying into her apron and mumbling, "How could I have known?" and other endless protestations of innocence.

"Be quiet, Patsy," Lester said with an authority he must have learned from the duke while standing at his door.

She sniffled and lowered her apron.

"Please, Your Grace," she began.

"Let Lord David do the talking," Lester ordered once again.

David nodded to Winthrop, who stepped up to the desk where the duke sat. "Your Grace, it has just come to my attention that Patsy was the one who was assisting the men who made such a misery of Lady Olivia's life."

"I was not assisting them. I thought I was helping a courtship."

"Nonsense," Winthrop said, echoing the reaction of the rest of the listeners. "How is it assisting a courtship to supply the baskets and deliver Lady Olivia's clothes, all for money?"

Patsy gave up all pretense of tears. "We all know that Miss Lollie had no hopes for marriage. That all she can think about is the kitchen. I thought this was a very romantic way for her to be compelled to marry and to think about something but how to make the best dishes."

"You thought?" Lord David said. "Exactly who gave you authority to make such a choice for her and her family?"

"I am a woman, and I know what a woman feels better than anyone else in this room."

"Patsy," Lester said, with such disappointment that Michael thought he must really care for her. "You did it for the money. At least tell the truth now that you are caught."

"And that is all your fault, Lester. You would not marry until we had enough money. You have been saying that ever since we started meeting in the old castle."

In the basket room. Michael looked at Pennistan, who nodded, apparently having the same thought.

"It's been two years. We would never have enough money if I waited for you to earn it." She straightened and tried not to look guilty. "So I did it."

Lester stepped forward. "Your Grace, I cannot apologize enough. We hand in our notice."

Patsy looked shocked. The duke nodded.

"In order to lessen gossip I have accepted positions for us at the Gateway Inn. I will be managing the tavern and Patsy will work as a maid as she did here."

Patsy looked furious at his declaration.

"We will also forgo the usual one-year pay that is given to employees, or Patsy may well feel that this change is a reward for such disloyal behavior."

The duke inclined his head.

"The one boon I would ask, Your Grace, is that I not be denied the occasional chance to visit when Lady Olivia is baking cinnamon buns."

"I will think on it, Lester." The duke's expression was unreadable.

Patsy could not hold her tongue. "You like Lady Olivia even more than her cinnamon buns."

Lester took her arm and marched her to the door. "At the moment, Patsy, I like everyone more than I like you." Once he had pushed Patsy out the door, he turned, bowing to the duke and to Lord David. "Until today, it was a pleasure working for you, sir." He left with an impressive dignity.

No one spoke for a moment. For his part, Michael was sorry that Pennford was losing Lester.

"Make no mistake, brother," Lord David said, "this was about jealousy more than anything else.

"Since Olivia is about to be married, I do not believe we will have to worry anymore about defending her honor. That will be Mr. Garrett's responsibility."

41

OLIVIA WAS CUDDLED up next to Michael on the settee in his parlor, having just given a very interesting demonstration of how quickly she learned.

"I love you, love you, love you."

"I hope so, my dear. I would not like to think that you would behave like this with any man."

"Oh stop acting as though this is no more than a casual coupling." She looked into his eyes and insisted he be honest. "Can you not feel the connection deepen each time we are together?"

"Yes, darling girl, and it is absolutely terrifying." Amazing how those lovely green eyes could pull the truth right out of him.

"You said that once before. Why are you terrified?"

"Olivia." He took a moment to adjust her décolletage so he was not quite so distracted. "If I am the right man for you then Big Sam should have married the princess. I have no future, no place to live but this gatehouse, no kitchen for you to cook in."

"Can you not have faith that it will work out?"

"Oh, I have faith in many things, Olivia, but I have always been taught that virtue is rewarded and you are the first sweet taste of virtue I have ever known. And even that I have corrupted."

She jumped up from the settee. "Never, ever call our lovemaking corruption. It is not. I know exactly who to talk to about this." Olivia took his hand, pulled him off the settee and out the door.

She waved and called out to people as they headed to the village. Michael pretended she was in charge and tried to figure out who would have all the answers. When they went up the vicarage walk he thought it would be Mrs. Blackford. But no, it was not ten minutes before they were settled in the vicar's office talking to Reverend Drummond himself. Michael had to clear off a second chair, though Olivia had insisted she was more than willing to sit in his lap.

"It is a pocket miracle," the vicar said without a second's hesitation.

"Exactly," Olivia agreed. "That was one of the most memorable sermons you ever gave, sir."

Mr. Drummond nodded his thanks to her.

"Money is a factor, but not the most important one." Surely that was what a pocket miracle was, Michael thought.

"You are too literal, young man," the reverend said with some apology, even though that was God's honest truth.

Olivia looked at the vicar who nodded as though she was one of his prize pupils.

"Michael," Olivia said, "a pocket miracle is something that can be easily explained in the normal course of events. However, you know, in your heart, that it is a gift from God."

Michael smiled at her and she grinned back.

"I cannot tell you how many times Revered Drummond said that we should not hesitate to ask for a miracle. That is exactly what I did. And you found me."

How could he not go willingly? Michael took Olivia's hand and squeezed it. "To be perfectly accurate, I would say that *you* are *my* pocket miracle."

She wrinkled her face in that silly expression of pleased embarrassment that was the first thing he had loved about her.

"I give you both my blessing," Reverend Drummond went on, "but you already knew I would. The one you will have to convince is the duke. Do you want me to plead your case? Or come with you when you talk to him?"

"No, thank you, Reverend. I will speak with him."

"I was going to say yes." Olivia looked at Michael with some affront.

Clearly love was one thing, perfect understanding another.

"Reverend, it is what the duke wants for Olivia. He has spoken to her about it. But I will observe all the conventions and ask permission as any gentleman would."

Michael turned to his almost-fiancée. "Olivia, if you are going to have a say on everything I do, I hope you understand that I have a say in what kind of buns you make for Sunday breakfast."

Olivia narrowed her eyes, prepared for combat. The vicar forestalled it.

"What he is saying, my lady, is that the enormity of this aspect of commitment has this moment struck him for the first time, and it is something that you will have to discuss in more detail."

She relaxed a little and Michael breathed thanks for the man's understanding.

"Personally, I find it an admirable commitment that may well be the biggest challenge your marriage faces. I would advise that you have these discussions after you have been together in the most intimate way. It is a time when you are least guarded and most honest."

Michael watched Olivia blush and did his best to nod with appropriate solemnity. The vicar had been married. The man knew what he was talking about.

"I want the two of you to have complete faith that you will be happily married before summer. You will have a place to live, Mr. Garrett, you will have an income and the duke will give you his blessing." He stood up.

"That would take more than a pocket miracle, Reverend Drummond." Michael was almost annoyed at the casual way the priest was dismissing their worries.

"Yes, it will, but I am certain that when the time is right, this living will be passed on to you."

"This living? That is impossible, sir." Michael added the last word with a bow, well aware of the rudeness that had been startled out of him.

"That is why it is called complete faith. Pocket miracles come to those who have even the slightest hope in God. In your case it is not as difficult as it seems, but yes, more than a pocket miracle."

Olivia nodded, though her expression was serious. She actually believed him.

Michael did not. This was a man who went out at night to look for lost sheep.

"Your father is a bishop, my boy."

Michael looked at Olivia who shook her head, denying she had told the vicar. "The duke has spoken to you about this?"

"I went to him when I realized who you were. He already knew." He said it as though it was stating the obvious.

"Garrett is a common enough name. How did you connect me with the bishop?"

"It came to me in a dream," Drummond said with all the certainty of an Old Testament prophet. "That sort of awareness often does these days. I do believe it is one of the true joys of aging for me."

"I see." Michael was not sure he did.

"We must take it on faith, Michael. At once the easiest and most difficult thing to do. Will you?" The promise in Olivia's eyes was amazing.

"I will." It felt like as much of a commitment as a marriage vow. Michael could not remember the last time he had taken anything on faith. Then he realized he had begun that list when he accepted that Olivia loved him.

Reverend Drummond came to Olivia and took her hand in both of his. "You have been blessed in this life and have shared it with the world around you, Lady Olivia. Mr. Garrett will be your greatest support, as you will be his. Your greatest joy and, I will be as honest as a widower can, your greatest exasperation. Believe me, it is worth the effort."

"Thank you, sir." Her voice was clogged with tears.

He nodded and patted her hand one last time. He took Michael's hand in both of his. It was awkward, felt strange. Michael had expected no more than a handshake.

"Olivia is a treasure. She is your treasure now. Guard her with all the good in you. Love her with all the power your heart holds and, Mr. Garrett, listen to her."

He spoke the last with a smile of such understanding that Michael had to smile back. Either that or cry himself.

Michael and Olivia walked arm-in-arm up the road from Pennsford to the castle. It was, at last, a perfect spring day. Who cared if it was already summer?

The walk took much longer than usual, as there were any number of spots where it was necessary to stop and admire the flowers or the green-tipped trees and share a kiss.

They approached the gatehouse as the sun bathed the castle in a golden light exactly as it had the evening he had first arrived at Pennford.

"This may be the coldest, wettest spring we have ever had, but it feels like the most glorious spring of my life."

"I think it must be as Saint Paul says, that love makes all things new."

"See, you are already sounding like a man of God," she said on a laugh.

"If that's so I will declare this day one of rest."

"Oh yes, and we can spend all of it in bed." She raised his hand and kissed it.

"Very enticing, but I think you would be missed in the kitchen." He pulled her off the lane with a gentle tug and kissed her in case she thought his words a rejection. He pushed her curls off her face and framed it with his hands.

Olivia pulled him back onto the lane. "If we stop dawdling there will be enough time before Cook wonders where I am."

"If you wish," he said, pretending that giving her pleasure was a noble gesture on his part. "It would be pure joy if nothing disturbed us from now until the banns are announced. We could use some peace."

No sooner were the words out of his mouth than one of the grooms hurried over to them.

"You must come immediately, Mr. Garrett. The most extraordinary thing has happened! Troy has learned to count!" Apparently it was so extraordinary the groom did not even notice that the night guard was holding hands with the duke's sister.

Olivia laughed and pulled on his hand. "Hurry, Michael." When he shook his head she let go of his hand and went ahead of him. She was back before she had gone far. "Michael, if Troy can count, do you think she can learn her letters?"

"Do not even suggest it, Olivia. The next few years would be a circus. And Pennsford is quite lively enough as it is."

"Not only are you beginning to sound like a man of God, you are beginning to act like one." She paused only a moment. "Stodgy."

"Sensible."

"Solemn."

"Sane."

"Somber."

"Sagacious."

"Oh that is excellent. You win this time, wise one."

She blew him a kiss and hurried ahead.

Michael watched her dance along, her pink gown billowing behind her as though it could hardly keep up.

As much as he might tease Olivia, it was clear that his life was going to be anything but quiet. She would see to that, if the people of the castle ever considered making his life easier. He thanked God for it as he followed the heart and soul of his world into the stable to see exactly what Troy could count.

Epilogue

MICHAEL WATCHED Olivia putter about their vicarage bedroom. He wondered if she did it to tease him or because she truly could not settle to bed without being sure that everything was in its place. He never complained. It was such a pleasure, anticipating that moment when she would come lie beside him.

She was as adventurous in lovemaking as she was with food. He thanked God for it every day. And every night he hoped that God was not shocked at how much they enjoyed each other. No matter what new ways they found to tease and tempt, it always ended the same. Want became need and loving each other was the only thing that mattered.

Olivia blew out that last candle and replaced it with a new one. Once under the covers, she drummed her feet to loosen the covers, never mind that by the time they went to sleep they would be loosened enough.

"Now, tell me, Michael, where did you find Reverend Drummond?" She was lying on her side, watching his profile.

Michael stared at the canopy so that he was not too distracted to answer his wife. "He was in the haunted room in the old castle, talking to the air."

"Or the ghost."

"I knew you would say that, and Mrs. Blackford agrees with you." He glanced at her. Just a glance. Her eyes had a devilish glint and he found he gave in to this temptation so easily.

"I spent some time discussing whether he wished to give the sermon this week, and after that he asked if I had decided what to do with the extra loaves and fishes. I assume he was referring to the Gospel feeding of the multitudes and assured him it was all taken care of. When I left to come back here, he was in the castle chapel at his prayers."

She leaned closer and kissed his bare shoulder. "You are so kind to him. Thank you. He seems to be content?"

"Yes, it was inspired of the duke to suggest that he move to the castle and act as chaplain."

"A pocket miracle," Olivia reminded him.

"Yes, it was."

This was another part of their evening ritual. If it had been his idea that they share a bed, for the first few months at least, it was Olivia who always had a dozen questions for him before they kissed each other good night.

He would grumble that it kept them from what they wanted to do most, but in time he had his own questions. As Olivia pointed out, in bed they had each other's complete attention.

"Olivia, have you heard anything more? Where is Jess now?"

"Still in Sussex." She flopped onto her back and reached over to take his hand beneath the covers. At least he thought it was his hand she was reaching for. "It will be almost a year since he left London. At least now we have a place to send letters. He is helping Gabriel, and after that he is off to see Rhys Braedon and his family."

"Does Rhys Braedon gamble?"

"No, so far Jess has avoided the gaming and will tell no one why. He can be so exasperating. You think I am impulsive? Jess has made it an art."

"At least you know why your letters never reached him."

She let go of his hand and moved so that he could reach out and pull her close.

"Michael, did David tell you where Lyn is these days?"

"In France at the moment. He will be back in time for Parliament."

She buried her face in his chest. "He will grieve for a long time, Michael, but I am hoping that he will marry again."

The thought of losing his wife, as the duke had, kept Michael silent a moment. He could not imagine the pain if he lost Olivia. Grief was too tame a word.

"So, my dear." He turned to face her, with only a few inches of white linen between them. "Where are Michael and Olivia?"

"In bed together." She answered him cautiously, biting back a smile.

He kissed her forehead, her eyes, her nose and her

mouth. "Then, tell me, why are we talking about other people?"

Olivia fell back from him. She threw her arms out and her bare breasts peeked out from her unbuttoned nightgown. "Michael, why are we talking at all?"

Author's Note

THE RESEARCH for *Lover's Kiss* was wide and varied and, as always, lots of fun. Lady Olivia's obsession with food was not the norm in Regency England, especially among the ton, and for the daughter of a duke, it was unheard of. It is proof of her singular passion that Olivia made a place for herself in the kitchen. Her position followed her even there, as she did not cook for the household but pursued her own interests.

The briefly mentioned historical figure, Antoine Carême, is considered to be the first celebrity chef. He trained under Talleyrand and worked for Napoleon, the tsar, the Prince Regent and the Rothschilds. How lucky for me that his year in England actually did coincide with Olivia's one London Season.

Bendasbrook makes his appearance in this book with a nod to the superb science fiction writer Lois McMaster Bujold. He is my version of one of the best characters in all of fiction—Miles Vorkosigan.

Elaine Fox, friend and writer, deserves endless thanks for her willingness to brainstorm and read and comment and critique. Lavinia Klein and Marsha Nuccio are right up there with Elaine. They are, as Marsha calls our group, Lifesavers.

Anke Fontaine helped with Troy's movements and any horse-related details, especially whether even a genius horse could fit through a cottage door. Thanks also to Kalen Hughes for her expertise on so many things Regency, and to Pam Rosenthal and Tracy Grant for their willingness to share information on the subject of habeas corpus, barely mentioned in this book but of great importance then and now. And to Evelyn Payson for her help with Anglican Church history and details, several of which I stretched for the purposes of the story. The Beau Monde chapter of RWA is a group of talented women who are endlessly generous with their knowledge. Thank you.

Finally thanks to my husband, Paul, who will eat whatever is put in front of him, or find his own dinner, and to my editor, Shauna Summers, and her assistant, Jessica Sebor, whose input and support make any project better.

About the Author

MARY BLAYNEY lives in southern Maryland within sight of the Chesapeake Bay, an hour from Washington, D.C., where she was born and lived a good part of her life. In an area filled with history, her favorite events are millions of years apart. The Battle of St. Leonard Creek—the first step toward the attack on the Capital in 1814—took place a few miles from her home. Each year the event is reenacted and a bit of the period she loves so much comes to life. The Calvert Cliffs are filled with fossils millions of years old, many of which can be found on the beach nearby. When not distracted by the beach or the history of the area, Mary spends her time making up the history of the Pennistan family. Her next book for Bantam Dell is in the works now. For more information on her career and previous books, check her website at MaryBlayney.com.